Morning Light

A Door County Love Story

Enjoy

Michael Pritzkow

Michael Pritzkow

ISBN: 1493535315
ISBN 13: 9781493535316
Library of Congress Control Number: 2013920072
CreateSpace Independent Publishing Platform
North Charleston, South Carolina

Dedication

To Ted and Jeannette Hoeppner of Ephraim, Jessie Downer, Susan Springman, DuWayne Statz who have all supported my writing in their own special way, and my editor, Brenda Windberg.

Chapter One

Peter Franklin saw her as he waited at the counter of Wilson's Ice Cream Parlor. How was it that he had never noticed her before? He stopped at Wilson's every day.

Her beauty mesmerized him, the perfect example of the All-American look that set Wilson waitresses apart. Sparkling white teeth, long hair, and a beautifully shaped athletic body, she was a sight to behold.

Peter studied her as he waited in line. She smiled at each customer and seemed genuinely friendly to all. His heart rate kicked into high gear. *Would she be friendly to me too?*

A single drop of perspiration caught his eye. He watched as the drop slowly trickled down her neck to the swell of her right breast, hesitated, and then disappeared between the hollow of her cleavage. His mouth went dry. Oh, to be that drop and caress that breast, he thought. He leaned closer to the counter, closer to her.

Then, as if that wasn't enough, he noticed her eyes. She had the most amazing green eyes with little flecks of gold around her iris. They seemed to urge him closer. He watched as her eyes darted to him, then gave him a quick wink. Was she giggling? He smiled back, but she had already returned to scooping ice cream.

Peter licked his lips, suddenly desperate to spend some time with this girl. Finally, it was his turn, but he had the wrong server. His hopes plummeted. *I want the one with the green eyes.*

1

Behind him, a frazzled mother with four energetic boys offered an answer to his problem.

Turning to her, he asked, "Would you like to take my place? I know how hard it is to take care of kids when they're wound up. I used to babysit for my neighbor back home in St. Louis."

For a second, he thought the mother was going to cry. "Oh, thank you. I am at the end of my rope. I just want to give them a treat and get out of here. Nothing is easy with these four."

They both laughed.

Pleased with himself, Peter smiled and moved in front of Annie. "Hi."

She turned to him, ice cream scoop in hand. He thought he saw her mouth the words. "Finally."

Peter leaned on the counter, inches from her lips. Neither said a word, their eyes transfixed. Then she wet her lips, breaking the spell, and smiled.

"That was really considerate of you to let that mom and her kids go before you."

"Oh, it was nothing. I know how much fun kids can be at that age. Besides, I wanted you to wait on me."

"Really?" She seemed to blush a bit. "All the same, it was nice of you." She dipped the ice cream scoop in a small pail of water and gave him another smile. "What would you like?"

Body tingling at the thought of what he'd *really* like, Peter cleared his throat. "Can I ask your name?"

"Annie. Annie Wilson. No relation to the owners of this place, I'm afraid." Her arm made a sweeping motion. "What's yours?"

"Peter Franklin. I'm from St. Louis. My family's been coming up to Ephraim every summer since before I was born."

"Well, Peter Franklin, it's nice to meet you. Now what can I get for you?"

He looked down at the ice cream scoop in her hand, and then back to her intoxicating eyes. "I guess I'll have my usual, a root beer malt."

"OK, one root beer shake coming up." He watched Annie turn and grab one of the big aluminum mixing cups behind her, "Wait," he said, "not a root beer shake. I want a root beer malt! My dad got me hooked on them. They're great!"

A surprised look appeared on her face, followed by a smile. "I don't think I've ever made a root beer malt before."

His heart beat faster, here was his opening. Peter matched her smile. "It's pretty simple. You make it just like a vanilla malt, except you put lots of root beer syrup in the mixer instead of vanilla extract." He leaned a little closer, smiled a little bigger. "Then you add your plain malt mix, ice cream and milk, mix it all together and voila. You have Peter Franklin's root beer malt."

She gave the cutest little shrug. "I don't think I've ever tasted anything like that before." Perfect! Exactly what he hoped she'd say. "Since you haven't had one, why don't I buy you one?"

She hesitated, then shook her head, but her smile never faded. "That's really nice of you, Peter, but I just can't leave now, at least not until my break."

"When is that?"

"In about ten minutes."

" I can wait. When you're ready for your break, make the malts." He turned and looked through the front window and pointed across the street. "I'll just sit under that big tree and wait for you."

She sighed, and her eyes scanned his face. "Why not?" she finally said with a toss of her head. "You seem nice, and the malt sounds yummy. I'll meet you across the road in a bit."

Peter wanted to cheer, but he held himself to a grin. "Perfect. I know you'll love it."

Ten minutes later, as she made the two malts, Annie's pulse turned jittery. She glanced across the street, noticed Peter's lean, muscular body, and imagined a ripped set of abs underneath his white polo shirt with the little green alligator on the chest. The tan sailing shorts,

3

upturned collar, leather topsiders, and Ray Ban aviator glasses gave him a distinctive look. Yep, *he comes from money.*

Her heart revved to a different beat. His kind, the wealthy kids, made her uncomfortable. They seemed to have nothing better to do than laze around all summer and act like jerks. *Must be nice not to worry about money.*

Then with malts in hand, Annie crossed the street. Butterflies claimed the pit of her stomach, and she thought about the first time she'd seen him, earlier that week. There was nothing special about that. All the "girls" at Wilson's noticed good-looking guys when they came in, and Peter was better than most. Yes, she thought, there was something special about him that pulled at her all week wanting to meet this guy. His eyes were a bright topaz blue. She could tell he spent most of his time outside by the way the sun had bleached his brown hair and peeled his nose. All in all he was a nice package.

Everyday, when he would come in, she would stop what she was doing and watch him for a few moments. It still puzzled her. Why him? She knew she got more than her share of attention from the male population that came into Wilson's. She knew that, but for whatever reason, he was different. She was excited to meet him and find out why she was drawn to this particular guy versus the others that came in every day. This was her chance and she wanted to make the most of it.

Reaching the tree across the road, she handed him his malt and sat next to him on the grass, next to the water's edge. "I threw in some extra root beer syrup, so I hope it's good?"

Annie watched Peter bring the aluminum-mixing cup to his nose, savoring the strong aroma of root beer. He raised the cup to his lips. She hoped the thick creamy taste would bring a smile to his face. She held her breath.

He grinned. "This is wonderful! Are you sure you haven't made this before?"

Her face broke into a huge smile. "Peter…I'm a professional ice cream mix-ologist. I'm supposed to make it good." They laughed.

She moved the cup to her mouth, instantly thrilled by the flavor. "Wow. I love the taste of the root beer. It is good, if I do say so myself."

Sitting by the water's edge, they looked across the bay at Peninsula State Park. The Park's limestone bluff was a perfect backdrop, rising several hundred feet above the water's edge. Home to Eagles, they gave the bay its official name, Eagle Harbor. Sailboats moored throughout the bay gave it a picturesque look.

Peter smiled and turned back to Annie. "So, you live here in Ephraim, and your name is Wilson, but your parents don't own Wilson's. What do your parents do?"

"Well, Mom used to work at a gift shop here in Ephraim called Cabin Craft. She had to take a leave of absence on account of an accident, but she'll be back working soon, I hope. Dad works in Sturgeon Bay at Deacon Yachts. They build custom power yachts and sailboats. Matter of fact, see that big black sailboat in the bay with all the varnished wood?" Annie pointed across the water.

Peter nodded.

"It's called *Falcon*. It's the pride of Lake Michigan. My dad helped build it. He told me it's got electric winches, roller furling head and main sails along with an autopilot. The owner can sit in the cockpit and control everything. It was designed that way so he could sail it alone."

Peter stared in disbelief. "Amazing, it must be at least fifty feet. He can sail that boat all by himself?" He took another gulp of his malt and turned back to Annie. "I love sailing more than anything in the whole world."

Annie's skin tingled when he leans closer.

"Anything, that is, except one of your root beer malts on a hot June day."

She laughed. "Wow, I'm honored."

Peter winked and glanced back at *Falcon*. "Seriously, I'd give anything to sail on that boat."

Annie chuckled. "Fat chance of that. The owner is rich. Unless you're rich too?"

Peter blushed. "We're well off. I mean, my parents are well off. I don't work."

He doesn't work! Life's not fair. Why can't I have that? The summer people that stay up here and come from wealthy families are so lucky. Peter seems nice for a rich kid, not arrogant like some that come into Wilson's. He's really good looking too. I think I want to spend more time with him. It just doesn't seem fair that I have to work my butt off at Wilson's and he's out playing. I wish my family had more money.

"I'm sorry," Annie said. "I didn't mean that to come out the way it did. It's just that I need to work." She paused. "What did you do today, Peter?"

"Today, I played golf across the bay at Peninsula State Park. After I finish this wonderful malt, I'm going sailing."

"It must be nice to play all day." She said.

"What? Sorry I didn't hear you."

"It's nothing, just me mumbling." She touched his arm. "Your boat?"

"My Sunfish, it's over there by the pier. The white one." He pointed to a half a dozen sailboats pulled up on the shore near the boat dock. "Do you sail?"

The question made her heart leap. "No, but I'd love to learn." Tilting her head slightly, she fluttered her eyes at him. "Would you teach me? It'd be fun, and I promise I'll be a good student."

"I'd love to teach you. Do you know how to swim, just in case we tip over?"

Annie grinned up at him, then got right in his face. "Do I know how to swim? I know how to swim better than you!"

Peter smiled. He looked out at *Falcon*, then leaned in close, almost touching. "Okay, Miss Smarty, let's just see who's better. How about tomorrow, before work, we have a race out to the *Falcon* and back? We'll take off from the municipal pier here, swim out to *Falcon's* anchor chain, touch the chain and then swim back to the pier. First one to touch the pier wins. How's that? We'll just see who's faster."

What have I gotten myself into? I wanted to meet this guy, but now I have to get wet too. "Okay, but what are we swimming for? I'm not going to swim all the way out there and back just for fun. I want to race for something." She watched his eyebrows crinkle like someone deep in thought but then she watched his eyes. He had beautiful eyes. They were roaming across her body. In spite of the mandatory Wilson's outfit of navy blue shorts, red and white-white checkered blouse, and white tennis shoes, she knew what got to boys. She shook her long blond hair, then gathered it in her hand and pulled it over her shoulder. Then she re-positioned her legs from a Yoga sitting pose and stretched her long, tan legs out, touching Peter's knee with the toe of her tennis shoe. She watched Peter's eyes move down to her legs, and then when they moved back to her face, she loosened a top button of her blouse showing off more of her ample breasts. When she did that, Peter smiled. She could tell Peter was very interested. She knew he was having trouble concentrating on a worthy prize besides her breasts. Good, she wanted to keep him interested.

Annie sat up straight. "I know! How's this? The loser has to do whatever the winner wants for the whole day. Kind of like a slave. That includes making lunch, not just buying it. You do know how to cook, don't you?"

"Yes, I know how to cook. I make a mean tuna sandwich."

"OK, I'm off tomorrow. Let's race tomorrow morning, say seven a.m. Is that too early for you?"

"No way. I'm usually up early to get a tee time and play golf."

"OK, then it's set. I'll see you here tomorrow, at seven." Annie got up from the grass. "I better get back to work. If you're finished with the malt?" She looked down at Peter with a big smile and touched the tip of his nose with her finger. "If you're not here tomorrow morning at seven, I'll just assume you're afraid of being beaten by a girl."

Peter just laughed.

Chapter Two

At 6:45 a.m., Peter leaned his bike against the big oak tree across from Wilson's. Then he took a deep breath at the sight of Annie in the early morning light. God, she's got long legs. Then he watched as she bent over, reached into her backpack, grabbed a couple of rubber bands and made a ponytail. Did I see a tiny hot pink bikini bottom? I hope the rest is a small bikini under that sweatshirt. "I think I'm in love," he laughed.

"What are you laughing at?" she asked.

"Oh, nothing."

"God, what a morning this is." Annie stood with her hands on her hips. "Look at the water. It's eerie with the mist floating above like that, and not a ripple. I love this time of the morning."

"Yes, the sights are beautiful this morning, and the water looks nice too." He flashed her a smile.

"What?" she said, and then it hit her. "Boys!" she muttered. "Come on; let's get this over with. You're going to have a lot to do this morning after I beat you."

The two walked to the end of the municipal pier. Eagle Harbor faced northwest, exposed to the favorable side of Green Bay. "I love to come out on this pier when the weather gets nasty," she said. "The large waves come rolling into the bay, and then smash into this massive pier. I can feel it shake sometimes."

What is she talking about? The weather? The pier shaking? I'm shaking just being with her. God she's beautiful. Annie took off her sweatshirt and shoes. Peter tried not to stare, but he couldn't help

8

thinking of a sleek leopard, lean, powerful, and dangerously beautiful. His mouth opened, but nothing came out. He knew she had a nice body from what he observed yesterday, but wearing a bikini. WOW! Hot pink matching top, while not as tiny as he was hoping for, it sure shows the outline of her nipples. I love nipples or at least I think I do. Maybe a taste this afternoon?

Looking to the heavens, he mouthed, "Thank you, God."

Annie interrupted his spiritual conversation. "What are you looking at?"

"Nothing. I was just loosening up my neck. See?" He moved his head in circles, then up and down.

"Oh. Okay." She took a deep breath. "One last time. We swim out to *Falcon*, touch the anchor chain, and swim back here. First one back wins."

"Yep, pretty simple rules" Peter started pulling his T-shirt over his head when he heard, "Ready, Set, Go" and then a splash. Startled, he peered out through the neck hole of his T-shirt. "Hey, that's not fair!"

Throwing his shirt on the pier, he kicked off his deck shoes, took a couple strides, and then made a long graceful dive. As he moved through the water, he knew he could make up the lost ground. After all, he was a strong swimmer and she was a girl...a beautiful girl, but still a girl and not as strong. No problem.

After just a few minutes, he realized he had misjudged Annie's swimming ability. When she touched the anchor chain first and passed him on the way back, he decided he was in trouble.

The race lasted about twenty minutes. He looked up from the water, his hand on the edge of the pier, and saw her grinning. As he pulled himself up, she handed him his towel. "You're a pretty good swimmer for a guy," she said. "You probably didn't know I was Door County freestyle swimming champion last year, did you?"

Peter laughed. "I think I've been had."

Smiling, Annie leaned over and gave him a peck on the cheek. "You're a good sport."

The kiss was nice but he wanted more. Her breasts were right there. He could almost touch them but then she stood up.

"By the way, I want tuna sandwiches and Cheetos for lunch. And I think root beer is my new favorite beverage."

Peter nodded and toweled himself dry. "When do you want me to pick you up for this day of servitude?" he said with a grin.

"How about nine thirty? That should give you enough time to make everything."

"And what do you want to do?" He slipped on his deck shoes and T-shirt.

"I want to go to Newport Beach and paint. Did I tell you I love to paint? I've wanted to paint there all spring and now it's summer. We need to get there before the crowds to pick out a good spot." Looking up at the sky, she said, "The light should be great today." She bent down, grabbed her sweatshirt, and slipped on her tennis shoes.

He chuckled. "By the way, that's the same lunch I was going to ask you to make for me. One last question: Where do you live?"

"Three Fourteen Tamarack Trail; it's the road behind Hotel Ephraim, the white house with the swing." Annie smiled and then said, "Just look for lots of painting stuff on the lawn; it should be easy to spot." She paused and studied him. "Peter, I'm looking forward to today."

With a sigh, he watched her get on her bike, wave, and ride home. He was looking forward to the day too, even if she made him work his butt off with all the things she had planned. Most of all, he hoped he had enough energy to do the things he thought about last night in bed. That's what he really wanted.

**

There was no mistaking Annie's house. Painted a traditional white, with a wooden swing under a covered porch, a one car detached garage sat to the left of the house that backed up to a tamarack woods and marsh.

Kind of a small house he thought. Not something mother would approve of. He could hear her make her usual comments; "They probably are not the right kind of family for us, Peter." He hated it when she said "us" when all he cared about was himself. I hope this works out today.

Peter noticed how much quieter it was back here, and cooler too, away from the main highway. He liked the porch with its swing. He pulls up in his mother's Cadillac, and parks it on the gravel driveway next to the wood-trimmed Chevy station wagon, and he sees the pile. His mouth drops open.

Did Annie have ALL her painting equipment on the front lawn? It sure looked like it to him. He hoped she didn't need it all. He just wanted to be with her, and maybe see a little more of her body. Actually he wanted to see a lot of her body. Was this her way of making him pay for losing the bet?

He ambled over to the pile. "Shit, shit, shit," he said as he looks at the pile. Just then, Annie came out of the house wearing short cutoff jeans, a red tee shirt with Wisconsin stenciled across the chest, and a white sailor's hat turned upside down. His pulse quickened. She toted the morning's sweatshirt, a beach bag, an old blanket, and a canvas director's chair, along with a big smile. "I think that's about it, unless you can think of anything else we'll need today?"

"Maybe I should borrow a pick-up truck," he said, grinning. "I only hope I have enough room in the car for you, Annie,"

Pushing her sunglasses up on her nose, she tilted her head and looked at him with a quivering lip. "It's not that bad, is it?" Then she laughed. "Besides, it's not every day I have someone to help me lug this stuff around."

"Ok, I know the deal," he said. "In your opinion, does this count as work? You gave me static yesterday about not working. This looks like a lot of stuff just for a silly painting."

She glared at him. "It might be a silly painting to you Mr. Big Shot, but it's what I love to do and you," she paused, "have to do what ever I want."

"Sorry. It's just, I didn't think you would need all this stuff."

Five minutes later, they were loaded and ready to leave.

"What's Newport?" Peter asked as he turned the key and backed out of the driveway.

"It's a State Park farther north with a nice, gentle beach with dunes, rocks, and lots of trees. They'll make a good backdrop for scenes I intend to paint. Let's go."

The drive over seemed to fly as Annie chatted and gave directions. Newport Beach meant heading north out of Ephraim along Highway 42. Driving through Sister Bay and Ellison Bay, they eventually turned east off the highway and headed toward the Lake Michigan side of the Peninsula.

As he drove, he couldn't resist teasing Annie about her swimming before he was ready. "I think it would have been close if we started at the same time. You are fast."

"I said, 'ready, set, go,' and you just weren't ready."

And so it went until they drove down the beach road. The turn-off to the beach was more like a farm path. Grass grew high enough between the two ruts so it hissed against the underside of the car. Peter drove slowly so he wouldn't bottom out his mom's Cadillac.

"Stop! This is it!" Jumping out of the car, Annie danced around, arms raised, and yells, "It's perfect. It's just perfect." She grabbed her bag and a blanket and sets off. "Come on, Peter. You can get that stuff later. I know just what I'm looking for."

She hurried ahead, talking over her shoulder. "I need a view of the water, a curving shoreline, some rocks jutting out into the water, and some trees for background."

"Oh, is that all?" Peter said as he finally caught up. I sure hope she's good. I had more important things on my mind concerning Miss Wilson like wrapping my arms around that great body. Maybe even finding out if she has a mind. I'm not sure I could handle an airhead.

"Don't be an old poop!" She looked down the beach. "Oh, one other thing. I'd like to be up a bit on a sand dune for a better view.

Finally, if we could get behind some juniper bushes to break the wind, that would be great too. That way, sand doesn't blow onto my paper."

"I hope this paradise isn't too far from the car?"

"Oh, quit your complaining. You lost the bet. Besides, its beautiful here."

About a quarter of a mile from the car, Annie found her perfect place.

Peter liked that it was secluded. Maybe, if he let her paint for a while, he could turn her attention to other things.

Annie spread the blanket out, placing a rock on each corner. Then she put her beach bag in the center. Finished, she gave Peter a hug. "I'm so excited. The light is perfect." She grabbed his hand and gave it a squeeze. "I'll even go back to the car with you and get the tripod, paper, and paint box." She hooked her arm through his and gave him a tug. "Let's go, I want to get started."

Peter smiled. "Let's walk down to the water first. I want to see how cold the water is on this side. You know, Annie, this side of the peninsula's water and air is about ten degrees cooler than the Green Bay side. The prevailing winds on Green Bay blow the top water towards the western shores of Door County where Ephraim is. On the east side of the Peninsula, like here, the prevailing winds blow the warmer water away towards Michigan."

"I know that, Peter. I've lived here my whole life." Then she stepped in the water. "Oh, it's cold," she squealed. "Look, I have goose bumps all over."

Peter smiled. He knew how he could make those goose bumps go away. He'd like to cover her with his body like he was a blanket. Hold her tight and kiss her on the warm sand. "I noticed."

"I hope it gets warmer this afternoon so we can swim." Annie smiled back. "Are you still going to teach me to sail this summer when I'm not working?"

"Isn't that why we had the race…to make sure you knew how to swim?" He nudged her with his hip. "Guess you'll do OK if we tip over…. and we will." Peter fixed his eyes on hers. "I think I'm a good teacher." I've never had a prettier student than you, he thought.

Annie smiled.

Moments later, they reached the car. Annie grabbed what she needed to get started and headed back, leaving Peter to get the rest. By the time he got the first load to the spot, Annie had her tripod set up and just finished matting, taping, and wetting the paper. She was ready to paint. When Peter arrived with the second load, he noticed, she was lost in her art. It's nice to have a passion like my sailing. He flopped down on the blanket, and closed his eyes.

"Carrying all your equipment across the sand has made me tired." Half asleep, he asked, "What are you going to paint?"

"Oh, I don't know…something small." Annie looked at the water and shoreline. "Something to get a rhythm going, to get my fingers and brush working as one. I don't know if anyone else does it this way. I see lots of people warm up like this in sports or music. It just helps me to get a feel for how I'm going to paint."

Peter grunted and fought to keep his eyes open. Annie didn't seem to notice. "When I feel things are right, I'll start on something I want to paint."

"So what do you want to paint now?" Peter yawned.

She pointed down the beach. "I like how the trees and rocks reflect on the water, the gentle curve of the beach. I know there isn't a boat out there, but I think I'll put a sailboat flying a spinnaker just coming over the horizon."

Peter laid his head on the blanket, eyes closed. "Sounds nice."

"It's only going to be eight by eleven inches, so it won't take me too long to paint. You rest now. I don't talk much when I'm painting, but when I get done I get very excited. Matter of fact, I'll probably talk your ear off."

Peter's eyes snapped open. "Oh my god, what did I get myself into?" Laughing, he rolled over, looked once at the water, and closed his eyes again.

**

A hand softly rubbed his back. Peter slowly opened his eyes and rolled over. What he saw made him smile. Annie's face came into focus, hovering a few inches over his face, her eyes looking deep into his. Her long blond hair framed her beautiful expression. With the help of a soft breeze, the tips of her hair gently caressed his cheeks.

"I'm done with the painting," she whispered.

He rolled over on his side, propping his head on his hand. "Let's see!" He stared at her work.

Annie watched his eyes dart back and forth across the painting as he took it in.

He looked up at her. "WOW! This is nice. I mean, you're really good. I never expected you to be this good when you said you were an artist."

Annie just stared at him, eyebrows high.

"I mean, this really looks good. I'm not saying that just because I want you to like me. It really is good."

"I'm glad you like it. It means a lot to me."

"How did you learn to do this?" Peter sat up now, interested.

Annie smiled. "As a kid, I used to draw a lot. Door County's a Mecca for artists. It's often referred to as the Cape Cod of the Midwest."

Peter nodded. "I've heard that."

"The local artists really helped me. Before my mom's accident, artists would come into the gift shop where she worked to see how their art was selling on a consignment basis. They were always nice to me, and once they knew I was serious about art and painting, they'd invite me to their studios. If I saw them at the beach or in town, I'd ask them questions, usually about some painting technique. Even now, I'll ask their opinion. They're usually very generous with their thoughts."

Peter smiled. "Golfers are like that too. Everyone's an expert, trying to help you with your swing."

Annie shrugged. "Just about everything I learned as a painter, they helped me with."

"You're very good." Peter held the painting up again. "This paint looks different?"

Annie laughed. "That's because its watercolors. I love watercolors. I mix the colors with water and actually wet the paper with this large brush, then let it shrink and dry." She held the brush up for Peter to see.

"Then I just paint what I like." She turned toward the water again. "I haven't sold anything yet, but I will. I can feel it. I have to. I need to make money if I want to go to college. We had to use most of my college money to pay for my mom's hospital bills. She fell and hit her head while riding her bike to work. Since then, she has a hard time keeping her balance, and her memory is not as good as it used to be. Without her working, money is tight. It's not like we're going to starve, but I need to work at Wilson's and save every penny."

"Painting is my one luxury, but I don't have much time to spend painting like I used to." She sighed. "I'm not as lucky as you when it comes to money."

"From what I've seen so far, it won't be long before you're selling lots of paintings. I wish I could help you with your art in some way. I guess right now all I can do is feed you and be your servant, carrying all your stuff. If I had lots of money, I'd give it all to you." Then he leaned over and kissed her.

She sighed. "Thanks Peter, I appreciate the thought...and the kiss."

Peter nodded and changed the subject. *It's my parents that have the money. Not me.* "Hey, I'm hungry. You ready for lunch?" He handed Annie the painting.

Annie nodded. "Yah, I'm starved."

He gave her a tuna sandwich, Cheetos, and opened her root beer, and then did the same for himself. It didn't take long for either to finish their meal.

"Thanks, Peter. That was really good. I love tuna sandwiches."

"You're welcome. It's an old family favorite recipe."

Peter pointed down the beach. "The water must be warmer now. There are lots of people swimming."

Looking at the tops of the trees, he noticed them bending slightly toward the shore. "The wind shifted, so the top water must be moving in. Why don't you paint something small and then let's go swimming? I have to get the car back by two o'clock so Mom can play bridge with the ladies in Sister Bay."

"Okay." She started painting the shoreline.

An hour later he returned and looked at the painting and asked, "Is that me?"

"What do you think? When you walked down to the water to skip rocks again, I painted you in and added a small sailboat on the horizon. I just finished when you came up from the beach."

"Thanks, Annie. Now I can tell my friends back home that I was a model over the summer." He leaned over and gave her a quick kiss on the lips, then he turned and started running toward the water, waded in up to his chest, and dove in. Breaking the surface, he yelled, "It's really warm."

Annie walked down to the water. He came up to meet her. He grabbed her hand and, together, they dashed in. Her body tumbled under the water, and when her head broke the surface, she screamed at Peter. "You lied to me. It's still cold."

"I know. I can see you're cold." Peter moved close, wrapped his arms around her body and pressed against her. "Does this make you feel warmer?"

"It does, but don't get any ideas."

"Hey, I'm just getting back at you for starting the race before I was ready. Besides, you don't seem as cold now." He leaned back and looked down at her breasts. I sure would like to do more, he thought. Is it too soon?

"I do feel warmer," she said.

"Good." With that, he pulled her close and gave her a long slow kiss. Before she opened her eyes, he grabbed her hand and pulled her toward the beach. They laughed then ran to the blanket and flopped down. They laid on their backs and looked up at the blue Door County sky. Neither said a word. Instead, they breathed in time with the sounds of the waves lapping on the shore.

Annie spoke first. "This sun feels so good. I love lying here just letting my mind wander."

Peter grunted, and then closed his eyes. The sun felt good on his chest. He moved his hand a small distance and bumped her arm. He liked feeling her close. *She's probably thinking about painting. God she's beautiful.*

Minutes later, Peter rolled over on his side and watched Annie's chest rise and fall. Gently, he touched a finger to her arm, and then slowly traced it down to her fingers. When he did it again, more slowly, he noticed Annie get goose bumps.

"Peter! What are you doing?"

"Nothing, just seeing if you were asleep. I guess you're not."

"No, I'm not!"

"Good." He leaned over and brushed his lips across her cheek, then moved to her neck, then back to her lips as he moved his chest onto hers. He felt her arms slide to his back, pulling him to her. *Ahh.* His body responded as he pressed against her, letting her know she excited him. He kissed her for a few minutes more before slowly rolling on his back. Eyes open, he stared at the sky.

Annie lay silent.

Oh shit, did I move too fast? Did she feel my arousal pressing against her? Maybe she didn't like the kiss. His stomach tightened.

She too, looked up at the sky. Her face held no expression.

"Are you all right?" Peter asked.

"Yes. It just took me a while to decide if I liked you kissing me. It's so easy for people with money to do whatever they want to the rest of us." Annie turned toward him, eyes red. "I feel intimidated by you, because you come from a wealthy family. I'm uncomfortable with that, really uncomfortable." She paused. "But you surprised me by being a nice guy."

Peter took a deep breath. "I can't help that my parents have money, but do you like me kissing you?"

Annie blushed. "I think I do, but don't think you can kiss me any time you want, Peter Franklin." With that, she sat up. "I think it's getting late. If you want to get your mom's car back by two, we better go. Remember, you have to haul all this stuff back."

"Yeah, lots of fun," he muttered.

"Oh, didn't I tell you? There's an old tractor trail just behind those bushes." Annie pointed to a large grouping of juniper bushes hiding the road. "Why don't you drive the car down here? It will make it a lot easier to load up this stuff."

Peter sat up with a jerk. "You mean you let me carry all this stuff here when you knew there was a road just thirty feet away?"

"You lost the race, Peter. I wanted to get my money's worth." She giggled and gave him a peck on the cheek. "Besides, a little hard work is good for you." Her giggle intoxicating, Peter tickled Annie until she jumped up and ran away from him.

"Hurry and get the car," she called from a safe distance. "You owe me dessert too. We can stop at the General Store in Ellison Bay and get some ice cream."

**

When Peter pulled up next to the cottage at Hotel Ephraim, his mother was waiting for him. He pulled in front of her and turned off the engine, his stomach tightening at the sight of her tapping foot.

"You're late," Patti Franklin said, glaring. "You know I play bridge today. I hate being late. You better have a good excuse."

Grinning, Peter showed her the painting Annie had painted of him and the sailboat.

"Mom, I met this gorgeous girl yesterday, we had this race this morning to see who was a faster swimmer. I lost, and the loser had to do what the other person wanted. She wanted to go up north to Newport Beach and paint. See, that's why I have this picture and was late getting back with your car."

Peter's mom just smiled. "I'd like to meet her someday. I hope this one comes from the right kind of family."

"Let it go, Mom. Remember the last time you did that?"

"I can't talk about it now. I'm late for cards. We'll talk later about this."

"I'm going sailing now," he said, "but I'll be back for dinner." *Why does she have to keep sticking her nose into my love life? I'm not going to let her wreck it for me this time.*

Peter jumped on his bike. His thoughts centered on when he would see Annie again.

He smiled as he peddled. *She did want to learn to sail.*

Chapter Three

Dennis Jamison thought how lucky he was to find his summer job at Sturgeon Bay's Deacon's Yachts. Fortunately, Darrell Wilson, Yard Supervisor, liked him right way. Dennis smiled, remembering when Darrell told him he hired him because he saw excitement in Dennis's eyes, and that he reminded him of himself, twenty-five years earlier.

After just a couple of weeks of work, two women walked up to Darrell and Dennis as Darrell was explaining how he wanted some trim work installed on a large motor yacht.

"Well, what a pleasant surprise. What brings you two down here?" Darrell gave each a peck on the cheek.

Betty Wilson grabbed Darrell's hand like a love struck teenager. "Annie drove down because she needed more art supplies. I came along for the ride and thought, as long as we were here, you could take us out for lunch."

Darrell broke out in a big grin. "Now this is the best thing that's happened to me all day. You bet, let's go." Then he looked at Dennis, who just stood there, taking everything in.

Darrell turned toward him. "I'm sorry, Dennis. This is my wife, Betty, and my daughter, Annie. This is Dennis Jamison. Dennis is one of the new guys we hired for the summer. He's from Milwaukee. He seems to be doing a good job so far..."

Dennis listened to Darrell, but his eyes focused on Annie's face. When he heard Darrell say, "…I guess we'll keep him," he laughed.

"Ok, girls, let's go have some lunch. I'm hungry." He looked at Dennis. "Finish up here, and then go have some lunch. I'll check your work later."

Dennis simply nodded as Darrell, Betty and Annie turned and walked off. He stood and watched: his eyes focused on Annie and her sexy walk. His imagination ran wild as he thought about her eyes, her long legs, and what that body might look like naked. He couldn't quite remember the last time someone stopped him in his tracks on a first meeting.

He let out a deep sigh and watched the three walk away. Just before Annie reached the corner, she turned, looked over her shoulder and waved goodbye to Dennis, and then disappeared.

"Man, I'd like to see more of that!" he said aloud, and then sanity hit. Dads like Darrell are very protective of their daughters, he thought. Besides, the man was his boss.

What the hell. I've got lots of time to think about how I'm going to get to know Annie Wilson, my way.

The days passed, and with each day, Dennis got better at his job. He knew he was over the hump when the guys started asking if he'd like to join them for a beer after work. And when he found himself talking about boating on his time off, he knew the boat business was in his blood.

He felt good about having a passion for boating. It gave him something to think about and work toward besides getting laid. Working with his hands gave him great satisfaction, not to mention the pride he felt when he finished a job. It made no difference to him, whether he installed a piece of wood or he did varnishing work, he loved what he was doing.

Most of the boats Deacon's built cost over a million dollars. A majority were motor yachts, but sailing yachts still accounted for about thirty percent of the business. Dennis quickly came to understand that he had to do the job right the first time, so he became a perfectionist in every area. He asked a lot of questions. He got to work early and stayed late. He knew it was a job, but to him, it was fun.

One Friday, just before quitting time, Darrell walked up to him as he was putting the finishing touches on a yacht railing.

"Hey, Dennis. If you aren't doing anything this Sunday afternoon, maybe you'd like to join Betty, Annie, and me for dinner?"

"You bet I would. I'm getting mighty tired of hamburgers and pizza." His mind flashed back to the image of Annie swaying as she walked away, then turning and waving to him. His whole body warmed at the thought. "What time should I get there?"

"Why don't you come around two thirty? Annie gets off work around then. She works at a local ice cream shop in Ephraim. Have you been to Ephraim before?"

"No, but I know it's just up the road."

"We dress casual on Sunday afternoons, so wear what you want. If it's hot, you might want to bring a swimsuit. We're just going to have chicken on the grill, nothing fancy, but it'll be good. Betty makes a great cherry pie. Matter of fact, her potato salad is pretty good too. Annie can show you around Ephraim when she gets home."

Dennis nodded. *Ahh, Annie.*

"Here's the address. See you Sunday."

"Thanks."

**

Dennis could hardly wait for Sunday. Though he didn't have much money, he bought some new 'Topsider' deck shoes and carefully washed and pressed his nice polo golf shirt and shorts. He wore his Ray Ban aviator sunglasses because he liked the look, and the wire frames wrapped around his ears so they wouldn't fall in the water.

When he arrived at the Wilson house, Darrell came out and greeted him. The Weber grill stood in front of the garage with a large bag of charcoal leaning against its leg.

"Annie's not home yet, so I thought I'd wait to start the coals. Want a beer or a soda?"

"Beer would be great."

Darrell handed him an Old Style. "Must be busy at Wilson's. Annie's usually home by now. It'll give us a chance for some man talk."

Dennis nodded, and they shot the shit about work, and what he liked best about Deacons. "Every day is so exciting to me," he said. "I literally jump out of bed each morning, ready to learn something new."

Darrell smiled and got himself another beer.

"I didn't know boating could be that invigorating," Dennis said. "I think I'm hooked."

Darrell laughed, and then they clinked their beer bottles together. "To boating."

The crunch of gravel echoed as Annie turned into the driveway on her big Schwinn fat tire bike. Dennis put his beer down. Let the games begin; this is why he really was up here, not the food.

Leaning the bike inside the garage, she walked over and kissed Darrell. "Hi, Dad." Then her eyes moved to Dennis. His blazing blue eyes held her attention. His muscular chest filled out his shirt nicely, and the snug shorts showed off his strong muscular legs and more. She looked up and smiled. "Hi, Dennis. It's nice to see you again." *He looks like a jock; must have played football in school.*

"Nice seeing you too, Annie."

After a few minutes of small talk, she turned and walked to the house. "I'll be out in a little while. I just have to get out of these clothes and get into something comfortable."

"Honey, do you think you could give Dennis a tour of Ephraim before dinner? He's never been up this far north in Door County."

"Sure, but I am really hot and sweaty. I need a swim. How about after dinner?" Looking at Dennis, she said, "Did you bring a suit, by chance?"

He smiled. "I did."

"Good. Dad, could we go swimming for just a little bit? We won't be too long, and the water is warming up for the first time this summer."

"That sounds okay to me." Darrell pointed at the grill. "I haven't started the coals yet. I'll wait about fifteen minutes and have another beer. Maybe I can convince your mother to come out of the kitchen and enjoy the afternoon while you two swim. Dennis, you can change in the bathroom next to the kitchen."

Dennis nodded and moved toward the house.

"If you want something to drink, Dennis, it'll have to be soda. They don't allow beer at the municipal beach."

"That's fine. I'll take a couple of sodas," Annie said.

A few minutes later, Dennis came out of the house in his suit.

Annie came down a few minutes later in a bright cobalt blue one-piece suit with two towels around her neck. She liked him even more in his swimming suit. She watched Dennis give her the once over.

Dennis broke into a big smile.

He definitely likes me by that smile, even in this old one-piece suit.

Darrell looked at Annie and Dennis and just smiled. "Ah, youth," he said. "The coals should be ready in about fifteen minutes, and it should take about thirty minutes to cook the chicken, so be back here about three thirty."

"Ok, come on, Dennis. We can walk; it's only a block and half to the beach. Do you have a towel?"

"I do."

"Good, let's go."

They started down the road toward the beach.

"Dad tells me you're from Milwaukee." *God, he's good looking.*

"Actually I'm from Shorewood, a suburb just north of Milwaukee. It borders Lake Michigan. It's a nice enough area."

"Have you lived there your whole life?"

"Yes. I went to the local grade school and high school. I feel pretty lucky to have a job at Deacon's. Two of my buddies got jobs there, too. The three of us have a very small apartment in Sturgeon Bay."

Annie nodded. She could tell Dennis was excited about his work. *I wonder if he has a girlfriend up here? Maybe that's the real reason he came to Door County.*

"They're letting me do some real work on the boats now, but I'm still learning," he said. "I really enjoy it. Your dad's great to work for. He's helped me a lot."

"Dad's pretty good with the guys. He got his start just like you. He went on to school and came back each summer to Deacon's, and my mom. They met up here."

"Really!"

"Mom worked at the boatyard doing bookkeeping and secretarial work when she was in high school." Annie smiled. "They always seem so happy with each other. The thing I like best is that they laugh and talk a lot."

"They sound like great parents to me."

"They are! They respect my opinion, even if we don't agree. And if they're really serious about something that affects me, I really don't argue because I know they have their reasons."

"You never argue?"

"I didn't say we never argue. I just don't fight it too hard. I think they are great parents. I hope I can do as well when I have kids."

They crossed the road to the beach.

"I wish I could say my parents were that way." Dennis paused, looked to the sky and then at Annie. "That doesn't mean they're bad, but with Dad, it's his way or the highway. We had some good arguments, mostly Dad and me. Mom tried to stick up for me, but Dad was the boss. It made for some hard feelings."

Annie reached over and touched his arm. "Hey, I'm sorry to bring all this up on the walk. We hardly know each other. I'm sure you'll be up for more Sunday dinners if I know Dad. He remembers what it was like to be away from home that first summer."

Dennis looked at her and smiled. "I'd like that. It is different being away from home. It's the simple things, like eating in a family setting, that I miss."

Stopping at the edge of the parking lot, Annie surveyed the beach and the water. "The nice thing about coming here later on Sunday is it's not crowded."

Dennis decided he liked it without crowds too, but for a different reason.

Annie spread one of the beach towels out on the sand, dropped the other, and then looked at Dennis. "Let's go!"

They both ran into the water up to their waists and dove in. Dennis came up screaming, "It's cold. I thought you said it was warming up?"

Annie just laughed. "It'll get really warm in a few weeks. Now it's just invigorating."

"Thanks, I'll remember that next year!" Dennis headed back to the beach and the warm towel.

Annie laughed as Dennis splashed back, grumbling. She kept swimming a while longer and then got out.

Dennis held her towel as she came toward him. Once again, he couldn't help but notice her body. He felt himself become slightly aroused as he thought of what she'd be like. He knew he wanted her, but not right then. She didn't seem like the others that succumbed to his charms, and there were many, but he had all summer. He smiled with that refreshing thought.

"Now I feel better." She toweled herself dry. "I guess you aren't used to the cool water yet," she said with a smirk. "You'll get used to it after a while."

Dennis shook his head. "I don't think so. I used to swim in Lake Michigan at Atwater Beach back home when I was younger. I never got used to it then, and I'm not going to get used to it now."

"We'll see." Annie took a stick and started doodling in the sand. "What other things did you do back home?"

"I worked some, and played lots of sports. You know, the usual, baseball, football and basketball. I made just enough money to go out and have a good time," he said with a sly smile.

Annie winked at him. "Oh, I can imagine what your good time involved."

He laughed, then looked her in the eye. He didn't know why, but he really wanted this girl to like him. "My parents worked hard, but we never had a lot of extra money. Mom works at a bank, and Dad is a mechanic at Miller Brewing Company. He does maintenance work on the trucks, fleet cars, and anything else that needs fixing. That's how I got an interest in working with my hands." He paused and then smiled. "What do you like to do?"

"I love painting and drawing. Wilson's taught me that I don't want to be a waitress all my life. I'm sick of not having money. I want to be a famous artist and sell paintings for lots of money," she said. "I guess I have a lot of practice ahead if I'm going to do that, but I'm only nineteen. How old are you?"

"Just turned twenty. I'm going to the Milwaukee School of Engineering this fall."

The two fell silent, and then Dennis asked, "What about sports?"

"I'm a pretty good swimmer." Annie smiled. "Outside of that, I like biking and fishing with Dad, but painting is my number one thing."

Glancing at her watch, she jumped to her feet. "We should start back. Dad doesn't like it if he has to wait. He loves to barbeque, in case you haven't noticed. If his coals burn down too low waiting for us, watch out!"

Dennis tried not to let his disappointment show. "Then we better get going. I don't want him mad after he asked me to come for dinner."

"Dad does a great job of cooking brats and chicken, but just make sure you save room for Mom's cherry pie. It's the best."

"I'll remember that."

For Dennis, dinner with the Wilsons was casual and perfect. Darrell and Betty were great hosts, but it was Annie who made sure he enjoyed himself. She kept him involved in the conversation, explaining whom so and so was when Darrell or Betty started talking about someone in the community or relatives. The food was great, and Betty's pie was to die for.

Darrell patted his stomach. "Annie, why don't you give Dennis that tour of Ephraim and Sister Bay since he didn't see much before dinner? He's probably sick of us and would rather spend time with you." He winked at Dennis.

Darrell, you're a prince. Hoping his huge smile didn't make him look dumb, Dennis turned to Annie and nodded.

"Ok, I'll give him the grand tour."

"Don't be too late. Dennis has to drive back to Sturgeon Bay tonight," Darrell said. "I'll see you tomorrow morning, young man."

"Thanks again, Darrell, and Mrs. Wilson. It was a wonderful dinner." *Finally I can get out of here and make some moves on Annie. I love teasing but eventually I'll get her.*

Chapter Four

Dennis led the way to his beat up, rusty orange VW Bug convertible. "The car runs better than it looks," he said and laughed. "Where to?"

"Let's go to Sister Bay first and work our way back," Annie said. "That way, you can drop me off at home and head back to Sturgeon Bay when we're done."

"Okay," Dennis said. "Where to in Sister Bay?"

"Let's start with Al Johnson's Swedish restaurant. It's a main attraction. The food is great, but most people remember it because of the goats on top of the restaurant's sod roof."

"Really?"

"Yeah, it's pretty neat."

They got to Al Johnson's and, sure enough, the goats were on the roof. The place was packed as usual. Looking down along Main Street, people walked and shopped, enjoying the many gift shops and restaurants. The late summer evening gave the area a carnival atmosphere. Parents or grandparents shepherded their kids, and cars slowly cruised down the street, enjoying the view of the water and boats at the marina.

After the short tour of Sister Bay's downtown, Annie thought they should play miniature golf at the Red Putter. They got a score card and colored golf balls, then walked to the first hole.

"Dennis, do you play golf?"

"This isn't golf."

"Sure it is." Annie grinned and moved the putter back and forth in a practice stroke. "It takes skill, touch, and timing to hit a golf ball just hard enough to go through the windmill without getting it knocked into the water. It takes skill and vision to shoot to the most strategic spot, so you can make your next shot. You don't play much miniature golf, do you, Mr. Jock?" She stared at Dennis as she tossed her pink golf ball up and down.

He smiled. "It really doesn't look that hard."

"We'll see. Do you want to bet?" she said with an arch in her brow.

Dennis laughed, certain he was about to be taken, and just as certain that he didn't care. "Sure. How much?"

"A buck for eighteen holes, and the loser buys ice cream at Wilson's."

"Okay, you're on!" *At least she's competitive. Should be an easy buck.*

After eleven holes, it pleased him that it was still a tight game. Annie was better on the holes that required playing angles or laying up in the right spot for the next shot, while he did better with the straight shots and holes that required more power.

On the twelfth hole, the windmill hole, Annie got through on her first try, avoiding the water hazard and the rotating windmill blades, putting her in position for an easy two putt.

"Nice putt, Annie. That was really good." Dennis took his time lining up his bright green golf ball, and then stroked the putt. It looked great, but, just when it looked like it was going to roll right through, the wooden windmill blade whacked it and sent it into the water hazard. "Shit," was all Dennis could say.

"Too bad." Annie giggled.

Sighing, he replaced the ball in the drop area and stroked it again. Whack, whack, and whack, three more shots into the rotating wooden blade and into the hazard. Finally, he two putted for a ten, while Annie two putted for a three. One look at the beautiful girl to his side, however, and his frustration slipped away.

Annie studied him. "I can tell you don't like to lose," she said.

He shrugged. "You're right. It is harder than it looks, but I lost fair and square." He paused, expecting to say nothing else, but the words just kept coming. "I don't like to be embarrassed. That windmill embarrassed me, and that's what got me mad, not losing. But I got to hang out with you. You're fun. Come on, let's get that ice cream." With a smile, he pulled a dollar out of his wallet and handed it to her. "You're pretty good at this miniature golf."

"You might say that. I do get my share of ice cream and dollars from guys who think I'm easy, like you." She winked.

They climbed into the Bug and drove the short distance to Ephraim. It was a perfect night to have the top down. Annie looked beautiful with her blond hair blowing back, a big smile, and her green eyes sparkling. Dennis had a hard time keeping his eyes on the road.

As they rounded the bend leading near the water's edge, Annie suddenly said, "Pull in here!"

"Why, what's here?"

"Just pull in. I want to show you Anderson Dock and The General Store. It's one of the oldest buildings in Door County, a real landmark. The water in the slips is deep, so bigger boats can tie up here. See, look at these big cruisers and sailboats." They walked around the graffiti-covered wooden warehouse and admired several of the yachts.

"I bet we built some of these boats at Deacon's," Dennis said.

"Maybe." Annie sighed. "I love to fantasize about living on a boat."

"I know what you mean," Dennis said. *I'd love to fantasize about living on a boat with you.* "I work on boats like this all day, and they're neat. It's fun to meet customers and hear about their dreams."

Annie stared at a forty-foot sailboat. "See this one, Green-Eyed Girl?" she asked.

"She's a beauty," Dennis answered.

"The owners stop in Wilson's for ice cream once or twice a week. Sometimes, I dream one of them will ask me on board and give me a tour. In the dream, they say, "Would you like to sail with us out to Chambers Island or to Gill's Rock?" She looked toward the water and sighed. "So far, it's only been a dream."

Dennis gave a little laugh. "It's all right, Annie. Dreams are cheap. Let's go to Wilson's and get some ice cream."

She leaned over and gave him a kiss on the cheek.

"What was that for?" I knew it wouldn't take long before she'd want something more.

"For being a good sport," she said.

Dennis looked at Annie. "We can do better than that," he said and pulled her close, kissing her first on the lips and then slipping the tip of his tongue between them. He felt Annie shudder, he felt her body heat increase to his touch. He hoped she was feeling a warm tingling throughout her body, like others told him they experienced when he kissed them. She seemed to linger at his touch, and then he felt her press herself against him. He knew she liked the feel of his lips to hers. Slowly, she pulled back.

She surprised him next when she said, "You're a good kisser. I've never felt something like a buzz run through my body when someone kissed me." Looking up at him, slightly dazed, she mumbled, "That was very nice, Dennis, but now I need something cool." Fanning herself, she said. "Let's get that ice cream."

He looked at her and smiled.

They found a parking spot near the Eagle Inn, and walked the block to Wilson's. Rita Gallagher, Annie's best friend, was working behind the ice cream counter when Annie and Dennis walked in.

"Hi, Rita."

"Hi, Annie. What can I get you?" Rita said, her eyes focused on Dennis.

"This is Dennis Jamison. He is one of the new guys working for my Dad at Deacon's this summer."

Rita nodded. "Hi."

"He's buying. He lost a dollar to me playing mini-golf. Windmill got him."

"Another one, poor guy," Rita said with a smile.

Annie watched her sizing up Dennis, and she knew her friend liked what she saw.

"What would you like?" Rita asked.

"How about a double scoop of chocolate chip in a cone and you?" He said.

"You're cute!" Rita giggled. "I might just take you up on that offer."

Dennis arched his eyebrows.

Annie looked at him, wide-eyed. *He just kissed me and he says that to Rita?* She gave a measured smile. "You better watch it, Dennis. Rita's a wild one!"

Rita stuck her tongue out at Annie. "What do you want?"

"Oh, I'll have a plain vanilla cone."

Rita finished making Dennis's order. Handing the cone to him, she asked Annie, "You been out with that Peter guy?"

"We're going out this week. He sails and plays golf all the time," Annie said, thinking it must be nice not to have to work and just ask Mommy and Daddy for money when you need it. "Not like us." *But he was nice to me the other day, even when I was on his butt about being wealthy. I wish I wasn't so testy about money. Maybe I'm afraid of not measuring up to the same standards as his rich friends.* "He said he was going to teach me to sail this Wednesday when I'm off. I'm really looking forward to it. I think he's safer to be around than Dennis here."

"Safer?" Dennis looked at her with a smile. "Did that kiss scare you, Annie? I hope not."

Annie blushed as Rita gaped. *It does bother me how turned on he got me with that one kiss.* "I have an idea. Maybe I can talk Peter into taking us all sailing? We could rent one of those boats across the street big enough for the four of us. Dennis, would you like to go sailing with Rita and me if I can talk Peter into taking us?"

"That would be fun." He looked at Rita, and his eyes settled on her ample breasts. "If she wears something besides that uniform."

Rita followed his eyes and smiled. "I just hope you're as good as you think you are," she said. "I might be too much for you, Dennis."

"I'll be enough for you. You can bet on that," he said and winked.

"If you two are done?" Annie said, her hands on her hips. "Dennis, pay the lady. Rita, here's the dollar Dennis lost to me at golf for your tip."

"See you later, Dennis," Rita said.

Annie nodded and waved goodbye. She and Dennis walked across the street to one of the picnic tables, then sat down and watched the sun's last rays settle lower in the sky. Ten minutes later, the sun slipped behind Eagle Bluff as they sat looking at the boats, Horseshoe Island, and the ruffled water of the bay. A big black sailboat came up to its mooring on a slight breeze, rounding up and lowering its sails.

"What a beautiful boat that black one is," Dennis said as he finished his cone.

"It's *Falcon*. Isn't she a beauty? Deacon's built her in the sixties," Annie said with a smile. "My friend Peter, the guy who's going to teach me to sail and I hope will take us sailing. He and I had a race last week, out to *Falcon* and back. I won." A big smile crossed her face. "Because he lost, he had to spend the whole day lugging stuff around for me while I painted. I know he wanted to race just to spend more time with me and it worked. We had a good time together."

Dennis laughed. "If you were a gun slinger and wore a pistol on your hip, I bet you'd have several notches cut into the handle with all the bets you've won from innocent guys like me."

"I might," Annie said with a smirk. "I'm competitive. I can't help it if you boys want to bet!"

Dennis leaned his elbow on the table and looked at Annie. "Let me see if I have this right. Peter is going to teach you how to sail. Then after he teaches you to sail, you're going to talk Peter into renting a sailboat and taking us all sailing."

"You got it. You've got to pay for half of the boat rental. Are you okay with that?"

"Sounds all right to me." He looked towards Wilson's. "Rita looks like she can be a lot of fun."

"So can I!" She punched his arm. *Remember me?* "She's really a handful. The red hair fits her. I like Peter and I like you too. You know, a girl has to keep her options open, but you'll have fun with Rita."

"Options?" He laughed. "Where is she from?"

"From Madison. She and her family came up to Door County for the summer when she was younger. We've known each other for years, and we decided that we'd work at Wilson's together this year." Annie paused. "You two should get along well. She's competitive, and she plays soccer and volleyball at school, so she's in good shape."

"So I noticed!" Dennis said with a big grin.

"I saw your eyes roaming over her body. You guys are all the same."

Dennis didn't say anything. He just winked at her.

Annie laughed, but she understood.

"I'll make sure Rita and I can get off at the same time and day next weekend. I'll tell Dad and he can tell you. We can meet here at Wilson's…okay?"

"That sounds fine to me."

Pointing to Wilson's second floor, front window, Annie continued, "Rita lives there, above Wilson's, in the so-called dorm rooms."

"Wow, how many girls live up there?"

"I think eight, but it looks like a dozen. It's really messy, as you might imagine. I try not to go up there." Annie took a deep breath. "I think you'll like Peter. He's nice like you." *But not as damn sexy as you.* "We should all have a good time."

Dennis nodded. "I'm looking forward to it. Heck, if you and Rita look sexy enough, we might just talk about you all afternoon and save sports and boating for some other time."

They both laughed.

"I better take you home before your dad gives me a hard time for keeping his daughter out too late."

"I doubt that," Annie said with a grin.

They walked back to the car. Dennis opened the door for Annie, then walked around the front of the car and got in.

She turned toward him. "Dennis, I really had a good time with you. I'm looking forward to next weekend…when we go sailing."

He turned and pulled her close, kissing her harder than before.

She moaned. *Oh my, my body never felt like this when Peter kissed me.*

Dennis relaxed his hold on her, and she slowly pulled back.

Savoring the moment, she opened her eyes and looked at him. "See, I'm not scared of you."

He smiled. "You will be when my hands roam all over your enticing body."

"Oh, aren't you bold. We'll just have to see…next time."

**

Driving back to Sturgeon Bay that night, Dennis's mind drifted back to Annie. Who is this Peter guy? Someone who means more to Annie than me, he thought. That's probably why she set up the double date with Rita.

The image of Rita leaning over the cooler to scoop the ice cream flashed in his mind. *Now that was a nice little package, with those mischievous eyes. I hope she's wild like she says she is.* He smiled, his thoughts focused on Rita, and then he stretched out, getting comfortable in the old VW Bug convertible car seat, as the warm summer wind pressed against his face and hair. *I should be able to get on a more physical level with her.* Besides, he thought, with Rita there are no worries about Darrell and my job.

Annie popped into his mind. *I've got plenty of time to get into her pants.* He laughed. Hadn't she bumped into him a couple of times when they were playing golf? He could feel her breasts brush against him. She knew what she was doing. She was a teaser all right, with a body and wit to boot. He smiled, he knew she could be his any time he really wanted her, but for now, it would be Rita. *It was a great night to have a convertible.*

**

The next day, Peter stopped by Wilson's for his malt fix and to see Annie.

"Oh hi, Peter. I was just thinking about you."

"Really! Ready for another race? I hope this time we'll start at the same time."

Annie stuck her tongue out at him. "You'd still lose."

Peter raised his eyebrows.

"You'll just never know how fast I can swim until it's too late," she said. "Are you still going to teach me to sail Wednesday?"

"Sure," he said with a big smile. "What time works for you?"

"How about three?"

Peter nodded. "I'll look forward to it."

Annie reached over and turned off the Mixmaster. Grabbing the can of whipped cream, she gave Peter's malt a shot. "Here you go."

"Thanks."

"See you Wednesday. Like to talk but," she turned and counted three customers waiting, "work."

Peter waved and headed outside. As he walked to his Sunfish, he couldn't help but be excited about sailing with Annie. He saw her just about every day, but that was at Wilson's. It wasn't like he could really talk to her there.

His thoughts turned back to their time at Newport Beach. They really did have a good time. He thought about lying on the blanket kissing. He had girlfriends back home, but they didn't make him feel like he did with her that day. He just wanted to be with her. He wondered if she had a boyfriend or even several? She never mentioned anyone that day but she is beautiful and she does see a lot of guys like him at Wilson's. At least that day she was all mine and it was fun.

Will she be the one he loses it to? He thought. Was he too young to think that on their first date? To touch her, smell the citrus fragrance of her hair and body when he held her close. Her kisses were delightful. He could have held her in his arms all day. Physically, she turned him on too. He definitely liked the feel of his manhood pressed against her. He thought she liked him. She acted like it. Hadn't she asked him to teach her to sail? Yeah, Wednesday!

**

Annie got home that night and, as usual, went down to the beach for a swim and unwind. She stood on the beach, admiring the view she never tired of, with the limestone of Eagle Bluff on the left, Horseshoe Island in the center, and the Village of Ephraim to the right. Finally, her eyes focused on *Falcon* as it rode on its mooring. She loved staring at that yacht. It looked as powerful as its name implied, with its gleaming black hull, richly varnished trim, and tall mast.

Entering the water, she slid below and swam toward the anchored raft, currently holding court to three sea gulls. They gave her the evil eye, squawked, and took off. She watched as they circled low and, on their fly-by, scored a direct hit on the raft. She laughed at the whole scene.

It took a couple of minutes of splashing water onto the raft before she could stretch out and get some late afternoon rays and relax. Her mind wandered as she half dozed on the gently rocking raft. She thought of Rita peppering her with questions all day about Dennis, wanting to know what happened before she met him Sunday.

"Annie, he is so good-looking. Don't you think he's good-looking?" Rita asked.

"Yes," Annie said. *He's Good-looking and very exciting.*

"Did he kiss you?" Rita asked

Annie smiled but didn't answer.

Rita got even more animated. "Come on, tell me! How good was he?" she asked, wide-eyed. "Did you think I was too forward with him?"

Annie just shrugged.

"Was he better than Peter?" Rita pressed.

That stopped Annie cold. She felt an attraction for both, but Dennis caused electricity that ran through her body when their lips touched. She didn't get that when she kissed Peter.

When Peter held her at Newport Beach and kissed her, it felt good, but more like a flannel nightgown on a cold night. Dennis just had that bad boy, cocky attitude about him that intrigued her and somehow drew her toward him like a moth to a candle. He brought something out in her she wanted more of but wasn't sure she was ready for yet.

Of course, she didn't tell Rita all these things. Her friend was her buffer against Dennis until she could sort things out. She knew that wasn't fair to Rita, but she also knew her experiment with the four together would lead to a good time, so why not?

And then there was Peter. He brought out feelings different from what she felt for Dennis. Peter made her smile and feel…. comfortable? He was good looking in that All-American way she liked, but his family and their money made her uncomfortable, second-class even. She wasn't comfortable with any wealthy people ever since her horrible run in with those two rich mothers and their wretched kids on the beach long ago when she was five or six. She still had feelings of being second class. Did she fit in even now? At least with Dennis, they were on the same social level.

But she sensed Dennis was a bad boy, not to be trusted. He didn't miss a beat flirting with Rita after just kissing her. Peter was kind, funny and gentle. Dennis got frustrated if things didn't go as planned. She saw that at the windmill, but just as fast, he seemed to let it go. Dennis's looks did attract her, she had to admit, and when he kissed her… Electricity!

But I trust Peter more than Dennis.

Laughing, she realized she wasn't in such a bad situation after all, not with two good-looking guys interested in her. Why can't girls play the field too? She sat up and shook her long hair from side to side. Life was good.

She got up and dove into the water, enjoying the swim back and thinking about both men.

Chapter Five

Wednesday moved at a snail's pace. Annie was so excited about learning to sail. Then again, maybe she was excited just to be with Peter.

She talked Rita into coming ten minutes early, so she could go home and change. She decided to wear a modest bikini, jogging shorts, an old pair of sunglasses and a "Cubs" baseball cap. She probably would take some shit from Peter because it wasn't a Cardinal's hat. She smiled to herself. It was nice to keep him off balance, she thought as she pulled the bill snug on her head and tugged her ponytail out the small hole in the back of the hat.

As she rode her bike to the boat dock, she spotted Peter in his swimsuit, T-shirt, aviator sunglasses, and cap. He waved.

"Great afternoon for sailing," he said as she pulled up. "I brought some towels that we can store in the watertight compartment in case we tip over."

"Tip over?" she said, alarmed. "You're just kidding, aren't you?"

"Not really," he smiled, "but it shouldn't be a problem for a champion swimmer like you."

"You do know how to sail, right? You aren't bullshitting me, are you, Peter?"

"You have to push the envelope when you're learning, Annie," Peter said. "That's where the fun is. Besides, if you don't tip over, you really haven't learned to sail."

She stared at him.

"A Sunfish is meant to be sailed on the edge, and that means tipping it," he continued.

She smiled. "You mean somewhere between fun and disaster."

"Don't worry, Annie, I haven't lost anyone yet."

"Great."

"Okay, let's get going," she said as she slipped her shoes off. "I told Mom we'd be home for dinner at six-thirty sharp. You're coming for dinner, aren't you?"

"It shouldn't be a problem. Yes, thank you."

"Dad hates it when the time line for dinner changes and he has to start barbequing later; mentally, it throws off his timing with the coals and cooking. It's a religion with Dad, and the beer is his sacramental wine. You'll like my mom and dad…they haven't forgotten what it's like to be our age. That's why they look like they're in love now."

"That's nice," Peter said. "It's been a while since I saw my parents even kiss."

"I didn't bring it up to make you feel bad. It's just the way it is with my parents. I hope I act the same way they do after so many years of marriage."

"Well I know I'll act completely different from the way my parents act." He said. "Let's talk about something else, like sailing."

"Oh! Is this your boat?" she said.

"Yep."

Peter unlocked the boat chain, and dragged the boat into the water.

"Annie, would you hold the bow while I put the rudder in place and raise the sail?" As Peter assembled the boat to sail, he explained a few things about the Sunfish and sailing. Annie listened, then looked at him with a quizzical look. "I didn't understand any of that."

Peter smiled. "You'll see how it works once we get going." As he raised the sail, he told her about all the parts of the boat.

Her head was really spinning now. "Are you talking in code or something?" she said, but Peter seemed to ignore her.

"One other thing, in sailing we don't use the word ropes. They are called sheets or lines."

"Oh, I see," said Annie, trying not to laugh. She didn't want to hurt his feelings, and all she wanted to do was get out on the water and go sailing. She knew she'd pick it up fast.

"Peter, do you think you could tell me all this stuff while we're on the water? We have to be home by six-thirty, you know."

"Oh yeah, I forgot. Get in the cockpit, and let's go."

Annie got in while Peter steadied the boat. He pushed off and hopped in as he pointed the bow just a little off the wind to the starboard side, pulling the main sheet in to tighten the sail against the wind. They started moving gently through the water. Small waves lapped against the hull of the Sunfish with a pat, pat, pat, sound. Just about that time, the boat started tipping slightly.

Annie's stomach lurched, and she grabbed Peter's arm. "What's happening?"

"The boat's just heeling over a bit, nothing to worry about. Put your feet under that strap and lean your body back like this." He leaned back, and Annie did the same. "Our weight equalizes the pressure on the sail so the boat flattens out."

She smiled and tried to relax.

"Believe me, you'll like to heel over after a while. It will be more exciting and faster. If the wind gets too strong, and we can't counteract the wind's force by shifting our body weight or letting pressure off the sail, then we tip over...that's part of the fun. You'll see. Matter of fact, I'll tip the boat over on purpose just so you get used to righting it. It's really simple, and the real fun with this boat is sailing on the edge between tipping and keeping it upright."

"If you say so, Peter. You're the Captain." *I hope sailing on the edge is as fun as he makes it sound. He better know what he's doing.*

Annie started enjoying herself once they got going and she realized they weren't going to tip. For the next forty-five minutes, Peter and Annie sailed out to Horseshoe Island, then northeast toward Sister Bay. As they started back, he asked, "Would you like to sail the boat?"

"I thought you'd never ask!" Could she catch on to sailing as fast as she did painting? She loved the wind and the elements of nature all coming together to move the boat through the water. They switched places, and Peter pointed to a house on the shore. "See that yellow house off the bow? Move the tiller so the leading edge of the sail is on the center of that house. That's how you steer a straight course."

Annie caught on fast. The wind picked up slightly, and the boat heeled more and more. Peter controlled the main sail tension, trying to get the boat to sail on the edge, while Annie continued to sail on a straight course. So excited, she squealed as the boat tipped and flattened out as if she was riding on a roller coaster.

"Peter, this is sooo much fun," she giggled. Suddenly, a puff of wind hit the sail, and Annie screamed as the boat tipped over.

In an instant, she surfaced and laughed as she treaded water. "What happened? What did I do wrong?"

Peter swam next to her. "You didn't do anything wrong," he said, smiling. "We just got hit with a puff of wind that put us over the edge."

She grinned. "You did say that might happen."

"Tipping over is all part of sailing with this boat. Now I'll show you how easy it is to right it."

Peter pushed the boat so its bow was into the wind. Then he made sure the rudder was straight and the lines were not tangled. "Now grab the edge of the hull and step on the end of the dagger board. The boat should pop upright," he said. "When it does, we pull ourselves into the cockpit, turn the boat slightly off the wind, and start pulling the sail tight until we start moving. Are you ready?"

"Yep." *God, I hope this boat pops up.*

"Okay, here we go."

They took it one step at a time and up it went. Thirty seconds later, they were moving through the water.

"That wasn't so bad," Annie said, and she pointed the boat toward Eagle Bluff.

As they got closer and closer, the wind died down to the point that they hardly moved.

"What's happening? Why are we slowing down?"

Peter pointed to the limestone bluffs. "The shoreline and bluff are blocking our wind. If we turn around, we can sail out to Horseshoe Island again and come back not so close to the bluff."

"Sounds good to me," Annie said and they came about.

After circling Horseshoe Island again, they spied the *Falcon*.

"Let's sail to the *Falcon*," she said. "I'd like to see it up close."

"Okay," Peter said.

It took them about ten minutes to sail alongside her. They approached downwind. *Falcon's* hull blocked the wind as the Sunfish just barely moved along the hull, and they marveled at the beauty of the varnished teak. The boat seemed huge at water level.

"I don't know what it is about this boat, but I just love it. Someday, if I'm ever rich, I'd like to buy it," Annie said.

"Annie, if I ever have enough money, I'll buy it for you."

She smiled at him, leaned over, and gave him a kiss. "I'll remember that promise."

Peter let go of the main sheet with his left hand, pulled her close, and kissed her. Lost in the moment, he opened his right eye just in time to see the anchor chain approaching the Sunfish. "Shit!" He grabbed the tiller and quickly turned the boat away, narrowly avoiding a collision with the chain.

"Was it worth it, Peter?" *I'm starting to like this guy. Be careful, Annie.*

"Of course," he said with a smile. "You're my first mate on this boat."

"Peter, if you buy me that boat, I'll be your first mate for life, or the duration of the cruise." She laughed.

"So you'd just like me for the material things? Is that what you're saying?"

"Well, you are a pretty good kisser too."

"Why, thank you," he said. "Would you like to practice some more?"

She giggled and nodded. Right in the middle of the kiss, the wind shifted and the boat tipped over. Annie came up spitting water and laughing. "Did you do that on purpose?"

"No! The wind shifted."

Peter paddled over and gave her another kiss as they treaded water. Hidden by the boat's hull, they kissed for what seemed like minutes until they heard a fishing boat motoring up to them.

A concerned voice filled the air. "You two all right? The Wife and I saw the boat tip over and thought you might be in trouble."

"Oh, no trouble here, just some tangled lines. Thanks for your concern." said Peter.

"See Martha? I told you they were all right. Just some teenagers having fun."

"Yes, Frank," she said with a laugh. "Just some teenagers having fun. Now let's get that ice cream you've been promising me."

Annie and Peter giggled as the fishing boat motored away.

"You know, ice cream sounds like a good idea, Peter."

"You buying?"

"You bet."

They got the boat upright and sailed it back towards Wilson's.

**

Walking into Wilson's, Annie spied Rita. Standing in line, waiting for Rita to serve them, she told Peter, "I want you to meet Rita, my best friend. Did I tell you we are going on a double date Sunday afternoon with Rita and Dennis?"

Peter spun around, turning to Annie. "I'm sorry, what did you say?"

"We're all going sailing now that I'm an expert sailor." She laughed. "I thought it would be fun. Peter, your mouth is open."

He squinted at her. "I'm just surprised by all of this. I don't even know Rita or Dennis. You just learned how to sail…"

"Does that mean you don't want to go?" Her heart sank. *I hope I didn't go overboard and assume too much?*

"Of course not. I love sailing. I like spending time with you, or can't you tell? I just don't know Rita or Dennis. Are you sure they are going to like sailing?"

"I'm sure. Besides, you're going to meet Rita in a few seconds, and Dennis works with Dad at Deacon's in Sturgeon Bay. I know you two will hit it off. You can talk about sports. That's what guys usually do anyway, don't they? I've got it all figured out. You two rent the boat. You've got lots of money to sail and play golf, right? Rita and I will take care of the food and beverages."

Peter nodded. "I guess I have enough money," he said, but he didn't smile.

"Dennis is going to pay for half so it won't be that much. Besides, if you're going to buy me that sailboat like you promised, you better get used to sailing me around."

"I guess it sounds fair. Let's meet Rita and get that ice cream."

Annie saw Rita wave as she and Peter walked up, then she laughed when she noticed they were wet. "God, it looks like it was a perfect day to go sailing…and swimming too."

Peter and Annie just smiled.

"What would you two like? Let me guess, root beer malts?"

"No, a couple of small cones. Just a little snack before we go to my house for dinner. Rita, have you met Peter before?"

"No, not formally, but I've seen him in here making "cow eyes" at you when you weren't looking."

Peter grinned. His already sunburned face got redder.

"Nice to meet you, Rita," he said. "Annie tells me that we're going sailing Sunday, if that's okay with you."

Now it was Rita's turn to smile. "Sailing would be great! I was really envious of you two this afternoon. It looks perfect out there."

Annie turned to Peter. "It is. Peter is a really good teacher." She ran her finger down his arm and smiled. "I didn't realize sailing could be that much fun, even when you tip over!" She cocked her head at him and winked.

Rita's eyes lit up. "I can hardly wait to go. What time Sunday?"

"How about ten thirty?" Annie said. "That will give Dennis time to get up here and for us to get ready."

"That sounds fine to me," Peter said. "I'll go across the street now and reserve the Flying Scott for the day."

"Right." Annie said.

"All you two have to do is lay back and look beautiful and sexy. Dennis and I will do all the work. That's what you ladies do best, isn't it?"

"Right." Both answered in unison as they glared at Peter. "We can't cut them off already, can we?" Annie said, laughing.

"Well, you can cut Peter off if you'd like, but I'll just have to wait and see about Dennis." Rita licked her lips. "That boy looked pretty hot." She sighed. "I better get back to serving the customers or I'll be out of a job." She waved and said, "I'll see you Sunday, Peter. See you tomorrow, Annie." Rita turned to the next person. "Can I help you?"

"Yes, if you're done with your chit chat, I'd like a Banana Split," the gray-haired lady said.

**

As she and Peter sat at her parents' dinner table, Annie causally mentioned that they were going sailing Sunday with Rita and Dennis.

"I like that Jamison kid," Darrell said. "He works hard."

Peter looked at Darrell and Betty. "I'm sure we'll have a good time. Rita seems like a nice girl."

Betty coughed and looked at Annie, eyebrows high. She smiled at Peter and said, "Rita is one to look out for."

"Oh, Mother! She's not that bad. Rita just likes to have fun. Besides, she has an image to maintain. Aren't redheads supposed to be wild?"

"Oh, that explains it. Now I understand!" Betty said.

They all chuckled, except Peter, who just looked questioningly at the three.

Annie turned to Betty. "Enough, Mother. What's for dessert?"

"Our own Door County cherry pie. Do you like cherry pie, Peter?"

"I love it."

"Good. You get an extra big piece because Darrell doesn't need any more weight."

"Oh, Mom. Dad looks great for someone his age."

"Gee, honey." He turned toward Annie, shoulders slumped. "I don't know if I should thank you or cry."

"You know what I mean, Dad."

"Yeah, I do. Thank you. One piece, Betty."

**

After dinner, Annie and Peter walked to the hotel's private beach to watch the sunset. Several guests were doing the same thing, so they slipped over the stone retaining wall, out of view of the other guests, except those sitting on the pier.

"Peter, I really had a good time today."

"Me too. What was your favorite part?"

"Oh, the sailing. Just at that moment when you pull the sail tight, and the boat heels ever so slightly, and I can feel it move through the water on its own. The little pat, pat, pat sound the water makes, lapping on the side. That's the best. What was yours?"

"I think I liked when we were sailing close to *Falcon* and I gave you a kiss."

Annie smiled and got close to his face. "What did you like better, looking at *Falcon* or kissing me?"

"Ah, let me think." He paused, then leaned over and kissed her, pressed her mouth open with his tongue. Annie gave a slight whimper and held him tight. She felt herself getting warm, and when her hand slipped to Peter's lap, she felt something else as well. Gently, they pulled back, and then Annie nuzzled her cheek into his chest.

Finally, Annie sighed and looked into Peter's face. "That was nice. I really did have a good time today…besides the kisses." *It surprised her how comfortable she felt with Peter for knowing him such a short time. Now if she could feel as comfortable with his family's money?*

When she didn't say anything more, he asked, "What are you thinking about so hard?"

"About today, and about the day of the race when we went up at Newport Beach."

"We could do that again, as long as we find someplace close to a road. I love watching you paint. You're very good."

"Thank you." *Does he really think I'm a good painter? I might just take him up on his offer. I know he likes me. I see how he looks at me.*

For the next few minutes, they both just sat there, holding hands, not saying anything.

Finally, Annie turned toward Peter and squeezed his hand. "Stop by Wilson's tomorrow, will you?"

"Don't I always?"

"Most days you do. You might have to wait for me to get a break, but we could split a root beer malt."

"Is that a bribe?"

"Take it any way you like."

Peter leaned toward her and gave her another kiss. She pulled him closer, pressing her body against his and holding him tight. After a while, she slowly pulled back. "We better go," she said, feeling weak-kneed as she stood.

He turned briefly, arranging himself so he could walk. Annie smiled. She liked the effect she had on him, but she felt excited herself. *A little competition, Dennis? Maybe more than you think.*

Walking home, hand in hand, she knew she would think about Peter tonight. She had no doubt he would be thinking about her.

Chapter Six

Rita asked Annie to come to the dorm room over the restaurant and help her pick out what to wear for the double date.

"What do you think Dennis would like me to wear?" she asked.

"As little as possible," Annie said, and then held up one of Rita's string bikinis.

Rita giggled at the thought. "That might be okay later, but what do you think for now?"

Annie looked at her mischievously. "Do you want to impress him and get him hot?"

They giggled.

"Oh, I guess I'll be a little conservative, even though it's against my nature. How about I wear this tiny bikini, these cutoffs, and my white Wisconsin T-shirt?"

Annie nodded.

"That way, if I get wet, he'll see through the T shirt. He'll like that! I can always peel the clothes off and drive him nuts if we don't get wet."

"That might work, but I think you'd keep his attention all day even if you wore a gunny sack," Annie said with a smirk.

Giving her friend an appraising glance, Rita said, "What have you got underneath your T-shirt?" She tugged at the hem.

"The same suit I usually wear. Peter has seen me in this, but not Dennis. It's an old pink bikini. Besides, I'm not trying to impress anyone like you are." Annie knew this was a lie, because she did find Dennis exciting. So exciting that the idea of the date made her a little uncomfortable. "You're the one we've got to get Dennis interested in," she said. "That way, the four of us can spend the summer together." *And I can sort things out between the two.*

"It wouldn't be much of a summer without a little romance, right?" Rita said.

"Right," Annie said. "Let's go over to Bill's grocery store and see if I can sweet talk Bill, the owner, out of some beer. He remembers what it was like to be young."

Rita looked surprised. "Why doesn't he sell beer?"

"Dummy, don't you remember? Ephraim is dry."

"Oh, I forgot. Just a couple of cans for later…to loosen us up." Rita winked. Annie got a big smile and nodded.

**

Finished with shopping, they walked across the street to the boat dock and met Dennis and Peter, who were already in the process of paying for the boat, signing the rental contract, and getting checked out at the marina.

The boys had introduced themselves before the girls arrived, and Peter was explaining all about the Flying Scott. It was Dennis's first sail, so he had a lot of questions.

"This is a special treat for me, to finally get a chance to sail," Dennis said. "I am really looking forward to learning."

Annie and Rita stowed the food, beer, and soft drinks in the little cuddy cabin's cooler. Annie looked at Dennis, and then she draped her arm around Peter like a long lost brother. "You've come to the right place, Dennis. If Peter can teach me, he can teach you."

Peter pulled Annie closer. "Thanks. I'll take that as a compliment."

Rita smiled and excitedly started giving a play-by-play broadcast. "It's a gorgeous morning for a sail." She paused and held up a finger. "The wind is blowing from the prevailing Southwest at five to eight knots…I think. With just a few clouds in the sky, the captain and crew are ready."

"Enough already!" Annie said. "Let's get going and you can explain all this stuff to Dennis as we sail."

"Ladies, your chariot awaits. If you'll take a seat near the bow, Dennis and I will push us off," said Peter.

Peter explained about the centerboard, rudder, and sails to Dennis. It didn't take long to get into a rhythm as they sailed on a reach toward Sister Bay. The girls settled into girl talk, with an occasional look over the tops of their sunglasses to see if the boys were paying any attention to them.

Annie chuckled at Peter's explaining the finer points of sailing.

"It's very comfortable, and the preferred way to sail. Look how our passengers are stretched out in the cockpit. They are not screaming or anything. They seem very relaxed and beautiful."

Rita and Annie smiled. "We were wondering when you guys would get around to us," Annie said.

"Yeah, what are we, chopped liver?" Rita added.

Dennis smiled. "I don't think I'd ever call you chopped liver, Rita. How come you're all covered up? It's warm out here." With that, he pulled his T-shirt over his head, revealing his muscled chest and arms.

Not to be outdone, Peter pulled his shirt off too.

The girls hooted. Rita started chanting, "More, more, more."

Dennis persisted. "It's nice out. Let's see what you're hiding under those shirts!"

Annie and Rita looked at each other. Slowly, they took their shirts off as Rita hummed the melody from "The Stripper," twirling her shirt around over her head before she threw it at Dennis.

"Now, isn't that more comfortable?" Dennis said. "When you've got it, flaunt it, and you two have it!"

The girls smiled, and Annie blushed just a little as she looked at Dennis and then Peter, who smiled broadly back at her.

"Is that enough for you, Dennis?" Rita asked.

"For the time being," he said.

That got hoots from everyone, and then they all fell quiet.

"Where do we want to eat?" Peter said finally. "It's almost noon."

Dennis looked toward shore. "Where are we?"

Peter pointed to the right. "We're just off Ellison Bay. See that spot on the shore? We could head there and eat on the beach, or turn around and sail back to Horseshoe Island and eat there. Then we could still sail toward Chambers Island and back before we have to turn the boat in at five-thirty."

"That seems like a lot for the first time out," Annie said. "Let's just head into Ellison Bay."

Everyone nodded. It took about twenty minutes to tack into Ellison Bay. They tied the boat up, and found a picnic table nearby. Annie and Rita got things ready while the boys rolled the mainsail down onto the boom.

"We've got tuna sandwiches, ham and cheese, Cheetos, and some of Mom's apple pie."

"What's to drink?" Dennis asked.

"I have root beer and Coke. And for this afternoon's sail, I have a special treat; some Schlitz, the beer that made Milwaukee famous," Annie said.

Dennis patted her on the back. "Good job. I'll get a bag of ice at the general store in town before we shove off, so it'll be really cold. Maybe some more soda too, if you think we'll need it, Peter?"

"Yeah, beer sounds good, but I don't want to get too looped. Maybe another soda."

"Wise move, Captain Peter," Dennis said. "It's got to be at least eighty degrees by now."

**

After lunch, Dennis and Peter headed off to get the ice and soda. Rita couldn't contain herself and started talking as soon as they were out of earshot. "Did you see Dennis's body when he took off his shirt? Oh, baby! I'd like to run my hands over that."

Annie felt herself getting warm just thinking about Dennis and what she'd like to do, but then she thought about Peter. While she didn't get the rush thinking about his body, she knew he still got her excited.

"I wish he wasn't so damn interested in sailing!" Rita sighed.

"Geez, Rita. Loosen your top just a little and lean over a few times. Let him see more of your ample assets. I guarantee you'll get his attention."

"You're right." Rita started making adjustments. "How's that?"

Annie nodded. "It looks just right. I'll get Peter to sail over to one of the islands that's just above water. We can anchor and swim around. I'm sure we can get them to carry us on their shoulders and throw us around. Guys like to show off how strong they are."

Rita smiled. "We've got beer, too. That'll liven things up for us all. Great plan, Annie."

Annie made a couple of changes to her straps to show a little more skin for Captain Peter's enjoyment, too. She didn't want Rita to have all the fun.

"I knew you'd know what to do," Rita said.

"Oh, I'm sure you know what to do too. If you don't, I bet Dennis does!"

"I hope so," Rita said with big eyes.

"Oh, yes!" Annie said. "I think he's like a cat, waiting to pounce. We just can't see his tail twitching yet."

"Well, if I get him interested enough, I'm sure I'll see something twitching."

Annie wiggled her finger at her friend. "Oh, you're wicked but good."

Rita flashed a big smile. "What about you and Peter?"

Annie didn't answer right away. "Peter has his own ways, which I find are more subtle, but effective. He's got my juices going a few times. He's just a little more cautious with his emotions and letting himself go, but I think I can get his tail to wag, too!"

Rita's eyebrows darted up, and they both laughed. "Quiet now, here they come.

Hi, boys, looking for a good time?" she said in her sexiest voice. "We've got all you're looking for right here. That ice will cool us down nicely." She grabbed a cube and rubbed it across the top of her breasts. "Ah, that feels good." Then she winked at Dennis.

Smiling, Dennis looked at Peter. "I think we came to the right place. Say, if you two ladies want some fun and action, your yacht awaits."

Peter took their hands and helped them into the boat. He looked at Dennis, giving his best gravely Blackbeard voice. "Aye, we'll make them walk the plank when we're out of sight of land if they don't do what we want! Aye ye mates, let's shove off."

They tacked out of Ellison Bay and started back toward Horseshoe Island. A half an hour later, Dennis said, "Let's break out the grog and have a ration. What say ye, crew?"

"Sounds good to me." Rita reached for the beer and passed them around.

"Ah, this tastes good," Dennis said.

Peter had a few sips of Annie's, not wanting to be a stick in the mud. Turning to Dennis, he pointed at the tiller. "Do you want to sail on the way back?"

Dennis's eyes lit up. "You bet!" He finished his beer in a couple of swallows and they switched places.

The wind picked up as they maneuvered to a close haul. The boat started heeling over, water splashing over the bow. Everyone got wet. They shifted to the high side of the boat, putting their feet into the hiking straps and leaned back slightly with Rita next to Dennis, and Annie next to Peter.

Peter gave Dennis suggestions on steering. "See the dark green house on the shore? Put the leading edge of the jib on the center of the house." At the same time, Peter handled the main sheet and cleated in the jib controlling the front sail.

With the boat balanced, Rita and Annie moved their arms around the boys and snuggled, pressing their breasts against the boys' backs. It was a mellow crew, and the touching created a sexual tension they all felt. The beer tasted good, the sun and wind did their magic. After about two hours, they reached the Strawberry Islands.

It was too early to beach the boat there, so Peter suggested they sail back to Horseshoe Island. As the island's horseshoe shape came into view, he said, "The state built a really large pier for boats to tie up to, so I say we go swimming off the pier."

"Sounds like a good idea to me, Peter," Annie said.

"There won't be many boats there this time of the day, especially on a Sunday," he said, but when they rounded the point of the island, they found one boat, a Boston Whaler, tied to the pier. "I hear voices on the back side of the island. Sounds like they're fishing."

Peter took over the tiller from Dennis and steered the Flying Scott toward the pier. It only took a few minutes to dock and tie up the boat. "This is great; we can swim, fool around, and have a short sail back before we have to turn the boat in."

Rita whispered to Dennis, "I like the fooling around part." She set down her beer, put her towel on the pier, ran to the edge and jumped in, doing a cannonball. The water exploded, and everyone got wet. When she came up for air, she yelled, "Come on, Dennis, don't be a stick in the mud. You look like you can swim."

"Yeah, I can swim," Dennis said. He stepped to the edge, curled his toes over it, and gracefully dove into the water. He came up under Rita and pulled her down. When they both came up, she splashed water at him.

"You shit!"

He laughed. "It serves you right. You teased me all afternoon. You got me hot, and now you're going to pay!" He grabbed her close and kissed her as they treaded water.

"I wasn't sure," murmured Rita, "if you were interested."

"How could I not be interested in you, Rita?" And then his hands slipped under her bikini and caressed her breasts. He smiled.

After a few minutes, they swam toward the shore and climbed on the dock after she adjusted her bikini back over her breasts.

Dennis looked toward Peter and Annie and said, "Looks like they want to be alone. Let's move over to the far side and give them their privacy."

"Their privacy? How about ours?" Rita said with a grin.

Annie and Peter laid on their backs looking at the sky, their bodies touching from shoulder to ankle.

"What do you think that cloud looks like?" Peter pointed to a fluffy one overhead.

"A horse's head. And that one looks like a VW Bug."

He laughed. Rolling on his side, he kissed Annie's shoulder.

"Umm" she said. She rolled close, snuggling next to Peter. Running her hand lightly down his arm until her fingers intertwined into his, she leaned in and they kissed gently. He pulled her closer, her breasts pressed tight against his chest. Peter pressed his hips against her. His rising excitement matched hers. Soon their tongues probed and danced, as they made small moaning sounds.

Suddenly, Annie rolled away and stood up. "Peter, I need to take a swim, and by the looks of your suit, so do you."

"Not *now*, Annie!" Peter pleaded. "You feel so good. Come back."

"I will, but first I need to swim...now! Let's get in the water, Peter. Please?"

"Okay, if you insist."

He got up, grabbed her hand, and they took two quick steps before they jumped. Their screams were drowned out by the whoosh as they hit the water.

"God this feels good," Annie said. She turned toward Peter, treading water. "Is your stiffy gone now?"

"It is, now. Thank you for your interest."

The two swam around for a while, enjoying the cool water.

Annie swam onto Peter's back, wrapping her arms around his neck. Moving her mouth close to his ear, she whispered, "Let's get out and see what Rita and Dennis are doing." They heard Rita giggling, and other muffled sounds echoed from the far end of the dock.

Rita and Dennis were lying on the dock. Dennis was on his side, his head propped up in his hand. He kissed Rita, while his free hand moved in small circles on her left breast. Rita moaned louder and louder.

Annie and Peter just stared. Dennis looked up, his eyes focused on Annie, and he winked.

Holding Peter's hand, Annie squeezed it so hard he turned and looked at her. Her whole body blazed with fire as she stared back at Dennis. Finally, she turned to look at Peter. He coughed and cleared his throat.

Annie regained her composure and said, "We didn't interrupt any-thing, did we?"

Dennis chuckled. Rita quickly moved to adjust her clothing.

"No," Dennis said. "Rita and I were just getting better acquainted." They both sat up. "Is there any beer left?" he asked as if nothing had happened.

Peter went to the boat and got the two remaining cans of Schlitz, two cans of Coke, and the bag of Cheetos. "We can have a snack before we have to start back," he said.

"Great!" Annie could see that Rita was flushed, and her top was still very loose. She looked at Dennis's swimsuit, but saw nothing to indicate he was aroused. I wonder what it takes to get Dennis excited. I sure have no problem with Peter in that area. Dennis turned me on just with a kiss and a touch. I wonder what he likes? I might need to give him a try, if nothing else to give Rita a little competition. I think I have that right. Didn't I set this double date up? Still, she was surprised because she thought Rita would turn him on. She did with the others, but then, Dennis didn't seem like the others.

Interesting, Annie thought. This will make for some new interest-ing conversation tomorrow.

After consuming the Coke, beer and Cheetos, Peter looked at his watch. "Time to head back," he said. The others protested but started packing.

Annie knew her parents expected her around six, and Peter's parents probably the same, but she knew Rita and Dennis had no such limitations. Rita would push her freedom to the max. She assumed Dennis would be a willing subject for Rita.

It didn't take long to get back to the pier and then to Wilson's. Dennis and Rita were hungry, so they ordered fries, cheeseburgers and Cokes. Peter and Annie just had Cokes and split an order of fries.

"Dennis, do you want to stick around for a while since it's early?" Rita asked.

"Sure, we can find something to do before I have to head back to Sturgeon Bay," he said.

Rita ran her fingers through her windblown hair, leaned close to Dennis and said in a loud whisper, "I know this really neat place over at Peninsula Park that's very romantic. Does that interest you?"

Annie stared at Rita, mouth open. "Why don't you tell Dennis exactly what you think?"

Rita smiled back. "He knows what I think already, don't you, Dennis?"

"Yes, I know what you're thinking, and I agree one hundred percent. We need some time together, so we can appreciate the nice view of Ephraim."

"See? I told you he knows."

"What a great day," Annie said. "Thank you, Dennis and Peter, for getting the boat. I hope the four of us can do more sailing and spend more time together."

Rita chirped in, "I'm all for that."

"I can always make time for sailing with two lovely ladies," Peter said. "Dennis, you're getting the hang of sailing."

"Well, you're a good teacher."

Annie studied the two guys. "Why don't you see if you both can get off one day next weekend and let's do it again? We can go out to Chambers Island and to Fish Creek. We can start earlier and really get some sailing in."

The other three nodded in agreement.

"Great," Annie said. *Maybe I can tease Dennis like he teased me with Rita. I need to make up my mind about him. Do I really want to get involved with him or stick with Peter?*

"We better get going home, don't you think, Annie?" Peter looked at his watch.

Dennis got up, and Annie went over and hugged him, but one hug was not enough for Dennis. On the second hug, he pulled her closer so he could feel her body and she his. This time, he kissed her lightly on the cheek but at the same time, Annie felt him press his chest and hips firmly against her while his hands lightly cupped the sides of her breasts. Annie moaned.

Still trembling from Dennis's hug, she went over and gave Rita a kiss and hug too. "See you tomorrow, Rita." *I can only imagine what's going to happen tonight and I'm jealous.*

**

She grabbed Peter's hand and they walked home. Peter talked about how much he liked Dennis, how the four really seemed to hit it off, and how Dennis picked up sailing fast. He thought Rita was wild and fun. He agreed with Annie that they should be perfect for each other.

Annie chuckled. *If he only knew how much I liked that hug. Did he see how Dennis touched me? Is he just being nice?* Then she looked at Peter. "I'm looking forward to hearing about what happens tonight at work tomorrow. I'm sure they both are going to pick up where they left off."

"Are you envious of them?"

She didn't say anything for a moment. Looking at the road without lifting her eyes, she murmured, "Yes and no. We're doing just fine. I don't want to do anything I'll regret later."

"Yeah, I know. I know you're right, but…"

"But what?" Annie saw Peter jump at the edge in her voice.

"Oops." Trying to make it right, he said, "You know, guys are always ready for more…more adventure."

She stopped. Her pulse jumped as she turned on him. "Is that what you call it? Adventure!" Her voice rang hot and she jabbed her finger square on his chest. Rich or poor, they all want the same.

Peter shook his head and said nothing more.

She tried to calm down as they continued to walk. "I just don't want to wreck things by going too fast." *I have dreams and I don't want to fuck it up with you or Dennis by doing something irresponsible now.*

Sighing, Peter said, "I like being with you, Annie. You really turn me on, or didn't you notice this afternoon?"

"Yes, Peter, I noticed! Just to set the record straight, you excite me too." *Although not as much as Dennis.*

"Really? I thought so." He put his arm around her and gave her a kiss.

"That's what I mean, Peter. I love kissing you, holding you, and being with you, even if your family has lots of money."

"Geez, Annie, can't you cut me a little slack, and like me for me?"

"It's a hard hurdle for me to get over. But it's my problem, not yours." She ran her hand on his cheek and then lightly kissed him. "I'm sorry."

**

Back in town, Rita and Dennis had unfinished business.

"Let me go up to my room," Rita said as she pointed to the second level of Wilson's. "I'll get a blanket and a couple of beers and be right back."

Leaving the picnic table across the street, she raced to her room, but not before grabbing a bag, putting some ice in it, and then racing upstairs to the dorm room. She put two beers from her secret stash in a plastic bag, tied a knot around the bag and rolled the blanket around the bag of ice and beer. Satisfied, she went to her dresser and pulled out a slightly wrinkled white blouse. Pulling the T-shirt over her head and taking the bikini off, she put on the blouse and tied the ends at the bottom. She put a little perfume behind her ears and between her breasts, looked in the mirror one last time, ran her fingers through her hair, and flew out the door.

**

Dennis had parked the car in front of Wilson's and was waiting. Rita jumped into the passenger seat with a big smile.

"Ahh, I like your blouse. No bra." He leaned over and gave her a kiss. "That was fast. I thought it would be at least ten minutes," he said.

"I know you've got to get back to Sturgeon Bay early, so I tried to be fast." She squeezed his arm. "More time for romance."

Dennis smiled. "Where is this place?"

"It's just off the eleventh fairway. If you look across the bay where the tenth green is, you can see it." Rita pointed across the bay. "See the flag on the green? Move up the bluff and a little to the right. See the limestone bluffs and birch trees?"

He nodded and glanced back to the road.

"There's a nice flat spot in those trees, back from the ledge and out of the golfers' sight. That's where we're going," said Rita. "I went on a walk with a golfing friend of mine a few years ago when I noticed the spot. I kind of tucked it in the back of my mind for future reference. Today's the day to try it. I hope it's not full of our favorite state bird."

Dennis looked at her. "State bird?"

"You know…the mosquito!"

He laughed. "Oh, that one. I think I have some spray in the trunk. I'll bring it along."

It was perfect, just the way she remembered it. She spread the blanket on the grass, sat down, and placed the bag of iced beer in front of her. Dennis sat down next to her and reached for a beer.

"Let's share. We'll keep this other one cold until we want it," Rita suggested.

Dennis popped the can, handing it to Rita. She had a few sips and gave it back.

"Isn't it beautiful here?" she whispered, almost as if in a trance. "You can see all of Ephraim stretched out. There's the fire station, Wilson's, the village hall, the two churches, the hotels and resorts, the Yacht Club, and Anderson Dock. It looks magical with the sun setting behind us." She gave a slight sigh. "I never get tired of this sight. I just love it up here."

"It is beautiful, Rita, and so are you."

Dennis leaned over and gently kissed her on the lips. He kissed her again, this time their tongues met. He heard her catch her breath and then moan as she exhaled. Slowly, he pulled away and kissed her cheek, nibbled on her ear, then her neck, and back again to her lips.

"Oh, Dennis," she whispered.

He gently pushed her down on the blanket and ran his hand to her stomach. She was lean like a tigress. He felt her stomach muscles flutter as he moved closer to her breasts. He untied her blouse. He knew just how to kiss her here and there, just the way he knew she wanted to be kissed. Dennis sighed, "Ah, Rita."

Chapter Seven

The next day, Annie could hardly wait to get to work. She wanted to hear all about Rita's evening. She was busy getting the tables ready for the day's business when Rita came floating down the steps, smiling.

"What a gorgeous morning," she said in a singsong voice. By this time, the other girls were clunking down the steps also. "Another day in paradise," one of them said while the others grunted.

Annie hurried to Rita. "How was it?"

"Oh, Annie, it was wonderful. It was everything I hoped it would be. I can't tell you now, but when we have our break, I'll fill you in."

"Did you stay out all night?"

"I would have, but no. He had to get back to Sturgeon Bay for work this morning, but when you know what you're doing, it doesn't take all night to make someone feel really special. Dennis knows what he's doing, that's for sure. I'm getting excited just thinking about it."

"I bet you are," Annie said in a soft voice, trying to hide her jealousy.

"I'm really looking forward to this weekend," Rita said. "I told Dennis he should drive up some evening. He said he was usually tired after work. When he does go out, it's for a few beers with the guys. He said he really looks forward to that because that's when he learns a lot about boats and their construction. If he doesn't get up here this week, I'm going to be really horny by Saturday."

"Rita!" Annie said, and then smiled. *I'm getting horny just talking about him myself.*

"Oh, it's easy for you, Miss Smarty. You have Peter up here all the time."

"I guess you're right. Anyhow, I'm looking forward to hearing all the lovely details."

Rita just smiled and nodded.

"I'll talk to you later," Annie said.

**

It was a busy Monday morning as Peter entered Wilson's.

"Hi, Peter."

Peter turned and saw the daughter of one of his parents' closest friends, Rhonda Smits, and two of her girlfriends.

"What brings you to Wilson's on this nice day?" Rhonda asked.

"I usually come in here to have lunch and something to drink. My girlfriend works here, so it gives me a chance to visit her for a short time."

"You have a girlfriend, up here? She works at Wilson's? Geez Peter, I thought you could find someone who didn't have to work. You should go out with me, not someone from up here. We could be together and play with the St. Louis gang. Your mother talked to me about us this past winter and thought we'd be perfect for each other."

"No, Rhonda. My mother doesn't run my life although she thinks she does. Annie's my girlfriend, she works here, and that's fine with me."

"Well fine then. I'm here to get a hot fudge sundae, and my friends want ice cream cones. Maybe your friend can wait on us," she said, looking around.

"Here she comes now." He watched Rhonda and her two friends check Annie out as she carried a tray of silverware from the kitchen. He couldn't help but smile when he saw Annie, but then he noticed Rhonda was glaring at her. *Jealous, are we?*

Annie looked at the three and then noticed Peter. "Hi Peter," she said. "Early today, aren't you?"

"I am. Say, I'd like you to meet Rhonda Smits and two of her friends, Penny and Sally. Their parents are close friends of mine, here and in St. Louis."

"Nice to meet you. What would you three like?"

"I'd like a hot fudge sundae with two cherries," Rhonda said, "and my friends would each like a double chocolate waffle cone. Think you can handle that?" she said with a smirk.

Peter noticed the surprised expression on Annie's face, but she said nothing and nodded. He sensed that after that comment, she did not like the three, but that was all right; he didn't like them either. They were stuck up, he thought.

Annie started their order. First she made the two cones, which she handed to Penny and Sally and then she worked on Rhonda's hot fudge. The hot fudge warmer and cherries container where located at the far end of the granite counter.

"I'd like lots of whipped cream too," Rhonda called.

Peter watched Annie pile extra whipped cream on the sundae. From her demeanor, he knew she didn't like waiting on the three. She worked as fast as she could, most people who came into Wilson's were nice and patient, but not Rhonda. Annie turned to deliver the sundae, and that's when Rhonda saw only one cherry.

"You forgot my extra cherry!" she shrieked. "I specifically asked you for two cherries and you forgot the second one." She turned to her friends and, in a voice loud enough for all to hear, said, "They must be really hard up for help this year if she's the best they could find. Just so she'll listen better next time, I'm not going to give her a tip." She turned toward Peter. "Your girlfriend is not a very good waitress."

Her two friends nodded.

Peter glanced at Annie. *How's she going to handle this?*

"Oops, I forgot. My mistake," she said. "I'll fix that in a jiffy." Annie seemed to force a smile. She moved back down the counter, put the second cherry on top, and walked back toward Rhonda. It was a huge sundae.

"Here you go," she said. Nearly back to Rhonda, and rushing, she stumbled on the edge of a box sticking out and her right arm shot out trying to regain her balance. In a flash, the sundae splattered onto Rhonda's sparkling white tennis dress.

"Oh my God," Annie said. "I tripped. It was an accident. We'll pay to get it cleaned."

Rhonda screamed. She looked down at her outfit, now decorated with whipped cream, hot fudge, melting ice cream, and the two cherries. The sticky red fruit clung to the whipped cream before succumbing to gravity. Rhonda wailed as she wiped the mess with her hand, causing everything to land on the floor with a plop. "Look what you did to my new outfit."

Annie hurried around the counter. "Let me help,' she said. "I'm really sorry." She took a wet rag and tried to wipe the front, but it only smeared more. "I'm really sorry. It was an accident."

Rhonda batted Annie's hand and rag away. "You clumsy bitch! You'll pay for this. I'll make sure of that. I'm going to tell my Daddy all about this."

"It was an accident," Annie said again, but Peter thought he saw a trace of a smile on her face.

Rhonda turned to her friends. "Let's get out of here. I'm all sticky. I want to go home and get cleaned up."

As they walked out, Annie called, "I'll be happy to make you a replacement sundae anytime." Then she popped a cherry into her mouth. "I'll be right with you, Mr. Franklin, as soon as I clean up this mess and wash my hands."

After about five minutes, she came back to Peter. "Nice friends you have," she said. "I might have been thinking about doing it, but it truly was an accident."

He smiled. "I know it was an accident. Besides, they aren't my friends. I never liked Rhonda or her type. I'm forced to be social to her because of my parents."

Annie nodded. "Seeing you today makes things better." She leaned over and gave him a kiss on the cheek.

He beamed. "How'd things go with Dennis and Rita last night?"

"I think they went very well. Rita came floating down the steps this morning on cloud nine. I can't wait to hear all the details. Rita said she couldn't wait to see Dennis again."

"Wow, he must be special for her to say that."

"I guess so." Annie shrugged. "Do you want something to eat and drink?"

"Yes, a cheeseburger and root beer, please."

"Sorry I can't chat, but we're really busy today, especially after this accident, and it's lunch time. I'll call you when it's ready."

It took a while to get his stuff. When she gave him the food, he gave her a kiss on the cheek and walked out.

**

The wind never came up that day, so Peter walked north to Anderson Dock and fished. It was one of those days. It didn't help that he didn't catch any fish. As he walked home, he stopped at the boat rental business across from Wilson's. On a whim, he asked the man behind the counter if they had any part-time jobs available. *It'd be nice to make my own money for a change.*

"What type of job are you looking for, young man?" He asked. "I'm Mr. Peterson, the owner."

"Oh, anything connected to boating. I'm a sailor and just like being around boats."

Mr. Peterson looked at Peter over his sunglasses. "We are looking for someone to help check people in and out on the boats. Where have you worked before?"

"Ah. Well, I've never had a real job like working around boats. All I've really done is babysit for neighbors back home."

"I don't know Peter. There's a big difference between babysitting and checking people in and out on the boats I rent here. I need someone that can handle money and deal with adults. It's great you like boating and being around them but this is a business, not summer camp."

"I can handle them. I have been around some of the most obnoxious people you'd ever want to meet. My parents belong to a big Country Club in St. Louis and I play golf in club events and tournaments with a lot of them. Sometimes they bend or break the rules and I have to call them on it. They don't like it. Especially, when someone my age does that, but I can handle myself with people like that. I don't get intimated when I know I'm right. I'll protect your interest just like I protect the interest of all the honest golfers in the club event and tournament."

"You think you can do that for me. Protect my interest?"

"No problem, Mr. Peterson," he said. "Another big reason. It's really the reason I want a job. I'm tired of asking for money from my father. I want to earn my own money. My dad can make my life miserable at times, especially when it's about money."

Mr. Peterson just looked at Peter. He didn't say anything for about fifteen seconds. "How old are you?"

"Nineteen."

"Nineteen. That's old enough I guess. Why don't you come back tomorrow morning, say eight? I want to think about it tonight."

"Thanks, Mr. Peterson."

Peter floated home. To get paid for being around boats, he thought, it doesn't get any better than that.

**

It wasn't until Rita and Annie actually were finished with work that they could really talk. Annie invited Rita home for a snack and a swim. Betty made some rhubarb pie, so Annie and Rita had a piece and then headed for the beach.

They swam out to the raft. There were some kids playing on the raft, but as Rita and Annie swam out, the kids' mothers called them in.

"Thank God for small favors," Rita said.

They stretched out on the raft, comfortable on their stomachs, eyes closed. Finally, Annie couldn't wait any longer. "Well, what happened with you two last night?"

Rita sighed, "We went to this spot on the golf course that overlooks Ephraim. It was just at sunset. It was beautiful. I brought a couple of beers I had stashed to help set the mood. We had a couple of sips when he started kissing me, really gently. That surprised me, because he was a little rough when we were in the water yesterday, not that I minded it." She giggled.

Annie didn't say a word. She remembered seeing his hands on Rita's breasts, and then kissing her. She remembered how electric she felt when Dennis kissed her that first night.

"First he kissed my lips," Rita said, "then my neck and ear. Then he started French kissing me, which drove me mad. I laid back on the blanket. He untied my blouse, touching my stomach and…" She sighed. "I was so hot, Annie. Then, just when I thought it couldn't get any better, it did. I never had anyone make me feel that way and kiss me there!" Rita giggled again. "He was so good. After that, I would have done anything. I wanted him to feel good, too." She smiled.

"And then what?" Annie asked, starting to feel warm.

"I started rubbing his crotch and could feel him get excited. Finally, I unzipped his shorts and wow." She paused. "I guess I did a good job. At least he said I did."

Rita was quiet for a few seconds before she continued. "Anyhow, we just laid there for while and then we finished the beer. If we smoked, we would have lit up a cigarette, just like in the movies. Finally, he said he better get going, so he drove me back to Wilson's. He gave me a kiss good-bye and said he was looking forward to next weekend. I was spent. I mean, I have never felt that way in my whole life. I loved it."

Envious, Annie nodded and pressed her legs together. After a moment, she asked, "Didn't you get nervous or anything? What if he tried going all the way?"

Rita smiled and chuckled. "I didn't get a chance to get nervous because it just seemed to happen. Nothing was forced. I was in a love zone. He could have done just about anything to me at that point and I would have said yes. It was just perfect what he did. I suspect he would have liked to go further, but for our first date, I think we were both happy. I know I was."

Annie laid her head down so Rita could not see her eyes. "I know Peter and I will get there too. I guess I'm just nervous about getting pregnant if we go too far." She turned her head back toward Rita.

Her friend reached over and touched her shoulder. "I understand."

Annie sat up. "Let's swim back. I need to cool off."

"Me too. I got hot just talking about it."

"Do you want to come home with me and have dinner? I'm sure Mom and Dad would love to see you. I know we have enough food."

Rita said, "I'd love to."

They got up and dove in.

**

That same day, Dennis felt great as he worked, but he had trouble concentrating all day. He couldn't help but think about Sunday as he worked. "That Rita was something!" he muttered to himself, "She's funny, exciting to look at, and fun to be with. No hidden agenda with her, that's for sure. She sure has a nice body and likes to be touched." He liked that too.

At least now he knew how to take his time and pace himself when he got into a situation like he had with Rita. He thought back to his junior year in high school, to the life-changing event he suffered through. He was so embarrassed by what happened.

Connie was pretty hot stuff. She was a cheerleader. Everyone wanted her, but she wanted him. Why not, he was all-conference, and captain of the football team his junior year. She made it her business to be with him because she knew he'd be Homecoming King and then she'd be Homecoming Queen.

The relationship was working fine until her parents went away for the weekend. We had the whole house to ourselves. Then we went upstairs to their bedroom.

Dennis started sweating as he remembered everything as if it were yesterday. God, he had been so excited. Looking back at the situation, it would have helped to have a beer, but he was an athlete, and he couldn't drink. He followed the rules back then, especially when it came to sports. He laughed about it now.

Connie came out of the bathroom in a little teddy. God, she looked hot. They got into bed, and he started doing all the things he thought he was supposed to do. He had never been that far with any girl.

Connie was rubbing him, and he was feeling her breasts. His hand drifted lower, touching her in all the right places, just like the magazines said to do. Her hips started to move.

"Let me make you wet." she said, and slid down his body and ran her tongue up and down his cock. That's all it took. He couldn't control himself any longer and his load exploded on her face. She screamed and some shot in her mouth, but he couldn't stop.

Incensed, she jumped out of bed and ran to the bathroom. He heard her spitting, gargling and crying. When she came out and stood over him as he struggled to pull his briefs up.

"Look what you did. You were supposed to make love to me like in the movies. Here, I even got us a rubber." She grabbed a foil packet from under the pillow and held it in front of his face, shaking it "I expect something like this from a freshman in the backseat of a car, but not from *you*, Dennis." In hysterics, she picked up the rest of his clothes and threw them at him. "Hope it was good for you, because it sucked for me. Go! Get out! Now!"

He never felt so humiliated. He hated the way he felt at that moment. Right then and there, he promised he'd show that bitch, and all women, for that matter. He promised himself he'd never lose control again. He was going to become the most skilled lover he could be. Now, he never really let himself get too excited with any of them until he was ready. He liked it when they pleaded for more. Rita did.

He thought about Annie and Rita. Rita was fun and didn't hide what she wanted. He liked that. She wanted to please him and she did. Yes, he could play with Rita and enjoy the summer, but he was the boss. Then there was Annie.

Annie was the one he wanted to toy with, and she excited him, but in a different way. She had intrigued him from the first moment he saw her at Deacon's. The time they spent together that Sunday afternoon and evening told him one thing, he had to have her.

Right now, she liked Peter. He could see why. Hell, he liked Peter, and he needed a friend like Peter, too. He could wait for Annie. Push her buttons. He knew, sooner or later, he'd get his chance, and he'd make the most of it.

Peter and Annie wouldn't be forever. Besides, he didn't want to jeopardize his working relationship with Darrell, just for a roll in the hay.

Chapter Eight

Waiting on the stoop outside Wilson's for Annie to finish her workday, Peter felt excited. His reward came in the form of a big smile when she saw him.

"What brings you here now?" she said. "You don't usually show up this late. Is the golf course closed or something? No wind?" She looked at the bay. "No, there seems to be plenty of wind, so that can't be it."

"I've got great news," he said. "Mr. Peterson, the owner of the boat rental place across the street, just gave me a part time job checking people in and out on their boats."

"Oh, Peter, I'm so happy for you."

"I even get to teach sailing. Can you believe it, getting paid to do what I like?"

Annie squeezed his hand. "That's great."

"My own money. No more groveling to Dad to get spending money. Self respect."

"Good for you, Peter." Annie's eyebrows rose. "I just hope we can coordinate our schedules."

"I don't think that will be a problem. I know something else you'll like," he said. "We should go back up to Newport Beach again and try that painting stuff. I know this spot that's secluded. You can paint and we can...you know. Just a suggestion," he said with a sheepish smile. Then he watched a big smile appear on her face.

"I'd love to paint up there again. Maybe even more than paint. I'm off Thursday. Would that work?"

"Sounds like a plan."

They walked hand in hand up the road to Anderson Dock. They sat on the dock, watching boats come and go. Green Eyed Girl pulled alongside the dock wall, so they walked over and sat on a bench in front of the boat as the owners tied her up for the evening.

"You know, Peter, I have this dream about going out on this boat. I don't know what it is about her, but I just like her looks."

"It looks like it could go any place your heart wants to go," Peter said.

"In my dream, we cruise over to Chambers Island or to Gills Rock, then over to Washington Island, then we sail back at night with a full moon." Annie paused. "God, would that be exciting. The people who own her come into Wilson's almost every day. Almost like you, Peter. I heard them talking about sailing her from Ephraim to Ft. Lauderdale and back each year. What a life."

Peter squeezed her hand. "There's still plenty of the summer left for your dream to come true."

Annie sighed. "I guess so. Let's start back to the house."

**

The next days passed quickly. Peter enjoyed working for Mr. Peterson and being around boats. He never tired of talking to the customers, whether they wanted to rent a paddleboat, a fishing skiff, a sailboat, or a runabout. Every customer had one thing in common; he or she loved the water.

His job also required him to determine if the person had enough experience to handle whatever boat they were renting. If it was a simple paddleboat, he made sure they understood the dangers of the water and where they could or could not go. Though he hadn't been on the job long, he'd already gone out several times to rescue someone who had tipped over a boat or to tow back sailors who sailed too far out and couldn't get back when the wind died.

That Thursday, Mr. Peterson approached Peter as he finished his work. "I've been watching you," he said. "I like what I see. Have you sailed bigger boats?"

"Not really," said Peter.

"Who taught you to act the way you do around customers?"

"What do you mean? Did I do something wrong?"

"No, you seem to really care about them having a good time, and you take care of my equipment. I like that."

"Thank you, Mr. Peterson, but I'm just doing my job," said Peter, relieved to hear the compliments.

"I have a proposition for you. I want you to start working at my Sister Bay marina three times a week. I'll pay you a little more for working up there. I know it's farther away, but I want you to get used to working with larger boats. I have a charter business there, and I want you to get involved with that. How does that sound? Think you're up to it?"

"Oh, wow! You mean it? That's great. Yes, I'd love to work there."

"Good. Talk to Jim Erickson, he's my manager there. I'll pay you extra for working in Sister Bay. Jim will fill you in about the boats and chartering. I need someone to help out when Jim's doing special projects for me during the summer, and I think you're the one."

"Really! I don't know what to say except thank you." *Well dad, I guess I'm better than you thought, and I didn't need you or Grandpa's help. I hope you aren't planning on me ever working for you. You can't make me. I won't let you. I can't wait to tell dad. He'll probably be pissed. I am so excited.*

Mr. Peterson took off his sunglasses, smiled, and put his hand on Peter's shoulder. "You finish out the week here and then start working in Sister Bay on Mondays, Wednesdays, Fridays and on Saturday mornings, if we need you. Tuesdays and Thursdays, you still work here."

Peter nodded as he followed Mr. Peterson back to his pickup truck.

"You'll still work half days at both places," Peterson said as he climbed into the truck. "You'll check new people in, go over the operation of the boat and its equipment. Then, when the customer brings it back at the end of the charter period, you'll make sure there is no damage or loss of equipment. Fridays and Saturdays are probably the most important days of the week for us. Make sure that's okay with your family."

"I don't think that will be a problem." *I don't think they really care if they see me or not, they're in their own little world.* "Just so I get one day on the weekend to go sailing."

Mr. Peterson turned the ignition key, put the truck in gear. "I'll talk to Jim and set everything up for Monday. He might come down here tomorrow morning and go over things with you." Then he chuckled. "His bark is worse than his bite, but he's the best in the business."

"Thanks, Mr. Peterson." Peter watched the truck slowly pull out on to the highway, still unable to believe his good luck. How great to work and be around big sailboats. He might only be able to spend afternoons with Annie, but that was a small price to pay for this opportunity. They'd just have to meet later. She'll understand, wouldn't she? She'll have to, that's all. This is too important to me.

**

Excited to tell Annie about the job, Peter remembered he was going to spend the afternoon at Newport Beach with her that day. He raced home and got his mom's car. If his mom needed to go anyplace, he thought, she could just get a ride from another summer guest at the hotel. If she knew he was using her car for a date with Annie, she'd say no, just to mess up his love life. I think she enjoys creating misery.

When Peter pulled up in front of Annie's house, she didn't have nearly as much equipment this time. "How come you're traveling light today?" he said.

"I didn't know what to expect last time. Now I do." Annie grabbed a shopping bag. "I got some snacks and soft drinks."

The trip seemed quicker to Peter this time. There were some people around, but it was still pretty quiet. They set up fast. Annie set the blanket down and put rocks on the corners, then got her palette out and started mixing colors.

"Anything you want me to do?" Peter rubbed his hands together.

"No, I think I'm all set. Go ahead and do whatever you want."

"Okay, I'll just walk the beach. Maybe find some drift wood or a bottle with a message inside." He waved and headed down the beach.

After about thirty minutes, he was back and started swimming.

"How's the water?" she yelled.

"I must be getting used to it, it doesn't feel too cold." Peter got out and laid on the blanket so he could watch Annie paint. "How's it going?"

"I don't know. I just can't seem to get into anything."

"Why don't you take a break and lay down here with me?" He patted the blanket.

"Like that's going to inspire me."

"It might. It sure would inspire me!"

She looked at him. "Okay, why not? You wouldn't take advantage of a poor defenseless girl, would you?"

"I might. I would. Lie down and let's get friendly."

Annie cleaned her brushes in some water and covered her paints so they wouldn't dry out, then snuggled next to Peter.

He leaned over and started kissing her and running his fingers through her long, blond hair. Slowly, he kissed her neck.

"Ummm," she moaned. "You're giving me goose bumps."

"Let's see," he said, raising her tee shirt to look at her stomach.

"Peter!"

"You're right, you do have goose bumps. I better warm you up." And with that, he rolled on top of her with his elbows outside her shoulders and his legs between her legs.

"Peter, what are you doing?"

"Just warming you up. Aren't you warmer now?"

"Yes, but that's not what I had in mind."

"Oh, how's this?" He lowered his head and gently gave her a slow kiss. Their tongues intertwined, and he rested his hand on her breast, tracing circles around her erect nipple.

In a soft whisper, he heard her say, "Peter, we can't do this. We both want to, but we can't." Peter rolled off, breathing heavily. "It's just…when I'm with you, I want more." He laughed and brought his face closer, so that their noses almost touched. "I mean…it feels good to kiss you, and I want to touch you more, Annie." He sat up, looking deep into her sparkling green eyes. "I know we've been together only a short time, but you're everything to me."

Tears filled her eyes. "I know, Peter. We just have to take it slow and easy. Our time will come…. just, not now."

He reached over and grabbed her hand. "Come on then, let's walk the beach and cool down. I want us to have fun today. I want you to paint some more."

He pulled her up, and she rested her head against his chest.

"Thank you, Peter, for understanding," she said. "I really want to do more…"

He gave her a hug. "My mind says you're right. You'll just have to convince another part of my body," he said.

Laughing, she looked down at the bulge in his shorts and shook her finger at it. "Bad boy, bad boy!" She looked at him with a twinkle in her eyes. "How's that?"

"Oh, now I feel better. Thanks."

They walked up the beach, hand in hand. He watched Annie bend over and grab something at the waters edge. "Look." She said, holding it up for him to see. "I found a piece of glass worn smooth by the water and sand. Isn't it beautiful? It's shaped like a large diamond. It has some lettering still faintly visible. PE. Just imagine if this was a diamond. We'd be rich!" said Annie.

Peter kept walking. "I'm looking for a bottle with a treasure map in it. If I found a million dollars in gold, I could buy you *Falcon*."

Annie slipped her arm through his. "We could sail back and forth from here to Florida like those people on 'Green Eyed Girl.' It would be a grand life, wouldn't it?"

"Yes, it would." Peter smiled. "If it's with you."

"As long as we're dreaming, I could paint pictures of boats and towns along the way. I could sell them at the marinas. Everyone loves the beauty of boats and water."

"I think they love what that beauty represents, Annie. They love the idea of freedom."

"Let's start back," she said. "You got me in the mood to paint again."

Annie started painting as soon as they got back, but after a while, she gave an exasperated sigh. "I just can't get it today."

"Why don't you try something else?" He pointed down the beach. "How about that family over there? They look like they're having fun."

A father and his son played Frisbee in the water, while the mother read and the daughter sat at the water's edge, building a sandcastle.

"You're right, Peter, that really captures the essence of summer in Door County."

Annie worked feverishly on the painting for about ninety minutes and was just finishing up as the mother and daughter meandered their way up the beach. The little girl ran behind Annie and looked at the picture, and then she ran back to her mother.

Annie heard her yell, "Mommy, Mommy! Come quick. Look, she painted a picture of us."

The mother walked up and looked at the picture. She brought her hand to her mouth as if she were going to cry. "Is that us?"

Annie smiled. "Actually, yes. I thought your family captured Door County and what summer is all about. Do you like it?"

"Like it? I love it! Would you sell it to us? It would be perfect above our fireplace. How much do you want for it?"

Annie's mouth dropped open. "I...I don't know..." she stammered.

The woman turned and yelled to her husband, "Frank, Frank! Come over here quick."

It took Frank a couple of minutes to get things together and walk over. "What is it, Doris?"

"Look at this," she said, pointing at the painting. "This girl just painted our family. She said we captured what summer is all about up here."

"She's right. I like it." Said Frank. "Would you consider selling it?"

Annie stared at Doris and Frank. She looked at Peter with excitement in her eyes as she thought about her first sale. "If it means that much to you, of course."

"How much do you want?" asked Frank.

Annie lowered her brows, thinking hard. "It's a one of a kind. How much do you think it's worth?"

Frank reached for his wallet and pulled out two bills. "Would you take two hundred dollars?"

Annie's mouth went as dry as sand. She coughed to clear her throat. "I think I could let you have it for that price. There is just one thing I have to do yet." She bent over and signed her name in the lower right corner.

Annie watched Doris as she slid her arm around Frank's waist and kissed him on the cheek. "Thank you, honey."

He turned and kissed the top of her head. "You're welcome. I'm excited about it, too. Look, she even made me look skinny." They all laughed.

When the family left, Peter got up and gave Annie a big hug. "You're a professional artist now."

She looked at him, tears filling her eyes. "I can't believe it finally happened. I never expected this today."

"Well, get used to it, kid. You are on your way."

"You know, you get credit for part of my success."

"I do?"

"If you hadn't pointed out that family, it would never have happened."

"So, I guess I'm your inspiration?"

"Yes, you are. You're my inspiration and something else." She wrapped her arms around his neck and kissed him.

The drive home was a heady experience. Peter and Annie fantasized about her career in art. "Maybe a gallery? Paris?" she said. They talked and laughed, reliving the whole afternoon. They got to Annie's house and burst through the front door.

"Mom! Mom!" she yelled.

Betty, cane in hand, shuffled into the kitchen. "What's wrong? Are you hurt? Is everything okay?"

"Look," Annie said as she held up the two one hundred dollar bills.

"What's that for?"

"I sold a painting to a family ..." She explained what happened.

"We'll have to celebrate," said Betty. "I know I have some champagne around here." She left to find it.

"You know, Annie," said Peter, "if you can find what people are passionate about and paint it, you'll have lots of buyers. This was a great lesson in marketing your art."

She looked at him, pondering what he'd said. "You mean I should go around and ask people if I can paint for them?"

"Indirectly, I guess. You could put fliers up," Peter said. "Paint what people love."

"I need to think about that."

"Yes, you do, especially now that you know how much the paintings are worth. Two hundred dollars is good money."

"That's more than I make at Wilson's some weeks. I need to make lots of money if I'm going to school this fall. It took me little over an hour and a half to paint that picture. That settles it; I'm going to be an artist!"

"Annie, you 'are' an artist."

**

The next day was bright and sunny. Peter was halfway done with his shift at South Shore when Jim Erickson arrived and introduced himself. At about 5'10", strong and stocky, Jim looked like a wrestler. He had dark brown hair with a little gray, and he wore a navy blue tee shirt, blue jeans, and a sailor's folding knife in a leather case attached to his belt. Aviator sunglasses and a faded Yankee's baseball cap made him look a little less intimidating.

"How's it going today?" he asked.

"Okay," Peter said. "We have all the boats going out this afternoon. I guess everyone's trying to get one last sail in before his or her vacation is over. This morning, we rented three fishing skiffs and one Sunfish."

Erickson looked him in the eye. "Mr. Peterson said he offered you a job working in Sister Bay."

"Yes, he did."

"You should be prepared to work your ass off. You're going to start with all the shit jobs first. If you can handle those, then and only then, will you really start learning about the real boating business. I don't want some kid working for me for just one summer. I want someone who can work several summers. When I get done with you, you'll be able to run a boating operation for anyone." Jim stepped back and studied Peter for a few seconds. "Mr. Peterson sees something in you he likes. He's a pretty good judge of character. He saw it in me twenty years ago, and I'm still here."

Peter didn't say anything, not that he had a chance. *Does he really see something special, in me? Is this my future, the boating business? Several summers working here, he said. Boating? I'd love that. It'd sure be different than the family business. I'd like that even more. I'd be away from mom and dad and their controlling attitude. That's good.*

Jim took off his sunglasses. "You still want to work for us, Franklin?"

Peter looked him in the eye. "Absolutely, I'm not afraid of hard work. I'll be ready Monday."

"Good, that's what I wanted to hear. You be there at eight a.m. sharp!"

Jim got in his truck, waved, and took off.

Peter watched him drive away. "Whew. So far so good." Now all he had to do was get through this day.

**

As was often Annie's custom after work, she swam out to the municipal beach's raft. On this particular day, Rita joined her and, after arranging their bodies to take advantage of the afternoon sun, they each relaxed. Neither seemed to hear the squawk of sea gulls, the high-pitched sound of powerboats, or the squeal of children playing on the beach. Each was lost in their own thoughts and enjoying the gentle rocking of the raft.

Finally, Rita broke the silence. "What a day for a Tuesday. It started quiet enough but then got crazy. I thought my arm was going to fall off scooping ice cream. I never really got a lull until my shift was over. My right arm is going to be so strong after this summer," she said as she made a muscle. "This fall, I will probably beat most guys in arm wrestling and win a lot of drinks."

Annie laughed.

"How was your day?" Rita asked. "I didn't get a chance to talk to you."

"I was in the small dining room today. It wasn't as busy as your area, but it had some interesting moments. The usual small kid's birthday party this morning. You know how much I like that. Then, later in the day, it was just steady."

Annie rolled on her side, facing Rita, her arm bent, holding her head up. "I did eavesdrop on an interesting conversation," she said in a low voice.

Rita rolled over, her eyes bright with anticipation. "Really? Let's hear it. Gossip has been kind of slow lately."

Annie sat up, suddenly energized. "I waited on these two women wearing very stylish jogging outfits, right out of *Runners World* or some magazine like that. Sounded like the kids and husbands went back home after a week and the two were staying another week. They sat at the small table in front of the window. You know, the one with the view that looks out over the bay?"

Rita nodded.

"I had just walked up to take their order when these two extremely good-looking guys pulled up on their ten-speed bikes; they looked like bronze gods, strong chests glistening with sweat. They parked their bikes in the rack in front of the window, grabbed their tee shirts from a small daypack, and wiped the sweat off their faces and chests before putting the shirts on.

"One of the ladies, with short blonde hair, turned toward her friend and me and said, 'Don't you just love the way bike shorts accentuate the package of the male anatomy? Come to think of it, the rest of their bodies aren't bad either.' 'We all laughed."

"I guess I was too busy today. I usually don't miss the good ones," Rita said with a smile.

"I took their order," Annie said, "and when I came back with the food, I arrived just as the two were starting a most interesting conversation. Luckily, the dining room wasn't too busy yet and it was relatively quiet, so I could listen. The blonde said, "Remember those two good looking biker boys we saw earlier? Wouldn't it be fun to do something wild and crazy with them, something you always fantasized about doing?"

Annie paused as Rita sat up. "Then her friend said, 'What are you talking about?' The blond continued. 'Have you ever thought what it would be like to let yourself go? To be wild, with no inhibitions?'

"The brown haired woman picked up her friend's glass, sipped it and set it down, then said, "I don't think there's any booze in it." She smiled at her friend. 'What are you talking about?"

Rita moved closer to Annie "Then what? What did her friend say?"

"Well, I was really intrigued, so I slowly started cleaning tables, even though they were spotless. I mean this was not a normal Wilson's lunch conversation. Anyhow, the blonde said, 'Don't you ever get bored with Tim?' "Tim must be her husband," Annie interjected.

"Then the blonde said, 'I know Tim is good to you and the kids, but don't you sometimes think you'd like a little something more?' Her friend looked at her, almost frightened.

'Sometimes I think there is someone better out there. Someone that's got the full package, the spark that keeps me excited. When hands caress my body and I get goose bumps and all I can do is moan. It's been a long time since I've had that feeling. That's what I miss.'"

Rita sat wide-eyed as Annie continued.

"Her friend put down her cheeseburger, sipped her coke, and looked at her friend, steely eyed. 'You mean you got married to Don, but you weren't really in love with him?' she said. "I tried to remain invisible and clean another table within earshot."

"The blond said she didn't know. She thought she was in love with her husband. She said he was good looking and all that, he was a good dad and husband, everything a woman could want and yet... she paused and didn't finish. Then her friend snapped at her. 'What? What more could you want?' The blonde's eyes got teary. 'I don't know except I know I don't have it. I'm missing something. I guess I want that spark everyday. I don't have that. My life is a routine. I hate my routine! You only live life once. I think it could be better.'"

"Her friend coughed to clear her throat. "You aren't thinking of getting a divorce, are you?' The blonde reached across the table and patted her friend's hand. She smiled, but not a happy smile, and then said, 'No, I'm not going to get a divorce. I guess I wish I had been more selective choosing a husband. Maybe I should have taken a little more risk in love. I should have looked for someone who doesn't mind getting down in the mud sometimes. Someone to keep me on my toes, and a smile on my face.'

"Her friend gave a sigh of relief. She said she didn't think she could handle starting over with someone new because their families were so close and she really liked her husband. And then the blond said that she liked her current husband too."

"I would have stayed and listened to more, but some other customers came in and, by the time I finished, the two were ready to leave. You know, Rita, they gave me two tips."

"Two tips?"

"Yeah, one was money, and the other was to look for someone to keep me excited, on my toes, my whole life."

**

Dennis showed up on the weekend at 9:00 a.m. Peter was waiting for him at the boat rental pier. He described his new job at Sister Bay, and Dennis was genuinely excited for him.

"That's great!" said Dennis. "I haven't been around boats as long as you, but I get the sense this is going to be my business."

Peter put his hand on Dennis's shoulder. "You build them and I'll sell them."

Dennis laughed and gave him a high five.

"Here they come. Man, they look great," said Peter. He could feel the anticipation, just like he did before a big golf match or sailing race, but in this case it was a date. He couldn't wait to get going, competing, male against female, male versus male. Was he competing against Dennis? He didn't think so. Dennis was with Rita and he was with Annie, but Peter wasn't blind. He saw how he looked at Annie too. He was pumped. Yeah, male against male over two hot dates. "We are two lucky guys." He said.

"Actually, Peter, I like to think they are two lucky women."

"You would say that." He laughed.

After Rita and Annie placed their beach bags in the cockpit, Peter asked, "Where to, girls?"

Annie adjusted her baseball cap so her ponytail slipped through the hole in the back. "I thought we were going to Chambers Island and Fish Creek this time. We could see where the wind takes us?"

"Great plan," Dennis said.

"Whatever you say, Dennis." Rita just smiled and leaned over, giving Dennis a long, sensuous kiss. "I needed that after not seeing you all week. Did you miss me?"

"Of course I did. Can't you tell?"

"Well, I hope so. You'll just have to show me later." Grinning, she pinched his cheek.

"Oh, cut it out, you two," Annie said. "You're making me sick."

The wind was from the southwest at about five knots. The high bluff blocked most of the wind until they sailed out past Horseshoe Island, where they made a tack to the west. Keeping out about one and one-half miles, they stayed out of the shadow of Eagle Harbor bluffs moving past Nicolet Bay, Pirate and Little Strawberry Island. They had enough wind to move at about three to four knots. The wind and waves picked up as they made their way toward Chambers Island.

"If this wind direction holds at this angle, we can sail to the southern tip of Chambers and anchor behind the point," said Peter. "Then we can picnic for a while and either sail to Fish Creek or back to Ephraim."

"That sounds like fun," Annie said as she looked at the island off the bow in the distance.

Dennis looked at Peter in awe. "You've got it all plotted out in your mind already, and we just started sailing. I'm really impressed."

The girls nodded.

"It's really nothing but geometry, Dennis. After you've sailed for a while, you'll visualize your route, too. That's why I love sailing. You've got to plan. To think how you're going to get from point A to point B. If you're in a powerboat, you make sure you have enough gas, food, drinks, and away you go. With sailing, you've got to use what nature gives you."

Peter looked at Chambers Island as the Flying Scott rose to the top of a wave. "To me," he continued, "the fun is going from Point A to point B. I get bored when I reach my destination. The journey is what I love."

Annie cut in. "I love the journey too, Peter, but I hope we can eat and swim soon. I'm getting hungry. I bet the water is warm in the shallows."

"I'm sure it is. You know Chambers is an island, but did you know that on the island there is a lake, and on that lake is another island? Kind of neat, huh?"

"Very neat," Rita said. "How long until we get there, Peter?"

"About an hour. Can you hold off eating until then?"

"I guess we'll have to," Annie said, and they settled back.

It actually took them an hour and a half, but it was worth it. The tip of the island created a natural curved harbor. Dropping the sails as they glided in, they walked the boat close to shore and anchored. The water was indeed warm, very warm, for a change. They swam and then they ate. After that, they decided to sail toward Fish Creek and get some ice cream at a little shop near the water. It wasn't Wilson's, but it was ice cream.

"Dennis, do you want to try sailing us to Fish Creek?" Peter asked

"Sure, I'll give it a whirl."

"See the different tone of the waves on the water where the small waves meet the bigger waves?"

Dennis pointed to a line on the water. "You mean there?"

"Yes, that's the wind line. When we hit that area, the wind is going to hit the boat and heel us over. Hold the course steady and, after about a hundred yards, tack toward Fish Creek, okay?"

"Aye, aye, Captain!"

"You handle the tiller, and I'll handle the sails. You girls might want to shift over here. It's going to become the high side of the boat pretty soon. We'll need your weight here, anyway, if we're going to try to keep the boat flatter on this close haul. Annie, do you want to handle the jib?"

"Sure."

"I'll tell you how tight or loose to make it. Just do it the way I showed you before."

"Okay."

"Get ready, here comes the wind," Peter cautioned.

The girls giggled until the wind hit.

"Oh!" Rita screamed as the boat heeled over. She looked at the incline meter with some concern, then started calling off the numbers with increased intensity. "Ten degrees, fifteen, twenty, twenty-five degrees! Are we going to tip over?" she said, with panic in her voice.

Peter shook his head. "No," as he let some of the main sheet out. "That should relieve some of the pressure on the main sail and help flatten the boat a bit."

"Thanks, Peter," Rita said. "I thought I was going for a swim for sure."

"I just wanted you to get involved too, Rita," he said with a toothy grin.

"Gee, thanks. This is much better, but I don't feel much like ice cream right now."

"Don't worry. Once you get on land, you'll feel better."

About one hour after leaving Chambers Island, they reached the Alibi Dock. It was packed with boats, so they moved off to the east near the boat launch area and anchored in a shallow area. The four jumped over the side and waded ashore.

"The boat should be okay there while we get that ice cream and see the sights. Rita, are you feeling better?" Peter said.

She nodded and put her arm around Dennis, then stood on her tiptoes and gave him a kiss. "That's for being such a good steersman."

"Helmsman is the correct term, I think," Dennis said.

"Whatever."

Dennis smiled. "I might need another kiss. The price just went up."

"Okay," Rita said. This time, her kiss was more passionate and lasted longer.

Annie watched. "Are you guys ready? Geez!" She squeezed Peter's hand. "Did I ever tell you I like being with you?" she said.

"No, but you could show me."

Now it was Annie's turn. She ran her hands across his chest, around his neck, and pulled him down where she hungrily kissed him. When she released him, he flashed a big smile.

"Now that's what I call showing your appreciation. I think you got my motor running. I'm ready to shift into another gear."

"I thought you were a sailor, slow and steady?" She said smiling.

"I saw how you looked at Dennis a couple times. I can be exciting too, if you let me?"

"What are you talking about? I'm with you, aren't I?"

"I know."

"Hey, I thought you guys were in such a hurry," Rita yelled.

Annie and Peter ran up to Dennis and Rita. The four walked up the street to get ice cream and browse. As they ate their ice cream, they walked into one of the many gift shops and looked at some shop's jewelry.

Rita spied something. "Annie, look at this. It's a small sailboat on a gold chain."

"That's really neat," Annie said as she leaned down close to the glass.

"Do you really like it?" Peter asked

"I sure do! It's so simple. A gold sailboat with its sails set. I think I'll get Mom to bring me back next week when I get paid and buy it. When I wear it, I'll always think of the four of us being together and the good times."

Rita hugged her. "That's nice. We do have a good time, don't we?" They all nodded.

Slowly, they walked back to the boat. On the way back, Dennis got Rita a cut-off tee shirt that appeared just a little small to everyone, except Dennis. "I think I'll wear it on the way back." She said. She pulled it on, then reached underneath, untied the strings to her bikini, and slipped it off. "Now I feel more comfortable. How do I look?"

Dennis stared at her. He didn't say anything.

Peter cleared his throat. "What's the matter, Dennis? Cat got your tongue?"

Dennis smiled, not taking his eyes off Rita and the "Door County" printed across her chest. He put his arm around her and pulled her close. "I think I'll just let you and Annie sail the boat back, we'll just enjoy the ride. I want to give Rita the special attention she deserves since I didn't get to do that on the way here. How's that, Rita?"

Annie grabbed Peter's hand. "Peter, do you think I could sail the boat back?"

"I think that's a great idea. You really haven't sailed since we went out a couple of weeks ago. This will be a great ride back because we'll be on a reach all the way. It's the smoothest point of sailing with the exception of sailing straight downwind. It'll be like sailing downhill. Besides, you're my First Mate."

They got to the boat, raised the sails, and pushed it out to where they caught a little wind. Dennis and Rita sat forward on the starboard side, and Peter and Annie sat on the port side. Annie handled the tiller, while Peter handled the jib and mainsheets. It took about 20 minutes to get out into the stronger winds for the ride back.

"Annie, see the wind line?" Peter said and pointed off the starboard bow.

"Yes."

"Just be ready for the boat to heel over. Dennis and Rita, you might want to move over to this side now before the wind hits us."

They scooted over.

"Get ready, Annie. Here it comes."

The sails made a snapping sound as the wind filled them. Just as Peter predicted, the boat heeled over, and they accelerated like a car shifting gears. The girls yelled and spray flew back.

It didn't take Annie long before she was sailing a straight course.

"Look at that wake line behind the boat. It's as straight as an arrow. You are really doing a great job handling the boat Annie. I'm really impressed how fast you've picked this up. We'd make a great team sailing to Florida and back like that couple on Green Eyed Girl."

"We would, wouldn't we?"

"Yes, we would." He looked into her eyes at that moment and saw something that made him take her in his arms and kiss in a tender way and he hoped it would come true.

"This is so neat, Peter. I see why you love to sail so much."

"Now keep the leading edge of the jib just off the shoreline. We should be able to sail this course for at least an hour. Enjoy, Annie," he said but he was thinking about a long voyage, with her.

Peter leaned back and enjoyed the ride himself. First watching Annie, and then, the sights of Peninsula State Park as it passed on the starboard side of the boat. He rubbed Annie's back and neck as she handled the tiller. Then his hand reached around her back and started to cup and rub the side of her breast.

He saw her look at a smiling Dennis, who saw what was happening, and then she whispered in Peter's ear, "That really feels good, don't stop."

He watched her nod at Dennis. "We can play that groping game too," she said, loud enough for all to hear.

Peter got a big grin, and then watch Annie's eyes shift to Dennis in time to see him wink at her. Yeah Dennis, I bet you'd like to have your hand on her breast too.

The boat was really moving through the water as the wind picked up more strength. Even Dennis and Rita stopped their groping to enjoy the ride.

"Peter! What's that humming sound?" Annie asked. "Is something broken? It sounds like it's coming from the centerboard or keel."

Peter smiled at the concern on their faces. "No mates, that's the sound of perfection. The boat is perfectly balanced and it will make that sound when you're in the zone. Good job, Annie."

"Really? Thank you."

"Yep, you're in sync with the wind, waves, and water. It doesn't get any better than this, guys."

They continued past Eagle Point, past Horseshoe Island, until it was time to tack into Eagle Harbor. Annie passed the tiller chores to Peter. She handled the main and jib sheets. It took another half hour to sail to the Ephraim Municipal Pier.

Collecting their gear, they moved to a picnic table under the big tree across from Wilson's and drank the last of their sodas.

"Anyone hungry?" Rita asked.

"I could go for a little something," Annie said.

"Let's go to 'Tony's' in Fish Creek for Pizza," Rita said.

"Sounds good to me."

The four piled into Dennis's Bug and headed off.

Chapter Nine

S itting at 'Tony's' and waiting for the pizza, Rita said, "I feel like I'm rocking back and forth in the booth."

Peter laughed. "That's your sea legs."

She looked at her legs. "What's wrong with my legs?"

"Your inner ear is still used to the rocking motion of the boat." Holding up a glass of water, he tipped it back and forth and then held it steady. "See, the water is still moving back and forth, but the glass is still. That's your inner ear. You'll be okay in a while."

"Thank you, doctor," Rita said.

When the waitress came, Dennis ordered a pitcher of beer. She smiled.

Everyone's eyebrows went up when the waitress brought the pitcher to the table. She winked at them. "You all look mighty thirsty and sunburned. Out on the water today?"

They nodded.

"I bet this here beer is going to taste mighty good, right? Oh, by the way, you're all twenty-one, aren't you?"

Of course, they all nodded.

"I can't believe we got this beer, she didn't even card us," Peter said

"Oh, that." Dennis smiled. "I ran into Janice at a bar in Sturgeon Bay last week when I was drinking with the boys after work. She was there with some of her friends and I bought her a beer."

Rita glared at him. "You went out with the boys and bought her a beer? Fuck you, Dennis. You could have come up and saw me. You're a real asshole!"

"Hell, if I didn't run into her, we wouldn't be having beer. I think it was a good trade off. Nothing happened." Then he leaned over and gave a reluctant Rita a kiss.

Rita punched him in the shoulder as she pulled back. "You better start coming up once in a while during the week. I'll make it more worth your while than drinking with the boys!"

Dennis chuckled and glanced at Janice.

He poured them each a glass of beer but he could see both Rita and Annie glaring at him.

"Come on, I just had a couple of drinks with her when I was out with the boys. I think if I remember correctly, she came on to me."

"I don't think I believe you Dennis." Rita said. "You better start coming up a little more often or two can play the game. There's a lot of Dennis Jamison's out their that would love to get there hands on these." And then she cupped her breast.

"Touché'" Annie said and laughed.

Peter brought the glass to his lips and took a mouthful. "God, I'm not sure beer ever tasted this good before."

Dennis held his half-empty glass in front of him, admiring the beer. "You're right. The sun and the water really made me thirsty. And maybe I will have to come up here more often." Then he winked at Rita.

About ten minutes later, Janice brought their pizza. "Is there anything else you need?"

Dennis smiled. "Why, yes, there is. How about another pitcher of beer?"

"Okay, but this will have to be your last one. The manager was questioning me if you were old enough."

"That's fine. It just tastes so good."

The four dug into the extra-large, thin crust, supreme pizza. The second pitcher arrived and took just a little longer to finish. Peter and Dennis split the check and included a very generous tip.

Walking out to the car with a slight stagger, Rita, Annie and Peter were all laughing.

Rita turned toward the building, spread her arms, and yelled at the top of her lungs, "Tony…I love you, wherever you are!"

Laughing, they all climbed into the car.

**

Driving back to Ephraim, Dennis pulled the car over on the shoulder of the road near the practice area of the golf course.

"It's too early to call it a night. Let's get out and sit for a while." He got out, opened the trunk, and got a couple of blankets. "This'll give us a good view of Ephraim and me a chance to sober up a little. I hear there is a great place for making out around here. Not as good as some I know about," he said and winked at Rita, "but still pretty good. I guess I don't want the day to end."

Rita grabbed his arm and pulled him close. "I'm still a little mad at you, but that brings back good memories, if you know what I mean."

They walked to a spot at the end of the practice range near the 10th tee, out of view from the golfers but with a nice view of the Village.

"It's getting dark so the golfers should be done practicing. We shouldn't get hit here." Peter said.

They spread out the blankets; Rita and Dennis on one, and Annie and Peter on another. Rita cuddled close to Dennis. Annie and Peter did the same. After a while, Dennis and Rita started making out.

Peter looked at Annie. "You're beautiful." Then he leaned over and kissed her.

Annie sighed. *If Rita and Dennis can do it, so can we.* She reached for his hand and moved it to her breasts. It was all the encouragement Peter needed.

Running her fingers through his hair, Annie whispered, "Oh, Peter, it feels so good. Don't stop. I wanted to do this for so long, but…."

He kissed her hungrily, not letting her finish.

When Annie opened her eyes later, she saw Dennis watching her. He smiled at her. She noticed Rita's brief shirt pushed up. With no bra, his hands roamed over her breasts, gently rubbing her nipples.

She heard Rita say, "Oh, Dennis," and then watched her body slowly start moving to his touch. "Yes, don't stop!" She heard Rita say, as she moved closer to Dennis. Then Annie watched her friend's hand caress his growing bulge.

She heard "Rita," and then watched her hand slide underneath his suit and grab his manhood. "Ahh," he groaned softly. "Yes, that's good."

In the fading light, Annie unfastened her bra and then shuddered as Peter kissed her breasts and she rubbed his bulge. *For one moment, I want to feel what it's like to be a woman, to have Peter touch me, to be reckless. Why not let Peter have his fun like Dennis and show Dennis I can be just as wild as Rita. That's what I want to do, but I can't. I'm afraid.* Why am I not ready yet? Annie rolled away from Peter. She felt Peter's hand hold her's and squeezed it.

Neither said anything.

Rita and Dennis's activities slowed. Annie noticed Rita's shirt still hiked up, revealing her erect nipples. She quickly pulled it down when she saw Annie staring. Annie wondered if she saw tears on her cheeks.

They lay there for a few minutes, composing themselves. A slight breeze caressed the four, gently cooling them before Dennis broke the silence.

"We better get going. It's close to ten. By the time I get home, it'll be late. I need my beauty sleep," he said and stretched his arms.

**

Peter and Annie walked towards Annie's house. Peter stopped and turned toward her. He grabbed her hand, squeezed, and looked into her eyes. "I have to get this out while I have the courage," he said. "Annie, I love you."

She sighed. "Peter, I know you do." She knew she should say, "I love you too," but she couldn't. One reason she couldn't say, "I love you," was because she felt she wasn't good enough for Peter's family, especially his mother. He'd never invited her to his house for anything. He kept her away from his family and their friends. I'm second-class in their eyes, she thought.

Another reason was she wasn't sure Peter could keep her excited like Dennis did when he kissed and touched her. She never felt electricity like that from Peter. Sure, he got her excited tonight, but she wanted what the lady at lunch wanted, someone who could keep her excited forever. She could only guess how much voltage Dennis could bring to her body. But did she trust Dennis. Not like Peter. She didn't think Dennis would help her with her dream of being an artist. At least with Peter, she was pretty sure he'd support her efforts any way. He had in a limited sort of way already. She was so confused. Hell, she was still a virgin. All this sex stuff was only a guess. Why was life so difficult? She wished she could climb into her mother's bed, have her mother wrap her arms around her, and then tell her what to do about Peter and Dennis. What am I thinking? Mom couldn't tell me. She'd have no clue how to handle Dennis. There was no one to give her answers, no one but her. She didn't say anything except, "I'm sorry Peter." She started crying. "I can't tell you I love you…at least not tonight. I'm so confused."

"Confused? Confused about me? You sure didn't seem confused on the golf course a few minutes ago! What changed?"

"I can't talk about it right now," she choked out, "I'm sorry." She pulled her hand away, turned and ran the remaining hundred feet to her house.

**

Peter was excited to be in Sister Bay the next morning, Monday. He thought about Mr. Peterson warning him about Jim Erickson, "His bark is worst than his bite." I'll see if that's true in a few minutes.

"Franklin! In here." Jim called as Peter walked through the marina. When Peter stepped into the office, he pointed to the coffee pot. "You want some before you start?"

Sheepishly, Peter said, "I really don't drink coffee, Mr. Erickson."

Jim laughed. "You can't be no boater if you don't drink coffee. Here's a mug you can use while you're here. If you don't like it, buy your own. One other thing…"

"Yes?"

"Don't call me Mr. Erickson, that's my father's name. Just call me Jim."

"Okay, Jim."

Jim moved to the door. "Now let's get started. Get some coffee and follow me."

Peter got half a cup of coffee with lots of sugar and cream and walked out with Jim to the shop.

"Here's where all the tools are. When you're done with the tools, you bring them back here. No excuses. If you lose a tool in the water, write down approximately where you think it went down. We know tools are going to go overboard, but we dive under the boats all the time to check for damage to the keel, rudder, and hull after they come back from a charter, so it's no big deal to spend a few minutes looking for a tool. Every tool has its place, and a place for every tool. Remember that; drill it into your head. You'll get used to the procedure fast, or you won't be here long. Understand?"

Peter nodded. *There sure are a lot of rules working here, not like in Ephraim.*

"This is another important area." Jim pointed to a board showing each slip in the marina. "This is the key board. When you are done working on a boat, you lock the boat up and immediately bring the key back to the board. Each key has a foam float with the name and slip number written on it. Hang it back on the board. Don't screw this up. You do, and you know what happens."

Peter nodded.

"It's not that we're hard asses, but boating is about discipline. Little things can cause huge consequences. Lake Michigan is littered with boats and equipment because people took things for granted or didn't follow procedures. The tool and key procedures take a little time to follow, but over the long run, they save hours of time looking for things and lessen frustration. Got it?"

"Got it." Peter knew Jim was right. He had heard or read sea stories about the very thing his new boss was talking about. He was determined to follow the rules.

Jim spent the next hour and half showing Peter around the marina, introducing him to all the guys and gals in the shop and store. He explained what days Peter would be working at the marina. "Everything okay so far, Peter?"

"Yep."

"Good. Let's get working. Mr. Schultz just brought his Sea Ray back after being out all weekend. Take the mop, pail, sponge, cleaning supplies and clean the boat. Before you start cleaning, go with Buddy Martin over there and have him show you how to fuel it up. Some take gas and some take diesel. Buddy will show you how to tell the difference. When you are done with the fueling, write the total cost on the slip and give it to Jean in the service department."

Jim put his hand on Peter's shoulder and looked him in the eyes. "All this is new to you. You're going to have questions, that's normal. Ask them; don't start anything until you know exactly what you're doing. You'll save yourself time and us money by asking questions and getting the answers. Our goal is to do it right the first time. That way, the customers are happy and so are we."

Peter nodded. "Makes sense to me."

"You see something that might need to be repaired, tell us. We'll call the client and see if they want it fixed. Better to fix it here at the marina than towing them in from the lake or have them break down in a storm. Are you starting to see a pattern here, Peter?"

"Yes, Jim, it makes a lot of sense to me. I like helping people, and I sure don't want anything nasty happening to them out there," he said pointing to the open water.

"Good boy. I believe you. Now, let's go to work. When you are done with Buddy and the fueling, start cleaning up Mr. Schultz's boat. When you're done with those two jobs, come and find me. I'll inspect your work. We have a certain way we do things here, and I just want to make sure you are doing it our way. Try your best. That's all anybody can ask."

Jim turned and walked toward the shop. Peter walked over to Buddy.

"Okay kid, I hope you last longer then the other two did. They only made it ten days. Jim can be a son of a bitch."

"Only ten days?" he said, as they walked to the gas dock.

"Yep. Here's how we do it...."

It took Peter about three hours to clean Mr. Schultz's Sea Ray the way he thought Jim would want it. He put away all the cleaning supplies and went to find Jim.

"Peter, the only thing I can see you need to do is make sure the water spots on the windshield are wiped off. When that's done, snap the canvas cover over the windows and fold the deck chairs. Put them in the stern locker. Good job!"

"Thank you," Peter said with a big smile.

"You even scrubbed the water line, didn't you?"

"Yes. It took a while, but I got the dirt and oil film off. I did it the way I'd want it done if this were my boat."

Jim put his hand on Peter's shoulder. "That's exactly how we want you to think of all our clients' boats. Stop doing that and you know what happens."

"Yes, I have a pretty good idea."

"Take care of them as if they were yours. I think that's enough for your first day. Go punch out, and we'll see you Wednesday."

"Thanks, Jim. See you Wednesday."

**

Rita and Annie were abuzz all day, talking about the day and evening before and how great it was for them both. When they got their break for lunch, they went out and sat across the street on the municipal pier, shoes off, feet dangling in the water, slowly kicking without making a splash.

Rita popped the last of her sandwich in her mouth. "That Coke tasted good." She paused. "Did I hear some moaning coming from you guys last night?"

Annie smiled and looked out toward Horseshoe Island. "Are you sure that wasn't you and Dennis?"

"Oh, hell, I knew we were moaning, but you were, too!"

"I couldn't help myself. I hated being Miss Prissy." She was quiet for a couple of seconds before she continued. "What's wrong with that? Isn't that what young love is all about, discovery…. uncharted discovery?"

"You got it."

Annie took a deep breath. *I'm confused with whom I want. I like both for different reasons.* "Peter said he loved me last night."

"Really?" Rita said. "That's exciting. I wish Dennis would say something like that. I know he likes me, but he likes himself more. He hasn't said anything except that he likes being with me. Do you think he likes me for my mind or my body?"

Annie eyed her friend, and Rita burst out laughing. "You don't have to answer that. But he makes me feel good, and he sure is easy on the eyes."

Annie looked down at the water. *You're right about that.*

"I envy you, Annie. It's nice to know where you stand."

"I know. Peter is the most caring person I ever met. He made some comment the other day about how his mother wasn't sure if I'd fit in with their family. That set me back. When I asked Peter about it, he didn't say much except that he probably shouldn't have said anything, but then he asked me to a summer party. I'll have to get something fancy to wear so I fit in."

"Wow," Rita said. "As if his family isn't tough enough, now you have a party to worry about and impressing all his rich, snobby friends."

"Right," Annie said in a soft voice. "I'm so insecure about measuring up. I don't know if Peter is worth it. Someone like Dennis would be better. He's more from my side of the tracks. I wish I could make up my mind. I really like Peter. I'm so confused." She gave the water a hard kick.

Rita's expression grew serious. "Dennis is mine, Annie. Remember? I see how he looks at you, but he's mine."

Annie hesitated. "I don't know what you mean. He looks at me?" When Rita didn't say anything more, she continued. "Rita, I just mean Dennis is from a working family like mine. I need to decide if I can fit into Peter's world. That's what I mean. I know Dennis is yours." *I'm so confused about everything.*

"Oh," Rita said. "Sometimes, it just seems like there is something between you and Dennis."

"There's nothing between us, Rita." Annie turned her head, her gaze aimed up the shore toward Sister Bay. "I wonder how Peter's first day is going. It's funny not seeing him at the pier. I miss that. Did you ever notice how strong his legs are?"

Rita nodded. "He's got a nice six pack, too!"

Annie giggled. "Yeah, he's got a nice package. You know, Rita, we are two lucky girls."

"You're right," Rita said, "but then again those boys are pretty lucky, too. They've got two hot chicks!"

The next morning, Darrell came over to Dennis's work area. "How's it going?" he asked.

"Pretty good. George is showing me how to install the hatches and portholes so they don't leak. It's not hard, but it takes time. George is a good teacher, but he sure does like to chew and spit. I almost grabbed the wrong Styrofoam cup. Man, that would have killed me."

Darrell laughed. "Sounds like you guys had a good day sailing yesterday."

"We sure did," Dennis said.

"Well, keep up the good work, and when we have a shakedown cruise, I'll see if you can go along for the ride," his boss said with a smile.

"Wow, that would be fucking great. Pardon my French."

Darrell laughed. "I'll see you later."

Dennis's mind drifted to the previous day. The two couples making out on the blanket. He liked that excitement. It was one of the things that drove him. God, that Rita has a body. She looked great in that cut-off shirt.

He thought of Annie. Also a good body, and interesting to toy with. It drove him wild to watch her and Peter getting it on. "Maybe someday," he muttered.

I know she's interested in me, otherwise she wouldn't have watched while she was kissing Peter. I saw her eyes widen when I started kissing Rita's nipples. I guess she wanted to see the master at work.

Dennis looked up and saw Charlie Koch coming over. "Dennis, can you give me a hand with this cowling? I need you to hold this sheet metal for that cruiser over there."

As they worked on the cowling, Charlie glanced up with an appraising look. "How's your love life up here, Jamison? Getting any? A guy like you probably has women all over the place."

Dennis just kept working.

"Come on, don't tell me you're pining away waiting for Snow White!" said Charlie.

"Nah, I've been seeing someone up in Ephraim, a friend of Darrell's daughter, but that's about it."

"Really? I don't believe you." Charlie shook his head. "We're meeting at the Canal Bar Thursday night after work. Ladies' night. Half price beers for women. That usually brings in the foxes. Why don't you meet us there? This is different than a few beers after work, if you know what I mean? There are usually about eight of us from work that go. See if you can shake loose to join us."

"Maybe," Dennis said.

"I think you'll have fun, even if it's just us guys. Then again, you might find someone and not have to drive up North."

"Thanks, Charlie. I'll think about it. It does sound pretty good. It would be a break from fishing and hanging around the shop." After a moment, he flashed Charlie a smile. "Sure, why not? Where's the bar?"

Charlie rubbed his hands together. "Now you're talking! It's on the north side of the ship canal near the coast guard station. We usually get there about six thirty. Gives us enough time to clean up and grab a burger or something."

"Okay, I'll see you there." I can have a little fun and still be with Rita.

Chapter Ten

The next few days moved along at a steady pace for everyone. Annie and Rita worked at Wilson's, and often Peter joined the two after work to go swimming or biking. One night when Annie worked the evening shift at Wilson's, just Rita and Peter went swimming. After a quick dip, the two got situated on the raft.

"Peter, do you think I'm attractive?"

"Yes. You're very good-looking."

"Attractive enough to go out with?"

With that question, Peter rolled on his side. "Rita, why are you asking me these questions?"

"I'll get to that in a second. Peter, would you kiss me?" She moved closer, so that their bodies were almost touching. "I need to know something."

"Rita, I'm going out with Annie. I don't think it would be right."

"Oh, don't be so prudish. I know you have the hots for Annie. I really need to know something!"

"Well, okay." He leaned over to kiss Rita, thinking it would be just a peck on the lips, but to his surprise, Rita really kissed him. Her tongue swirled with his, and she pulled him close and pressed her breasts against his chest while her free hand moved lower on his body and started rubbing, creating a growing bulge. He forgot who was doing the rubbing for a while and just enjoyed the sensations. When he pulled back and opened his eyes, he was embarrassed.

"I'm sorry, Rita. You made me forget who I was with."

She placed one finger to his lips and smiled. "Hush, I was the one that wanted you to do this." She looked into his eyes, then down at his hardness. "I just wanted to make sure I could still turn someone on. I think I still have it by the looks of your swimming suit."

Peter laughed. "Annie is right, Rita. You are a wild one. If I wasn't with Annie, I'd love to be with you."

"Really! That's nice to know. I wish Dennis was more interested in me. I know he cares when he's up here, but I worry about him being down in Sturgeon Bay. I don't believe that crap about fishing and going to sleep because he's too tired. I don't trust him. He'll go after anything in a skirt, even Annie. Did you ever notice how he looks at Annie?"

"What do you mean?" He said as his stomach did a big flip-flop.

"You're so trusting, Peter. I see how Annie looks at Dennis. And I see how Dennis looks at her. I'm not saying they've done anything, but there's something there."

"Geez, I never noticed." He felt sick as he remembered a few smiles directed at Dennis when they were sailing. He thought it was just a way to show she was happy but now?

"It's a girl thing. We have radar that can pick up vibes like that," she said, smiling.

"I did tell her I loved her the other day and she didn't say anything."

"Hey, she's just cautious. She told me about that, but I know she cares deeply about you. Besides, if she dumps you, there's always me, and now you know what I can do to you." She patted his suit. "Don't worry, Peter. I just wanted to find out if I still had what it takes. You're a keeper!"

He laughed. "You've definitely got it! Now let's swim back. I need to cool parts of my body." *Annie and Dennis?*

**

Peter loved working at the marina in Sister Bay. He learned more about the servicing of gas and diesel engines, as well as how to change halyards, splice rope, and how to properly varnish. Varnishing alone could take up a whole summer, but Jim wasn't that mean.

Though Peter was in pretty good shape, he still lost weight from spending so much time in the tight engine compartments or the boat cabins on days when it reached 80 and 90 degrees. Still, he loved what he was doing, and Jim was a good boss. He was demanding but fair. Everyone there was friendly and helpful.

Being around larger boats all week got him thinking about getting a bigger boat than his sunfish. He started looking for a boat with a cabin, so he could do some overnight sailing and live on it for a few days. When an ODAY 20-foot sailboat came in later in the week on a trade, Peter fell in love with it. It looked perfect, with an outboard, a jib, 150 Genoa, and a mainsail with two reef points. Peter was so excited that he stopped Jim that same day and asked what he thought about him purchasing it.

Jim put his hand on Peter's shoulder and looked him straight in the eye. "You know, Peter, when you own a boat like that, you get a better understanding of what our clients expect, want, and need. That's why we think it's a good idea for all our employees to be involved in some way with the water."

"Makes sense to me," Peter said.

Jim smiled. "You come to the office when you're done with your work today, and we'll sign the papers and work something out for you. How's that?

Peter was like a kid at Christmas. "That's great. Thanks, Jim. You won't be disappointed."

"I know we won't."

Peter started cleaning his boat as soon as he finished signing the papers with Jim. It didn't take long for word to spread through the marina that Peter bought Red Baron. Everyone came over and checked it out. He stood back, admiring his clean boat. He got a root beer from the vending machine and poured just a little over the bow. "I christen you Red Baron, pride of Door County," he said, and then he drank the rest.

Maybe he could borrow the car and take Annie and Rita out for a cruise tonight. He was so excited he thought he'd burst.

**

Rita and Annie headed out to the raft after work. "What do you suppose the boys are doing now?" said Rita.

"I don't know. Peter is probably golfing or something. Sometimes he'll come over and we'll go down to the beach and talk."

Rita giggled. "Talk! I bet you do more than just talk?"

Annie smiled. "We do talk, but that doesn't mean we don't fool around once in a while too. It gets pretty busy at the beach around sunset. It's the guests, Peter, the mosquitoes, and me. What do you think Dennis is doing tonight?" Annie asked.

"I hope he's fishing like he says. He might be going out with the boys and having a few. He does that sometimes after work. I hope that's all he does." Rita sighed. "Sometimes he says he just likes to stay at Deacon's when things quiet down because he can study the boats. Other times, he says he's so tired when he gets done with work, he just goes home and relaxes."

"Do you believe him?" Annie asked.

"I don't know," Rita said in a shallow voice. "I don't think it makes any difference. I can't control him. He always seems restless, not tied to anyone. You know what I mean?"

"Well, Rita, you're wild too. So you tell me."

"Yeah, I guess you're right. It's just that I don't seem to be as wild as I used to be. I only see him on the weekend, and that isn't enough for me. I need more action." She smiled. "Maybe I'll take some of those cute college guys up on their offers."

"You wouldn't!"

"I might." Rita shrugged. "A little jealousy never hurt anyone."

"You've got a point there. I have to share Peter with sailing and now work. That's tough."

"Yeah, it is. Maybe he'll grow out of it?" Rita said.

"I doubt it. He really likes sailing, and now I know something surprising about his family and why he likes working so much."

"I'm listening," Rita said.

"Seems Peter's grandfather made his dad come into the family business. It's been very successful, and still is, but Peter's grandfather made life horrible for his dad. He always belittled Peter's dad, telling him he would never amount to anything without his help and if he didn't give him the business and basically run it, Peter's dad and his family would be a failure. Peter's grandfather died a few years ago, and it seems his dad took on many of his grandfather's domineering characteristics.

"Now his dad is acting the same way toward Peter. Peter said he was thankful his dad is not up here every day. Usually he's up every other weekend, and then only four or five days. Every time he asks for money, his father belittles him. If he doesn't come in first in a sailing race or golf, his dad gives him a hard time. He's never physically abusive, but says he's psychologically abusive. Peter told me that's why he loves working for Jim and Mr. Peterson, because they treat him great, plus he has a chance to prove himself and make his own money."

"That's hard to take, especially from a parent," Rita said. "And he's so nice."

"Yeah. Sometimes money comes with its own special costs." Annie looked at her watch. "We better get going. Do you want to come for supper?"

"Sure your mom won't mind?"

"You know my mom and dad. They sure aren't like Peter's. You know Peter has never invited me to his cottage for dinner or anything. Makes you wonder. I'm not sure I even want to meet either of them. Come for Supper. They love seeing you."

"Okay."

**

The girls were on the swing when Peter walked up.

"Guess what?

"What?" they said in unison.

"I bought a boat today." Then he saw them drinking beer. Annie handed him a beer.

"What's this for?"

"I guess it's in celebration of your boat, now. Dad gave us the beer earlier and figured you'd be along soon. To the boat," Annie said. The three clinked the long neck bottles.

Peter sat between the girls. "I knew your dad was nice."

"He loves boats." Annie said. "He'll be excited for you. I think he wished he could have a boat himself. He and mom never had enough money for a luxury like a boat. Then I came along. I guess I became their boat. Secretly, I think Dad will probably wonder how someone your age could even buy something like that?"

"Well, if he asks I'll tell him I used some of my babysitting money and the rest, I'm working off this year and next. They trust me. I'd never disappoint them."

"I'm not insinuating that you'd do anything like that." She said.

"He'll probably think my parents bought it for me. No way I'd let that happen. I hate asking for anything from my parents."

"Well, You can tell him all about it." Annie said. "He'll enjoy some man-talk tonight. He might have some ideas for you."

"That would be great. I'm always open for suggestions. I just hope it was him that was wondering how I could pay for it and not you two?"

"That's not nice to say, Peter. We're happy for you." Annie said.

"Yeah. We're happy for you. What's its name?" Rita asked.

"Red Baron! The pride of Door County." They all chuckled as Peter continued. "It's not as big as *Falcon*, but it's big enough for me and, I hope, for you guys."

Betty called out, "Dinner's ready."

After dinner, the idea of sailing came up. The three decided a short evening cruise the following night would be fun.

**

The next day, Peter was waiting with his mom's car when the girls got out of work. High excitement filled the air on the drive to Sister Bay. They got some ice for the small cooler, and some soda and chips.

As fate would have it, there was no wind. Unlike the Sunfish and Flying Scott, Red Baron had an outboard. Soon, they were motoring out into the waters of Green Bay.

"I love the Port-a-Potty," Annie said. "Now I don't have to jump in the water to go to the bathroom."

Rita tried her hand at steering the boat and found she liked it. "I'm in command now," she said. "I'm the captain of the "Love Boat!"

It was a beautiful sunset. They toasted the sun as it dipped below the horizon. They relished this new experience. Being farther north along the peninsula, Ephraim's bluffs did not block the spectacular view. The multi-colored horizon was very romantic. Peter had two women with which to enjoy the moment. With an arm around each, he felt like he was in heaven. He turned to each and gave them a kiss. Rita giggled, but Annie did not. *Touché Annie just in case Rita was right!*

"Thanks, Peter. This was nice," Annie said. "Rita and I think you made a great investment." Then Annie gave him a long romantic kiss.

"Hey, that's not fair," Rita said. "I'm getting horny watching you two."

"Poor thing," Peter said. "Next time we'll bring Dennis, OK?"

"Sounds good to me."

They slowly motored back to the marina and tied up at the slip. After grabbing a snack at Al Johnson's, they dropped Rita off at Wilson's.

"Thanks for the cruise, Peter. It was really fun." Getting out of the car's back seat, she walked around to his open window, where she threw her arms around his neck and gave him a big wet kiss.

"If you get tired of Annie, you come and see me. We'll do some things I've read about and have been dying to try on Dennis, but he isn't around."

"Rita! Goodnight!" Annie said. *Does she really mean that?*

Rita laughed and walked into Wilson's.

"Wow, she's wound up tonight," Peter said. But she's a good kisser. He said smiling.

"Really?" She paused. "I think she just misses being with someone. Too bad Dennis can't come up here more often," Annie said. "Once a week isn't enough for her." *I'd like to see him more myself.* "I think she's going to start seeing other guys."

Peter's eyes got wider. "I don't know how Dennis is going to feel about that, but then he's probably not pining away until the weekend."

**

Dennis felt like shit Friday morning. He'd gone to The Canal Bar Thursday night to meet Charlie and the guys. Charlie was right, there were a lot of women there. It didn't take long for a few to come up to the group and start talking smart.

Everyone was out on the deck enjoying the beer and the view. It was hot, with no wind. The beer went down fast and easy. Some days, you just can't get enough beer, Dennis thought, and last night was one of those days.

Dennis saw Stacy and Darcie when they arrived. Probably up from Chicago for the weekend, he thought. He watched the two, as they seemed to be checking out those on the deck. They were pretty obvious in their gestures when they spotted Dennis. After a few minutes, they came over.

Stacy smiled, as she got close. "We think you are the best-looking guy here, so we wanted to introduce ourselves before some other woman got your attention. We decided you were just what we needed tonight."

"Some young stud," Darcie said.

Dennis pushed down his sunglasses, looking over the top edge. "Well, ladies, here I am. Can I buy you two a beer?"

"Sure, why not?"

Both in their mid to late twenties, Darcie had jet-black hair with brown eyes, about five feet six, while Stacy had short blond hair, blue eyes, and stood about five feet ten. Both begged his attention, dressed in short cutoffs, lacy bras and very sheer silk blouses. One had a thick gold necklace while the other had a large diamond pendent hanging down between her full breasts. Dennis's eyes were drawn to more than the diamond pendant. If that wasn't enough, they wore gold bracelets and expensive gold watches.

"What do you do?" he asked, as he looked them over, wondering if they were for real or just toying with him.

Darcie smiled. "We both work for large law firms in Chicago."

Stacie piped in, "Our husbands are in Canada fishing, so we thought we'd come up for the weekend, and do a little fishing ourselves. We're hoping maybe to catch a big one like you. What do you think, Darcie?" She played with Dennis's chest hair through his open shirt.

"He sure is handsome. Looks like he's strong too." Darcie ran her fingers down his forearm. "You think you can handle the two of us, stud?"

"I'm sure I can. It's you two I'm worried about." He snickered.

Darcie leaned in and whispered in his ear, "I hope so." She placed her hand on the inside of his thigh and squeezed, then ran it up and across his chest to his chin and slowly turned his head, so she could give him a deep kiss. "But first, big boy, I think we all need just a few more drinks" She put her platinum American Express card on the bar.

After about an hour, Stacy said, "Lets' go, I'm ready for some action." She grabbed his hand and the three left for a cottage just down the beach. When they got to the cottage, it didn't take long for them to get out of their clothes and get comfortable. True to his word, Dennis did not disappoint.

At about 3:00 a.m., the trio went skinny-dipping in Lake Michigan. The water rejuvenated Dennis enough so he could keep Darcie and Stacy busy until sunrise. When it was time for him to go, the two women got up and ran their hands over his body one last time. He was spent.

"Dennis, you are the best fuck we've ever had," Stacy said in a soft voice. "You get to Chicago, you call us anytime. We'll get the room, if you bring this along." She gave it a squeeze.

Darcie went over to her purse, got her business card out, and slipped it into his front jean pocket. "Now don't you forget us, Dennis? We'll be here for a couple more days. If you want to try some more tonight, just leave a note under the door. I hope you can make it, because you sure know how to please me."

**

About 3:00 p.m., Peter came into the shop looking for Dennis. He found him varnishing one of the big power yachts. He took one look at Dennis and started laughing.

"Holy shit, man. You look horrible. You all right?"

"Yeah, I'm all right. Someone in the next apartment kept me up all night screwing, so I got about two hours sleep. I'm beat."

"You look it. I had to get some stuff for my mom at some store down here. She couldn't get it because today was her bridge day. She couldn't miss that big event, so I had to go. I got some exciting news I wanted to tell you about, so the trip down worked out fine." Peter told Dennis about his new boat. "You want to go out sailing Saturday and Sunday? It would be fun. I know Rita misses you," Peter added with a frown. "Although I don't know why. What do you say?"

Dennis squinted at him with tired, red eyes. "What time?"

"The girls get done with work at three, so we can sail that afternoon or evening. If you want, we can sail Sunday, too. Annie and Rita are off the whole day. You and I can stay on the boat Saturday night. That way, you don't have to drive back and forth to Sturgeon Bay. We can get a leisurely start Sunday."

Dennis nodded. "I'll see you Saturday."

"I can hardly wait for you to see my boat. It's a beauty."

"I bet it is," Dennis said, "but if I can't make it, I'll tell Darrell and he can tell Annie."

Peter watched Dennis walk toward the bathroom. He sure looks tired, Peter thought. I don't believe that story for one minute. I hope whoever she is, she's been worth it. Rita's pretty hot. If I weren't with Annie, I'd be all over Rita, that's for sure. Oh well.

Chapter Eleven

That night, Peter decided to spend time with his family. He'd hardly seen them since he got the job at the marina, but his mom and dad didn't seem to complain about the nightly absence. Tonight, when he said he wanted to spend time with them, they actually seem pleased. They went for a whitefish dinner at the Greenwood. After dinner, Peter's dad surprised him.

"Let's go see this boat you bought. I suppose you expect me to pay for it?"

"No Dad! I'm paying for it. It's all worked out already. I'm paying for it with my wages over time." He said, feeling proud.

"Oh, it's about time you paid for something."

"Oh, Ken, try to be happy for Peter," his mother said.

The entire family piled into the car and drove up to the marina. Once there, Ken Franklin was impressed with the boat. "Peter, I think you made a sound investment."

"Really, Dad?" His dad never gave him compliments. "Let's go for a ride. It is very stable."

"Why not?" his dad answered.

The lake was flat, so Peter took his parents for a short motor ride. His parents sat in the cockpit facing the setting sun, while Peter sat on the other side facing Sister Bay's shore. His mother seldom went out on the lake, but instantly fell in love with the evening experience.

"Peter, I don't know when I've ever had so much fun on a boat. Isn't it romantic, Ken?"

She leaned over and gave Peter a kiss and then Ken. "Don't look so surprised," she said. "I'm happy!" Peter could not remember when he had seen his mother this happy. Even his dad smiled at her.

But the magic was short lived for Peter when his mother asked, "Are you still seeing that girl that works at the ice cream place in Ephraim? What's her name?"

"Annie, Annie Wilson. Yes mother, I am."

His mother sighed. "Didn't you say her mother is disabled, or something, and her dad works at a shipyard? What are our friends going to think? I think you can do better, honey."

"Like stupid Rhonda? Why can't you stay out of my love life? You've wrecked everyone I've ever been interested in. I'm just warning you. Right now Mother. Don't start your meddling with Annie."

"We'll see?" She said in a huffy voice.

**

Saturday afternoon, Rita saw Dennis dozing in his car, under a large maple tree. "Annie, there he is. God, just look at him. I am having a hard time not running out and giving him a big kiss."

"So why don't you? I can cover for you. Just make sure it's a quick kiss."

"You're a saint."

"Go!"

Rita ran over. With the convertible top down, she gently slid her arms around Dennis's neck, feeling him stir.

He slowly opened his eyes. "Hi," he said as his lip curled into a gentle smile and his eyes twinkled. "Is it three-fifteen?"

"No. I couldn't help myself. I had to come out and give you a quick kiss. I really missed you, Dennis."

"I missed you too," he said and then yawned.

"You aren't tired are you? I hope you weren't out fooling around to all hours?" Rita's joy was replaced with concern. "I'm looking forward to spending time with you. I'm hoping we can spend time a lot of time in each other's arms."

"Me too." Dennis said as he tried to stifle another yawn. "I just didn't sleep well for a couple of nights. I was working late on a boat up from Chicago named Dar-sea. It had twin screws and a huge top deck." He smiled. "It was hot work and I'm tired."

"Well, I hope you get a second wind." She said, "Or I'll be pissed." Then she smiled. "Wait until you see Peter's boat. It's really neat, and he's so proud of it."

"I bet."

"I better get back." She gave him a deep kiss.

**

Peter and the girls showed up at the same time. Dennis was jerked to a state of alertness when all three started talking. Rita was the most excited, bounding into the front seat, tossing her beach bag on the floor. She wrapped her arms around Dennis's neck and gave him a long sensuous kiss. If Dennis thought he was played out from the past two nights, one part of his body didn't get the message.

Sitting up straight, Dennis turned to Annie and Peter in the back-seat. "Ready?" He revved the thirty-eight horsepower VW engine and shifted into first gear. They stopped in Sister Bay to get some food and drinks and then headed to the marina.

"What a great looking boat," Dennis said.

They loaded the supplies and made sure the gas tank was topped off. Motoring into the wind, they raised the mainsail and the bigger jib. The winds were light from the prevailing southwest. Sailing northwest with no particular destination in mind, they all got comfortable. Rita had her back to the bulkhead of the cabin. Dennis lay on his back with his shoulders between Rita's thighs and his head on her stomach. She smiled and gently rubbed his chest and shoulders while Dennis, in a semi daze, made sounds of contentment.

"Why don't you guys get a motel room or something?" Annie said, irritated after watching Rita and Dennis's touching get progressively more explicit.

"Geez, Annie, it never bothered you before," Rita said. "I'm just happy to have my man here. Besides, you have Peter. You can do the same thing and it wouldn't bother us. We're adults."

Peter looked at Annie, then at Dennis, and saw him smile. "I think Annie's just uncomfortable with you guys doing it right in front of us. Isn't that right, Annie?" When he saw her glaring at Dennis, and Dennis smiling back at her, he remembered what Rita said to him on the raft. *Now I know what she means, there is something between them. But what?*

They sailed for about an hour and a half before changing their heading. All were enjoying the sounds of the water and waves against the fiberglass hull, but the mood of the evening had definitely changed.

It was 8:30 p.m. when they finished their sail. After securing the boat for the night, they headed to the Sister Bay Bowl for some burgers and fries.

Peter looked at his watch. "It's ten-thirty. We should get going. Dennis, why don't you drop Annie and me off first? You are welcome to sleep on the couch at the cottage, or you can sleep on the boat."

"The boat sounds pretty good, maybe Rita and I could sleep there. Otherwise, I'll just sleep in the car. The seat folds down, and I'm so tired I could sleep standing up."

Rita gave him a quick peck on the cheek. "I'd love sleeping on the boat. We can sleep in the nice V-berth. The dorm room is so hot. It would be a nice change to sleep with Dennis."

Smiling at Rita, he said, "I have a blanket in the trunk, just in case it gets cool."

Annie yawned. "What time are we getting together tomorrow?" she said as she rubbed her eyes.

"Nine?" Peter said. "I don't think I'm ready to have you guys be the first ones to sleep in my boat. If anyone's going to sleep in it the first time and make love, it's going to be me and, I hope, Annie." Then he looked at Annie. "How about us?"

"No Peter, I'm not ready for that yet," she said. "Besides, I'm tired. I want to go home."

"Fine." Peter leaned away from her and stared out the car window. *If it were Dennis asking her, would she say yes to sleeping on the boat and making love?*

"I guess it's the car for me tonight," Dennis said.

Sunday morning was quiet; a light mist was in the air, which seem to mirror the emotions after the four's first confrontation. They met at nine, but decided not to go sailing.

Then to the surprise of all, Dennis said, "I think I'm going to go home early. I'm exhausted."

"What!" Rita said, surprised. "Did I do something wrong?"

"No, I'm just tired and want to go home and sleep."

"Oh. Are you really going to go home or are you going to work on that boat from Chicago? What was her name? Dar-Sea, I bet she did have a bigger upper deck. Yeah, go home and sleep asshole."

"My aren't we testy this morning." He said. He tried to kiss her but she pushed him away. "Okay, have it your way." He got in his car, waved to Annie and Peter and drove off.

"I bet you're sorry to see Dennis leave too?" Peter said.

"What does that mean?"

"Rita and I think there's something going on between you and Dennis. I don't have any proof and I hope I never do."

"Are you two smoking some grass this morning? What the hell is going on?"

Neither Rita nor Peter said anything.

"I'm going back to bed." Rita said.

"I guess I'm going to play golf. I need to hit something." Peter said, and started walking home.

"What about me? I didn't do anything!" Annie yelled at the two, but both kept on walking.

Chapter Twelve

Annie had mixed feelings about the mid-week party at the Smithback's. The house sat on the bluff overlooking Eagle Harbor. The invitation-only party seemed to be the social event of the summer for the St. Louis and Ephraim younger elite, so it was even more important for Annie to prove to Peter's mother she could fit in. Ever since Peter invited her to the party, she had been trying to find just the right dress that fit her budget and looked great. She finally found a smart, short, black sleeveless dress at a slightly used clothing store in Sturgeon Bay. She knew black never went out of style, even if it was from last year.

Excited about her find, she borrowed a red pair of shoes from Rita and a red patterned, silk scarf from Joan, one of the girls living in the Wilson dorm. After an hour getting ready, she finally felt comfortable with the way she looked. She gave her hair one last look in the mirror, then a light touch of red lipstick, and she started down the stairs.

Peter pulled up to the Wilson's house in his mother's washed and polished car. Betty and Darrell sat on the swing; Betty sipping lemonade while Darrell had a beer.

"Hi, Peter," Darrell said.

"She should be coming down shortly," Betty said. "I was just in her room ten minutes ago and she was fussing with her hair. She is so nervous about this party. I hope she has a good time." Before Peter could answer, Annie stepped out on the porch. All eyes turned.

"Annie you look wonderful! I don't think I've ever seen you in a dress before," Peter said with a smile.

"I can get dressed up for special occasions. I guess this is a special occasion, isn't it?"

"It is to me. I've never taken a date to one of these parties before," he said, "so this should be fun."

"Maybe you should go alone." She said panicky.

"What? I'm not going anyplace unless you go along. Come on, don't be stupid about this. You'll be fine."

"Do you think I'll fit in? Really. It's important to me that I fit in with your friends."

"You'll fit in just fine. Most everyone is really nice, and they all just want to have fun," he said. "We're going to have a great time, and the food will be excellent. They even have a band so we'll be able to dance." Peter glanced at his watch. "We better get going or we'll have to walk a mile once we find a parking spot."

**

It did not take long to drive to the road, but they did have to walk a long ways to the house. There was a big tent in the yard next to the house, set up with a long table of food. Several tables and chairs were under the tent and scattered around the lawn. Everyone congregated around washtubs full of iced soda and an iced barrel of beer.

Peter introduced Annie to several of his friends. After about forty-five minutes and a couple of beers, Annie started to relax. She began to agree with Peter that the people were just as nice and friendly as him.

Then it happened: Rhonda Smits showed up with her two friends, Sally and Penny.

"Well, look who's here? Are you helping serve the food? That is what you do at Wilson's, isn't it? You can't be here as a guest." The three laughed.

Annie felt her face grow red, but she wasn't sure if it was embarrassment or anger. She felt everyone look at her.

"Back off, Rhonda. Annie is my guest," Peter said.

"Oh, I'm sorry, Peter. I forgot you're slumming this year. Hell, look at that dress. If I'm not mistaken, that's last year's style. Nice looking, but really…last year's style?"

Annie watched the others in the group snicker. She was wrong. They weren't nice or friendly. What she really wanted to do was slap the ones that were snickering, but she'd try to be nice for Peter's sake. She didn't want to embarrass him.

Rhonda studied her, and then smiled. "I'm sorry, where are my manners? I see you're almost out of beer. Let me get you one. Kind of funny, me serving you, but then that's just the way I am, just trying to be friendly." She went over and poured a glass of the foamy liquid and walked back. As she got close, she faked a stumbled and tossed the full glass of beer onto Annie's face, dress, and scarf.

Annie screamed.

"Oh, excuse me," she said in a low voice. "I must have tripped on a root or something. It was an accident. Isn't that what you said to me?"

Annie stood there, not knowing what to do.

"Shit." Peter pulled out a handkerchief and handed it to her. He glared at Rhonda as he said, "She's not one of the well-liked people here, but she has to be invited because of her parents. I'm sorry."

Annie wiped her face and did her best cleaning the silk scarf and dress. She tried to keep her feelings in check.

One of the female guest said, "Come on, Peter, I know where some seltzer is for her dress and scarf so it doesn't stain." She grabbed his hand and started to lead him into the house.

"We'll be right back with a rag and seltzer. Don't leave," he called back over his shoulder.

Annie felt like a freak at a sideshow with everyone looking at her. She heard Rhonda talking to some of her catty friends. "She deserved it after what she did to me earlier this summer. I hope her dress is ruined like my tennis outfit. Mine wasn't some old rag, either. It was new."

Annie turned and walked away. When she reached the road, she started crying and running. She didn't know where she was going to go and she didn't care. All she knew was that she wanted to get away from all of them. She hated all those people, and that included Peter. He was one of them, and always would be. She didn't fit in. *And she never would.*

**

She didn't know how long she walked, but when she saw Anderson Dock, she decided to sit on the dock and try to calm herself. It was always one of her favorite places.

As she turned and started to walk into the parking area, leading to the dock and warehouse, she heard a familiar voice. "Annie! Annie!"

Then she saw the familiar orange VW bug and the smiling face of Dennis Jamison. Oh great, she thought, he'll see I've been crying. She watched it slow, stop, and then back up to the blare of horns and the swearing of drivers. The parking lot was packed with cars waiting for the evening's sunset. Seeing this, she heard Dennis say, "Wait there." She watched him drive a few hundred feet and find a parking spot.

He got out and started walking back toward her. Why was he up here? He must have called Rita. He probably was going to buy her dinner, but now?

She watched him walk closer. He had his shirt off, and she remembered it was a workday for him. He must have stayed later than Dad, she thought, probably working on some project that had to be finished.

Annie saw the sweat glistening on his muscular chest, like he had baby oil all over it. Without thinking, she licked her lips and let out a small, "Aha." Her whole body felt flushed. The sound of the crushed gravel against his work boots heightened the sensation as he came closer. The resistance of the past summer seemed to ebb away. The strong desire she'd always felt for Dennis from that first kiss rose from the pit of her stomach. Her breasts swelled and beads of sweat trickled between them. Her breath quickened.

Standing in front of her, he looked into her eyes. He looked concerned. "You look like you've been crying. You're all dressed up. Why are you walking dressed like that, and where's Peter?"

"Let's not talk." Annie took a step closer to Dennis, sighed, and let herself go. She rested her hands on his damp, tan chest, felt the hairs slide between her fingers as she lightly scraped her nails upward. A small sound escaped as her hands continued their journey. Finally, she locked her fingers behind his neck. Looking into his knowing eyes, she hungrily pulled him down to her waiting lips. She pulled his chest against her waiting, wanting body, her mind screaming. *How can I be doing this? I know how he treats women. This isn't fair to Rita. How can I look her in the eye after this? And then there's Peter. But I'm really not good enough for him or his family. Dennis and I are on the same level.*

Dennis's lips grazed her neck. She closed her eyes and turned off the voice in her head because right then, right that minute, she wanted Dennis Jamison.

**

Dennis drove to Fish Creek and luckily found a small motel room with an uninspiring view. He wasn't here for the view, he told himself, just the bed. He was grateful he didn't have to take Annie all the way to his place in Sturgeon Bay. She might recover her senses and change her mind. He'd been waiting for this all summer and when he least expected it, boom, it happened.

He parked the Bug in front of the small yellow cabin, reached under his worn black car seat and opened a cardboard box containing a toothbrush, razor, and six condoms. He grabbed two.

He saw her stare at the condoms and then back at him.

"I was hoping you had something like that," she said and smiled.

When he opened the motel room door, he was relieved to see it was very clean, with a nautical look. He took her by the hand and led her in.

"Is this ok?"

"It's fine, Dennis. I was afraid we were going to do it on the golf course or someplace like that. I was hoping my first time was going to be someplace better than that." She turned and kissed him. "Thank you."

"You deserve better than that, Annie. I want this to be special for both of us. I've wanted you since the first time I saw you. You probably don't remember."

"I remember everything about meeting you that day." Her eyes seemed to sparkle. "You were hot and sweaty, and just looking at you got me excited."

He laughed. "Is that why you turned and waved at me just before you turned the corner?"

She nodded again.

He smirked. "Right then, right at that moment, I knew I had to have you, and here we are, finally."

"Finally," she said and then laughed, breaking the tension. "You were pretty carnal. I was getting wet just looking at you that day, just like now."

"You did? You are?"

He felt her arms slip around his neck and pull him to her lips. He slid past her wanting lips and made love to her with his tongue. He felt her shudder and squeeze him tight. When she pulled back, she said, "Dennis, make love to me."

She turned her back to him. He slowly lowered the zipper and then slid the black dress off her tan shoulders and watched it pile at her feet. When she turned around, he gawked like a child looking at presents under the tree at Christmas. Her breasts swelled above the cups of her bra, her nipples pressed out the black lace. He kissed her again, but this time he reached around with his two fingers and expertly unfastened her bra. When he stepped back, his heart was pounding.

He pulled back the summer comforter and top sheet and lowered her to the bed. Then he hooked his thumbs over the elastic of her panties and slid them off.

"Oh, Annie. You're beautiful." Dennis quickly unbuttoned his shirt, kicked off his shoes, and, in one motion, slid his jeans and underwear off.

He lowered himself to the bed where he feasted on her breast, circling her nipple with his tongue, and then plucked it out further with gentle sucking. He rubbed her other nipple with his thumb and forefinger until he heard her moan, then kissed down her stomach until he reached the soft folds of her treasure spot. He spread her legs and slowly started kissing her, his tongue expertly moving up and down, and then plunging his tongue in and out of her. At the same time, his hands moved up to her breasts, massaging her nipples with his thumbs and fingers. Soon her hips started to move rhythmically up and down in time with his tongue. Thrilled, he watched as her head moved from side to side just as she moaned and tightened her legs around his head.

"Oh, Dennis."

Dennis was hard as he'd ever been. "Are you ready, Annie?"

"Yes. Yes."

He moved on top and slowly entered her, first the tip and then gradually more until he was finally completely inside her. He moved slowly with her, letting her get accustomed to his size, and then he started moving faster.

"Oh, Dennis. Oh, oh, ahh," and then she squeezed him tight.

He continued to move faster inside her, until she tightened around him again. When he saw her green eyes flutter open, he looked into her eyes, smiled and said, "This is for you, Annie," and he let out a long groan.

Chapter Thirteen

Driving home after making love with Dennis, Annie was excited. She wasn't a virgin. She had finally done it and with Dennis Jamison. He had an exciting body, and he made her feel special and wonderful for the first time.

Suddenly, Rita's voice was in her head, and her spirits fell. She thought of the rumors she heard this summer. Dennis was no saint, that was for sure, but she sure wouldn't have to worry about being accepted by his friends and relatives. He fulfilled her lusty passion in a way she knew the inexperienced Peter could not. Well, she couldn't go back, she thought. *Hell, she wasn't a virgin anymore!*

That night, driving home from Fish Creek, the radio was playing a Carol King song, *Will You Love Me Tomorrow?*, which seems to say exactly what was on her mind. *Will he love me tomorrow?*

As Dennis dropped her off in front of her house, he smiled. "Annie, this'll be our own little secret. Rita and Peter don't need to know." Then he kissed her goodnight and drove off, leaving her standing in the middle of the road in the dark.

Now what am I going to do? She started to cry. There was no going back indeed.

**

Peter was waiting when she arrived at Wilson's the next morning.

"I feel horrible about what happened," he said. "I searched the Smithback's house and property after I came back with the seltzer and washcloth, but you were gone. Then, after finding out you bolted away, I drove around for another couple of hours trying to find you. Where did you go last night?"

"I just wanted to be alone. I was very mad at you and your stupid friends. I just don't fit in with you and your crowd." She stood on the steps, looking at her feet, then she turned around and looked at *Falcon*, bobbing at its mooring.

"You know, Annie, not all the people up here are like Rhonda Smits. You just needed to give my other friends a chance."

Annie shook her head. "When I was a little girl, five or six years old, playing at the beach with a new water color paint set my mother got me for my birthday. I had a white writing tablet for paper, not even real artist paper like I use now. My mother knew I liked to draw and paint so she got me this cheap painting set, you know the black tin hinged box with 6 colors and one brush.

It was my first time painting. So I'm sitting there, at the beach, crossed legged in a yoga position painting Eagle Harbor and a couple of sailboats. You can easily imagine how crude the picture looked, but it was my first time. Mom was having fun watching me paint, and I was having fun painting until..." she paused and bit her lip.

"I was having fun until two moms and their bratty kids showed up and disrupted everyone. They entered the beach area, talking loud, making fun of the locals and how they dressed. It didn't take long for their four brats to see me, and come over to see what I was doing. They started laughing when they saw my painting.

One of the girls said it looked like finger painting and she could do much better. Then one of the boys, with lots of freckles and red hair, grabbed the paper and threw it into the air, laughing. It floated toward one of the mothers, who picked it up and looked at it. She said, 'He's right, honey, you should start all over, because this is horrible.' Then she crumpled it up and went back to reading a book. That's when I started crying and mom got up and walked over to the mother, grabbed her paperback out of her hand, looked at the cover and title and then said to the mother. 'This looks like a boring book. Why don't you read another.' And then threw the book into the water."

"Wow," Peter said. "I can't believe they didn't discipline their kids besides saying that too? Good for your mom."

"They didn't! My mom kissed the top of my head, gathered my painting stuff, and we walked down to Wilson's and had an ice cream. My mom thought that might heal things, but it didn't." Annie let out a big sigh. "That's why I don't like your kind. All they care about is themselves. I'm not what your parents want. They'll continue to make it miserable for me, just like the two families at the beach. I think we should call it quits."

"Come on, Annie. I'm not like that," he said.

"I want you to leave me alone for a few days. I need time to sort this out," she said, knowing it was much more than that. *Dennis was a great first time lover, and she was thankful for that, but he was also someone not to be trusted. Was she to be trusted?*

**

That afternoon, Annie finally saw Rita. She only hoped Rita wasn't able to put two and two together. As it turned out, she didn't even ask Annie about the party. Rita was really mad at Dennis.

"He calls to say he's coming up to take me out to dinner. I was so excited; I spent an hour getting ready. You know me. I never do that. Then the asshole never shows up. He probably found some easy fuck and stayed in Sturgeon Bay."

Annie's stomach tightened. All she could do was look down at the ground and say nothing.

**

Days passed with Peter stopping every day at Wilson's and asking Annie to meet him to try and make it work. Finally, Annie gave in and said it was all right for him to stop by the house that night and visit.

She sat patiently on the swing, waiting for Peter to show up. When he did, she leaped up and gave him a big kiss.

"What happened? What did I do to deserve this? Are we back together?"

"I'm in a good mood. I followed your advice about painting and I got a commission to paint a big powerboat docked at Anderson Dock. They want their boat and the weathered Anderson warehouse in their picture. They saw my sign at Cabin Craft about custom paintings. Tomorrow after work, I'm supposed to go and talk to them, get a better idea of what they want. I'm so excited. This could make me some big bucks."

"Oh, I thought it was about us." His shoulders sagged as he said it, and he kicked the ground. "The painting deal, that's great too. Someday you'll have your own studio. You're on your way."

"I know. It's really exciting." She paused. "What do you want to do now?"

"Let's take a walk."

They took a lazy walk towards Wilson's. Peter ordered his usual root beer malt. They split it. Sitting out near the municipal pier, they talked about nothing in particular.

"Are you all right?" he said. "You seem different today, more attentive."

"Can't I just be happy to see you?" she snapped. "Even after the disaster at the Smithbeck's, I miss seeing you." She paused. "I'm struggling with what to do. I'm sorry."

"Can we head back?" Peter said. "I'm really tired. It was hot working on the boats today."

"I guess so. I thought you'd be more excited for me, and happy to spend time with me. Are you sure it's not something else?" *I hope he didn't find out about Dennis.*

"No, what else is there? I'm just tired," he said. "You need to figure us out, Annie. It can't always be about you. I have feelings too. Figure us out and then let me know."

They walked back to Annie's house, each lost in their own thoughts. When they reached Annie's house, Peter simply said, "Good night, Annie." He turned and walked away.

"Aren't you going to kiss or hug me goodnight?" Annie called.

"No."

**

The next day after work, Annie met with Bill and Charlene Tenny, who owned the Carver motor yacht she was to paint. She talked to them for about an hour, asking several questions until she knew just what they were looking for. She said she would have a preliminary sketch of the boat and background in a couple of days, and after that it would take about a week to complete the painting. They were comfortable with that.

While she was there, the couple that owned 'Green-Eyed Girl' watched what was going on at the Tenny's boat. As she was leaving, they inquired about Annie painting their boat, too. She held her excitement. "I'll have to check my painting schedule, but I think I can fit you in."

She explained the process to them, and they seemed pleased with the idea. They gave her a crisp one hundred dollar bill as a down payment.

Thrilled, Annie raced home and excitedly explained her painting coup to Betty and Darrell. She couldn't believe her good fortune. She had two or three weeks of painting to look forward to before the school payment deadline. She figured to make four hundred dollars on each of the paintings. "Life is good," she told herself.

She started planning a strategy. She'd make custom paintings of houses, favorite scenes of Ephraim, Sister Bay, and other points of interest. She thought that, if people brought in their favorite photos, she could paint from the photo and paint the family into a scene like she did of the family from Chicago.

**

That night, Peter and Annie sat at the end of the hotel pier and kicked at the water.

"Thanks for coming tonight," she said, "I'm sorry how things ended the other night."

"I'm sorry too. I don't know what it is, but things seem different. I want to get back to the way it was, so I'm glad to be here."

"It feels like old times out here on the pier." She said. Especially after Dennis didn't come up at all to see Rita or Annie. Gradually, she realized that Peter was the real deal and she should try again. She missed being with him.

"What's going to happen this fall for us?" she said, getting the ball rolling. "What about schools. I am limited to where I can go because of money, but I know what I want."

They talked about the plans they had. They talked about schools they had applied to.

"I'm going to go to a school that specializes in the arts someday," she said. "I'd love to study in Paris someday."

"Let me tell you a story about my dad and me. It might explain where I'm going." He kept his head down, looking at the shimmering reflection of the night in the black water. "You know that he took over the family business from my grandfather. My Grandfather was an asshole to my father and made life hell for him, belittling him every chance he got. Now my dad is doing the same to me. I know he loves me, but I'm stopping the vicious cycle right now. Otherwise I'll spend half my life doing something I don't want to do, just to please my dad. I'm not going to do that."

He gave the water a big kick. "I'm going south to The University of Miami."

"Miami!"

"I want to be around sailing and the boat business. Mr. Peterson encouraged me to pursue this area of work. 'You'd be a natural at it, Peter' he said, and that's all it took for me. From now on, it's about me. What I want to do. I want to build my own business, make my own money, be successful."

Annie smiled at him. She didn't have the parent problems like he did, but she did want to make lots of money and to have status. Isn't that what money and fame brought? She knew she wanted to be a painter, so the trick was to figure out how to make lots of money in the art world.

As for a degree, she thought graphic arts or something like that would be good for now. She, too, wanted to go someplace away from home, just to see a different part of the country. Paris was one of her dreams. She knew she could always come back to Door County because her parents were not leaving. She loved Door County, but it was time to take a chance and see what the rest of the world was like.

Maybe she'd like it out East because of the concentration of art in the New York area. She might even try Chicago. There were a lot of schools there, and it was only seven hours away, but still far enough away from home. It all hinged on money, and she maybe had enough for a local state school.

"Maybe I can get a scholarship later, but right now I'm accepted at the University of Wisconsin, in Milwaukee. My grades are good enough for any school, and once I get some schooling under my belt, I could always transfer to some other place."

"I'll check on schools in the Miami area," Peter said with a smile. "Then we could be together."

"That would be nice, Peter. I'd really miss the winters in Door County and Wisconsin," she said, smiling. "I'd have to wear a tee shirt or bikini most of the time. Darn. I think I could handle that!"

He leaned over and gave her a kiss. "That would be great."

"It would, but it'll have to be next year. I can't afford it unless I get a scholarship." *I do miss being with him. Not his friends or his parents, but him.*

"Well, it's something to think about." Peter looked at his watch. "It's late, time to head home."

**

The next day, Annie started her work on the paintings and this settled her mind. She finished two sketches in a few hours. One sketch was a view looking out across the bay with Anderson dock, the old warehouse with its charming graffiti, and the boat. The limestone bluffs in the background completed the picture.

The other sketch was a close up view from the state park's bluffs, looking across the harbor at the boat, the warehouse and the dock. The Anderson General Store was in the background. The toughest part was making everything fit to scale.

Satisfied with her work, Annie walked home. She'd stop back later and see which sketch Bill and Charlene Tenny liked best. It took her about three days to paint the Tenny's Carver and they were overjoyed. The next painting was Green Eyed Girl.

**

The summer passed with its own fast paced rhythm. When Mr. Franklin's birthday came up, the Franklin family went to Ellison Bay to have dinner at Clayton's Supper Club. Surprisingly, Annie was invited to join them, but Patti Franklin was very cool towards her.

Ken and Patti Franklin ran into the Hoeppner's, fellow Hotel Ephraim guests. When they found out it was Ken's birthday, they started buying them cocktails to celebrate.

Relieved, Annie and Peter headed to the Ellison Bay municipal pier to see the sunset and be alone.

"How's your painting coming of 'Green-Eyed Girl'?" Peter asked.

"The Tennys were overjoyed with their painting. They showed it to every boat owner on the dock." She giggled. "I've got six referrals because of them. Business is so good that I don't really need to work at Wilson's but a couple hours a day. I'm charging four to six hundred a painting now."

"Wow," Peter said.

"Actually, 'Green-Eyed Girl' is finished. I'm going to deliver it to the Pelzwalkers tomorrow morning. Afterward, let's go for a bike ride through the park. Will you pick me up and drive me to Anderson Dock around eight-thirty?"

"Sure, no problem.

"How's the charter business?" she asked. "I got so wrapped up talking about painting I forgot about your work."

"It's good. I told Mr. Peterson about going to school in Miami, and he said he had a good friend who owns a small charter business near there. I think he said his name was Mahoney. He said he'd call and see if he could get me some part-time work while I was going to school."

"That's great."

"He said the guy was around sixty, his wife had just died, and he was getting tired of the business and needed some help."

"That's perfect, Peter."

He nodded. "That's why I want to go to Miami. I'll get a good education and get into something I love. I really like the people associated with boating."

"Yeah, without the referrals, I'd be painting everything and anything instead of concentrating on what people want."

"I like the way we're both doing things we care about. Let's head back to Clayton's and see if Mom and Dad are ready. I might have to drive."

Annie laughed. "Oh, come on. Really?"

"If Mom starts singing "Poke-a-dots and Moonbeams," watch out. I'm taking the keys."

When they walked into Clayton's, Ken and Patti were singing that very song, as a duet. Peter walked up to his dad and took the keys off the bar.

He turned to Annie. "See?" Annie bent over laughing, while Peter just shrugged. "My parents do have fun moments. I just haven't seen it often."

They got back to the cottage around 10:30 p.m. Peter knew his mom and dad were a little tight when Ken and Patti said to Jeanette in a slightly slurred voice, "Come on, honey, time for my last present."

Holding hands, they walked into the cottage, closed the door and turned off the lights.

Peter and Annie watched and chuckled.

"I know they do it, but it's always difficult for me to visualize."

"I know what you mean." Annie smiled.

"Yep, let's head to the pier and let them finish their business."

It was still warm for almost 11 o'clock. They finished the beer they'd grabbed from the refrigerator as they left the cottage. Peter pulled Annie close. Pressing his body to hers, he gave her a long kiss.

Annie whispered in his ear after their lips parted. "Down, big boy."

"I know. It has a mind of its own. You feel so good in my arms, the night, the stars….what can I say?"

Annie laughed, "How about time to walk home?"

"In just a little while," Peter said. Let's get friendly. He started to unbutton her blouse, moving his hand to her breast. "I need more of you Annie."

"I need you to kiss me too," she said, "if you're going to touch me there."

**

Peter pulled up to the Wilson's house the next morning as the Moravian church bells stopped ringing for the 8:15 a.m. service. Annie was waiting. She placed the painting in the back seat and climbed into the

Cadillac. It was a perfect morning. A light breeze stirred up wavelets in some areas, while others looked like mirrors. The sky was a bright blue, devoid of clouds. There was no traffic as Peter came around the bend, passing the majestic Evergreen Beach resort.

The Pelzwalkers were just finishing their coffee and Grape Nuts with raisins when Annie and Peter walked down the dock to their boat. Marge saw them coming first.

"Joe, here comes Annie and her boyfriend with the painting. I can hardly wait to see it."

Bill and Charlene Tenny saw them coming, too, and walked over to see. Charlene gave Annie a peck on the check while Bill shook Peter's hand.

Joe finally came up from the cabin with a cup of steaming coffee. Annie introduced Joe and Marge to Peter.

"Okay, we're ready. Let's see the masterpiece," Mr. Pelzwalker said.

Matted on stiff matting board, Annie had draped the painting with a big beach towel. "Ta-Da," she said and pulled off the towel.

Marge clapped her hands. "Oh my, it's better than I ever expected."

Joe sucked in his breath, his eyes misting. "It captures everything about the boat and this place."

Annie had painted 'Green-Eyed Girl' with its sails set as she rounded up to come alongside the dock. On the edge of the painting stood the warehouse, with Eagle Bluff in the background, but the focal point was the beauty of 'Green-Eyed Girl'. The golden teak, the cream-colored hull with green trim, Joe at the wheel, and Marge standing on the bow, preparing to step off the boat to tie her up; it was just perfect.

"It looks so natural, so every day," Charlene said to Joe and Marge. "I told you she was good." Joe reached into his shorts and pulled out a roll of money. Peeling off five one hundred dollar bills, he gave them to Annie, and then said, "Here's an extra two hundred. It's worth it!"

"Oh my!" Annie said.

"Annie, I don't know what to say," Joe said as he put his arm around Marge. "We are so happy with the painting." He looked at Annie and Peter, both beaming with pride and excitement. "Say, what are you two doing today? Marge and I were going to sail up to Washington Island, have lunch and sail back. If you aren't doing anything, why don't you join us?"

Annie's eyes got big as saucers; she jumped up and down and hugged Peter. "Really? You mean it? I've dreamed about this all summer. We'd love to go, right, Peter?"

"Absolutely."

Joe said, "I think we have enough food and drink for an army. We're about ready. Let's stow that painting in a safe spot and get this show on the road."

The wind was from the prevailing SW. It was so light, they raised the main sail at the dock and motored away toward the north. Once they got away from the influence of Eagle Bluff, the wind started to pick up to about ten knots. They turned the diesel off and settled in for a nice reach to Washington Island. Marge gave Annie and Peter a tour of the boat. It had rich teak above and below the deck, a true "blue water" cruiser, with all the comforts of home.

Peter marveled. "I could live on this boat forever. Someday, this is what I want."

Annie put her arm around him and gave him a kiss on the cheek. "It's nice to have dreams, isn't it?"

When they got topside, Joe had the autopilot on and was easing the sails for the reach. 'Green-Eyed Girl' moved past the Little Sister Shoals. The knot meter showed six.

"Peter, you want to take over?" Joe said, smiling.

"I'd love to," Peter said as he leaped to the wheel.

"You know how to sail, I assume?"

"Oh, yes. I work over at Peterson's Marina in Sister Bay. I handle the charter business for Mr. Peterson and Jim Erickson," he said, trying to sound important.

Joe studied Peter. "I'm impressed."

"I've never sailed anything this big. I have an ODAY 20, but I've never really sailed anything with wheel-steering."

"Just drive it like a car. Turn right to go right and left to go left." Joe flipped off the autopilot. "She's all yours, just steer a heading of ten degrees or stay out a couple of miles from shore. Either way, we should be good."

Peter looked at Joe. "I'm real familiar with this area up to Ellison Bay, but past that? I've never gone that far."

"No problem, it's fun to have someone who likes to sail beside me. Marge loves sailing and will handle the boat in a pinch, but she'd rather do all the other things. That's why I have the boat set up basically to be sailed by one person."

They sailed on a reach for a couple of hours before they approached Washington Island.

"If you'd like, we can sail around the island and come back through "Death's Door."

Peter looked at Joe, puzzled. "Death's Door?"

"It's a channel between Washington Island and The Door Peninsula. You get currents and wind from Green Bay and Lake Michigan. They meet in the channel. It can get mighty nasty at times, and many a ship has gone down in those waters. Matter of fact, an Indian tribe was going to attack another on Washington Island, but a storm came up, capsized their canoe's, and several braves were lost. Hence the name, Death's Door. Don't worry, the weather today is good."

Peter smiled.

"We have a great boat, and we have a fifty horse power diesel. Many of the ships that went down didn't have engines. Back then; cargo schooners were totally at the mercy of the wind, without engines and a current pushing them toward shore, that's when they usually got into trouble. Now we would just kick in the Iron Wind and power away to get away from trouble, they could not and piled up on the reef, shoal or shore.

"The ships back then were between sixty and one hundred twenty feet long. It would be neat to build one of the old ships like the City of Baltimore is doing now."

"They're building a replica of a Baltimore clipper?" Peter asked.

"Yes, they are. The Baltimore clipper was a Topsail schooner named Chasseur, known as the Pride of Baltimore. It participated in the war of 1812."

Peter was enthralled with the story.

"I'm a history buff. When it comes to ships and anything to do with the water, I'm your man."

"That's neat, Mr. Pelzwalker. They should build something like that up here in Door County. The people could get behind a project just like the people of Baltimore."

"Sounds like a good idea, Peter. Who knows? By the way, call us Joe and Marge."

Annie and Marge came up from below with some cheese, fruit, and lemonade.

"That looks great," Joe said. "I could use something to drink besides coffee, and I'm starting to get hungry."

"You're always hungry," Marge said with a wink.

"We're going to sail around Washington Island and back through Death's Door. We should be back around dinner time, so I don't think your parents will get worried."

"Don't worry about them, they're used to us being late," Annie said, smiling.

"We're really having a good time. It's something Annie's been dreaming and talking about since she saw your boat." Peter said.

Marge patted Annie's hand. "I'm glad we could make you happy. You sure made us happy with your wonderful painting. It's going to go above the mantle when we get home. This boat is really our favorite home, but we needed someplace for the children and grandchildren. We'll get a place in Florida and live on 'Green-Eyed Girl' in the summers up here. So you see, Annie, your painting will help us make that transition."

They spent the rest of the day and early evening sailing with Peter at the helm. Joe was content just enjoying the ride for a change and fiddling with the sail trim. Later, they all had rum and cokes as they passed Ellison Bay on the return part. They finally motored the last three quarters of a mile as the wind dropped. That day, friends were made for life.

Chapter Fourteen

Rita seemed very depressed and angry when Annie saw her on Monday.

"Why so glum, Rita?"

"That asshole Dennis never showed up all weekend. I know he was screwing around down at Sturgeon Bay. I'm getting sick of him and his ways. Two can play that game. There are plenty of guys that want to go out with me. I don't want to, but that's going to change. Tommy Jacobson has been after me all summer, and I'm going out with him tonight."

Annie moved close to Rita and put her arm on her shoulder.

"I really like Dennis," Rita continued, "but I just can't keep feeling like I'm second banana to all his future conquests. Maybe he'll come around. I know he likes me. He's told me as much, but he says he's not the type who thinks he can settle with just one girl right now. I thought I could handle that, but when he doesn't even show up on the weekend that's it!"

Annie nodded; she remembered how he stood Rita up the night she lost her virginity. God, he was good. She could see how Rita wouldn't want to give him up. If she thought he'd change, she'd probably have worked harder on him herself, but he was a womanizer, plain and simple. He wouldn't change.

"Besides, it's getting close to the end of the summer," Rita went on. "In a couple weeks, everything will change when I go to school at UCLA. I'll meet lots of surfers, listen to the Beach Boys, and probably never come back to Door County until I'm old and gray."

"I guess you're going Hollywood," Annie said. They looked at each other and laughed.

"You're right. I may be over-reacting, but things are going to change. I just want to prepare myself, so I don't get too hurt by that shithead."

"Well, have a good time tonight. I think you're going to find it hard to find someone you like better. No way Tommy is going to be better than Dennis. Try not to wear the poor guy out on your first date."

"Annie, how can you say that?" Rita smiled. "I'm of the weaker sex, and he'll probably take advantage of me...I hope so. See you later or tomorrow."

Annie understood Rita's concern, but she knew the effect Dennis could have on women firsthand. She could still picture his body, bare-chested. *She'd love to run her hands and nails across his chest right now. Have him grab her, kiss her, and take her. Just picturing him now made her warm. Dennis Jamison, you're trouble and you know it.*

**

Tuesday was early shift day for Annie and Rita. "I like working the early shift," Annie said. "Time goes fast getting everything ready for the day. There is so much to do."

"I know what you mean. Doing set up and working the lunch crowd and the short afternoon makes the day fly by. Then we're done and can enjoy the rest of the afternoon." Rita said.

"Rita, do you want to have an ice cream cone. I'll make us one as soon as I finish here." Annie was just finishing serving a table. "I'll meet you across the street at one of the picnic tables."

"Okay, I'll see you in a few minutes."

Ten minutes later, when Annie walked out with the two cones, she saw a big crowd huddled around Rita and older man lying on the ground. What is she doing? Annie thought. She watched as Rita had her hands on the man's sternum and was rhythmically pressing down while counting out loud. "One, two, three, four, and one..." Then Annie noticed a white haired woman, crying while at the same time a small poodle was trembling. The older lady was softly mumbling, "help him, please help him." Rita frantically kept up her routine. Annie dropped the two cones and ran over to Rita's side. "Can I do anything?" but before Rita could answer the Fire Rescue ambulance pulled up, and two firemen jumped out and took over.

"Rita, what happened?"

"I think he had a heart attack. I had just sat down and was starting to relax, waiting for you, when I saw this older gentleman and his wife walking their little white poodle. Suddenly, he grabbed his chest and said, 'I don't feel so good.' He went down to his knees, and then fell face down onto the grass. Then his wife screamed. I had taken a first aid course at my high school and learned CPR. I just did what I was taught."

"Wow." Annie said.

"Everyone stood around while the old man's wife screamed, 'Help him, help him! Can't someone help him?' I'm the only one that did." Rita slumped on the picnic bench. "I feel sick to my stomach."

Looking over, Annie noticed the color returning to the man's face.

"Rita Gallagher, do you realize you probably saved this guys life?"

"I feel like I just finished running a race and just barely won."

As she looked at the man and his wife, Annie could tell Rita was excited by what she had done.

"I can't belief I did that. Really, Annie, I save that guys life with these two hands."

"You did and I watched you do it. You're a Hero!"

The man's wife walked over and hugged Rita and started crying again. Annie watched the man open his eyes. She thought he looked confused and frightened.

Then a fireman came over, patted Rita on the shoulder and said, "You know young lady, you saved this man's life. He needed help right away and you gave it to him."

"It was CPR. I learned it last year in high school health class."

"Well, good thing you paid attention that day, otherwise he'd be dead."

They quickly loaded he and his wife and the dog, into the rescue squad vehicle and headed toward the Hospital.

Eventually, Rita and Annie went upstairs to the dorm room at Wilson's, where Rita cried. "I'm so relieved I did everything right." She said to Annie. "I saved a life. I just decided at this very moment what I'm going to study at UCLA this fall. I'm going to be a Doctor. That's what I'm going to do with my life. I'm going to be a Doctor!"

**

The summer was coming to a close with the three-day Labor Day weekend. After that, a lot of people would be going home, including Peter, Dennis and Rita. Annie and Rita were scheduled to work all three days. Peter's last day at the Marina in Sister Bay was Friday. Mr. Peterson had asked if he would work the three days in Ephraim.

"Of course," Peter said. He knew he was needed, and he wanted to earn as much money as possible to help pay for Red Baron.

Dennis's last day at Deacon's was Friday. Darrell had offered him a job for next year, and he accepted. He was looking forward to the long weekend before heading home and then school at Milwaukee's School of Engineering. He had talked to Rita. He had agreed the weekend before to spend their last nights together before she left for Madison and then UCLA. Tuesday would be packing day for her. Her mom was going to come up in the afternoon and pick her up.

Peter's family was going to stay until Wednesday and then make the 13-hour drive back to St. Louis.

For Annie, it was different. She was going to UW-Milwaukee. At least she'd see Dennis, she thought. He was also going to school in Milwaukee, but Peter was going to be in warm Miami and out of the picture until maybe Christmas.

**

Friday evening came, with the three waiting for Dennis at the marina in Sister Bay, but there was no Dennis at the agreed time. Tired of waiting for him to show up, Rita, Annie, and Peter sailed north to Ellison Bay and back. They had just tied up at the marina when Dennis finally made his appearance, slightly drunk, after too many goodbye beers.

Rita was mad. "What am I, chopped liver?" she yelled. She told him what a jerk he was for not being with them as soon as he could.

He explained, "I just couldn't leave the guys without a couple beers to say goodbye."

She finally understood how difficult it would be for him to just say goodbye and leave. She gave him a kiss. "I guess I understand. I don't want to wreck the last weekend we have together." That was the end of it.

"Thank you," he said and gave her a long kiss.

Peter and Annie clapped and whistled.

They drove to 'Tony's' to get a pizza. They asked for Janice, their favorite waitress.

They had a great time and left a big tip.

Before they were out the door, Janice shouted, "Hey, Dennis! How about a goodbye kiss?"

He grabbed her and gave her a kiss. Releasing her, he said. "See you next year, Janice. You take care."

Janice stood there, one hand to lips, the other waving.

Walking to the car, Rita turned to Dennis. "You are so bad, but I love you." They all laughed, climbed into Dennis's car, and headed toward Ephraim.

It was getting late and they decided to take Dennis's blanket and lie on the pier at Hotel Ephraim. For a change, it was quiet on the pier. The four amigos enjoyed the reflection of Ephraim: Wilson's lights, the Moravian Church, sailboat masts gently swaying, the amber street lights, and lights from businesses and resorts along the water's edge combined to give a special peace after a long summer.

"It's pretty late," Dennis said. "No one's around. Let's go skinny-dipping. What do you say?"

Annie looked over at Rita, who smiled and said, "I'm game! You guys go on that side of the pier. We'll stay on this side."

Annie and Rita took their clothes off, keeping their backs to the boys.

"We can meet in front of the pier and swim around, okay?" Rita whispered.

Peter jumped up and started taking his clothes off.

Annie started giggling.

Dennis said, "Okay," and started rolling over to the edge.

Rita started laughing. "Dennis, you look like a big log."

"I'm just saving my energy," he said.

Rita watched as he rolled toward the edge of the pier. He seemed to lose track of where he was and rolled right off.

Peter was completely naked by this time and cannon balled into the water. "Oh, does this feel good," he said, "I can't remember the last time I did this. It feels great without a suit on. You should try it, Dennis."

"I will," he said and then did a little jig in the water as he got his clothes off and threw them on the pier.

Peter cracked up.

Finally, the girls grabbed hands and jumped. They came up laughing and started moving toward the front of the pier with just their heads above water, even though it was only about 3 ½ feet deep.

At first, they swam around and splashed water at each other, but slowly they moved together and paired off. Rita put her arms around Dennis's neck, riding his back, while Peter and Annie did the same thing. They separated in front of the pier and moved to the right and left, into the darker shadows.

Annie slid off Peter's back, moving around to his front, sliding her arms around his neck and pressing her body to his. She kissed him. Peter felt her nipples harden against his chest, his enlarged manhood pressed against her as his hands slid down to the small of her back and pulled her tight. They blissfully sighed at the sensation and stayed in this position, looking into each other's eyes.

"I know what you want and you'll get it, I promise, but not here. Not right now. I have a special spot I want to take you to on Monday." She reached down and grabbed him, stroking him slowly until he finally let out a low groan.

Then Peter's hand moved between her legs, touching her, and then she kissed him deep and sighed. She looked over Peter's shoulder and saw Dennis and for a change, felt nothing for him. Then she whispered in Peter's ear, "That feels so good, Peter." *It definitely is getting better Peter. Monday!*

Finally, they parted, and the cool water rushed between them. They moved to the ladder, climbing the steps. Not hiding their bodies, Annie and Peter dressed. They held hands, sitting with their legs crossed, feet dangling in the water and looked out toward the open water.

They saw *Falcon* with its anchor light on. Past *Falcon*, there was the slow flashing red light, signaling the location of Horseshoe Island and above that, in the heavens above, the North Star. Time stood still for them, this Saturday night of Labor Day weekend.

Dennis and Rita appeared a short time later. After they got dressed, the four sat on the blanket. Finally Dennis said, "It's really late. You three have to work tomorrow, and I don't. Is it all right if I crash on your boat, Peter?"

"Sure, but you're welcome to sleep in my room, on a sleeping bag. Just drop Rita off and come back. I'll leave the door open."

"That sounds like a good idea. Your mom or dad won't wake me?"

"No."

"Okay, just let them know I'm there, so they aren't surprised in the morning."

Peter and Annie walked home and kissed. A few minutes later, Dennis crept into Peter's room, laid down on the sleeping bag and was asleep in seconds.

**

After Peter was finished with work, Dennis picked up Peter and drove to Fish Creek. It was a great time to have a convertible even if it was a rust bucket. Dennis dropped Peter off at the little gift shop Annie, Rita, and Dennis had visited when they sailed there weeks ago. Walking into the shop, he asked the sales clerk if the item he had called about earlier was ready.

After looking through several mustard-colored envelopes in a large shoebox, she finally found his packet. "Here it is. Would you like to see it?"

"Yes, I would." Taking the necklace and charm out of the envelope, he held it up to the light. "It's perfect! Just the way I pictured it."

Meanwhile, Dennis was in search of beer and soda at the General Store in Fish Creek. After being told he was not old enough to buy beer, he persuaded an older college guy to buy him the beer. The extra five dollars seemed to do the trick. He loaded the beer and soda in the Bug.

Peter was standing on the corner next to the C & C when Dennis drove up the street.

"Get what you needed, Peter?"

"Yep. How about you?"

"Yep. We have three six packs of beer and three six packs of soda. We're ready. Let's get the girls, times a wasting."

It didn't take long to get everything loaded into the boat at the marina and head out into the bay. There was a light wind from the northeast, so they had a nice reach to Horseshoe Island and then the Strawberry Islands. From there, they made a tack back north of Horseshoe Island and sailed into the lower end of Little Sister Bay

Harbor. Tucking in close to the shore in eight feet of water, Dennis threw the anchor out.

A couple of hours had passed since they shoved off. Rita and Annie were already in their suits. The boys decided they'd swim in their shorts. The water was very warm.

"This sure is different than June, right boys?"

"It sure is," Peter said. "Can't you tell my voice is lower than it was in June?"

Dennis piped in. "Yeah, I bet something else likes the warmer water, too."

Rita looked at him. "I knew you'd say something like that."

After swimming, the four stretched out on the boat. Dennis and Rita took a couple of cushions to the bow, while Annie and Peter stayed in the cockpit and relaxed.

Annie looked at Peter. "When are you leaving?"

"I think Wednesday or Thursday."

"Oh."

"Depends on the weather. None of us really want to leave early, but it's a long trip. Dad doesn't really want to drive on Friday with all the traffic."

In a voice just above a whisper, Annie said, "I hope you stay until later. I'm really going to miss you."

"You are? I'm going to miss you too, you know." He squeezed her hand.

"Yes, I know. Winters are long enough up here and in Milwaukee. Anyway, now they're really going to drag until next summer."

"It's going to be the same for me, you know!"

They were both quiet. Finally, Annie broke the tension. "It's neat that Mr. Peterson gave you a full time job in Sister Bay next year. I am going to miss seeing you at the Ephraim Marina. Maybe I'll see if I can get a job in Sister Bay at Al Johnson's or one of the gift shops there. I could put some of my paintings in the shops. Then we'd be closer. Who knows?"

"Yeah, that would be neat if you could. You're a real artist with several sold paintings." He smiled at her. "I know you'd sell more of your paintings. Why don't you ask people if they'd like something painted just for them? What do they call that in the art world?"

"A commission."

"Right, a commission. It might take a little more effort to get the business, but then it's sold, and you can take your time instead of just knocking off one painting after another."

She brought her hand to shield her eyes from the sun as the boat swung on its anchor. "I'll have to think about it. I like being spontaneous with my painting."

"Just a suggestion," he said as he kissed her hand.

"What are you guys talking about so intently? I don't hear much laughing," Rita asked.

"We're talking about school this fall."

"Oh, that's depressing," Rita said. "Say, how long until we eat? I'm getting hungry. This beer is giving me the munchies'"

Dennis poked her in the ribs. "Is that all you think about?"

"Noooo, Dennis, it's not. You know what else I think about."

Smiling, he said, "Yes, I like that."

Peter started moving about. "All right, let's get going. Dennis, you want to haul up the anchor? I'll motor out into the wind to save some time and we'll sail back to Horseshoe. We'll have a slow, easy reach again."

They found a spot at the island and tied up. Next, they set up near one of the picnic tables. Dennis and Peter got a fire going while Annie and Rita wrapped foil around potatoes and made a simple salad. As the coals got white hot, everyone had another beer but, this time, they took their time drinking it because they didn't want to get wasted and fall asleep.

Dinner was outstanding, with the steaks cooked to perfection by Dennis. Betty Wilson sent along one of her famous cherry pies for dessert.

"That was a meal fit for a king," Peter said.

As the temperature fell, a slight mist started coming off the water. There was no wind, and the lake had a slight swell running but no real waves or ripples.

"Put some more wood on the fire," Annie said as she rubbed her hands together. "I bet it's going to get cool later tonight. Besides, it's romantic, and this might be the last night the four of us will be together until next June if we all come back." *I sure hope we all do.*

"Sounds good to me," Peter said.

Peter and Dennis got up and started collecting sticks and dry timber. It didn't take long before they had a rip-roaring fire. The four spent the time talking about the summer and what they liked best. They had a radio playing. When they heard a song they all knew, they sang along. They tried to sing "American Pie," but settled for just the refrain. It didn't matter. They just wanted to have a good time and be together.

Around 10:30 P.M., Peter noticed the northern lights and, for the next two hours, all were spellbound with Mother Nature. It was like 4th of July in September.

"What a show," Annie said and the others agreed.

Dennis and Peter got up to get more wood, which resulted in much laughing, swearing and grunting as they got the wood piled next to the burning embers. After situating themselves away from the fire, the two couples snuggled in for the night with blankets and sleeping bags. Annie and Peter lay wrapped in each other's arms. It was impossible not to hear the muffled moans and panting coming from Dennis and Rita's direction.

Annie whispered, "Do you think they're making love? Rita told me she was going to be prepared for tonight, and then she pulled out two condoms. 'Just in case,' she said. She wanted the first time to be with someone experienced, and that sure is Dennis." She paused. "I mean, I assume that's Dennis." She saw Peter's brows furrowed. *Why did I say that? Does he know?*

"You know, Annie, I've never been with anyone but you. I've never gone all the way." She kissed him and said, "It makes a lot of sense to use a condom or some type of birth control." *Good thing Dennis had some that night. No way I want to be a mother now, with all I want to do.*

"That's for damn sure!" said Peter.

"Don't worry, we'll make love soon. I promise." Annie moved her head onto his chest and snuggled in. "Good night, Peter."

"Good night, Annie." *We'll make love soon. Didn't she say Monday? We're running out of time.* He pulled the blanket up to her shoulder with his arms around her.

It quieted down. Peace had come to Horseshoe Island.

As Peter walked Annie back to her home the next morning, he asked, "Can we spend some time together, just you and I? I know we can't spend the night together again, but maybe we can go for a walk or hang out on Red Baron for the last time this summer."

"I'd like that very much, Peter."

**

Back at the cottage, Peter had one of his parents' beers that were in the fridge on the porch. It was morning, a bit early for a beer, but he didn't care.

"Hi buddy, wasn't sure if I'd see you before you left?"

Dennis arrived just as he was finishing. They shook hands.

"Where are you guys going tonight?" Peter inquired.

"I think we'll try the Greenwood. They have great whitefish. I like whitefish now that I've been up here for the summer. What about you guys?"

"Annie's parents are cooking out tonight, so they invited me over. I think they're having grilled ribs and corn, kind of traditional."

"Sounds good to me," Dennis said.

"It does. We've been gone so much it'll be fun. Then we'll go someplace to be alone."

"Well, good luck on that. Make it a night to remember, buddy."

"I'll keep in touch," Peter said, "and if I come up to visit Annie at Christmas, I'll make sure I stop by and see you in Milwaukee."

They shook hands and bear hugged. Just before Dennis took off to get Rita, He asked. "Oh, one last question..." Peter looked Dennis straight in the eye. "Did you ever make love to Annie?"

Dennis coughed. "What? What are you asking me?"

"You heard me. Did you ever make love to Annie?" He took a step closer.

"You're asking me this on the last day of summer together?" Dennis hesitated. "I wanted to. If you two ever broke up, yes I would. That's just who I am."

"I don't know if I believe you or not. It's just something someone said earlier in the summer, but it's over now, and all seems good." Then he got right in Dennis's face. "If I ever find out you did, old buddy. I'll beat the shit out of you. I might be smaller, but I'm not a guy to fuck with. Got it?"

"Got it. See you next year. It's been fun up until now." Dennis turned and walked away.

Chapter Fifteen

Peter took a shower, got dressed in his white shorts and his favorite green golf shirt. He gathered the gift he got for Annie and a small bottle of perfume for Betty Wilson. For Darrell, it was simple, a six-pack of his favorite beer.

Peter walked the block and half to the Wilson's house. Darrell was out back, grilling the ribs and getting ready to put the corn on.

"Hi, Peter. Would you like something to drink?"

"Sure."

"Help yourself. Annie is getting dressed. She just came back from a short swim. She'll be down shortly. Are you excited to get back home to St. Louis?"

"Actually, I'm not. I really like it up here. The area is wonderful and so are the people. Mr. Peterson and Jim Erickson are great to work for, and I really enjoy the boating business. Next year, it's just Sister Bay and the charter operations with Tina Anderson. That should be fun!"

"That's great, Peter. It looks like you have it all figured out."

"Not really, but at least I have a job for next year and it's something I love."

Just at that moment, Annie came out the back door wearing a light blue and yellow flower pattern cotton summer dress that did the most to show off her body.

"Do you like it? Mom bought it this summer for a wedding. I thought I'd wear it since it's our last night together."

"Annie, I've never seen you look so beautiful except that morning we raced. Both times, you've taken my breath away."

Darrell cleared his throat. "Sorry, I didn't mean to eavesdrop but Annie's mom did the same thing to me. It must be the genes!"

"Oh, Daddy!" said Annie and they all laughed.

"How's dinner coming?" Annie asked. "I'm starved!"

"I guess it will be about twenty or thirty minutes. Maybe you guys want to go sit out front on the swing. I'll call when the food's ready."

"Sure you don't want us to keep you company?"

"No, I've got my beer, and if your mother comes out, we'll have a romantic conversation about Labor Day at Cabin Craft now that she's back working."

Peter and Annie walked around to the front of the house and sat on the swing. Peter pulled out the two small boxes. "I brought you and your mother something."

"Do you want me to get Mom, so you can give it to her?"

"Not right now. We can give it to her at dinner. I bought your dad a six-pack of his favorite beer. He looks like he might run out the way he's going tonight."

"That's Dad. He loves his beer, especially when he's grilling."

He gave Annie a brightly wrapped small box with a white bow on top. "This one's for you, Annie, I hope you like it."

Annie looked at Peter with excitement. He watched her hands tremble as she slowly peeled back the tape and unfolded the gold wrapping paper. He was trembling himself.

"Oh, it's from that little gift shop in Fish Creek." Her eyes darted to his. As she opened the box and lifted the small square of cotton, she caught her breath. "Oh, Peter, you remembered!" She held up the gold chain and gold sailboat to the light. "It's beautiful. It's just beautiful."

She gave him a hug and a slow kiss. Her senses were never more alive as her lips touched his and this time there was electricity. *You are so good to me. I wish I had more time than tonight to show you what I mean.* A tear trickled down her cheek as she pulled back from the kiss.

"I went back the next week and it was gone. I was so disappointed," she said.

Peter smiled. "I called the next day and they put it away, I had them do something special to it."

"You did?"

"Yes, look. See anything?"

Annie held it to the sunlight. Inspecting it closer, she noticed the name '*Falcon*' engraved on the side of the gold hull.

She laughed. "Peter Franklin, you are too much."

With a mischievous grin, he looked at Annie. "I told you someday I'd buy you *Falcon*. It's not the real thing, but it will have to do until I make my fortune."

"I love it, Peter. I'll never take it off until you buy me the real *Falcon*."

He slipped the necklace around Annie's neck, and then she turned to look at him.

A tear slid down her cheek. "This is the best present I've ever received in my whole life...it's so special." She gave him another kiss. This time, as their lips touched, Peter could feel the love. A profound sense of contentment settled over him at that moment, followed by a thrill of excitement.

Betty came out on the porch. "Sorry to break this up, but dinner is served."

"Mom, look what Peter got me."

"Oh, it's beautiful, Peter."

"He got something for you, too!" Annie handed her mother the box.

"Oh, Peter, you shouldn't have." She opened the bottle of perfume and put some on her wrist and neck. "It smells so good; maybe it will get your father frisky tonight?"

"Oh, Mom." They laughed as they went in and had their last summer dinner together.

**

Dennis and Rita had a fun-filled evening at the Greenwood restaurant that included a bottle of champagne that Dennis cajoled from the waitress. He explained it was their last night together until next summer. "I'd really like it to be special, and champagne goes a long way toward that end."

Their waitress, smiled as she looked at the two young people. "My husband and I had some when we were young, and it did make the night special! I'll be back."

When she returned, she had an ice bucket and champagne. "Never let it be said I got in the way of young love." Pop went the cork, and she poured the bubbly. "Hope you enjoy my selection. We'll give you the late season discount for lovers. I'll bring your dinner shortly."

Sitting in the car after dinner, Rita suggested they go back to the grassy spot on the bluff overlooking Ephraim. "I love that spot. I have such good memories of it." She moved her hand down to Dennis's leg, giving it a squeeze. "If you know what I mean."

"I do." Dennis said as he leaned over, gave her an amorous kiss, and slid his hand to her breast.

Driving over, Dennis couldn't help but think how exciting Rita looked tonight. With the top down, the wind blew her red hair and seductively billowed out her blouse. He loved looking at her exposed, tan breasts. Occasionally, he could see the outline of her areola peeking above her French bra.

He reached the parking lot and the overlook in record time. The fading sunset cast an apricot hue over the many white structures that made up the backdrop of Ephraim. Dennis spread out the blanket, and Rita moved to his side, embracing him. They watched as a gray shadow moved slowly across the village as the limestone Eagle Bluff defused the last rays of the sun.

"Dennis, I want this last night to be special." She kissed him. "I bought you a little present that I know you'll love, no pun intended." Smiling, she reached into her pocket and brought out three small aluminum foil packets.

"Rita, you're right, I do love the presents, but I think you're the best present tonight." He unbuttoned her blouse, and her chest rose to meet his touch. Rita unbuttoned Dennis's shirt and started kissing his muscular chest, and then began tonguing his nipples. When he let out a slight moan, she lowered her hands to his belt buckle. They slowly sank to the blanket.

He gently placed her down and gently started covering her with kisses. His tongue touched her closed eyelids gently feeling them move, then he nibbled on her earlobes. She moaned as he moved to her sensitive neck and turned her head in ecstasy. He pulled back to gaze at her naked splendor, and his lips closed and sucked on her ripe breasts.

Slowly he moved lower, trailing kisses to her small triangle, and feasted on her nectar. Her fingers gripped his hair and then he felt a rush overpower her as her legs closed tightly against his head and she whispered his name. He pulled back and then savagely kissed her lips as he plunged his manhood into her heated, wet body.

He moaned and then moved in long measured strokes, finding the areas inside her that gave her the most pleasure. His tongue did the same in her mouth, as they both turned up the heat on each other. His body moved against her, at the same time meeting his thrust with her own, and when he felt the squeeze of her walls, and heard her cry of her pleasure, he exploded inside her with a pent-up lust for the virginity she was giving him.

After making love for the first time, Rita savored the moment because it happen the way she had fantasized it would be all summer. From the moment she met Dennis, she hoped it would be this way and it was. She could go back to Madison and then LA fulfilled, looking forward to next year. Looking forward to seeing Dennis.

**

Peter and Annie finished dinner early. Annie borrowed Darrell's station wagon. "For our last night together, I want to take you to Cave Point," Annie said. "It's one of my favorite spots in Door County." She knew he'd remember her promise.

She and Peter walked to the car hand in hand. The drive was longer, but then they had to go across the peninsula and south of Jacksonport.

The place was deserted, just the way Annie had envisioned. "Cave Point is beautiful and exciting all rolled into one place, and tonight it's ours." She knew just where to go. There was one spot that she loved when she went there with her friends or family. That's where she took Peter.

They got there just as the sun was setting. The water had turned a pinkish blue. Spreading the blanket, Peter and Annie sat down on one of the limestone points, looking out over Lake Michigan. Being together and feeling the gentle vibration as the rolling waves pounded into the wave-worn limestone ledges and underwater caves, they were one with each other and nature. Surrounded by the familiar juniper bushes and pine trees that populated the eastern side of the peninsula, darkness surrounded them.

Annie pulled the extra blanket over their shoulders. "Peter, I just love the gift you gave me. It means so much to me. Every time I look at this sailboat, I'll think of you and this summer…I love you, Peter."

Peter was quiet for a while.

Did he know? Not now, please not now.

Placing his hands on her face, he kissed her.

Thank you, Peter. She moaned because of his kiss of love.

He kissed her again and again, her lips, her eyes, and her neck. His hands slid down to her breasts, caressing them, feeling their fullness.

"I want this night to be more special than it already is," she whispered. "Make love to me, Peter." She kissed him and then pulled back. "I've thought about this for a long time. It's the right time for us." Then, reaching into her small purse, she held out her hand. "Just in case. I hope you're not upset?"

"Oh, Annie, how could I be upset?"

With tears welling up in her eyes, she looked at him. "Make love to me."

As he tenderly kissed her lips, she slowly unbuttoned her dress, unsnapped her bra, and cupped her breast for his lips. She felt his tongue swirl around her nipples as his hands replaced hers and she leaned back. It felt wonderful and unhurried. She lay back on the blanket and unbuttoned the rest of the dress.

While she did that, she watched as Peter pulled his shirt and shorts off, slid down his underwear and finally kicked off shoes. He unwrapped the condom foil pack, rolled it on, and he was ready. He slid off her panties and shakily positioned himself above her, and then kissed her on the mouth as he slowly lowered himself.

"Ahh," they both said in unison as he entered her body for the first time, and they started to move. As his movement increased in intensity, her arms encircle and squeezed Peter. "Come with me," she said, and with a few more thrusts, he let out a low groan and pressed down on her.

With his head nestled against her, Annie sighed. *I love you Peter.*

Chapter Sixteen

Peter had been lucky to get a job at the marina, his second week of school in Miami, Peter mused, as he sat on a boat box. It seems like it was yesterday. What was that, seven years ago? Wow, time sure does go by when your doing something you love. He found out later that Jim Erickson and Mr. Peterson called the owner with a glowing recommendation suggesting that Mahoney hire Peter. Since then, the two had worked as a team. They were a perfect combination. Peter was outgoing, while Mahoney was an old curmudgeon with a twinkle in his eye. He was giving Peter his PhD in the charter boating business, like Jim and Mr. Peterson did.

One thing was sure he had learned about Mahoney. If Mahoney liked you, he couldn't do enough for you, but if he didn't, watch out. He'd been known to get mad at someone, and not rent to him or her. That's when Mary, his late wife, would step in and smooth things over. Now it was Peter that did the same thing when Mahoney got riled up with a customer. Since that first year together, Mahoney had turned much of the day-to-day charter operations over to Peter. Then, Mahoney made Peter an offer he couldn't refuse. The deal was to give Peter half the business if he'd work for him for five years. Then each year after the original five years, he would vest him twenty percent more until he owned the remaining portion. So after ten years, Peter would own the whole business. He was currently in his sixth year of the deal, and basically had 60% operating control, but still consulted with Mahoney before he did anything major.

Mahoney had his original office and still acted like he ran the place, but both knew that Peter was in charge. It was a great time for both, and business exploded. Peter added trawlers, powerboats, and catamarans to the sailboat fleet. He thought Mahoney would be upset when he suggested they change the name of the operation to Kick Back Charters but, instead, he loved the new name and the new boats.

Mahoney was a new man since Peter took over everything. It reinvigorated Mahoney. Now he came to the marina each day with a bounce in his step.

"I love the dollies who show up with the power boaters. Those guys seem to have more money to spend than the sailors. Hell, they even buy me beers. How good is that?" He looked at Peter with an all-knowing smile. "I guess those dollies are what you might call trophy wives or girlfriends." Chomping on his cigar, he continued. "From what I've seen so far, they all have a nice pair of 'trophies,' if you know what I mean."

Peter smiled.

"You know, Peter, I love teaching them how to cleat the line to the boat or dock; it makes for some great viewing."

Peter nodded. "I thought you might be getting bored with not running the place, but I guess you're making out okay."

"Yeah, it's a tough job, but someone's got to do it…. I just wish I was twenty years younger and had my health. I'd give those stinkpot guys a run for their money," Mahoney sucked in his gut and smiled.

"Just keep that thought, Mahoney," Peter said, patting him on the back then walked toward the office.

It was fall, and Peter looked forward to the season starting in earnest. He had just added some new boats to the lineup, and he was interested to see how things would work out for the coming season. So far, he was happy with the early reservations.

Peter was living his dream. This wasn't theory he learned at the University of Miami's business school. This was real. He was building it for himself.

He often thought about Annie. Usually, it was when he saw some-one who reminded him of her. A word, a phrase or a look would be enough. Sometimes, it was something he did that was similar to what they had done in Door County.

He missed her, that was for sure. He called her when he had a chance, which wasn't often, usually at night or on a Sunday. They could both talk late into the night on Sundays because Mondays were usually slow for each. He knew she was committed to her new art gallery, and loved the art business as much as he loved the boating business.

He also found it difficult to set aside time just to go sailing, just for himself. He missed the joy of the wind in his face, the feel of the boat as it glided through the water. He couldn't remember the last time he had sailed.

Peter sighed. He remembered a recent conversation with Annie about painting. "I love to paint," she'd said, "but I'm so involved with the gallery that I just don't find time to paint. I thought I'd miss it, but by the end of the day, I feel like I've painted all day. I'll get back to painting when the urge takes me, maybe when I go back to Door County. Right now, it's the gallery, my clients, and the artists."

Every call seemed to end with both trying to convince the other to come to Chicago or Miami so they could be together, but they knew they couldn't…. at least not now.

**

Annie's exposure to sculpture at *The Thomas Gallery* led her back to school to learn how to do sculpture. She enjoyed carving wood figures. The warmth of the wood spoke to her, and the smell of the wood was intoxicating.

Wood sculpture led to learning to sculpt in bronze. She loved the look and smooth feel of bronze created by Teddy Graboski, a local artist she'd met at The Art Institute. She met several people like him, since transferring from UW-Milwaukee to the Art Institute her junior year, and that's where she got her undergraduate degree. Teddy specialized in scaled down bronze casting of local cats and dogs. He told Annie, "I just walk around Chicago and take pictures of cats and dogs I see. Then I make a casting, and voila."

Nothing fancy, but the public loves them. The darn things sell like hotcakes.

Annie told Teddy about her gallery specializing in his type of art. "Why don't you display your sculptures there? I won't take a big percentage, and your sculptures fit my concept."

"I'd love to, Annie," Teddy said.

That was how she got several artists to sign on to her gallery. She called it *The Local Art Gallery*, based on the idea of featuring local artists. She started a separate area in the gallery called 'The Spot,' which gave customers and artists a chance to get together and design work.

While most artists didn't like doing work in 'The Spot' thinking it was beneath them, it worked. Both parties got a special satisfaction when they could agree on a project. It worked for Annie in Door County, and it worked in Chicago as well.

She started having open houses, providing refreshments on Friday and Saturday evenings and Sunday afternoons. Artists would set up small areas, almost like tents at summer Art fairs, with samples of their work. Customers, in turn, brought in photographs of what they wanted painted.

Sometimes, the artist even set up appointments to go out and see what the client wanted. It was an interchange of art and ideas which everyone loved, most of all, Annie. She carved out a separate space at the gallery and, on the weekends, it was the most exciting place to be. Annie developed a growing following for her gallery.

Thomas often stopped in to chat. It wasn't hard to figure out why he had one of the largest galleries in Chicago. He was nice to everyone, but especially enjoyed spending time with his former employee, Annie. He made it a point to stop in when he was in the area.

She knew he was fascinated with how others did their business. She knew he catered to the very wealthy. Usually opening his gallery only on the weekends or by appointment. It worked for him and it gave him a chance to enjoy art for the sake of art.

When Annie left Thomas's gallery to work on her own, she continued to stop in and talk to him about art and her dream of a unique gallery. Most of the time, Annie did the talking and Thomas listened. She knew he loved listening to all artists talk about their passions.

Annie was no different than the others, except she had that something that Thomas loved. He lit up with joy every time she came into his shop. "Sit down, have some coffee," he'd say, as he got her a cup and patted the couch for her to sit.

Thomas was a confirmed bachelor, not because he didn't like women, he just never got around to finding the right one. He tried several times, but he was comfortable being his own man. He did have one regret in his life, now that he was fifty-two, which was that he never had children. He often wondered what kind of child he would have had.

The first time Thomas saw Annie, he knew if ever he could create a picture of the daughter he'd never had, it would be her. It wasn't her looks alone that made him feel that way. Sure, she had unbelievable green eyes, a friendly smile, and a soft voice. Her long blond hair enhanced her natural beauty.

"She's enough to stop the heart of any man, any age," Thomas would often say to his artist friends. When he thought about it, though, what really made him love her was the way she treated people, with care and respect. They were soul mates from different generations. He wanted to take care of her in a very paternal way. He wasn't a dirty old man; he just cared for her.

**

One day in July, Annie looked up to find Thomas in her gallery. "Hi, Thomas. What brings you here on a hot summer afternoon?"

"I was hoping you had a cold beer. Could I mooch one from you on my way to my gallery?"

"For you, of course. What will it be?"

"How about a can of Old Style, if you've got one?"

"I think I do. It is pretty popular around here."

He popped the top and brought it to his lips, letting the beer slide down his throat. "God, that's good. Thanks, Annie. How are things going? Is business good?"

She got a big smile on her face. "Thomas, you know business is good. I owe a lot to your advice and counsel."

As usual, he nodded and drank as she talked.

"You told me to go with my gut feelings and I did. You know it's working and so do I." He smiled in acknowledgment.

"No one believed it would work, but it is. I love the way I'm doing business. I've got a head start on others that are trying to copy what I've started here. Thanks for having faith in me."

Thomas gave her a big hug. "Annie, you had faith in yourself, and that's all that counts. I've got to go. I've got a client coming at four-thirty."

She walked him to the door and gave him a kiss on the cheek.

"Annie, before I forget, call me next week. I've got something I'd like to talk to you about, okay?"

"Sure, how about Tuesday? You can buy me lunch."

"I'll look forward to it," He gave her hand a squeeze and walked out into the hot afternoon sun.

Annie closed the door. "I wonder what he's got up his sleeve."

**

Annie had more traffic than usual at the Gallery that night. She had to make an emergency call to the liquor store down the block. "I need four cases of Bud, three cases of Old Style, and six bags of ice. I'll give you an extra ten dollars if you can get it here in less than ten minutes."

She was busy and having fun. Everyone was having a great time. She'd sold ten paintings, so it was a resounding success. She was just saying goodbye to the Palmers and Burns from Duluth, who had each ordered a bronze sculpture of "Wolf Howling at the Moon."

"It captures the essence of up North," Liz Burns said.

At that moment, Annie noticed three people walk into her gallery. One was an obviously couple and a cute male friend. She walked over. "Hi, welcome to The Local Art Gallery, I'm Annie," she said to the three, and pointed over her shoulder. "There's cold beer and soda in the back. Help yourselves. If you have any questions, just ask."

The three thanked her, and headed straight for the back, and the beer. By the time, Annie found her way back to them, it was nearly 9:30 p.m.

"I am so sorry, folks, we didn't have a chance to chat." Annie said. "You are all welcome to come back tomorrow. I really have to close up, or I'll get in trouble with the cops, an ordinance about not being a bar."

Todd, Angelina, and Jack thanked her for having a great gallery and said they'd be back the following day. Todd and Angelina went out the door, but Jack held back. He took Annie's hand in his as he looked into her eyes.

"I didn't know art could be so interesting until tonight. I'm going to take you up on your offer and come back tomorrow. I've never bought any art in my life, but maybe you could help me decide what might be a good first investment."

"What's your name?" she asked. *He is really cute. I wouldn't care if he likes art or not, just to get to know him.*

"It's Jack, Jack Stevenson."

"Well, Jack, you come back tomorrow. It shouldn't be as crowded. I'd love to spend some time helping you." She gave his hand a slight squeeze and then released it. "Why don't you come about seven-thirty or eight? We can talk without being rushed."

Jack maintained his eye contact and just nodded. "I'll be here. Thanks again. See you tomorrow."

Once he was out the door, he punched his fist in the air and hooted, loud enough that people turned and stared. Annie watched him and giggled at his exuberance, thinking another visit from him could be interesting indeed.

Annie closed up and headed home.

It had been a good night. She sold a lot of art. She knew several of the artists had done well. It was always fun to see old friends and clients. She met several new people tonight she hoped would become clients.

At her loft, she poured herself some wine and kicked off her shoes. Jack and his two friends seemed like nice people, she thought. She was glad he was coming back tomorrow. That should be fun. It was always fun to get people started in art. He wasn't bad to look at either.

She reviewed the whole day as she sipped her wine, and then remembered she had to stop at Thomas's gallery on Tuesday. She got up and jotted the appointment down in her calendar. *I wonder what he's got up his sleeve.* Now all she needed was someone to share it all with. She didn't even have a cat or dog to greet her when she came home.

She touched the sailboat around her neck, and then reached for the phone to call Peter. It had been a while, and she missed hearing his voice, but more, she missed being with him.

While the phone rang, she flopped down on the old stuffed chair she bought at a garage sale years earlier when she was in college. Though really threadbare, it was like an old pair of jeans, so comfortable and well fitting, that she couldn't bear to get rid of it.

Finally he picked up.

"Hi. How are you?" she said.

"Hi, it's good to hear your voice. What's happening in Chi town?"

"I just finished with an open house at the gallery," she said, "I'm having some wine."

"How was the open house?"

"Really good. Lots of activity, new and old people…business is good."

"That's great."

"Yeah, it's great", then it hit her, "but what isn't so great is that I'm tired of coming home to an empty place." She started to heat up as she talked. She'd thought about their situation for a long time, especially lately. "It's been almost five years since we've really spent time together, and I miss not being with you."

Silence.

"Why don't you come down here?" Peter said. "You could open a gallery here. Besides, it's warm all year. Just think, no Chicago winters, no snow, no heavy coats. You could swim in the ocean and we could live on a boat. We could find a place at South Beach. It's a new trendy area, it'd be perfect for an Art Gallery. We could find an old building there cheap. A friend of a friend that is a developer is starting to buy real estate there. It's not very nice now, but once people start fixing up the buildings, others will jump on the bandwagon. It's right on the ocean. You could paint like you've always talked about, and we could be together."

"It sounds great, Peter, but you know I can't leave now. I just got things going the way I want them. Would you drop what you're doing and start all over again up here?" She waited several seconds. "Peter... are you there?"

"Yes. I'm here."

"Why didn't you answer me?"

"Because you know I can't leave what I've got built down here. This is my dream, too."

She fell silent.

"Annie?"

"Yes?"

"Are you all right?" he said.

She knew she wasn't because she was starting to cry. "No, I'm not all right. I'm sick of being alone. I'm sick of coming home to an empty place with no one to share my highs and no one to help me through the lows." She blew her nose with a tissue. "I love you, Peter. I know you love me, too, but it's just not working for us." Her voice cracked. "As much as I hate to say it, neither one of us is going to give in. It's never going to change! Our dreams mean more to us than each other. That's sad because we're so good for each other." And she started to sob.

"I don't know what to say. Let's talk about this tomorrow when we've had a chance to think about it."

Annie talked between sobs. "No, Peter...it's just not going to work....I...I can't wait any more...I don't want to wait any more...I'm sorry, Peter. I love you." She had thought about this moment for a long time, years. She knew what she needed to do as much as she hated to. She cut to the quick. "Peter ...this means goodbye. Good luck with the rest of your life and when you get up this way..."

Her crying grew louder, and between sobs, she choked out, "Stop and say hi," she said and hung up.

Looking out her windows at the Chicago skyline, through blurry eyes she saw heat lightening in the distance. Funny, she thought as she blew her nose. *This view is like me. Up close, everything looks great, but in the background, it's lightening. I sure hope things get better.* She got up and fell into her rumpled bed. Crying like a little kid, she slowly fell asleep.

**

Peter looked at his phone and slowly placed the receiver back in its cradle. He could not believe what just happened. He felt like he was going to be sick, but he knew Annie was right. They were both too headstrong, neither one wanted to give up their dream.

It was midnight in Miami. That might have been late in most cities, but things were just starting to roll in Miami. Peter grabbed his keys and decided he needed a drink. He didn't want to get drunk; he just didn't want to be alone.

When Peter walked in the door of Tommy's Bar and Restaurant, he saw a bunch of his friends in a cluster around the far end of the bar.

Right in the middle of the group stood Mahoney, holding court. He had everyone in stitches, telling tall tales of adventures he had accumulated over the years of being in the charter business. The stories weren't that good, but the way Mahoney told them, a cross between Robin Williams and Rodney Dangerfield, made them hilarious. It was just what he needed.

Peter was enjoying himself when he noticed he was standing next to a beautiful woman he didn't recognize. "Hi, I'm Peter. I don't think I've met you before." *What an original line.*

"Hi, I'm Paula."

They touched beer bottles instead of shaking hands.

"How do you fit into this group?" she asked.

"I'm in a partnership with our storyteller, Mr. Mahoney."

"Oh."

"We own a boat charter business here in Miami. This is our neighborhood watering hole. As you can tell by tonight's entertainment, Mahoney is the main feature. He should be quitting pretty soon. He's starting to slur his words."

Paula turned and looked at Mahoney and then back to Peter, nodding.

"God, he's going to feel like shit tomorrow," Peter said

Paula laughed. "He is pretty funny, and he just keeps going. I've been here for a couple of hours with Christina and her boyfriend, Juan. We're from Key West. My family owns a restaurant there. I just needed to get away for a while. I thought I might try to get a job here in Miami. I was a legal assistant in Key West. It paid the bills, but I was not happy."

Peter nodded.

"What makes me happy is sailing."

"Really?"

"Yes, having my captain's license allows me to get paid for showing people a good time. It's great when I can find work. Key West got too small for me. I want to sail full time. I've got to pay the bills, so I'll do something until I hook on to a more permanent position here. Maybe I'll hook up with a charter company? Know any?" she said, smiling.

Peter smiled back. "This might be your…" he paused to glance at his watch, "lucky morning. We're always looking for the right people. Why don't you stop down at the office tomorrow afternoon, and we can talk?" He gave her one of his cards.

"Gee thanks, Peter. What time?"

"Say three p.m. We should be done turning the charters around by then."

"Great. Can I buy you a beer?" she said.

Peter raised the bottle to the light. "Sure, but I'll buy. How about another green bottle?"

Chapter Seventeen

A nnie didn't want to do anything but lie in bed and feel sorry for herself. The light streaming in through the window finally awoke her. It was a beautiful day, she thought, as she lay on her side and watched a sparrow hopping on the ledge. I need to paint something, anything, just to get out and be among people, she thought.

She dragged herself out of bed, slipped on some jogging shorts and a crumpled-up tee shirt from the previous year's Art Fair. She wiggled her feet into her flip-flops. Grabbing a travel easel, paper, and her small paint box, she walked out.

Thank God it was sunny, she thought as she put her sunglasses on. She knew her eyes were puffy from crying all night. She stopped at Java Joint and got some coffee and a cranberry muffin. Heading down to Lake Michigan, she was amazed at the number of people on Michigan Ave. Why not? It was one o'clock on a beautiful Saturday afternoon. It made sense for a ton of people to be there. Life goes on, Annie.

Seeing all the people somehow gave her renewed strength in the human spirit. She went down to the water and started painting a small scene, a sailboat at anchor near Navy Pier.

As she painted, she remembered the first time she painted with Peter many years ago at Newport Beach. She felt sad thinking about it, but then something clicked. Her attitude changed for the better about Peter.

It's not as if Peter died. I can still talk to him if I want to. He's still my best real male friend. She touched the charm. The memories of their time together were still good. She smiled to herself.

Her thoughts shifted back to the painting, focusing on the water, the light and the boat. It didn't take her long, but when she finished painting, she knew she was going to be okay.

She packed up her stuff and headed home. Life was life. She would be just fine. Besides, she had another open house tonight. That was always fun and she met such nice people through her art.

She stopped on her way back and had an ice cream cone. It was not as good as Wilson's, she thought, but it would do.

**

It was a perfect afternoon at the Marina. Peter had seen Paula arrive about thirty minutes before their meeting. He caught glimpses of her walking up and down the slips, looking at his inventory of boats and taking notes. *Very good.* He liked that she got there early. There was a lot of preparation in sailing, especially when caring for others. *So far, so good.*

He found her attractive too, and so would the male charters. That was always a plus. After all, he was a male with all the standard male fantasies.

Very striking, he thought. She's tall, and lean, with an athletic body. He liked her brown eyes with flecks of gold around her pupils, and her brownish blond hair. She looked very sexy in white shorts, an orange University of Miami tee shirt, an Atlanta Braves baseball cap, and topsiders.

She's going to drive Mahoney and everyone else crazy, including me. God, I hope she's as qualified as she looks.

She came in to the office right at three p.m.

"Hi, Paula, how are you?"

"Great, but not as tired as Mahoney," she said, laughing.

"I saw him sleeping near the gas dock. He's got to get his beauty rest before tonight. He's a piece of work, but I love him," said Peter.

"I've seen quite a few like him around Key West."

"I can imagine. Why don't you tell me about yourself? I know you want to skipper, but tell me about your family and why you think you'd be qualified to work here at Kick Back." Peter leaned back in his swivel chair.

"My mother is Swedish and my father is Cuban. I have three brothers. I'm the only girl and the oldest. My mother, Inga, met my dad when she came to Key West to vacation. She got her law degree from NYU in January, and came down with a couple of friends to celebrate and get out of the cold. Dad's family ran a restaurant and fishing service in the old part of Key West. Dad saw Mom, Mom saw Dad, and it was love at first sight. Because of him, she stayed three weeks longer. He proposed, she accepted, and moved down a couple months later. I was born a year later. My last name is Guerrero."

"Thank you, but that doesn't mean you're qualified."

"I'm getting to why I'm qualified," Paula went on. "As you probably know, Cubans are very family- oriented. Since I was first born and the first grandchild of all the Guerreros, I got to do all the boy things with my dad and uncles while they waited for sons to be born. It was great. I suppose that's why I'm so independent today. Even after the boys came, Dad and I still had this special bond. It's about the water. I loved being on the water with him and my uncles."

Peter just nodded. *She's pretty and loves water.*

"Don't get me wrong, Mom made sure I was a good girl. School is important to her, so I had to do well at my studies. She set up shop in Key West and still practices law. Dad heads the family businesses, the restaurant, and the fishing service. My uncles supply most of the fish to the restaurants in Key West. The guiding business is very big in Key West. I'd go out with them when I was little. I was small, but I learned fast. I know what people expect when they go fishing. That's where I learned how to take care of boaters and fisherman."

"OK." Peter tried to stay focused on what she was saying, but her beauty distracted him.

"They can be very demanding," she continued, "especially when the fish aren't biting. I learned how to make a bad situation good. When I wasn't out on the fishing boats, I worked in the restaurant doing everything. I'm a pretty fair cook, especially with fish. It might be a simple meal, but I make it look great and taste better. The charter guests loved that."

Peter broke in and asked, "How did you start sailing?"

"I was good in school. You need to visualize how to get somewhere using angles and vectors liked I learned in geometry. You need to factor in the waves, wind and currents to get someplace with a sailboat. You just can't point the boat and put the pedal to the metal. It takes imagination. I like using my head. I must get that and the color of my hair, holding a few strands, from my mother."

"I know just how you feel," he said with a smile.

She laughed as she looked at Peter. "I better warn you now, I can get very excited at times. That's the Cuban in me. It goes as fast as it comes, and it's never directed at customers, in case you're wondering. It's usually directed at me, because I did something stupid. I guess I'm a perfectionist."

"I'm glad to hear that," he said with a smile.

"What else? I'm twenty-six. Never been married. I got engaged once, but it only lasted a month. He was too possessive. I drink, but not a lot. I don't smoke, and I like to have fun. That's about it. Here are my captain's papers and a list of references." She passed the papers across the desk. "These are people I've worked for and captained with."

Peter spent a few minutes looking over her papers, and he made a copy of her references.

"Thanks, I'll check these out. Now, if you have some time, let's go out and take a sail. It's a beautiful afternoon, and I really should see how you handle a boat. Are you comfortable with that?"

Paula smiled. "Sure, that would be great. I miss not being on the water, even if it's for a few days."

"Okay, I'll get a few sodas and ice and we'll pick a boat. Any preference?"

"Well, I've never sailed one of those cats before. That would be fun. I'm sure it's similar to mono hulls, but if you're going to have me captain one of these, then there's no time like the present to get some experience."

"Makes sense to me. Let's go."

They chose a 38-foot cat, which was the smallest one in the fleet. Peter spent about ten minutes familiarizing Paula with it.

As she looked around the boat, Peter heard her say, "I can't believe how much room there is in a catamaran compared to a monohull. I can see why it's so popular for cruising. What's the trade-off?"

"Cats don't sail upwind very well. There's a lot of windage, and you need a much bigger slip than with a monohull. You use two engines to back the boat into a slip, similar to a powerboat. Remember that when you bring her back."

Paula nodded.

"Once people get the hang of it, they love it. It's a great platform for most charter types who don't do a lot of hard sailing and like lying in the sun. Right now, it's our most popular sailing vessel."

"Interesting," Paula said. "I can hardly wait to see how she sails."

"Let's do it." Peter started the two diesels, letting them warm up. "I always feel more like I'm steering a power boat than a sailboat when I'm on a catamaran," he said, "because I'm under this hard canopy versus a canvas Bimini top. I'll handle the lines," he said, "you power her out into the channel. We'll set the sails as we motor out."

He watched as Paula easily handled getting the boat out of the slip using the two throttles. She looked at ease and beautiful, Peter thought, as she motored down the channel, into the bay.

"Paula, could you raise the mainsail?" He asked, curious about how she would handle a strange boat under the pressure of his watchful eye.

"Sure," she said, as she moved across the cabin top to the main sail halyard located on the mast.

He watched as she raised the sail with no difficulty. She sure didn't seem nervous, he thought. She moved with a simple grace and confidence that reminded him of Annie. He knew he had more than a passing interest in Paula because of the physical similarities, but he also felt comfortable with her.

She moved around the deck with ease. She went right to the roller furling headsail, releasing the sail and cleating it off. They were on a port tack, sailing down the channel toward the Atlantic.

"Nice job, Paula. Why don't you take over, and I'll get some Cokes for us."

He watched her get in the seat and check the instrumentation. "Compass heading 85 degrees, speed six and a half knots. Wind speed ten knots. This cat moves right along," she said as she steered with one hand on the wheel. "You're right, it really is a stable platform."

"Here you go, Captain," he said as he handed her a Coke with ice. "Found a lime in the galley, so I cut you a slice. Everything but the rum."

"Thanks," she said as she took a sip. "This tastes good just the way it is."

They settled into an easy conversation about boating, the charter business, and what she found most interesting about charter clients she'd had in the past. Peter told her about himself and his time in Door County, coming to school in Miami, and how he started working with Mahoney. He explained how he was buying the business from Mahoney, as well as his philosophy of service and his business.

"Have you ever stayed at a Four Seasons or Ritz Carlton?"

Her eyes got big, and then she got a little testy. "No, I haven't. I'm not made of money."

"I'm sorry, I didn't mean to insult you or anything. It's just that once you have stayed at one of those places, you'll understand what I'm trying to do here."

"I'm sorry, Peter. I shouldn't have reacted that way, but I come from a simple lifestyle and don't get a chance to stay at places like that."

"Well, maybe we can fix that."

"What do you mean?"

"Well, if you're going to work for me, you need to know what I want and expect of my employees. You just gave me a good idea. I want you to go to the Four Seasons here in Miami. I want you to see firsthand how they treat their customers. I want you to have lunch, dinner, and breakfast on me. This will probably be the only training you'll get from Kick Back, but their style of customer service should stay with you your whole life. It did with me after I stayed at one in Chicago a few years ago."

"Does that mean you're hiring me?"

"I guess so. I don't see any reason not to unless your references don't check out. You did warn me about your temper, and it did disappear as fast as it came. I can tell you know how to handle boats. I guess you'll have to cook for me, just so I know you won't poison the customers."

She smiled and gave him a hug. "I could cook for you tonight, if you like, but it will have to be at your place. Juan, Christina and I are staying at a hotel not far from here, but it doesn't have a kitchen."

Now he was laughing. "Paula, I was only kidding. You don't have to cook for me. You've got the job. As for the cooking, you can cook your favorite fish for me when you get a place of your own, but that can wait."

"Thanks, Peter. You don't know what this means to me."

"Yes I do, Paula. I can see it in your eyes."

She raised her glass of Coke. "To dinner, then."

They sailed for another hour before heading in. The sun was setting as they jibed the mainsail heading back toward the shipping channel and the marina. Finally, they lowered their sails and motored in.

It had been a good afternoon on the water, Peter thought. It felt good to share it with someone who obviously loved it as much as he did. As the sun's orange glow dipped below the Miami skyline, he decided he was going to enjoy being with her on a daily basis.

**

Annie finished painting and headed home to get ready for her open house. She felt better after she showered. She put on a light silk turquoise dress and gold hoop earrings giving her a classy, but casual, look. Glancing in the mirror, she realized she got a little sun today. She never wore much makeup, but decided a little peach-pink lip-gloss and a touch of glitter powder would give her a movie star look. She slipped on her favorite light tan sandals with the little gold stars on the straps. As always, she wore Peter's sailboat necklace.

With a shy smile, Annie gazed in the mirror, her fingers on the sailboat. "Well, Mr. Franklin, your loss is going to be someone else's gain, sometime."

She ran a brush through her strawberry blond hair, and then cupped her breasts, adjusting the cleavage and winking at herself in the mirror. Not bad, not bad. Grabbing her purse and keys, she walked to the gallery.

It was a gorgeous evening, and a nice crowd of people gathered on the streets. Annie knew she'd have another good night. She knew Rolando would have the beer iced and the food would arrive shortly. Several of the artists were already set up when Annie walked in the door.

Teddy was holding court with some of the new artists. "Yeah, it was Annie's idea to have an open house, but after she saw how the "non-art lovers" loved my work... she knew it would work. If it wasn't for me, guys, I'm not sure you would be sitting here now."

Annie came up behind him and cleared her throat. "Yeah, if it wasn't for Teddy here, none of this would have happened, I guess."

"Aw, Annie, you know I was only kidding," said Teddy.

She stared at him with a hard look, trying her best not to crack a smile, and then she started laughing. "Got you! Actually, Teddy did help a lot with this part of the gallery, because I knew it would work if we got the right artist like Teddy here and you guys. We should have a good crowd tonight, so be prepared."

It really was busy. Jack came right at seven-thirty, but Annie was swamped with business. He walked up to her and shifted from foot to foot, wide eyed. Finally, Annie finished talking to a couple from Libertyville interested in a large landscape.

"We'll be back," the wife said. They wrote a check for the painting and handed it to Annie. "If this painting doesn't work, we know the other one will."

"That's fine. I'll put a hold tag on this other painting."

Finished, she turned to Jack. "Hi, how are you tonight? Thanks for coming back."

"Man, you are really busy. I thought last night was crowded, but I think tonight's even bigger."

"I think you're right," Annie said with a smile. "I know you're here to talk about your first piece of art, but I'm so swamped. Could I impose upon you to wait a little while longer until I catch my breath? I really want to take some time with you."

Jack smiled at her. "I don't care if it takes ten hours, I'll wait."

"Great."

"Go on, take your time. I'll just have a few beers and browse around until things slow down."

"Thanks, Jack." One of the artists waved his hand frantically at Annie. "I promise I'll be back shortly," she said. She gave him a peck on the cheek. *That was spontaneous, Annie.*

"Shortly" turned into two hours. At nine thirty p.m., she found Jack near the tub of cold beer. She swore he was counting how many beers were left and was clearly feeling no pain. Then he started telling a couple about falling asleep in class after pulling an all-nighter at a local pub; he made his seven forty five a.m. class only to fall into a deep sleep. He was still asleep, with his head down, when the class ended. Still snoring for the next class, the next professor was so amused that he had a sign made: *QUIET, GRADUATE STUDENT STUDYING.*

When he finally woke up, the whole class applauded. His nickname from that day on was The Sleeper.

Annie leaned against the wall and listened. He is kind of cute, she thought. He's got a good sense of humor, and he's not afraid to meet people. Hmm, Peter's not in the picture anymore after last night. I might want to give him an art lesson after I close. He looks like he might be worth it.

Looking at her watch, she realized it actually was time to close. "Folks, as much as I'd like to keep this party going, Chicago's finest say I have to close up," she said loudly. "Thanks for coming and, if you decide you want something, I'll be open again tomorrow from one to four p.m."

As people started to leave, she walked over to Jack. "I am so sorry, but if you can sit right here for eight minutes until I lock up, I'll give you a very special art education lesson." She touched the tip of his nose with her finger and winked.

By the time Annie finished, Jack was nowhere to be found. Then she heard a thump in the bathroom. She waited near the door, smiling.

"There you are. I thought I scared you off." She moved closer to him.

"What? I went to the bathroom. Did I pee on myself? The way you're smiling..."

"Relax. I just appreciated how nice you were tonight. I asked you to come back and you did, right on time, and then I put you off, but you were very understanding and made yourself comfortable. I think that's really nice. And besides, I think you're really cute."

She leaned in and wrapped her arms around his neck, giving him a kiss that left no mistake about her intentions. Annie pulled back slowly, looking at him with fire in her eyes. "I don't know what came over me. I've never initiated a first kiss before."

"That's okay with me, Annie." Jack put his arms around her and pulled her close.

She liked the feel of his body through her thin summer dress. She could feel his muscular chest as he pressed against her breasts and felt her nipples become aroused as he held her. Without thinking, she pressed her hips against his and felt his interest. The kiss that followed was an explosion of passion and sexual energy that surprised them both.

After catching her breath, Annie reluctantly moved out of Jack's arms, turned off the lights, and locked the door. Turning toward him, she said, "Don't move, and stay where you are." She smiled at him as she walked across the gallery to a storage area, she knew held blankets used for protecting paintings.

Coming back, she looked at Jack as he stood in the darkened gallery. He looked unsure about what was going to happen next, but she knew. Annie spread four blankets, one on top of another, on the gallery floor; far enough back from the window, but close enough so the streetlights gave the room a warm glow. When she looked again at Jack, he was smiling. *Smart boy.*

She watched him grab a cold beer from the nearby cooler. He took a long drink, but she saw his eyes were focused on her as she moved around the gallery. Finished, she walked toward him, took the beer from his hand, and brought it to her lips. Slowly, she let the cold liquid flow down her dry throat.

Jack smiled. "Go ahead and finish it. I think I've had my quota for the evening."

She smiled as she drained the golden nectar. "God, that tasted good. I didn't realize how hot and thirsty I was." She lowered the empty bottle to her chest. She rolled it across the fullness of her breast, resting the bottle in her ample cleavage. "Oh, this feels good and cool."

She watched his eyes move, taking in her total package. She knew he was wondering what was next, and she didn't give him long to wait. Annie never broke eye contact as she slowly, ever so slowly, loosened her sundress. Jack's smile got bigger and bigger as she exposed more and more of herself as the dress unwrapped.

"I love dresses without buttons," he said.

When she finished opening her dress, she leaned in to Jack and pressed her body to his. She savored his long, slow kiss. Annie's arms dropped to her side and Jack cradled her face as he continued his kiss. She felt his fingers move through her hair, down to her tan shoulders, and then he gently slipped off the dress. As it fell to the gallery floor in a pile at their feet, she became more passionate. Finally, they separated. Annie lowered herself to the blankets. Looking up, she said, "Do you like what you see, Mr. Stevenson?"

Chapter Eighteen

Opening her eyes, it took a few moments to recognize where she was, and then she remembered the night's pleasant encounter. Annie grimaced with pain, understanding why her back hurt as her hand moved across the old blankets, then smiled as she felt Jack's warm body spooned behind her, his right hand gently holding her right breast. She pressed his arm to her chest, snuggling closer. She thought about what happened last night and why. *This is the way mornings are supposed to be. It felt good to wake up with someone next to her.*

She thought about Jack as she lay there. He was everything she craved in a lover. He had the passion of Dennis, the tenderness of Peter, and the good looks of both. *Annie, get hold of yourself, it was one night.*

After making love, they had stayed awake until 4:00 a.m. talking about schools, the art world, and his goals. Both knew in the wee hours of the morning they were lucky to meet each other.

That afternoon, she was still excited, as she had never been before. She needed to talk to Rita, who would understand. Even though they didn't see each other for months at a time, they talked all the time. She laughed as she thought of her phone bills, but she was her best friend. She could talk to Rita about anything, anything besides Dennis. If Rita knew what happened, she never brought it up.

Annie called her that night. "How's it going?"

"Hi, stranger. I was wondering what happened to you. You aren't sick or anything, are you? Wait, it's Sunday, I forgot. I get confused sometimes with my crazy schedule," Rita said. "How's work going?"

"Fine. I've been really busy with the gallery and all. It's really starting to work out just the way I planned it."

"Hey, that's great. How are you and Peter doing?" Silence. "Annie, is everything okay?"

"No and yes!" Annie answered.

"No and Yes? What kind of answer is that? Tell me!"

"Peter and I have called it quits."

"Huh?" Rita said. "I thought you guys were perfect for each other."

"It was just too difficult for us to carry on a long distance relationship. It's no one's fault. We both have our own thing going. Neither of us wants to pull up shop and move. Unfortunately, it seems our business and careers are more important than each other. As painful as it was, I decided to move on. Being alone without anyone to share the ups and downs of life reached a tipping point. I cried all Friday night."

"Annie, I am so sorry for you. For both of you."

"Yeah, thanks, but we'll survive." Then Annie remembered the rest. "I do have some good news!"

"Good news! What is that?"

"I met Jack."

"Jack!" Rita said.

"I just met him last night. I think it was love at first sight. Can you believe it?"

"Come on, Annie, you're kidding me; you never do anything that fast. I'm the one who's usually jumping into bed with someone on the first date."

"I know, Rita. Jack's a combination of Peter and Dennis, if you know what I mean. Jack's gentle, smart, and funny like Peter, and I really trust him. He's got the great looks and charisma that Dennis has. I think I found the best of both men in one guy. *Oh shit, why did I include Dennis?* Do you ever talk to Dennis anymore?"

"No, not really. I got fed up with all his bullshit and running around with other women."

Annie felt guilty. *I really need to tell her what happened between Dennis and me. She of all people should know how seductive he is.*

"He could be real sweet when he wanted to be," said Rita. "You know he sure excited me, but it was all for him. I finally got fed up. Shit, just thinking about him now gets me excited. You know what I mean, Annie?"

"I do. He had that ability. He knew it and used it." Annie took a deep breath. "What I'm getting at, Rita, is that Jack has that same ability to get me excited like Dennis did to you."

Rita sighed again. "That makes you a lucky woman."

It was like old times back at Wilson's. They talked about Jack and a new guy in Rita's life, Zach. They talked about two hours catching up on everything.

"You know, Annie, I saw where Northwestern Medical School has a six-month instruction program on a new surgical procedure I think I could apply for. I believe the Army will pay for it. If I get accepted into the program, we can spend time together, like old times."

"Oh, Rita, that would be great. I can hardly wait for you to meet Jack. I know it's only two days since we met, but he might be the one I've been waiting for."

"I hope so, Annie. It's not good to go through life alone. I'll call you when I know more about the school. Got to go, it's getting late. I'm on call in a little while. I love you."

"I love you, too." Annie slowly put the receiver down and looked out her window at the Chicago skyline.

**

The next evening, Jack cooked his specialty, macaroni and cheese with bacon. She'd laughed when he suggested it, but the joke was on her when she found it surprisingly tasty, especially with his favorite cold Budweiser.

That night, they took a walk along Michigan Avenue, and then on a lark, a romantic carriage ride.

"You know Annie, everything is happening so fast between us, but I know when I'm with someone very special. It reminds me of movies I've seen set during WWII. The soldier meets someone a few days before he's to be shipped out; they fall in love and get married. It happens. My parents knew couples like that, and they were still happily married. I feel that way about us."

Does he really mean all this? I think he does. I don't think I've ever been with someone like him before. As she rode in the horse-drawn carriage this warm summer night she had a feeling from his words and actions of the last few days, that this might be the person for her.

The next day, as morning peeked through the loft's windows, she watched as he propped his head up on his hand. She watched his eyes move across her body, looking at her as the sun came streaming through her window; its rays creeping across her naked body. She felt the light caress her face, and then move across the gentle rise and fall of her breasts. She made soft moans as he touched her. Finally, she raised her arms in a morning stretch. "Good morning, sleepyhead." She laughed at him and then kissed him. "I hope my breath isn't too bad."

She got up and shuffled in a slow meandering way to turn on the morning coffee. He laughed as she hurried back and climbed back into bed and then snuggled next to him. He kissed her, as the coffee aroma wafted through the loft and they made love at a leisurely pace. It was only the third day being together, but she wanted it to be like this forever.

Tuesday started hot and humid. Lake Michigan's cooling effect wasn't a factor since the radio already proclaimed it a scorcher with no wind. It was supposed to get to the mid-90s with high humidity.

Annie looked at her calendar while Jack took a shower. "That's right," she said with a smile. "I have a meeting with Thomas at his gallery today." *I wonder what he's got on his mind. It didn't seem like he just wanted to shoot the shit. At least it'll give me something to think about besides Jack.* "Life is good, thank you, God. I owe you one." She slipped off her robe and opened the bathroom door. "Want me to wash your back?"

**

Thomas was waiting for her when she arrived at 11:50 a.m. "I like a woman who's early," he said and gave her a hug.

"If you were from Wisconsin, Thomas, you'd know that we call that Lombardi time." Coach Vince Lombardi required everyone to show up ten minutes early, otherwise you were considered late. My dad loves the Packers and Coach Lombardi." She smiled. "Where are we going to eat? Some place expensive, I hope, since you're buying."

"Where would you like to go?"

"How about a Vienna hot dog, fries, and a root beer? I haven't had that for a long time," Annie said.

"Man, you're letting me off cheap. Let's go before you change your mind."

They walked a couple of blocks to a hot dog place and found a seat.

"Thank God it's air-conditioned, because it's ninety-two and still climbing," said Thomas.

"They'd have their shirts off at Wrigley field today," Annie said.

After a bit more chitchat over hot dogs, Thomas got down to business. "Do you know why I asked you to come to lunch today?"

"I figured you were going to give me your usual pearls of wisdom, or else you wanted to repay me for all the Old Style you consume at my place. Is that it, Thomas?"

He laughed. "That could be it, but it isn't."

She notices how he is looking at her, like her dad often did. Something's up, but what? Her stomach tightened.

"I've been watching you since you first worked for me. I like what I see. You've done a great job building your gallery into something you can be proud of. You treat everyone with respect and courtesy. The artists like working with you, and you do a great job of handling their various egos. Most importantly, you love the business."

Annie reached across the small table and patted his hand. "Thank you, Thomas, but you know you guided my career with your wise advice."

"It's funny you should say that because, when I see you and the way you act, I see me. You know I think of you as the daughter I never will have."

"Really? How nice." she said.

"I have an offer I'd like you to think about. I'd like you to think about combining our galleries and becoming partners. You don't have to come up with any money for this partnership. Your investment is your time and your current gallery. There will be no name change. It's the act of combining our energies for art that will make it work. I'll still do my thing, and you'll do yours, but eventually my business will be yours when I'm gone." He sat back and folded his hands solemnly. "I just don't want to see my life's work disappear after I'm gone. This way, I know it'll be in good hands, and I can continue to mold the business through you."

Annie put a hand over her mouth. Her eyes moistened. "Thomas, I don't know what to say."

"Say yes, Annie. I think we'll make a great team."

"Before I do that, I want to tell you about someone I just met who I think is going to be a big part of my life going forward. He might rob me of time I used to spend on the business because I didn't have anything else to do."

She talked about Jack for several minutes and, when she was finished, Thomas smiled. "I'm so happy for you. I see Jack only helping you, making you stronger, and giving you another perspective on life and business."

She got up, walked around the table, and gave him a big hug. "I guess you've got a new partner."

"I'm so glad you said yes. This takes a big load off my mind, Annie."

"Thanks, Thomas. I won't let you down." She gave him a kiss on the forehead and a hug.

Chapter Nineteen

Dennis had been in Charleston for a couple of years working for Deacon's new operation, which specialized in building sailboats geared for charter operations like Peter's. On the fast track at the company, he continued working for them full time after finishing college and turned out to be a whiz kid at productions and operations. When an opportunity to manage its Charleston presented itself, the job was offered to him. Being single meant he could easily move without the headaches and costs someone with a family might have.

Dennis loved Charleston. Everything was new to him. He found a nice place he could afford on the water, just off the main channel, something he could never have managed back in Wisconsin.

In addition to owning his first house, the women of Charleston excited him. With three colleges and a vibrant downtown with lots of restaurants and bars, he was having a great time. Nothing had really changed for him dating wise. "Love'em and leave'em" was still his mantra. Though they weren't all one-night stands, if they wanted more than one date, they played by his rules. If not, they were history.

He had been seeing Carolina for almost four months. A hairdresser he'd met over oysters and beer, she'd entertained Dennis with her funny stories of clients. With red hair and a great body like Rita, she did like to fool around, but that's where the similarities between the two women ended. Carolina was okay for the time being. Rita still excited him when he thought about their time in Door County and how he'd loved her wildness.

If Carolina didn't work out, there were always more. Eventually, she'd get tired of his ways. The only time his system backfired was when he was seeing Annie at UW-Milwaukee. Peter was out of the picture in Miami. It was the first time he changed his womanizing ways, and for five months, he was loyal to her, a record, but then he got bored. He started sneaking around with other women, got caught, and Annie was done with him. Looking back, he knew he made a mistake with her, but that was his life when it came to women. So many women, so little time, he thought with a smile.

Thoughts of Annie reminded him that Peter was flying in tomorrow to see the operations at Deacon's Charleston factory. Dennis was looking forward to seeing him. It had been awhile.

The next day flew by after picking Peter up at the airport. Dennis showed Peter around Deacon's operation in Charleston and the sailboats they built there. He could tell he was really impressed with the size and quality of the boats. In the end, Peter ordered two 38 foot, two 40's and two 44's. "This should get us started," he said, "I think I can get more orders for the charter/ownership program I implemented in the last couple of years."

With work finally finished, Dennis took Peter out to his place. They were going to have some huge T-bones, salad, and lots of cold beer.

"Dennis, this place reminds me of Harry's Tavern on Kangaroo Lake."

"You're right. I knew it reminded me of some place up north, but I couldn't put my finger on it. Harry was a good shit. Remember, he used to sell us those little Joe's for a quarter and a big bottle for 35 cents."

Peter laughed. "Didn't he just have one arm?"

"He did, you're right." Dennis nodded. "So, how are Rita and Annie? I haven't talked to Rita in a long time. Last I knew, she was still at UCLA becoming a doctor. I think she's still there?"

Peter looked out toward the water and then back to Dennis. "I haven't heard much about her except she's in the Army. Annie said she got the Army to pay for her medical school, and now she's obligated for six or eight years. That's about all I know." Peter raised the cold beer to his mouth and took a sip. "Didn't you keep in touch?"

"Not really, you know me. She got pissed off when I didn't pay enough attention to her. I was seeing other women on the side and she had enough. She broke it off even though we cared about each other. She deserves better than me anyhow." He shrugged. "So, Annie's doing great in Chicago with her own gallery?"

Peter nodded. "She and another guy are combining their operations so she'll eventually own several galleries."

Dennis looked out over the marsh. "You guys still trying to make it work?"

Peter looked down at the gravel at the base of the porch steps and kicked it. "We tried for a long time, but we're both too stubborn about who was going to have to move and start over again. It just wasn't going to work. We broke up a month ago. We're still friends. I still love her. I know she loves me, but sometimes it works out this way. What can I say?"

"Sorry to hear that. Any new loves on the horizon?" Dennis said, hoping to move the conversation forward.

"Matter of fact, there is," Peter said with a spark of excitement in his voice. "Her name is Paula. She works for me as a charter boat skipper and delivers boats for clients."

Peter spent the next few hours filling Dennis in about his business, Mahoney, and Paula. By the time the beer ran out, it was one a.m. "Time to call it a night." Peter said.

"Kind of reminds me of coming into the cabin at Hotel Ephraim and sleeping on your floor," Dennis said. "The tables are turned tonight. You're sleeping on my lumpy couch and I'm in a nice bed."

"Ahh, that first summer." Peter said. "So, there's something that's been bugging me since that first summer?"

"Ask away," Dennis said, though he felt his smile disappear.

"I wasn't off too much when I hit you for saying those things about getting into Annie's pants, was I?"

"You know how I am. I can't help it if the women want me." Dennis laughed, trying to make light of the situation.

"I don't know about you, Dennis. I guess you'll never change when it comes to women. Just for the record, Rita came on to me because you were fucking some babes in Sturgeon Bay. She was sick of the way you treated her. I could have done what you did, but I won't do that to a friend. I guess you and Annie were somewhat alike. You'd both deceive someone you care about just for a little cheap sex! You both make me sick when I think how you deceived Rita and me."

He threw his beer hard enough into the garbage can to tip it over. "I think I've had enough talk about the good old days." He suddenly stood up. "I'll find a place to stay in town, if you don't mind."

"Hey, don't leave. It's too late to find anything now. Besides, that was a long time ago."

"Go to Hell!" Peter said and walked away to calm down.

**

Later that month in Chicago, Annie felt herself glowing with positive energy. It was a good night at the gallery. Looking at Jack, she smiled. "You are my good luck charm, Mr. Stevenson. Ever since I met you, I've had record results. Is it fate?"

"I think it is," Jack said.

She watched him walk to the light switch and turned off the gallery lights, and then walk over to her. His arms wrapped around her, and then she felt his lips engulf hers in a long sensuous kiss.

"Wow, what got into you?" she said and tried to catch her breath.

He smiled. "Do you know what today is?"

Annie was slightly panic-stricken as she tried to remember. What was he driving at? She leaned over and gave him a quick kiss. "Yes, I do. It's our one month anniversary," she said.

"Oh, right, it is our one month anniversary, but that's not the answer I was looking for. Can't you think of anything else today might be?"

She scrunched up her face. "Jack, I can't think of anything else." Butterflies started to flutter inside. What's he smiling at? She felt his hand take her left hand in his, then reach into his pants pocket, and pulled out a diamond ring.

Before Annie could say anything, he said, "I can't believe you didn't know that today is the day we got engaged." Getting down on one knee, he said, "Annie Wilson, will you marry me?" He slipped the ring on her finger.

She looked at him, tears welling up. Pulling him close, she wrapped her arms around him, and kissed him with all the love and tenderness she possessed.

"I've been waiting for someone like you my whole life. I love you, Jack. I'd love to be your partner in life. Yes, I'll marry you."

**

"Rita, it's Annie. Did I wake you?"

"No, I'm just having a cup of coffee. I'm on call. What's up? Are you okay?"

Annie giggled. "I'm great, and I'm lying in bed with a slight headache after celebrating last night."

"Celebrating?"

"Rita…I was wondering…would you be my maid of honor?"

Rita let out a huge scream and then started laughing. "Yes, of course. I'm so happy for you. God, that was quick. Didn't you guys just meet?"

"A month ago to the day," Annie squealed. "We're in love! We want to spend the rest of our lives together. Jack didn't want to drag things out, and I agree. How does September sound for the wedding?"

"This September?"

"Yes. We thought we'd go out to Vegas and get married there."

"What did your parents say?"

"They don't know yet. You're the first to know. I'll call Mom and Dad next. I'm sure my folks will love Jack. Dad doesn't know investment banking, but he does understand hard work. Once he finds out how much Jack expects to make from investment banking, I think Dad will be okay. Mom will love him because I love him. She'll make a Door County cherry pie for him. Knowing Mom, she'll probably send him one every week."

"Are you going to call Peter?"

"Of course I am! We're still friends. At least I hope we're still friends. I can't believe he wouldn't be happy for me. I'd be happy for him."

Rita sighed. "I know, it…it's just so sudden. How about Dennis? Are you going to invite him?"

"Dennis? Do you want me to invite him?"

Rita thought about it for a while. "Yeah, it's okay with me. It would be nice to see the asshole after all these years. I'm sure he looks as good as ever! Maybe I should bring my new friend, Zach. That will keep him at a distance, or more important, it will keep me at a distance. I don't want to start up that relationship again after all these years. He was such a jerk back then, but he still gets me going just thinking about him."

"I bet." *Thank God I don't feel that way about him anymore. I've got Jack now.*

"Enough of that. I'm so happy for you and Jack. When you set the date, just call me."

"It's going to be pretty quick, Rita. I'm thinking somewhere around the 15th to 21st of the month."

"What about my dress? What color do you want me to get?"

"Just pick something up that goes with white."

They both laughed. "I'll find something, but don't you want to give me an idea of what color you might like? After all, you are an artist. Aren't artists usually concerned about getting the right color?"

"You're right." Annie thought about it a moment. "How about a light peach? That should go well with your red hair."

"All right, but don't you go getting mad at me if you don't like it when you see it."

"Don't worry. The only thing I'll care about is that Jack, you, and my parents are there. We decided to go to Las Vegas for the wedding because we thought it would be fun without a lot of fanfare. We'll have a quick ceremony and then party."

"Oh, this will be so much fun. I can drive over from LA in about five hours. I'm looking forward to meeting Jack."

"He's looking forward to meeting you, too."

"By the way, I got the okay to do some extra studies at Northwestern Medical School, so it looks like I'll see you guys for at least six months after you're married."

"That will be so neat. Jack is going to look for a job in Chicago. Investment banking is very lucrative, but also very time-intensive and stressful. He tells me when you start out, you do all the shit jobs. Grunt work, he says."

"Oh. He's going to be a high paid gopher," said Rita.

"You got it. It will be nice to have somebody's shoulder to cry on as I become an abandoned newlywed."

"I'll call you when I get all the information on Northwestern."

"Sounds good, Annie, I better get back to the sick and needy. I love you and congratulations. I'm really looking forward to seeing you and meeting Jack. Let me know what happens with Dennis and Peter."

"Okay. I love you too, Rita."

Chapter Twenty

Peter was back from Charleston and hard at work getting ready for the new boats from Deacon's when Mahoney came in to see how everything was going.

"You can't believe how nice the new boats are," Peter told him. "I can hardly wait to get them here. We should easily be able to sell them on the buy and charter program once we get them up and running."

Mahoney pushed his cap back. "Let's hope so. We put a lot of money down to get those boats, and we really don't want to tie up that much of our capital too long."

"I know, but I haven't steered you wrong yet, have I?"

"No, you haven't. You're the best thing that's happened to this organization, outside of me."

"You were the organization. I just gave it a little more life." Peter gaze moved to the many boats in their slips, "Speaking of life, where is Paula?"

"She's out on Sea Biscuit," Mahoney said. "Matter of fact, I think she's tying up right now. Give her a chance to check the clients off the boat and then you can jump her bones."

"Mahoney, you are incorrigible! But it is a good idea. She sure is beautiful. I'm really falling for her."

"Peter, now I'm speaking like a dad to a son because that's how I feel about you. Don't waste time waiting for things to be perfect, because they never are. If you love her, and she feels the same about you, get together. I had a great life with Mary. I wish she was still here, but she isn't. If I could find someone now, I'd wait a New York minute to ask her to marry me, because a person shouldn't be alone. But until I find that special sixty-five-year-old Miss America, I'll just have to be content manning the gas dock and helping all those young things tie up the boats. I sure hope it stays warm. I hate it when they put on those cover-ups."

Peter laughed. "You're too much. Thanks for the advice, Mahoney. You've got the job on the gas pier for as long as your heart holds out," he said and gave him a slap on the back.

"Thanks. I think watching the pretties will help me live another twenty years."

Serious thoughts crowded Peter's mind. *I have been thinking more about Paula. Especially after finding out about Annie and her future husband. Makes a guy think.*

He waited until everything settled down on the charter boat before he walked over and sat down next to Paula. "How'd it go? You look beat," he said.

"I am. It got really rough coming back. When we were about seven miles out, the wind shifted slightly from the northwest and that's when the seas picked up against the Gulf Stream. The swells grew pretty high, and they were steep and breaking. I'm glad we didn't have too far to go. Stuff started to fly around down below, so it's kind of messy."

Peter nodded.

"The people were happy I was along. They know how to sail, but they had never sailed on anything bigger than an inland lake and weren't used to what an ocean could throw at them. Throw in the fact that the tide was moving out, and it was dicey."

Paula got a mischievous look in her eye. "Want to help me clean up? I'll make it worth your while. Besides, I haven't seen you for a week. I missed you." She leaned over and gave Peter a long kiss. "Without you here, the week dragged."

"That's nice to hear." He got up and gave her a hug, lifting her feet slightly off the ground. "I missed you too! Sometimes management has to pitch in and help. This might be one of those times."

He put his hands on the hatch and swung down into the cabin. Then he helped Paula down. Sliding the hatch cover closed, he turned and looked into her eyes. "I think we need to check out the V-berth."

"I know what you have in mind, but the V-berth is really a mess."

"Oh sure, you're just tired, and you have every right to be, but I missed you so much. I just wanted to snuggle for a while and kiss you. Then we'll clean up."

Paula patted Peter on the back. "I am very tired. How about tomorrow night? We could go out for a nice dinner, a few green necks and home to my place. I'll be very friendly. How's that?"

"But I really missed you. It can't take too long to clean the boat. Then we can go out tonight." He leaned close. "I've got a secret to tell you. I'm really horny for you!"

"Okay, that's really nice but this boat's a mess. If you don't believe me, just go forward and look for yourself. It's going to take more than a few minutes to clean the V-berth. We threw most of the loose shit up there when the seas got rough."

"Okay, I will!" He opened the bulkhead door and stuck his head in. "Holy shit, it looks like a tossed salad of boating equipment. You weren't kidding." He turned around.

Paula had her T-shirt off and was unhooking her bra. She kicked off her deck shoes. With a twinkle in her eyes and a huge smile, she hooked her thumbs on her shorts and thong then slid everything down to the holly teak floor. "Is this more of what you had in mind, Peter? There is plenty of room here," she said, patting the main cabin cushion on the settee. "I missed you just as much as you missed me. Men don't have a lock on being horny."

It didn't take Peter long to tear his clothes off. Putting a board in the hatch for privacy, he turned back to Paula.

"Now what did I want to do?"

"Come on! Don't play with me or I'll get dressed."

"Yes, madam. Whatever you say."

They melted together. A week's passion exploded, their lips touched. They were home, together, where they felt most comfortable, in each other's arms, on a boat.

Their passion temporally exhausted, they savored holding each other, and napped. The motion and sounds of the water lapping against the hull created a private symphony for Paula and Peter that evening. Halyards caressing the mast, seagulls singing, the high-pitched whine of an outboard's prop through the water; all combined to serenade them. After what seemed like hours, they got dressed, cleaned the boat, and locked it.

"Let's get something to eat. Good sex always makes me hungry, and I'm really hungry," said Paula.

Peter smiled and took her hand as she stepped down from the boat. "If that's the case, you've earned two meals."

She playfully punched him in the arm. "I just might take you up on that."

"Let's go to Tommy's. I could go for some grouper, shrimp, and cold beer," Peter said as he pulled her close. It was a beautiful evening with a full moon just peeking over the horizon. It was going to be a perfect night.

This was what love was all about, Peter thought as he and Paula walked to the car. Mahoney was right; you don't need anything more than a good woman at your side to make everything right with the world. He had her, now what was he going to do?

"Paula, why don't we drive over to Key West? It's been a while since I've been there, and it would be fun for you to show me the place from your perspective. It would give me a chance to spend some time with you, away from the marina. Matter of fact, I'd like to meet your family."

She looked at him with eyes the size of saucers. "You know what you're asking? You're going to come under the scrutiny of my father, brothers and uncles." Now she was smiling. "You think you're ready for that?"

"Only one way to find out."

"Okay, you asked for it. We could go over tomorrow for a couple of days. I don't have anything going now for four days, so I don't think the boss will mind. Do you?"

"No, I don't think he will." He gave her a little kiss on her head as they arrived at Tommy's. When they walked in, it was like the first night they met, with Mahoney holding court. When he saw them, he raised his glass and kept on talking. They got their two cold beers, ordered the grouper sandwiches and some boiled shrimp, and then sat down to listen.

"I hope Mahoney's got some new stories," said Paula.

Peter just shrugged. "When he's on a roll like this, I envision him being like Hemingway, telling never ending boating and fishing stories. In fact, Mahoney told me that, when he was younger, he met the man himself."

Paula turned to Peter. "You know that my family fished with Hemingway a fair amount? Everyone who's lived in Key West for a while has Hemingway stories. My family's had restaurants and fishing boats since the forties, so they fed and fished with him. His favorite hangouts in Key West were Sloppy Joe's and Captain Tony's."

"I love his stories. I just wish I could have met him. I love The Old Man And The Sea, but the Nick Adams Stories, and A Moveable Feast give a snapshot of the real Hemingway, but that's my personal opinion."

Paula nodded. "You know Peter, Hemingway was just one of the characters of Key West. He's the most famous, but there are so many more. Wait until you meet my family. They're just as memorable, and they're alive!"

"I'm looking forward to it." *I did want to do this didn't I?*

Then he looked at Paula and he felt very much in love. Everything about her reinforced that feeling. Their bodies melted together as one. When one moved, they both moved. Peter loved to kiss Paula's neck and shoulders throughout the night. When he did, she let out a little sigh, even if she was asleep. She would press his hand to her breast as she slept, almost like a baby would hold a blanket to its body for security.

The next day, after making love, showering, and then making love again, they finally threw things together and drove to Key West. He actually was excited to be there. The trip down was educational and beautiful. Peter had the luxury of Paula's insight to the various islands and their history, plus just enjoying the scenery from a higher vantage point than the deck of a boat.

When they pulled into the driveway of her parents' small house, Peter was surprised to see the entire Guerrero clan waiting to welcome her home and meet Peter.

"I called while you were showering," Paula said with a smile. Once out of the car, she got hugs and kisses from her mom, dad, aunts, uncles and cousins. Then all eyes turned to Peter.

"Mom and Dad, this is Peter. Peter, this is my mom and dad."

"Nice to meet you, Mr. and Mrs. Guerrero."

No one said a word. No one extended a hand. Peter started sweating as if it was much hotter than 85 degrees outside. He didn't know what to make of the family, until he turned to Paula.

"Tough crowd!" he said.

This cracked up Paula's dad. He stuck out his hand and gave a warm shake. Then all the uncles and aunts closed in and shook Peter's hand, with the aunts patting him on the back.

Paula's dad put his arm around Peter's shoulder. "We just wanted to see what you were made of. You have to have a sense of humor in this family, because in Key West, life is not always fair. You'll do, Peter Franklin. Paula doesn't make too many bad decisions, and if she brought you to this mob knowing what we usually do, then you must be okay." He winked. "Let's have something to eat and drink. We all want to hear about you and your company."

Peter could tell by the hugs and kisses Paula got from family and friends, as well as how misty her eyes got as she greeted everyone, that she was happy to be home. He was glad he passed the first test with Carlos and her uncles. He was sure there would be other tests. He hoped he could charm them just as he charmed Paula when they first met at Tommy's Bar.

They had lots of wine, fruit, and shrimp as the afternoon slipped by. Small children were always nearby, and Peter marveled at how patient everyone was with them. There was plenty of laughter and storytelling. As it got closer to the dinner hour, the family started getting ready to go to the restaurant.

"Come on, Peter. You can see how the Guerreros do things."

It was about six blocks to the restaurant located in the old historic part of Key West. The place was really jumping. Peter marveled at how sunburned and happy everyone was, though he wasn't sure if it was the sun or the rum.

As a guy and gal sang old favorites in the bar, the waitresses delivered rum and cokes, gin and tonics, cold beer, and food. It was a gold mine, and very well organized.

As soon as Carlos walked into the restaurant, he was the model of efficiency. He talked to his staff and he talked to his customers, engaging them in simple conversation and always thanking them for coming to his family's business. Then he went back to the kitchen and spent a few minutes there making sure everything was going okay. Finally, he went to the bar and talked to his managing bartender, Paula's uncle Tomas.

Once he was satisfied that everything was going okay, he came back and talked to Peter. Total time: 25 minutes. He explained how his grandfather developed this system 75 years ago, and that he got most of his ideas from his father. Each generation passed on their knowledge to the next when the younger generation took over.

"I think the reason we're so successful is because we don't try to change a system that works. We tweak it here and there, but we never change what works."

Paula moved to Peter's side when she saw her father leave. "How you doing?" she asked. "Is Dad treating you OK?"

"I'm doing just fine. I really like your family. Everyone is very nice. I know I'm getting the once over from family, friends, and staff. I've even noticed several people walking past and looking me over. Everyone is great. I'm glad we did this."

She leaned over and gave Peter a kiss on the cheek while she slipped her arm around his back. "Mom said you're very handsome and that you must be smart to do what you've done with your business. Having brains and using them is very important to my mom. So, in Mom's book, you're okay."

"I'm glad your mom feels that way. Have you talked to your dad to see how he feels about me?"

"Only for a minute, in the kitchen just a little while ago. He just said that he thought you were very nice and he trusted you to do what was right for me. That's pretty good for my dad, so he must like you too."

Paula crinkled up her face at Peter and gave him another kiss.

"Do they like me enough for us to sleep together tonight?" he asked.

"I take back what I said about you being smart; I don't think they'd be okay with that at this stage, Peter."

"Just kidding, but you know I'll miss you."

"And I'll miss you too, but we can be apart for one night."

"I know." Raising his hand to her face, he caressed her cheek. "It's just that I don't want to be apart from you any more than I have to. Besides, I like waking up in the morning with you next to me. I don't need a blanket either. When I get cold, I just snuggle closer to you."

"Well, that's a pretty good reason right there," Paula said. "I'm sure Mom and Dad will understand and tell you to move right into my bedroom. They don't want you to get cold."

"That's what I thought, too," Peter said with a big smile. "Matter of fact, I think I am going to talk to your dad right now." He got off the stool and started toward the kitchen.

She grabbed his hand. "Peter, you aren't really going to talk to my dad about this, are you?"

He leaned over and gave her a peck on the cheek. "Maybe not, but I do need to talk to him about something. I'll be back in five or ten minutes, okay?"

He found Carlos helping move some produce from a refrigerator to the prep area.

"Carlos, would you have a few minutes to talk when you get done with this? It's pretty important. I could give you a hand, if you'd like."

"No, that's all right, I'm just finishing up here. The place is really hopping tonight, so I like to help when I see they need help, but we're just about done now. Give me a couple of minutes."

A man of his word, he was done in two minutes. "Okay, Peter. What would you like to talk about?"

"As you might imagine, I really care about your daughter. Even though we've only known each other for about six weeks, I love her with all my heart. I know she is the right person for me."

Carlos's eyes burned into Peter as he spoke. Peter was sure he knew something about passion; didn't he have the same passion for Inga?

"We have a passion for the sea and boats and, most important, for each other. I know she feels the same way about me as I do about her. You and Inga and your family have raised a wonderful daughter. Carlos, I am asking permission to marry your daughter. I have a good business that should provide a good income, and we can make it grow together. I promise you I will be a good husband and take care of her."

Carlos did not say anything but just stared at Peter. To Peter, those moments seemed like forever. Finally, Carlos smiled, grabbed Peter's shoulder, and looked deep into his eyes. "Peter, I believe that you love my daughter and will take care of her. I have noticed how she looks at you. I knew from the first moment you pulled up to the house this afternoon that you were the one for her. We welcome you into the Guerrero family. Have you asked Paula yet?"

"No, I wanted your permission first."

"I appreciate the courtesy. I'm sure you know that Paula's mother and I fell in love over a very short period of time. We are still very much in love, so it's not how long you know someone, but how you treat them each and every day. Do you have a ring?"

"Not yet."

"Wait here, I'll be back in a minute." Carlos went into his office and closed the door. He came out a minute later with a big smile on his face. In his deeply tanned hand was a beautiful diamond and silver engagement ring. "I had to get this out of the safe. Peter, you would do our family a great honor if you would present Paula with this engagement ring. It was my grandmother's, God rest her soul. She would have loved to have Paula wear it as her first great grandchild. As you can tell around here, we love tradition."

"I would be honored." Peter put the ring in his pocket.

Carlos gave him a big hug and a kiss on the cheek.

"I'm sure she'll love it because it's her grandmother's, but if she wants to pick something herself, I'll give it back to you."

Carlos looked at him, startled. "I know my daughter better than you on this. She'll love the ring. Go propose!"

**

Peter turned and walked through the double doors that separated the kitchen from the dining room and bar. Paula was talking to her cousin, Angel, when Peter came up. She introduced him, they exchanged a few pleasantries, and then he moved to rejoin some of his friends at another table.

"Well, what did he say? Did you ask about us sleeping together?"

"Kind of. He said he'd think about it and get back to me later tonight."

"That sounds like Dad. Oh well, you gave it the old college try."

"Let's go for a walk outside, maybe down near the water. It's so nice out this evening."

As they were walking out of the restaurant, they saw Carlos walk up to Inga and start talking to her.

"You don't think Dad is telling Mom that you wanted to sleep with me tonight, do you?"

"I don't know. They're your parents."

Just at that moment, Inga brought her hand to her mouth and looked over at Peter and Paula as they were leaving.

As they walked out the door, Paula asked, "Did she look mad?"

"No, I don't think so. She sure looked surprised, didn't she?" It was a beautiful night, just a whisper of a breeze, with the moon high in the sky. In the background, the music of Key West's many bars intermingled with the sound of palm leaves rustling in the night air. As they walked to the piers a couple of blocks away, a motorcycle revved its engine and someone yelled, "I want more rum."

Peter took Paula's hand as they walked among the boats. The magic of Key West was there. After a tour of the pier, they found a bench and sat down. Paula moved close to Peter and they kissed. She tilted her head, resting it on Peter's chest.

"I can hear your heart beating. It sounds strong and steady."

"I am strong and steady, Paula, just as you are. When we are together, we're just that."

She looked up at him. "We are, aren't we?"

"Yes, we are. What do you say we make it permanently that way?"

"What? What do you mean by that?"

"I mean I want to be with you forever. Paula, I want you to marry me."

She leaned back and looked at him. "You aren't kidding, are you?"

"No, I'm not." He reached into his pocket. "Paula, will you marry me?"

She looked at the ring, then at Peter, and gave him a long, loving kiss. When she pulled back, tears streamed down her cheek. "Yes, Peter, I'll marry you. I love you with all my heart."

They just held each other, not saying a word.

After a few minutes, Paula broke the silence with a chuckle. "When you went in the kitchen, you went to ask my dad, didn't you?"

"Yep. Do you recognize the ring?"

Paula held the ring up to the moonlight. "No, I don't, but it's very beautiful. Did you pick it out all by yourself?"

"No, your great grandmother did."

"What?"

"Your dad gave it to me. He asked if I would give it to you for your engagement ring. He said you would do the family honor by wearing it."

"Oh, Peter" She started to cry. "That's so beautiful," was all she could say between sobs.

When they walked into the restaurant, Inga came right over. Paula held up her hand, showing her mother the ring. "Peter just asked me to marry him and I've accepted. It's great Grandma Guerrero's ring. Isn't it beautiful?"

"Your father just told me. He presented Peter with the ring. Grandma is smiling."

Chapter Twenty-One

Peter called Dennis when he got back to Miami and told him the news.

"I want you to come down and meet Paula before the wedding, so bring one of your friends. I know you have plenty."

There was hesitation on the phone before Dennis answered. "You still want me to come down after what happened between Annie and me?"

"Don't ask me why, but yes. You're my friend, and I guess I'm just like all the women you left in the dust. I don't trust you as far as I could throw you, but for some reason, god help me, I like you." Peter paused. "I guess I know you'd do anything for me if it didn't involve women."

Dennis laughed. "Okay, I'll call you when I have a better handle on my available dates. And congratulations on your engagement." Then he paused. "Are you going to Annie's wedding next week?"

"Oh shit, I forgot about it. I said I would, and I haven't made plans or anything."

"It didn't take them long to get engaged and set the date, did it?"

"No, it didn't. That's what got me to think more seriously about Paula and me. But our wedding is off in the distance. I'll have to ask Paula if she'd like to go to Vegas for the wedding. Are you going?"

"Yes, I need a break, and Vegas is fun. I guess they got a special deal at the Four Seasons."

"Oh, I forgot it was at the Four Seasons. Now I know Paula will want to go. After I had her stay at the Four Seasons in Miami, she'd go anywhere to stay in one of their hotels. We'll both love it. It will be nice to see Annie and meet Jack. He's got to be nice if Annie fell in love with him, especially that fast."

"You should talk," Dennis said.

"You're right." Peter laughed. "Isn't Rita her maid of honor?"

"That's what I understand," Dennis said. "God, it will be sort of like old home week but under much different circumstances. I wonder if Rita's bringing a date? I hope not."

"It's going to be funny seeing Annie, knowing she found someone to share her life with and it's not me or you! I don't care, I guess. I'm happy for her," Peter said. "It will be fun for all of us to be together again, even if it's for just a short time. I better get plane tickets and my room while there is still time."

Annie and Jack planned a Friday wedding. They read somewhere that the weekend in Las Vegas really starts on Thursday, with most people coming in to town early to make the most of what Vegas had to offer. The marketing phrase "What happens in Vegas, stays in Vegas" was probably no lie, so they thought it was a great place to get married and have a good time.

Hell, it was a great place to go to even without getting married, Annie thought, as they arrived at McCarran International Airport. In this case, it was a special place for the whole wedding party. Annie knew her parents were looking forward to Vegas as their second honeymoon. Their first was in Green Bay. Todd and Angelina were always ready to party. Even though she hadn't talked to Dennis in a while, she guessed he was thinking of Rita. He called and said he was bringing a date, but she figured it was kind of like an insurance policy, just in case Rita showed no interest. Then there was Rita. Annie thought back to her phone conversation with Rita on Wednesday.

"God, he excites me," she said, "just thinking about him. Zach is ok, but he isn't Dennis!"

**

The unofficial gathering spot was the pool area. Everyone arrived early Thursday afternoon. Jack and Annie had arrived on Wednesday to set everything up for the Friday wedding. They had arranged for a separate area just off the pool at the Verandah restaurant.

The first to arrive were Rita and Zach. It was just like Door County years before, with Annie and Rita screaming, and jumping up and down when they finally saw each other. Jack and Zach looked at each other, shook hands, and laughed at the two women.

They had a cabaña to protect themselves from the September sun, but it was still stifling. They soon found themselves in the pool, drinking pina coladas at the pool's edge.

Darrell and Betty arrived, along with Jack's parents, Audrey and Jack Senior. Jack Stevenson was the president of several local banks around southeastern Wisconsin. They lived in the Lake Geneva area of southern Wisconsin. Like Door County, Lake Geneva was a big tourist area that most of Chicago visited at one time or another.

Todd and Angelina showed up next and wasted little time getting in the water and having drinks. Angelina hit it off immediately with Rita, and the two started talking about what they were going to wear that night in Sin City.

Todd slipped the pool attendant enough cash to reserve two more cabanas; there was plenty of room and shade for the guests to meet at the pool. Poor Thomas, his offer to pay for drinks, as a wedding present was very generous, Annie thought, but he was never going to believe all the drinks they ordered. Almost on cue, Dennis and his date, Carolina, arrived, followed by Peter and Paula.

Rita and Annie stopped talking and watched as Dennis and Peter approached. It had been years since Rita had seen either one. For Annie, seeing Dennis, and then Peter, was almost too much for her. She literally ran up to both to give them hugs and kisses.

"I am so glad you both could make it." Slightly misty-eyed, Annie looked at the two and thought back over all the years since Door

County. It seemed like just yesterday, but a lot had happened to them all since then.

Annie watched Peters eyes move to the golden *Falcon* sailboat he had given her in Door County the night they made love for the first time. She knew it looked very shiny. She thought, did he still think about her as much as she thought about him?

This was the right thing for them both, she told herself. *I know we still love each other and always will, but now it's a different love.*

Getting back to the moment, Peter turned to Paula. "Paula, this is Annie and Dennis."

Jack had slowly walked over. He knew about both Dennis and Peter as Annie had talked about them for the last few days.

Introductions were made all around. They moved under the cabana as the pool boys came and got more drink orders.

Peter introduced Paula to Jack and Annie as his fiancée, and the congratulations started all over again.

Even though Jack knew Annie loved him, in the back of his mind, he had been worried about this moment. He felt better now that Peter was engaged. He noticed Paula seemed similar to Annie in a lot of ways. He could see how Peter could be attracted to her. He also saw how Peter and Annie looked at each other even now. They probably love each other still, he thought, but he knew that Annie truly loved him, and Peter would never be a threat.

Annie gave Paula a big hug. With true emotion and tears in her eyes, she said, "Paula, you must be one special lady. Peter is a very special person, and I am so happy for both of you."

Paula, feeling Annie's emotion, just nodded. Her hand was pressed over her mouth, and she felt the tears welling up in her eyes, too.

"Thank you. We're both lucky to have found each other just like you and Jack did." She hugged Annie and then Jack.

Meanwhile, Rita slowly moved over to the group. She gave Peter a big hug and kiss. "God, it's good to see you."

Peter stepped back, holding both her hands in his. "Let me look at you, Doctor. You are fantastic, Dr. Gallagher. Say, do you make house calls?"

"Only if you get shot or are in an accident and end up in the ER."

Peter laughed. "On second thought, I'll pass." He turned to Dennis with a smirk. "Now, Dennis here might need your services someday."

"Thanks," he said

Rita moved toward Dennis. *Might as well get it over with.* An emotional electricity pulsed through her body, telling her what her mind would not. She knew she was getting warm and excited, and it wasn't the Vegas sun.

She had been waiting for this moment for some time, wondering how she would react. She thought about him a lot when she was alone, usually in the Doctors lounge as she tried to relax away from the ER. Just being this close to him brought back a flood of memories. Then he wrapped his arms around her and pressed her close.

"Hi, Rita. It's so good to see you. I don't know how you could look any better than you did back in Door County, but you do." She felt his lips press to hers, and after a moment's hesitation on her part, she relaxed and gave her lips to him. In that instant, she knew nothing had changed; that magnetism between her and Dennis remained. It made no difference today why they separated or what happened all those years ago. It was history and she wanted him.

It was going to be an interesting weekend, Rita thought. Rita stepped back, a little weak in the knees. She gave Annie a quick glance, and Annie smiled.

Zack walked over, looking none too pleased. She could read his mind. *The old flame is back.* Rita could tell Zach didn't like Dennis by his body language.

**

The evening had its own momentum from the pool. The group went to Caesars, The Mirage, The Desert Inn, The Flamingo, and Treasure Island.

They all stood on the boardwalk in front of Treasure Island and thoroughly enjoyed the pirate battle scene. Then it was downtown to Binions, The Golden Nugget, and back to The Four Seasons.

The gambling gods smiled on the group. Jack, Todd, Annie, and Paula won money playing craps. Peter and Paula won money playing blackjack. Zach, Rita, Dennis, and Carolina won a small amount of money playing slots, and Darrell, Betty and the Stevenson's played keno. All in all, it was successful. They all made it to bed before the sun came up, but not much sooner.

Rita and Dennis tried not to be obvious about their feelings for each other that first night. Hard as they tried, they both knew it was only a matter of time. Zach sensed the electricity between them, but knew enough not to make a scene. Carolina was just happy to be with Dennis and to be part of the wedding trip.

That morning, they all met poolside for breakfast, even if it was 11:00 a.m. The wedding was scheduled for 7:00 p.m. that evening, with the dinner by the pool patio at the Verandah. Rita, Paula, and Carolina went to the swim shop at the Caesar's Forum to get some sexy outfits for the next few days. When they finally showed up to meet Peter, Zach, and Dennis at the pool in their new outfits, they got all the attention they wanted from their boys and half the pool.

Rita, by far, got the most attention.

"How do you like my new suit? It's a one piece...kind of," she said with a laugh. "I just loved the way the turquoise ribbon material covers my breast and then crosses to form a thong. Just right for Vegas. Don't you think it's sexy, Dennis? What do you think, Zach?

She watched Dennis come over and gently pulled the ribbon back enough to glimpse a peek of Rita's breast. Zach wasted no time marking his territory. "Keep your goddamn hands off my woman!" And then he pushed Dennis vigorously backwards into the pool.

"Boys, boys. Simmer down, it's only a suit!" Rita was thankful Zach didn't punch Dennis, and she expected the worst when Dennis surfaced from the water, but Dennis realized his mistake. "Sorry. It just reminded me of our Door County days. I apologize Rita, Zach." Rita heard Zach mumble something under his breath but she was ecstatic with the effect the suit had on Dennis. *Point my side!*

Chapter Twenty-Two

Annie just laughed. Angelina whispered to Annie she was going to go back to the swim shop the next day to get a new suit. "Go for it, girl," she said.

"Damn right! After seeing Rita's suit, I'm going to get something to make Tony's eyes pop too! I'll make him so jealous with all the looks I'm going to get, he'll be eating out of my hand the rest of the weekend."

They all settled down and relaxed with a little swimming, sun, and drink. Pacing themselves made sense, so they could enjoy the wedding and all that was to follow.

Finally, it was time to get ready. Jack moved to Todd's room while Rita moved to Annie's room to get dressed.

Annie loved the dress Rita picked out. It matched perfectly with her simple but stunning white dress. Rita showed Annie the bra, and thong, garter and stockings she got for the wedding. "You know me, Annie; I needed something a little risqué just to get Zach's attention. Dennis's, too!"

"Dennis?" Annie's eyebrows arched. "What do you mean by that?"

"I just can't seem to control myself around him."

"I know. I saw how you two looked at each other. It's still there, isn't it?"

Rita looked out at the Vegas skyline. "Son of a bitch. Yes, it's still there."

Annie gave her a hug. "Good luck. I don't know how you're going to work it out, but I'm sure you'll both figure it out sooner or later. Just don't let them start a fist fight and wreck my wedding, ok?"

Rita let out a sigh. "I won't let that happen. I just need to figure it out this weekend."

"What do you think Zach's going to think?"

"Who knows? He's so full of himself, he might not even notice."

"Do you really think so?" Annie asked.

"No, he pretty sharp. I'll just have to let what happens, happen."

Annie said. "And the way you're going to look, it won't take Dennis long to get his antenna up and make his move."

Wetting her lips, Rita said. "I sure hope so. I'm ready. But enough about me; show me what you got for the wedding and tonight."

Annie opened the closet. "I went to Victoria's Secret in Chicago and got a lace no-show stretch thong, and white silk stockings to go along with a glamorous, lace garter belt. In keeping with the Vegas look and feel," she told Rita, "I chose a cocktail length silk gown with small pearls sewn into the top and a v-shaped neckline and v-shaped back, to give it a rich look, which makes the most of my body. I've always liked a classic white pearl necklace and matching earrings; very simple, but that's all I need, I think. What do you think?"

"It's just perfect," Rita said. "What about tonight?"

"When the time comes for Jack and me to be alone, it is going to be a lace antique white, Flyaway Baby Doll with matching silk panties and kimono. I want to make sure it's the best night of his life."

Rita nodded. "At least you'll have it on for a little while."

She laughed and then started to cry as she sat to put on her makeup.

Rita came over and gave her a hug. "Why so glum? You should be happy."

"I am. I really am." When she opened her hand, she had the sail-boat Peter had given her so many years ago. "You know, I never took this necklace off even once, since Peter gave it to me that first summer in Door County. I would touch it every time I thought of him. As you can see, it's very bright."

With a sigh, she wrapped the charm in tissue and placed it in her makeup bag. "A new era is starting. I'm just a little sad that's all," she said and then brightened up. "I'm also very excited to be starting a new life with Jack."

Rita bent down and gave Annie a kiss on her head. "You'll be okay, Annie. It's not like you can't think about Peter. He's your friend now. He's not your lover, that's all."

"I know. I really love Jack more than anyone I've ever known. I feel so complete with him. I can't wait for the wedding."

"You guys are so lucky. I hope I find that someone special like you did with Jack," Rita said, suddenly becoming very serious. "I see so much of what can happen when love goes wrong. That's why I'm so happy for you two. You'll always be on the other end of the spectrum."

"I know," Annie said in a soft voice. They both embraced and got back to getting ready.

There was a knock on the door. Rita opened it, and there stood Betty. "I'm here to help." She moved to her daughter's side and gave her a kiss, then held up a bottle of champagne. "Compliments of the Four Seasons," she said. "Your father and I haven't had this much fun in years. We decided that we are going to come out here every year for the rest of our lives. Everyone is ready for a good time in this city." She giggled.

Annie just stared at her mom and the half-empty bottle. "Mom, can we have some?"

"Oh, I'm sorry. I guess I got carried away." She poured them a glass. "We haven't had this much energy in our lives in twenty years. Your dad even checked to see if the hotel had any rooms with mirrors on the ceiling."

Rita and Annie started laughing.

"I mean it was like your dad was a twenty-year-old. I think he maybe got some of that Viagra stuff because he was a Wildman last night."

"Mother!" She knew Darrel and Betty were pretty passionate about each other, and they were never afraid to show their affection when Annie was growing up.

"You know, it might be your wedding, but your dad and I still know how to have fun, too."

Now Rita and Annie really started laughing. They finished the champagne, applied their final lipstick, and the three hugged and left to go downstairs.

**

When Darrell saw Annie, Betty and Rita, all he could do was whistle. "I have never seen three more beautiful women in my whole life." He gave Rita a peck on the cheek. He gave Betty a kiss on the lips and squeezed her hand. "Thank you, for giving me the most beautiful daughter in the whole world," he said, voice cracking with emotion. "She looks as beautiful as you did the day we got married. I love you."

Then he turned to Annie. "You are so beautiful, honey. You have been the best daughter any father could ask for. I am so proud of you and everything you have done your whole life. I know that you have found someone who will love and cherish you the way I love and cherish your mother. A father cannot ask for anything more. I love you, Annie." He leaned over and gave her a kiss on the cheek as a tear slid down his cheek. Clearing his throat, he turned to the three ladies. "Let's get this show on the road; we can't keep your future husband waiting. He's a nervous wreck."

**

The wedding took place at the far end of the swimming pool. The waterfall cascading from high above into the pool created just a hint of mist. Palm trees formed the perfect canopy, with the soft glow of sunset reflecting off the golden windows of Mandalay Bay. The atmosphere was perfect for a small intimate wedding. Annie and Jack had decided on 'Fields of Gold' by Sting. The song was playing in the background on Annie's stereo the first time they made love that night at the Gallery. It was their song. Both thought the lyrics matched what they meant to say to each other, about caring, and walking through life together, the fields of gold. Their vows were a simple pledge of love to each other.

The wedding was over in a Las Vegas minute, and then a nice dinner and several drinks at the poolside patio. After toasts and normal kissing of the bride and groom, the party broke up. Plans were made to start the night of partying at the House of Blues, located in Mandalay Bay's casino area.

The guys looked like they all came out of the Tommy Bahamas catalog, while the girls were a mixture of clothing that was pure Vegas. They wore a mixture of short, clingy silk that just showed the barest outline of a thong and the plunging, sequined neckline did the rest. Everyone was ready to party now that the wedding ceremony was out of the way. The Stevenson's and Wilson's tried to keep up, but by one o'clock they called it quits, while the young hit more clubs and casinos in the hired limos.

After going to the House of Blues, they went to the Hard Rock. Rita and Zach, Dennis and Carolina, Todd and Angelina, Peter and Paula, and Jack and Annie were on fire. Things were pretty good while they still danced as couples. By the time they reached the fifth club, the couples dance partners started to change.

Rita and Dennis finally got their chance to dance. The gods smiled down on them with their song being a slow song from the 70's, Carol King's, *so far away*.

Dennis realized, as he listens to the words of the song, he had to be together with Rita sometime before they left. Whispering in her ear as they danced, "We have to be together. I'll get us a room at Mandalay Bay for tomorrow. I heard Peter tell Todd that the guys were going golfing at the Desert Inn. I'll make an excuse I don't feel well or something, which should give us a few hours to get re-acquainted."

Dennis pulled back to look at Rita's reaction to his plan and heard her sigh, "Okay."

"Come on, you know you want it too," Dennis continued, "I think that should be a good start, don't you?" He smiled. "I'll give Carolina some money to go shopping. I'll tell her that I want her to get another outfit for tomorrow night."

Looking into her eyes, nothing more needed to be said. He pressed his body tight against her one last time. They were oblivious to all those around them as the song ended.

"It's going to be a long night," he heard Rita.

**

The next morning, the group somehow stumbled to the pool around 11:00 a.m. Dennis handed Rita a small note: Meet me at 1:30 p.m., room 13215.

The boys' left at 12:45 p.m., while everyone else stayed at the pool talking about how lovely the wedding was and how much fun they all had. Rita kept looking at Dennis, while still trying to stay tuned to the conversations around her. All she could do was to keep thinking about what was going to happen in less than 45 minutes. It reminded her of waiting for the school clock to say it was time for recess. Finally, she watched Dennis excused himself. Ten minutes later, Rita did the same. When she got up and took her purse, she looked over at Annie and smiled. Annie gave her a big smile and a discreet thumbs-up. *Let's hope so.*

Rita raced to her room and put on some perfume and body lotion to feel fresh and clean. A touch of lipstick and a run through her hair with her brush, and she was ready.

God, I feel like I'm back at Wilson's in the dorm getting ready to meet Dennis. She chuckled.

She reached the room at 1:33 p.m., thinking it was good to keep a man waiting. Especially someone like Dennis because she knew, once she walked into that room, she was powerless against his wants and her desires. She knocked on the door lightly. She felt flushed with excitement, her nipples hard, and her chest full. Her breath quickened as she heard his steps. She looked down, watched the doorknob turn and the door swing open. Dennis smiled, his muscular chest and blue eyes heightening her desire. "Rita, I've missed you."

She looked into his eyes; saw that his desire matched hers. "I know. I've missed you, too." She stepped in to the room. He slowly closed the door, and took her in his arms.

Chapter Twenty-Three

J ack and Annie got back to Chicago Tuesday afternoon. They were
exhausted but excited to be home. They called Thomas and told
him they made it back safe and sound. Annie invited him to dinner the
following week, so he could see the pictures, hear all about the wedding, and see where all the booze money he gave them as a wedding
present went.

"Are you sure I only bought booze for your party and not all of
Las Vegas?" He laughed. "I'm glad you had a great time. I'm sorry I
couldn't be there to help celebrate."

"I know. We missed you."

That evening, Jack and Annie looked forward to making love for
the first time as husband and wife in their own house. Jack stopped
and got a nice bottle of Pinot Noir, two t-bones, and cherry chocolate
chip ice cream, their favorite. They snuggled on the sofa and listened
to some jazz. Annie fell asleep on Jack's chest until they went to bed.

There, they made love slowly, tenderly, enjoying the moment. Jack
spent several minutes kissing Annie's throat and neck before nibbling
tenderly on her earlobes. He loved the soft sounds she made as he
touched her in all her favorite spots. When they were finished, they
held each other until they both fell asleep.

They never moved from their positions until the sun blasted into
the room the next morning. Annie sat up, stretching her arms and
back. Jack rolled over on his stomach, covering his eyes and smacking
his lips while he muttered, "Coffee, Coffee." She bent down and gave

him a kiss on his neck. She was looking forward to spending the rest of her life with him.

Shuffling out to the kitchen naked, she turned on the coffee maker. Starting back to bed, she saw Jack raise his head and smile as she walked back. Lifting the covers so she could snuggle close and get warm, he started kissing her. As his hand moved to her breast, she felt his excitement. He rolled on top of her; this time they made love with unbridled passion. When they were done, they both lay spent, their breathing rapid. Sweat soaked the sheets.

Jack looked at her with a smile. "There is nothing better in the morning than the fresh smell of coffee after you just made love." Now it was his turn to get up and get the coffee.

When he came back, Annie was smiling. She reached out and touched him.

"Watch it or I'll spill this coffee on you. You aren't ready to make love again, are you?"

"Well, he looks like he's happy to see me, and you're a young stud, aren't you?" Rubbing it gently, she looked up at him with a sheepish grin. "It is a renewable resource, isn't it?"

He gave Annie her coffee, took a sip of his before placing it down on the nightstand, and then bent low to kiss her lips and her breast. "Let's find out," he mumbled.

"Ahh," was all Annie could whisper.

**

Driving home from the Charleston airport, all Dennis could think about was Rita. He made love to Carolina several times in Vegas, but it wasn't even close to the excitement he felt with Rita for the few hours he and she were together. He was glad to learn that she was heading to Chicago, and Northwestern Medical School. He was almost too involved with the boat factory in Charleston to get involved with Rita, but maybe on a Deacon's trip he could fly into Chicago, meet up and then drive up to Sturgeon Bay. He did get up to Sturgeon Bay three or four times a year.

As plant manager, he had lots of responsibility and incentives. He was offered Deacon's stock through their stock option program if he could keep things profitable, so it was his chance to make some big bucks over the next few years. He knew Rita would make a lot of money as a doctor, but he wanted to make his money, too. He had his pride. Peter, Annie, and Rita owned a business or had the potential to make big bucks. This was his chance to do the same. He didn't want to blow it.

There would be time for him and Rita. But now, he'd just have to find some cutie down here to keep him occupied until then.

**

Jack had interviewed for two weeks with several investment-banking firms all over the country. He finally decided on a regional firm located in Chicago. He could get the national exposure he needed to build his career, but still spend most nights at home. He knew that he would be working 12-hour days, five to six days a week, but at least he'd be home at night with Annie. His office was close enough to the galleries that he could have lunch or dinner with her a few days a week. He still tried to help her on Friday or Saturday nights, just for old time's sake, but when things got busy, it seemed like they were ships passing in the night. It was exciting for both as they had good days and bad. Each was there for the other. For them, Chicago was the place to be.

**

Peter and Paula tied the knot in Key West on March 1, 1991. The Guerrero family overwhelmed the Franklins. They loved them as much as Peter did. They had such a good time, Peter's dad decided to spend an extra week in Key West fishing with Paula's family.

Dennis was wonderful as Peter's best man. Peter made sure Dennis was to be on his best behavior and not to be "Dennis" with any of Paula's relatives. Outside of that, Key West was all his.

Dennis was disappointed that Rita could not make the wedding, but understood she was a little busy with the winding down of the Gulf War and its many casualties there.

Annie was so busy with the new Gallery opening in Door County, and Jack was up to his neck with his first deal, that they could not make it down. Annie sent Peter and Paula a painting she did of Eagle Bluff Harbor from the pier in front of Wilson's.

When Peter saw it for the first time, he had to call her to let her how much it meant to him. "I'm going to hang it next to the first painting you ever painted of me. Remember the one you did at Newport the day I lost the bet?"

"You still have that?" Annie asked.

"Of course. It's one of my most prized possessions."

They talked for about an hour and half. Talking about everything and nothing. It was as if time had stood still and it was that first summer and they were lying on the blanket. They talked as friends whose life's horizons had expanded.

When Peter finally hung up, his eyes were moist, but his heart was not heavy. He just missed one of his best friends. He wished she could have been there on his special day.

Chapter Twenty-Four

In late fall of 2000, Peter got a call from Mr. Peterson. "Hi Peter. We need your help. We're going to build a replica of a schooner called the Garibaldi," Peterson said. "The ship was a seventy-eight foot, two-masted schooner, captained by a distant relative of mine who, unfortunately, was swept into the water in a storm back in 1880."

"This sounds interesting." Peter said.

"It's representative of the schooners that plied the Great Lakes at that time. It would be an attraction for Door County tourism as well as educational for children and adults. In tribute to my relative, Captain Peterson, I decided to help underwrite the first twenty-five thousand dollars of the cost for the project, and provide the use of one of my barns to house the building of the schooner."

Peter remembered talking to Mr. Pelzwalker years ago about something like this.

Mr. Peterson continued. "Peter, I would like you to be a board member, and a member of the advisory committee. We need someone with your skill and energy to make the project successful."

"I would love to help," Peter said, "but I don't know how much time and energy I can spend on the project." He paused. "Paula and I will donate five thousand dollars to help fund it."

Mr. Peterson was ecstatic. "That's a very generous contribution. Thank you. Jim Erickson is going to help, too. We really need to find a project manager. Do you know anyone?"

"What about Dennis?"

"I contacted him but he said he was too busy in South Carolina. He said he might be able to help later if he ever got transferred back to Sturgeon Bay, but that didn't look like it was in the cards any time soon. Dennis told me to contact Ken Judd. He said he's an experienced shipwright living in Maine. He and his wife, he said, want to come back to Door County."

"He's probably better for you than Dennis. Dennis has experience in fiberglass, not wood."

Mr. Peterson thanked him and agreed to contact Judd.

"When Dennis finds out I'm involved," Peter said, "he'd probably come up for a couple of weeks and help. You should ask Dennis if Deacon's might want to get behind the project? It would be great PR for them, and they are in touch with several retired shipwrights just like Judd, who would like nothing better than to get back at building a wooden boat like Garibaldi."

"That's a great idea. I could call Bud Sweeney and talk to him. They have lots of talent and equipment they might be willing to help us with." Mr. Peterson said.

"All they can say is no," Peter said.

**

With the project underway, Mr. Peterson ran a few ads in the *Door County Advocate*. He didn't know what to expect but when about 70 people applied after the first ad ran, not caring what they did. "They just wanted to be part of the project," he'd tell people. Door County was abuzz as spring came.

Annie got involved too. She painted a depiction of the future Garibaldi and started selling prints in her Door County and Chicago Galleries. Many of the shops in Door County did the same. T-shirts and bake sales were the order of the day as money was raised to get construction started.

Peter and Paula helped provide Mr. Peterson with a financial plan to keep the project on target. Jack got involved by approaching some of the investment firms he worked with to make contributions through their foundations. The project soon had enough money accumulated to start construction.

The warehouse at Peterson's marina was a beehive of activity as table saws, band saws, forklifts, joiners, adzes; clamps drills, drill bits and other tools were assembled. The ship took on a romance all its own. Participating in the many shipbuilding activities were local students and adults that helped make the project special. Fourth grade students and older were given the opportunity to help build something the size of Garibaldi and learn through the experience. Through Garibaldi, they learned about sailing, the environment, and history all in one operation. Students and general volunteers were put to work directly, since much work was needed to be done before the actual building started. A separate area was set up for the school buses. A tent was set up for the kids to have lunch and classes.

After months of work, finally the big day came to lay the keel, and it happened to fall on the week of July 4, 2001. The event kicked off the Sister Bay weekend of activities. A large semi carried the wooden keel to the shipyard from the lumberyard. It was decorated with red, white and blue banners. Once the truck reached Sister Bay, several of the children, Mr. Peterson, Mr. Pelzwalker, and the Judd's climbed aboard the truck and rode the last mile through town, in a parade to the building site.

The American Legion band played as the keel was hoisted from the truck and placed on a special platform. It had been a long and slow process up to this point, but now, the real building of Garibaldi could start. All those who had worked on the project up to that point stepped forward and signed their name on the keel.

**

Peter and Dennis flew into Milwaukee and planned to drive together to Sister Bay for the weeklong start of the actual building of the schooner. It had been months since they had been together, and it gave them a chance to catch up on old times. Dennis rented a red corvette, figuring he and Peter would have some fun for the week and the car would help. Fast cars and fast women is what Dennis liked.

While waiting for Peter's plane to arrive, he decided to have a beer at one of Milwaukee's airport bars. He had about 45 minutes until Peter's plane arrived from Miami, so why not?

His eyes always roving, Dennis enjoyed people watching, but he liked to watch the women in particular. One person who caught his eye was an attractive blond with an incredible figure. He thought she was probably an aerobics instructor.

Something seemed familiar about her, but just couldn't place it. He thought he knew her from somewhere. She was with another couple. When the couple got up to go to the airport snack shop, Dennis made his move. Walking over, he stood right in front of her. She couldn't help but look.

"Excuse me. I know this might be the oldest line in the book, but you look so familiar. My name is Dennis Jamison and I'm originally from this area, Shorewood, here in the Milwaukee area. I haven't lived here for years. I'm living just outside of Charleston, South Carolina now."

She got wide-eyed as he said his name. "Dennis, I didn't recognize you. I look familiar to you because we went to high school together. We even dated for a while. I'm Connie…" "English." Dennis said her name slowly, controlling his emotion. He felt the anger building inside of him as the events of the football night fiasco flashed back after all the years. The excitement in her eyes surprised him. She didn't seem like she remembered anything about that night, but he sure did.

"Dennis, you've changed. I would never have recognized you if you hadn't said something. Are you coming to the class reunion this August?"

"I don't know. I haven't received any information."

She got out a piece of paper. "Give me your address and phone number. I'll make sure you and your wife get an invitation."

He laughed. "I'm not married. I haven't found any woman I want to settle down with yet. Besides, I'm having too much fun just the way things are. Why change a good thing?"

Connie got slightly red. "Having fun is good. I sure do." She laughed as she looked at him, wetting her lips.

"How about you? Are you married?"

"Yes and soon no." She smiled. "I'm in the process of getting out of marriage number three. I'm going out to Vegas with my best friend and her boyfriend to party. Too bad you can't get away and join us."

"Yeah, too bad," he said, though he didn't mean it, despite her good looks. "I'm going up to Door County. I manage a boat factory in South Carolina for Deacon's Yacht. A friend and I are going up for the week. I'm waiting for him to get in from Miami."

About that time, her friends came back and said the plane was boarding. "I guess we better get going. Don't want to miss our plane to Sin City. It was really nice seeing you again, Dennis. I'll make sure I get you the information for the class reunion. Give me your address."

He nodded and then wrote the information down for her.

Then he watched as she took a step closer, rising on her toes and touching his cheek with her lips. He thought she only wanted to give him a little peck on the cheek for old time's sake, but instead he turned his face gave her a kiss with as much lust and emotion as he could muster. He had years of revenge on his mind, and there was no time like the present to start giving payback.

When he stepped back from the kiss, Connie looked confused. He held her for a few seconds. She seemed to have lost her sense of balance. As he stepped back and turned to go to the bar, she stood motionless.

"I'll look forward to getting that information," Dennis said. "Give me a call and maybe we can get together when I come up to work on the project again."

"Yeah," she whispered. Collecting herself, she said in a louder voice, "I'll send you the information as soon as I get back from Vegas. It was good to see you again, Dennis."

"Nice to see you too, Connie." *Yep, it was going to be a great summer up North.*

Dennis went back to the bar. "Give me an MGD in a frosted mug. I suddenly feel thirsty," he told the bartender.

Peter showed up about 25 minutes later.

"How was your flight?" Dennis asked as they shook hands.

"If you can believe it, it was right on time. It hardly took me any time to go through the airport to catch my plane."

"I was just finishing this beer. You thirsty?"

"You bet."

Turning to the bartender, Dennis said, "Give me and my friend here MGD's, please."

"Thanks," said Peter. "God, this tastes good after a long trip." He held the cold mug to his face and smiled. "Things don't get better than this, at least not in Milwaukee." They laughed, finished their beers and headed to Door County.

**

Jack and Annie woke to a gorgeous sunrise pouring into their bedroom. One of the beauties of the loft Annie had purchased so many years ago was the abundance of natural light that showered the rooms. As an artist, she couldn't ask for anything more. For two people in love, the gentle heat created by the sun's rays was a catalyst for the heat they generated on mornings like this.

Jack was up and getting ready for another long day. It was not uncommon for him to get up at 4:30 a.m., shower, grab a bowl of instant oatmeal and fruit, and scan the *Wall Street Journal* and the *Financial Times*. Then he'd walk the three quarters of a mile to his office in downtown Chicago.

Annie was half awake, feeling warm all over. She so enjoyed the warm tingling feeling after making love. Even though it was several years after their wedding, she still felt that thrill every time she saw Jack. They were so good for each other.

Not that they didn't have their moments, she thought. But when they did fight, it usually was a short spat. They had total respect for each other, and that's why they were more in love today than when they got married.

"Are you awake?" Jack asked.

"Kind of."

"I've got to work late tonight on the Johnson deal, so don't make dinner for me. We're trying to get this deal put together by September. Toby said, since I'm putting in more than the usual time, and he knows it's our anniversary that month, he is putting us up at the Plaza. Once the deal is put to bed, he wants us to take a few days off for ourselves."

"Gee, that's nice of Toby. It's only fair in a way. I hardly see you. Still, it's nice that he remembered our anniversary."

"I've got to get going." Jack leaned down and gave Annie a long kiss.

She loved the way he kissed her. He never was in a hurry to end it. She tried to get him to climb back into bed and make love to her one more time. "Jack?" She gently let her hand drift to his pants, but when he started laughing, she knew her plan failed.

He gently pulled back. "God, I wish I didn't have a meeting at eight. Otherwise, I'd jump in bed with you for another quickie."

"You look so dammed sexy in your white starched shirt and red tie. Why don't you try to come home early? I'll wear that teddy you like and meet you at the door with a cold Bud. I'll let you have your way with me and we can make love on the floor with just the city lights for ambiance."

He reached for her hand and kissed it.

"Did I paint a sexy enough picture for you?"

"You've got a deal." He kissed her forehead, grabbed his briefcase, and headed out.

Annie rolled over with a big smile on her face, thinking about the fun they were going to have that night.

Chapter Twenty-Five

Peter was just finishing a conversation with Mr. Peterson when Annie drove in to the shipyard. As she got out of her car, he couldn't help but feel the old attraction. She looked so beautiful, so alive. Her hair was in a ponytail, the end fit through the hole of a Garibaldi baseball cap. She didn't look like the 18-year-old he had loved years ago, but she looked more radiant than he could ever remember. He just smiled in appreciation.

He knew he loved Paula and had no interest in pursuing Annie sexually, but he still loved her. He walked out of the office toward her.

She turned her head, looking over the operation as she threw her backpack over her shoulder. When she saw Peter, she smiled and gave him a wave. "Hi, stranger," she said in a loud voice. She dropped the backpack and opened her arms to him, then gave him a hug and a kiss. "It's so good to see you. I missed you. I thought I'd come up for a few days, check on my Gallery, visit mom and dad and see how the project is going."

They each stepped back, held hands, and looked at each other.

Annie smiled. "Looks like married life suits you well."

"You too. How is Jack?"

"Working like a mad man, but he loves it. He wanted to come up. He loves it here, too."

"We all do," Peter said.

"He's working on a big case that is going to close in September, so his focus is on that. It lets me come up here with no guilt. I know he's not going to feel bad when I'm busy because he's busy. Did Paula come up?"

Peter shook his head. "No, she's with her parents."

"Oh, that's too bad."

"Dennis is up here."

Annie's eyes got big.

"We met in Milwaukee and drove up together in that red corvette he rented." He pointed to it parked across the street.

"How is the old rascal?" Annie said with a mischievous smile. "Seems he hasn't changed at all looking at the red car. Imagine!"

Peter kicked the gravel in the parking lot with his deck shoe. "He hasn't changed. He's been busy with Ken Judd. This is a new medium for him in boat building and he loves it. We'll have to try to get together for dinner at the very least. I still have Red Baron. Maybe we can go out for an evening sail, just like old times."

"I'd like that," she said. "As you might expect, I'm staying with Mom and Dad, so you can get hold of me there or just stop by my gallery in Fish Creek. It's right next to the ice cream shop in the building where you got me *Falcon*."

Peter looked at Annie's neck, expecting to see the small gold sailboat.

She caught his gaze. "I'm sorry, Peter. The day Jack and I got married was the day I took it off. Until that day, I never stopped wearing it. But you know I don't need that charm to remind me of you." She leaned over, giving him a light kiss on the cheek.

"I know. I never expected you to wear it as long as you did." He smiled. "Let's go sailing tomorrow night. We'll have dinner at the Bowl and go for a sail, okay?"

"Okay."

"I better get back to Mr. Peterson. He's probably wondering where I am." Then he paused. "Fundraising's a thankless job, but someone's got to do it, and I'm good at it."

Annie let out a sigh. "I better go find Dennis."

**

Annie started walking around the construction site. Finally, she found him. For her, it was déjà vu. He was selecting pieces of lumber for the next few frames to be built. Shiny with sweat, he had his shirt off, and his muscles rippled as he moved the lumber to a forklift.

She stood there, admiring. What a beautiful male specimen he was. A sigh slipped from her lips. She could still look! Her heart raced as he looked up and saw her.

He smiled, grabbed his shirt, wiping the sweat and grime from his chest and brow, and walked over. She saw him give her the once over and knew how Little Red Riding Hood must have felt when she saw the wolf. Unlike the warm, loving hug she gave Peter, Annie knew better than to do the same with Dennis. Instead, she extended her hand.

"Dennis, it's so nice to see you again. It's been awhile."

"It has. The wedding was the last time I saw you. I don't think I ever got a post-wedding kiss." Still holding her hand, he pulled her in close and gave her a hard kiss on the lips.

For just a moment, the past rushed back to Annie. She felt that old electricity run through her body. No! She thought. She pushed him away and stepped back, glaring at him. "I hope you enjoyed that, Dennis. I see you haven't changed."

With a mischievous smile, he looked at her. "That'll do. You're a married lady now, and I'm just the way I am. You know, Annie, I always had a special interest in you, but I understand. I just wanted you to know that I'm always here for you."

"That will never happen again, Dennis. Can't we just be friends?" She paused, letting the word 'friends' hang in the air. Then she said in a firm, steady voice, "If I feel that I can't trust you, then I can't be around you, and I really don't want that."

Dennis just looked at her, this time with a serious expression. "Annie, you are special to me, and I don't want that to happen, so I'll try my best to honor your wishes."

"Thank you. Now tell me what's happened over the last few years." *Was he finally changing?* They walked over to JJ's café and bar across the street from the building site and got caught up on their lives.

**

Peter looked forward to having dinner and sailing with Annie. He had Red Baron moved out of storage, rigged up, and cleaned by one of Mr. Peterson's new teenage helpers, Billy. Peter gave Billy a healthy tip because he knew how much work it was to clean and get a boat ready to sail. Billy sounded like Peter years ago, he thought.

"I love sailing," said Billy. "Working for Mr. Peterson is just about the best thing that could ever happen to me. I can hardly wait for the day to begin. I love working on the boats."

Peter smiled. "Do you have a girlfriend?"

He looked a little sheepish. Nodding, he answered in a quiet voice. "Yes, Sari who works at the Coffee Cup just up the street, near the Bowl. She hasn't sailed yet, but it's only a matter of time before I find a way to get her on the water."

"That's great," Peter said.

Peter picked Annie up in a borrowed marina pickup, and it felt just like old times. They couldn't leave until he had a beer with Darrell. Then Annie and he spent some time on the old front porch swing before leaving for an early dinner at Sister Bay Bowl.

Earlier in the day, Betty had baked a cherry pie and wrapped a couple of pieces for them to have on the boat. Peter brought wine for the evening cruise; everything was just the way he hoped it would be. A full moon and light winds from the southwest helped time stand still as they sailed into the evening.

After pie and some white wine, they both settled back and enjoyed the night. They remained quiet enjoying the wind and the gentle gurgle of water against the red fiberglass hull.

Deep in her own thoughts, Annie unconsciously moved closer to Peter, and he likewise slipped his arm around her.

Annie finally broke the silence and said what was on both of their minds as she snuggled against his shoulder like she used to. "Do you ever wonder what might have happened if one of us had given in so many years ago?" She felt Peter take a breath and slowly let it out.

"Yes, Annie... I do. I knew you loved me and I loved you, but we were so wrapped up in our careers. It's history now. I'll never change the way I feel about you, but I'm in love with Paula, just as I know you're in love with Jack."

"You're right. You can't go back, and I don't think either of us would want to give up what we've found."

Peter picked up the glass of wine he had near him. "Annie, let's toast to Paula and Jack. The other loves of our lives."

She laughed and gently touched her glass to Peter's.

They got back around 11:30 p.m. Peter took Annie back to her parents and then he headed back to his motel in Sister Bay.

When he got back around midnight, he noticed that Dennis's Corvette was not at the hotel. "Dennis, you haven't changed much in all these years. I hope you find someone who can tame you, because you just don't know what you're missing in life."

**

Morning came quickly. Peter liked to sleep with the shades open, so the morning sun could stream in and be his natural alarm clock. He looked out across the blue water of Sister Bay. "Another morning in paradise." He smiled as he slipped into a pair of old jeans, a clean T-shirt and headed down the block to Johnson's for breakfast.

He walked the few blocks along the shore. God, he loved this time of morning. "Not too many people up yet," he said out loud to no one. Arriving at Al Johnson's, he noticed that he even beat the goats this morning. Not only was Al's food excellent, he thought, but places like

Al Johnson's made Door County special. All you had to say was that you ate where the goats were and people knew the place.

Peter ordered the traditional Norwegian pancakes and berries and a cup of black coffee. He knew it was going to be a long day and he wanted something that was going to stick with him.

After finishing breakfast he called Paula to see how everything was in Key West. He loved the Keys. He wished he could move his charter operation to Key West from Miami.

More and more, he and Paula thought about opening a satellite office so they could justify spending more time there, but he worried about finding someone he could trust to run things. It was getting to be a pretty big operation, and he was either going to have to hire or be content to stay at his current size. He had about 30 boats, and that was all they could handle with the staff he had.

But it was something he and Paula had talked about. They were thinking of raising a family soon, and she really wanted to head back to Key West. He couldn't blame her. They were a great family, and he loved them deeply.

He had gotten inquiries from one of the big charter operations about merging or buying him out. The buyout would give he and Paula a handsome profit and the opportunity to move to Key West. He told them he wasn't interested at the current time, but maybe he would be sometime in the future.

His mind turned to Paula and her biological clock ticking away. He used to raise his eyebrows when she talked about it. She would always just stare at him and say, "What? You know that's true!" He'd say, "I know it's harder for you than for guys. We can make babies at any age...Want to try now?" She'd laugh, and he knew he dodged another bullet.

He did look forward to someday being a father, and he knew that Paula would be a great mom. With the extended family in Key West, he knew the kids would grow up in a loving world. It might not be Ephraim, but Key West was a pretty good place to raise a family.

**

Dennis was going to be sorry to leave Door County. He made a run down to The Canal Bar in Sturgeon Bay just for old time's sake. Having a beer on the deck, he eventually connected with an unhappy wife. She had a converted van that worked just fine. She loved country western music, especially George Strait. She heard him sing the song "The Fireman" and thought it only fair that Dennis be her fireman and help put out her fire.

The woman was burning inside for some good loving, so it served her husband right. He thought. Driving home that night, he thought he better buy that CD as a thank you to George Strait. He might even buy one of those volunteer fireman decals that he saw on pickup trucks.

She was a wild one and he was sure they really rocked her van. The drive back to the hotel from Sturgeon Bay was a little quicker with the Corvette, but he was still tired when the alarm went off at 7:30 a.m. He knew Peter was gone by then. He didn't have the distractions Dennis did.

Poor Peter. If he loosened up, he probably could make it with Annie. Dennis knew they both cared about each other, but he also knew Peter would never do the things he'd do if he had the chance.

His thoughts drifted to old times. Too bad Rita wasn't here, and then it would be like old times. Now there was someone who would get his heart going. He hadn't thought about her for a while, but she had a special place in his heart, if not some other place. Long term it wasn't going to work. Too bad, he thought, he had a great time in Vegas with her. It was the best sex he ever had with anyone. The special bond between him and Rita was the difference. He never had that with the others. He'd have to check with Annie or Peter on what was up with her. Maybe just a quick affair, it would be good for both of them. She wasn't like Annie, and he sure wasn't like Peter.

**

247

Rita's marriage lasted about two years. Zach's jealousy got to be too much for her. He couldn't stand the thought that she made more money than he did. His ego just couldn't take it. And she was going places he couldn't go. Eventually, it tore them apart and Rita filed for divorce.

After that, Rita applied to Northwestern Medical Center, was accepted, and moved to Chicago, where she buried herself in her work. Medicine was her life. She had no one she was involved with. She cared little about anyone other than Annie and Jack. She even seemed to block out thoughts about Dennis. She liked it that way.

When she wasn't working in Chicago, she did freelance work for Milwaukee's hospital system. Milwaukee was only 90 miles north of Chicago, so she could even commute if she wanted to. It kept her close to Annie and Jack, close to her parents in Madison, and gave her an opportunity to visit Door County with Annie when they could get away. Things were good for the three.

Chapter Twenty-Six

Dennis was back in the swing of things at the plant in Charleston after visiting Door County. Business was good; sales of Deacon's new boats were brisk. He had the factory running very efficiently.

It was Monday morning, about 10:30 a.m. local time, when he got the call.

"Dennis Jamison?"

"Yes."

"This is Doctor Olson at Columbia Hospital in Milwaukee. We've had a hard time getting hold of you."

Dennis gripped the receiver. "Yes...what's happened? Why are you calling me?"

"It's your mother, Dennis. She had a massive stroke yesterday, but we have things under control."

"Is she all right?"

"Yes, but she is going to need round-the-clock care. She is not in a life-threatening situation, but she needs care when she leaves the hospital."

There was a long pause as Dennis's mind raced.

"I know you are in Charleston, but I think you need to come back to Milwaukee so we can talk."

"I can be there Wednesday. Is that soon enough?"

"Yes, that should be just fine. Just call when you get in." The doctor gave Dennis his cell number.

Dennis sat at his desk, stunned. He never thought his mother would get sick. His dad had a heart attack and died ten years ago, but

Dad was overweight and smoked. He didn't take care of himself like his mom did.

There was no one else for her, just Dennis. He got an airline ticket. Then he talked to his supervisors at the plant and explained why he needed to leave.

"I'll probably be gone at least a week," he said. "Make sure you keep me informed. Terry Dothum is in charge while I'm gone."

They all wished him well. "We'll handle everything while you're gone," Terry said.

Next he called Bud Sweeney at Deacon's and told him what was going on.

"Don't you worry about anything, Dennis," said Bud. "You take care of your Mother, she comes first. You know we really have a first rate nursing home in Sister Bay. Scandia Village."

"Thanks, Bud. I didn't know where to start."

"I know you love working in Charleston, Dennis." Bud talked in a quiet, soothing voice. "I have a proposition for you that might solve several problems for everyone concerned. A couple of the important managers are getting ready to retire. I want to slow down myself. It might be the perfect time for you to move back to Door County. You can take over managing most of the operations while we're still here to help. The men know and respect you. You'd be close to your mom. Later, when the time is right, you'll manage the whole operation. Why don't you come up for a few days after seeing your mother and we'll talk about it?"

"Thanks, Bud, I'll do just that. I was worried about leaving you guys in a lurch if push came to shove with Mom. You've been so good to me over the years. Now I can just concentrate on Mom. I'll see you Thursday or Friday, okay?"

"Sounds good. I'll see you then, Dennis."

Dennis let out a big sigh.

**

Summer was almost over. Annie couldn't believe it was September already. She hardly ever saw Jack. He'd been so busy doing the due diligence on this major deal he brought to the firm. She was comfortable with it because she knew it was his responsibility to make sure everything was up to snuff with the Securities and Exchange Commission. This was by far his biggest case.

He met the owner of the company years ago when he was doing his graduate work at The University of Chicago's Business School. This deal was Jack's baby and she knew it was important to his career and her future.

Annie knew enough about what was going on to give her husband his space. She also knew when to give him encouragement when things seemed to be getting away from him. It was very stressful and exciting all at the same time. She knew he loved it and that, in a few days when everything was finished, they would have a whole week to themselves in New York. Jack had flown to New York on Wednesday to work with one of the other big investment banking houses on Wall Street. Annie knew she wouldn't see him until late Sunday. "We'll have a nice dinner at the Plaza's Palm Room on Sunday," he told her.

The weekend came and went, ending with a wonderful dinner Sunday night. Monday was Jack's big day. Annie laughed when he bounded out of bed like a kid on Christmas morning. For him, it was Christmas, and the company's IPO was the present under the tree. The company's stock was priced at $35 and traded at a premium all day, closing at $37. Everyone was extremely pleased.

That night, Jack and Annie went out on the town to celebrate. They had dinner on a fancy 120-foot yacht with the team and the company owners to celebrate the successful offering.

"This is so romantic, Jack. This is a nice way to kick off our anniversary week."

He leaned over and kissed the top of her head. Then he pulled her close, as they looked at the Statue of Liberty in the clear night. The two World Trade Towers looked so beautiful against the backdrop of the river and the city.

"Aren't they impressive?"

"What?" Annie asked.

"The Towers. Our meeting room is almost at the top of one of them. I have to go back tomorrow morning for an hour or two just to make sure everything is OK. I should be done around 10 a.m. Then we have the rest of the week to relax. Why don't you figure out where we want to eat for our anniversary?"

"Let's go to Greenwich Village, have a nice dinner and see a new play. I love that area."

"Okay. What are you going to do tomorrow morning?"

"I thought I would get up and explore Central Park. Then I'll do some shopping at Sak's, or I might go to Tiffany's and just look."

"You can do more than look. I need to get you something for our anniversary, so why don't you look for something you'd like and then we can go back together. I think we can afford it after this deal."

Annie brought her hand to Jack's face, gently slid it around his neck, pulled him closer and kissed him. "I love you, Mr. Stevenson."

He kissed her lips, her nose, and her closed eyes, and then held her close. "I love you, Mrs. Stevenson. We're so lucky."

They held each other, not saying a word. They didn't need to.

Back at the Plaza, Annie pulled back the drapes and gazed out over Central Park and the surrounding skyline of Condo's and expensive apartments. The lights were off in the room.

"It reminds me of being on the beach in Ephraim and looking at the twinkle of lights along the shoreline of the village, the Moravian church steeple, and resorts and private homes and the stars at night. The stars cover the sky from the horizon on up here too."

Jack came up behind her and slipped his arms just under her breasts, then held her close. "I love you," he said and started kissing her neck.

A chill ran down Annie's neck and she moaned slightly. She turned toward Jack. They slowly helped each other get out of their clothes.

Jack pulled the heavy bedspread off and placed it on the floor, so they could look out over the city as they made love.

Afterwards Annie said, "It feels like the night we made love for the first time at the gallery. Do you remember?"

"How could I forget?"

"I thought you were the sexiest man I had ever met. What I didn't realize is that I would fall in love with you as fast as you did with me. It was a magical night."

"Tonight is a magical night in a magical city."

"I'll never forget this night. I'll never forget what a special day this is for you and your career too. We're so lucky."

They lay in each other's arms and slept on the floor. At sunrise, they made love again. Jack kissed Annie good-bye. "I'll see you back here around noon. We'll find someplace nice to eat and then walk the city. Call me on my cell. I love you."

She got up and gave him a long lingering kiss. "Don't stay away too long!"

"I won't. Have fun shopping this morning."

**

"Rita, it's Annie."

"How are you?" said Rita. "Have you seen the news on New York and the Pentagon? It's horrible."

Annie started crying.

"What's wrong?" Panic rose in Rita's voice.

"Everything. I've…. lost him, Rita. I lost Jack in the World Trade Center. He had to go back for just a little while to wrap things up with his deal." Annie broke down. "We were going to meet for lunch…I came out of the Plaza. Everyone was looking up. Smoke was billowing out of the towers. I didn't know what was going on until I stopped someone and they told me." Tears came so fast she nearly choked.

"He was there. I called his cell phone. He was trapped on one of the top floors. He said he loved me. He said he'd be okay. Then he laughed and said he probably wouldn't make it for lunch. He said he'd call me when he got out and was safe. They were going to try to go to the roof. They hoped they could be air lifted off. He sounded so calm. He just kept saying, 'Don't worry. Don't worry. I'll be okay. I love you.'"

"Oh, Annie," Rita said.

"Twenty minutes later, the first tower went down. Then the second one went down... He never called, Rita," Annie cried softly. "I don't think I can live without him. I don't want to live without him," she whispered.

Rita gave a big sigh. "Annie, you know Jack would really be mad at you if he heard you talking like you are. Of course he would expect you to feel the way you do about losing someone you love. He'd say you have to go on. You're young; you have so much to live for." She paused, cleared her throat. "Annie, do you want me to come out? The planes aren't flying, but I can drive out and be there in less than a day. I have vacation time coming, so I can get away."

"Would you? I don't know what to do. Saturday is our anniversary."

"Where are you staying?"

"The Plaza."

"I'll be on my way in one hour."

"Thank you, Rita. I just need someone to be with. I'm all alone. I love you."

"I know. I love you, too. Try to get some rest."

"I'll try. When I close my eyes, all I see is towers falling. His last words were 'I'll be okay. I love you.'"

"Annie, I'm packing now. Call my cell phone whenever you need to, okay? I'll be there soon."

Annie hung up the phone. Looking out the window at Central Park, it was hard to believe last night they'd made love on the floor. She could almost feel Jack's arms around her. She'd never felt so alone in her life.

Chapter Twenty-Seven

It didn't happen often, but a client requested Kick Back to sail their boat back when he got uncomfortable sailing it back from Bimini. The events of 9/11 didn't help either. Two days later, after planes were allowed to fly again, Peter, Paula, and Frank Jetter, an experienced sailor and employee, caught a floatplane over to Bimini.

"OK, I verified with the weather service that conditions are right for a tropical storm. It is the middle of the hurricane season. Before leaving, I studied weather reports from the National Weather Service. I noticed one large storm over the Gulf of Mexico. It seemed far enough away not to cause a problem. No one that I talked to is sure if it would turn into anything more than a tropical storm. We'll have to keep a close eye on it to make sure it doesn't develop into anything worse."

Paula said. "I know. Hurricanes can pop up overnight from a storm like that. It doesn't take much to turn the Gulf Stream into a dangerous place."

Peter wanted to get going too as soon as possible, hoping to beat the weather to Miami just in case it got ugly. At least they didn't have to worry about the time of day when they arrived back in Miami. All the harbor entrances in Florida were well marked, unlike Bimini. The navigation markings for the islands were poor at best; it was always best to approach during the day.

If all went right, they'd be back home in less than a day.

The three arrived on time in Jamestown on the island of Bimini and soon were on the boat.

From that point on, nothing went as planned. First, they had problems with the two engines. There were air bubbles in the fuel lines, so the engines did not run well. No big deal, but it took time to get them running properly. Then they had to stow or tighten down everything that was not essential to sailing. It was close to four p.m. when they finally started back to Miami.

"We'll motor at first just to make sure everything is up to snuff and the equipment is working properly." Peter said.

An hour later, "The winds are starting to clock around to the southwest. Damn it, that's not good." Peter said.

"That makes me a little nervous." Paula said, "If a storm comes in from the west or northwest, it would create mountainous waves in the direction we need to go."

"I know. It could reach 30 or more feet high. The gulfstream current travelling north at four or five knots colliding with the wind could create huge waves that could be difficult to sail or even motor in. Not something fun to face in a 46-foot catamaran. The only thing going for us is experience and it was only 43 nautical miles to Miami."

"How come when were in dangerous weather like this, 43 nautical miles seems like forever?" Paula said.

They had motored for about an hour and a half when Paula talked Peter into raising the sails. They were on a beam reach, with the winds basically coming from the south. "Frank, steer a heading of 280 degrees. That should be a correct course for Miami and the marina."

"We can sail at eight knots vs. motoring at five, so it makes sense for now." Paula said.

The seas were manageable. Peter listened to the marine weather forecast again and the indication was that a tropical storm had indeed formed over the Gulf and was moving east toward lower Florida. He hoped they could get home before it turned ugly.

"Since things looked good at the moment, let's take advantage of the tolerable conditions and start dinner. I brought Dinty Moore beef stew, so I'll warm it up. Then I'll make coffee and put it in a thermos bottle. We'll need it later on. If the seas start to build like I think, it will be too rough to cook. The time to eat is when you first think of it, and when the weather is smooth enough to make it happen." He said to Paula.

"You're too much but I think your right. We better eat now because I think it's going to get rough."

Frank said. "I can always eat...anytime."

All was ready about 7:30 p.m., and then they enjoyed a nice dinner, even though the catamaran was rolling a bit. Paula had turned on the autopilot, which gave them a chance to eat together and talk strategy if the weather got nasty.

Frank was assigned the first shift, Paula the second, and Peter the third. The shift change would be two hours on, two hours backup, and two hours completely off watch.

Around 8:30 p.m., the wind picked up, shifting around more and more to the west. The seas started to build. They could still sail, but it was becoming more difficult with the waves cresting. The tops started to spill over with white foam, and the crests lit up like one of the chemical sticks kids wave back and forth on holidays. The catamaran moved through the water at about six and a half knots, and the warm, humid wind moved steadily to the west.

Paula and Peter were now on watch. Frank went down below to get whatever rest he could. Peter watched his wife as she sailed the boat up and slightly across the waves.

"I don't know how long we're going to be able to sail like this," she said. "Do you think we should bring the sails in or point more toward the north? We could sail toward Ft. Lauderdale instead of Miami and then bring it home once the weather blows through."

Peter thought about it for a while. "I think we should try to get home and get the boat tied up at our marina. We're about halfway there. We can motor the rest of the way if need be. It's going to be tougher to motor than sail, but we can stay on course. If we start pointing farther north, with this gulfstream current, we might drift way up north. I'd rather try to motor home."

"Yeah, I guess you're right," Paula said. "I just like to sail, and it's not often we get a chance to sail together, even if it's almost in a hurricane." They both laughed.

Twenty minutes later, Peter said, "Do you think we should reef the main or just bring everything in before it gets worse? You know what Sir Francis Chitchester said?"

"Yes, the golden rule of sailing…the time to reef is when you first think of it. Okay, let's just take the sails down. It looks like it's getting worse."

Paula edged the catamaran into the wind and tried to manage the heel while the catamaran climbed the waves. The water hissed like a deadly snake as it passed underneath the twin hulls. The waves were 12 feet and starting to break.

Peter put on his inflatable safety harness attaching a short lifeline to the base of the mast, just in case he lost his balance or was hit by a wave. With the Catamaran pointed into the wind, he lowered the mainsail and tried to tie it down to the boom. Paula adjusted the boats angle to the waves to 45 degrees in an effort to make it more stable for Peter on the pitching deck. The wind howled making a sound like a jet engine revving up for takeoff, then snatched the sail from Peter's hands, whipping it back and forth. His knuckles were skinned and raw as he tried to tie the mainsail on the boom. Streaks of blood spread across the white sails as he fought to gain control.

Shit, I'll have to soak this sail with bleach when I get back.

Paula, seeing that he was having trouble, flipped on the autopilot and made her way up toward the cabin top to help him. She yelled down to Frank, who somehow was asleep.

"Frank. Frank!"

"Yeah."

"Get up here and give us a hand."

"Ok. I'm coming."

Next she yelled to Peter, "Let me help. It's too difficult to handle alone!"

Turning to the still groggy Frank, she said, "You just steer the boat. I'll help Peter tie it down."

In seconds, the wind increased in intensity and the waves suddenly grew by five feet.

Paula looked at Peter. She yelled, "Just hold on for a second until I can get up there and help."

"Okay." He yelled. *She's not going to come up here without her harness is she?*

Paula turned around and made her way around the fixed fiberglass canopy above the cockpit. Peter heard a hissing sound like a train coming. He looked over his shoulder and saw a huge wave rising against the black sky. The curling white foam of the cresting wave looked like shark's teeth. He knew, in an instant, that it was going to collapse onto the boat. *This was going to hurt.*

"Paula! Hang on!" he screamed above the wind.

She turned and looked up, just in time to see the wave start to fall. She took one glance at Peter and reached for something to hold on to. When the wave collapsed on them, Peter wrapped his arms around the mast as best he could. Several tons of water dropped on him and ripped his arms loose from the mast and knocked the air out of his chest. He shot across the top of the cabin like a balloon bouncing across a sand beach. His safety line stretched to its full length, yet somehow didn't snap. It was the only thing that kept him from being swept overboard. He was dazed.

When he regained his senses, he looked for Paula, but all he saw was a black ocean.

"Oh God, Oh no. Please no!"

Peter saw Frank clawing his way back to the wheel. He had been tossed across the cockpit and was only saved by being thrown against the base of the traveler support in the far corner of the cockpit. Peter watched Frank claw his way to the controls, and then flipped on the autopilot. Peter tried to stand, but realized he was still dazed and decided to crawl into the cockpit.

"Paula? Where's Paula?" Panic engulfed him. He immediately threw the life ring and 'man overboard' pole out. He hit the MOB on the GPS. Taking control, he started a figure eight maneuver as best he could, trying to get back to where he thought Paula might be. *Please God please, don't let me lose her.*

Ten minutes later, he realized she was gone. She really had no chance when the wave hit her. She probably was off balance and out of position as she tried to get around the corner of the fixed canopy. When the wave crashed down, it probably drove her head into the corner of the fiberglass cover and knocked her out. He knew, in the best of conditions, it's difficult to find anyone. A head only sticks up maybe 18 inches. In 10-15 foot seas, with an unconscious person and total darkness, he knew it was almost impossible. Peter called a mayday, giving his position from the GPS. Then he put his head in his hands and sobbed.

**

The coast guard looked for two days, plotting the currents and wind vectors, but Paula's body was never found.

Peter and the Guerrero family had a memorial ceremony for her early on a Sunday morning. It seemed like most of Key West turned out. Many of those attending made their living from the sea. It was never easy to lose anyone, let alone a family member.

Father Phillip gave an emotional, uplifting service.

The Guerrero family held no grudge against Peter, knowing Paula's love for the sea and their love for each other.

Carlos came up to Peter after the service. "Peter, there is a hole in my heart that will never close. I will miss my baby, my Paula. I will miss never having bounced your babies on my knee. I thank you for giving me the honor of walking her down the aisle. She was so beautiful.... life... it is not fair sometimes."

They wept as they hugged. "You, Peter... are always, always part of this family."

**

Back at the Marina the following week, Peter was in his chair just staring, not really caring. He felt Mahoney's hand on his shoulder. He knew Mahoney loved him like a son he never had, so it wasn't a surprise when he ask, "How are you doing?"

"I feel empty. I don't want to do anything, see anyone, or talk to anyone. I've gone over everything. There are so many things I could have done differently, that she could have done differently. She should have had her harness on, that's our rule, but she didn't. If we would have kept on sailing, we would have probably lost the mast and sails, but we could have motored in. If we got Frank up just a bit earlier instead of doing it ourselves like we always do. All those things would have kept Paula alive. I know it's an accident. Things happen. I don't know what to do now."

Sorrow hung in the air like mist on a foggy night.

Mahoney put his hand on his shoulder. "Peter, we can take care of things here. You need to get away. Why don't you go to that place up north that you always talk about? What's it called?"

"Door County."

"Yeah, that's the place. Your friends are there?"

"Most of them."

Squeezing Peter's shoulder slightly, Mahoney spoke with a little more emphasis. "That's where you need to go."

"You're probably right. I'll think about it. Thanks, Mahoney. Thanks for being my friend and being here."

"Don't you worry about anything; we'll take care of everything. I'll whip these kids you hired into shape just like I whipped you into shape."

Peter looked at his friend. For the first time in weeks, he smiled. "I bet you will."

**

Annie was exhausted. Not only was she devastated by her loss, but also she was reminded of it wherever she looked. The news played and replayed the Towers falling. The debris from the Towers was all over the city. It seemed like everyone either lost someone or knew someone who lost a spouse, relative, or friend. The city and the nation were in a state of shock. Jack's company was in a state of shock, too. Toby, the president, and most of the investment banking team, had been in the Tower as well.

It was very difficult to get to Ground Zero. When Annie reached the area, she encountered thousands of people like herself. Initially, there was hope, but it quickly became apparent that there was little chance of finding survivors.

There was one glimmer of hope when a small group of fireman and workers were found protected by a single stairwell. As it turned out, they would be the last survivors found in the rubble. Recovery was slow.

Annie returned to The Plaza late on September 12, exhausted. As she entered her room, she saw Thomas and Rita.

"I called Thomas after I talked to you. We drove out together."

Annie collapsed into Rita's arms. Not saying anything, Thomas stepped close and pulled all of them together, giving each strength and comfort.

Annie sobbed. "Thank you. Thank you both so much for coming."

Tears trickled down the cheeks of all three as they stood in a tight cluster. After a few minutes, they moved to the sofa and chairs as Annie described the scene at Ground Zero. The area was crowded with relatives, friends, and volunteers, but the feeling was of sadness and despair about loved ones.

"Wherever you look, you see flyers with pictures of the missing. Each one asks for any information about husbands, wives, mothers, fathers, sons, daughters, friends and co-workers." Hope faded as the realization sank in that they were lost. Annie went to an identification area that was set up with pictures she had of Jack with a description of his University of Wisconsin class ring and his favorite Mickey Mouse gold watch he always wore.

She laughed, as she explained how he never wore his class ring until the Badgers won back-to-back Rose Bowl games. He used to rub it into the faces of his Illinois and Northwestern co-workers and friends. The Badgers had won, finally the last three times, 1994, 2000 and 2001. Then she started to cry as she realized that she'd never again hear him brag about that.

When she called her parents to tell them about Jack, her mom cried. Even her dad cracked as she talked. They were ready to drive out but, when she informed them that Rita and Thomas were with her, they were relieved.

"You come home, here to Door County," Betty said. "We'll take care of you."

"I will, after we find Jack." She sobbed and then said. "I'll call you later. I love you."

For the next few days, the three went down and waited for Jack to be found. The care and dignity the workers used when they found any human remains resembled an honor guard cortege.

On the fifth day, they found Jack's body. Annie, Rita and Thomas made arrangements for his remains to be cremated in New York City. Two days later, they started the drive home to Chicago.

Thomas drove his big black Mercedes while Annie cradled Jack's remains. Driving home in the back seat, Annie felt at peace for the first time in eight days, and she was able to sleep as she leaned against Rita.

Annie dreaded walking into their loft apartment for the first time. She thought she would be very depressed. She conjured up images of

Jack everywhere, and she worried that the good times, the love and laughter they shared in the apartment would flood her senses.

Even as she sat in the car, she could picture him working at his desk in the large open area. It was a special place for both of them. It was their passion area. Late at night or very early in the morning, he would work at his desk almost naked. Looking at him when he was like that would stir Annie's emotions. If she thought the time was right, she'd quietly move behind him as he worked. She'd slide her hands down his chest, kissing and nibbling his neck and ears. This was usually enough to secure his interest, and they would move to an old bear skin rug and make love.

Annie loved to rest her head on the head of the bear. The animal skin excited them both. Jack laughed at her when she bought the rug at an estate sale in Fish Creek. After it became their love place, he told her it was the best purchase she ever made.

Arriving home, Thomas and Rita went up to the loft with her to make sure she was okay. After a few hours and some more tears, Annie felt she could be alone without them.

What surprised her as she walked around the house were the positive vibes she got from everything of Jack's. He was there. Not physically, but spiritually. She felt at peace. Her favorite place when she wanted to feel close to him was now the bear rug, their bear rug.

Chapter Twenty-Eight

Dennis was waiting for Peter when he landed in Green Bay. It was Friday, September 28. Uncharacteristically, Dennis had a hard time controlling his emotions as he saw Peter walk down the ramp from the plane. He wiped tears and gave Peter a big bear hug.

"I am so sorry for your loss. Paula was such a good person. I …" He stopped because he couldn't go on. He knew he never had felt this way for anyone, at least not yet. For once, Dennis was not thinking about himself.

It was a beautiful fall day as Peter collected his baggage and got in Dennis's pickup truck. Green Bay's airport was on the small side, so it did not take long to get going.

"How was the flight up?" asked Dennis.

Peter stared at the countryside with the orange and yellow leaves rustling in the fall breeze. "It took forever to get through the airport in Miami. Security measures are unbelievable. It took me three hours before I got through. Thank God I had seen the news reports about the delays. I got there early, so I didn't miss my flight, but I can tell you hundreds did. It's a mess!

Once I got on the plane, everything was fine. The planes were on time and the service was great. It was just scary seeing armed soldiers in the airports. They mean business. Some guy made a joke about something and four security guards were on him faster than you could say 'go to jail', which is what I think happened to him."

"Things are a lot different everywhere," Dennis said.

"If you're from the Middle East, or look like you are, everyone looks at you funny. I know you shouldn't do that because they're Americans, too. Now I know how the Japanese Americans felt during WWII. It's a sad commentary on our times."

Dennis just shook his head in agreement.

"How's the Garibaldi coming?" Peter asked

"She's getting there," said Dennis, thankful to be talking about boats. "We're still framing. Once we get past that, we'll start bending wood for the sides. It's at least starting to look like a boat. I go up whenever I can. Mom is staying at the nursing home in Sister Bay. It gives me a chance to see her. She's doing okay, but it's going to take time. Thank God, Deacon's gave me a promotion and the job up here. I'm plant manager now. If things work out the way they should, I'll be running the whole place in a couple of years as guys retire."

"Fantastic. I'm really happy for you. I remember that first year when we all met and you were just learning about boats. You've come a long way."

Dennis smiled. "We all have. Here we are, right back in Door County. That is, everyone but Rita. I hear she's in Chicago and Milwaukee, splits her time between Northwestern Medical Center and Colombia Hospital in Milwaukee as an ER doctor."

Peter looked out the window, not saying anything. Finally, he asked, "How's Annie? How's she doing? Jack was in one of the towers when they went down?"

"Yeah, he was." Dennis sighed. "He was a nice guy. He treated Annie great. I'm not an expert on love, as you know, but I think they had the real thing. Darrell just shakes his head when I ask about her."

"He was a great guy. I wish I had a chance to get to know him better, but our paths didn't cross that much. Paula and I stopped to see them once on our way to my parent's house. We flew into Chicago, had dinner and spent the night at their place, and then we drove over to St Louis. I can see why Annie fell in love with him." He paused. "Is she in Door County?"

"Yes, at her parents. We could stop by if you'd like?"

"Let's wait. I need to settle in. Then I'll see her."

Dennis glanced at Peter as he drove. "You'll likely see her soon anyway. She's been coming down to the boat and working. She says it gets her mind off what happened."

"She's right. That's why I'm up here."

The orchards on the way up were thick with apples. To Peter, it was a blur.

Dennis watched Peter more closely. He knew he was probably thinking about Paula. "What are you thinking about? Paula?"

"The last time I saw her. Her face. The wave. I remembered her looking at me, then seeing the terror in her eyes as she saw the wave. When I looked again, she was gone. I keep turning it over and over in my mind, what could I have done to save her. She should have been wearing the inflatable harness and safety line. Sometimes I get so mad at her. She should have known better. She was a professional. It's eating me up. I know there is nothing I can do now to bring her back."

He wiped the tears sliding down his cheek, but he didn't care. Things like that didn't matter much to him anymore.

"Peter, where are you staying?"

"Well, I don't think I'll have a problem. It's almost October."

"Times have changed," Dennis said. "Fall is busier up here than the summer, if you can believe that."

The orange, red and yellow leaves hung on the trees. Set against a deep blue cloudless sky, it created a perfect fall afternoon. For a few minutes, Dennis thought, even Peter was able to forget the events of the past couple of weeks and enjoyed the scenery.

"Fall is my favorite time of the year," he said. "The colors, the crisp cool days and nights, the steady winds make it the perfect time to be in Door County. I wish Paula could have experienced this time and place."

Dennis reached over and rubbed Peter's shoulder. "Do you believe in reincarnation?"

"I really haven't thought about it."

Dennis went on. "Ever since I was a little kid and knew about life and death, I hoped that you just got reborn in a different form. You might have the spirit of another person mixed with you to make you unique. I don't know what I'm trying to say, Peter, but I believe in it."

Peter said, "It would be nice to believe that. I'd like to think Paula would come back as a majestic osprey or eagle, so she could soar on the wind. If that's the case, then she might see these fall colors right now." Peter wasn't sure he believed what they were talking about, but it did lift his mood a little. Paula might be soaring on the wind right now, waiting for him.

They decided to drive up the Lake Michigan side up of the peninsula, after passing through Sturgeon Bay. Dennis turned onto Highway 57 instead of his normal Highway 42 route.

"Hey, let's stop at Harry's and have a beer. I can tell you about my high school reunion."

Peter smiled. "Yeah, I remember Harry's. The four of us used to stop there and have Little Joe's beers, twenty-five cents for those little seven-ounce bottles. I don't suppose Harry is still around?"

When they reached Harry's, it wasn't Harry's anymore. Peter got out of the car. "Man, they fixed it up and it's bigger. It looks really nice. *Coyote Roadhouse*. New name, too."

Dennis tilted his hat back. "It sure does look bigger. Do you suppose the beer prices are the same?"

They laughed which seemed to break the tension for Peter. They went in to the bar and sat down and ordered some *Island Wheat* beer that was on tap.

"Did you know some of the grain used in this beer comes from Washington Island?" said Dennis.

"Really?" Peter held the glass up to inspect it for the first time. "Well, it tastes good. So tell me about your class reunion." He leaned his stool back to listen.

"Remember in July, when I met you at the airport in Milwaukee? While I was waiting for you, I ran into an old flame of mine. Her name was Connie. I really had the hots for her back in high school, but she embarrassed me once pretty thoroughly. I think she's part of the reason I'm so screwed up when it comes to women." He took a swig of his beer.

"Anyhow, she tells me about the class reunion and makes sure I get an invitation. Not only that, but she calls to make sure I'm coming. It's been a while since graduation, and I see a lot of old friends, men and women, but you know, it's really the women I'm interested in. About half are married, the rest are divorced or stayed single, saving themselves for that special person, I guess." Dennis starts laughing. "You know, Peter, kind of like me. I've just been saving myself for Ms. Perfect."

Peter laughed. "Right. It's getting deep in here."

"Well, anyhow, after a few hours of socializing, Connie comes over. She looks great. She's an aerobics instructor and a real estate agent for one of the local firms in Milwaukee. She has been divorced three times. First guy was a plastic surgeon, set her up great with this condo overlooking McKinley Marina. She got a great settlement. Second guy was a CPA. Then she meets this developer, and they get married, but he turns out to be abusive, so she divorces him. She's still having trouble with him, but she got a restraining order and things seem to be okay now. She doesn't remember embarrassing me back in high school. I played around with her Friday night of the reunion, keeping her interested, but still holding her off. I had her going, but I didn't want to piss her off because she is really good-looking and turns out, very athletic in bed. She was fun, smart and easy to be with. We hung around with some of our friends Saturday morning, and then we all went to the Brewers game in the afternoon. She sits next to me. She's going nuts. She wants me so bad, and I know it. Seventh inning stretch comes. She leans over and sticks her tongue in my ear and then whispers, "If you want me to do more with my tongue and the rest of my body, you'll get out of that seat, out of this damn stadium, and follow me to my condo where you can fuck my brains out." Then she smiles, tilting her head and batting her eyes, and says, 'Let's go play America's real favorite pastime: Sex'." He chucked.

"What could I do? I grabbed my ball and bat, so to speak, and went home with her. We've been screwing ever since." He takes a sip of his beer, looks out the window at Kangaroo Lake. "It's ironic. Now that I live up here, I have to drive to Milwaukee for sex. When I lived in Milwaukee, I drove up here for sex. Great country."

Peter is laughing so hard he's crying. "Thanks, I needed that, Dennis."

They finished their beers and took off. It was just the break they both needed to try to get back to some semblance of normalcy.

Getting in the car, Dennis asked Peter where he wanted to stay.

"Why don't you take me to the Evergreen Beach Hotel. It's close to the old Hotel Ephraim, which went condo. It's close to my roots."

Dennis glanced at Peter, smiling. "It's also close to Annie's house, isn't it?"

"I guess it is," Peter said. "I hadn't really thought about that."

**

After checking in, he walked down to the hotel's sandy beach looking out at the Park's limestone bluffs and Horseshoe Island. He sat on one of their pink Adirondack chairs trying to relax. As he looked up the shore, Peter saw Wilson's. He suddenly had a desire for one of their root beer malts. Why not, he thought, he hadn't had one in years. He buttoned up his canvas work jacket and started to walk. It felt good to be back.

It took him about five minutes to walk along the bay towards Wilson's. The air was clean and fresh. It was also getting cooler. It's October and I'm an idiot for not wearing a sweater, he thought, as he turned the collar up and pulled his coat tighter.

Eagle Bluff was alive with fall colors as he looked across the Bay. He stopped by the boat rental house where he got his start with Mr. Peterson but it was closed for the season. It was much bigger, and the area around it was improved. A modern steel and cement pier replaced the old wooden pier he and Annie had raced from. He could always count on catching a few rainbow trout or bass under the wood logs with the old pier.

He smiled as he turned. Walking into Wilson's was like stepping back in time. He did notice a few changes. The girls looked the same, but their outfits were different. They wore a Wilson's red T-shirt instead of a red and white-checkered blouse. And it was fall, so some wore blue or red Wilson's hoodies as well. They had expanded the outdoor seating, too. It was very busy, which surprised Peter, but then he remembered what Dennis said about the fall color season.

He decided to eat outdoors. It was pleasant and probably warm enough on the porch. As he opened the door to leave for the porch, Annie and her mother entered at the same time. Peter saw them first, by just a fraction of a second. Annie was looking down at the door-knob as Peter pulled it open.

"Excuse me, I..." Annie started to say and then she saw Peter, froze for an instant, and then embraced him and buried her head in his chest. They blocked the doorway, not caring what others thought. When they pulled back, both had tears running down their cheeks. They stepped back outside. For a split second, Peter forgot about his miseries. He felt happy holding her.

Annie was the first to speak. "What brings you here?"

"I came for the root beer malt," he said with a smile.

Annie laughed. "I should have guessed. You always did love those root beer malts."

"Hey, that's how we met or did you forget? What brings you here?"

"Ice cream cone. Mom and I were shopping and need a little something sweet."

"Hi, Mrs. Wilson, I mean, Betty. It's nice to see you again. Still making those great cherry pies?"

"It's nice to see you, Peter, and yes, I do. You'll have to stop over and have a piece."

"I will. I was just going outside to get a table on the porch; it's pretty busy inside. Would you two like to join me?"

"We'd love to," said Annie. "But you enter the porch seating area thru a inside door, at the end of the counter."

"Show me the way."

They found a table that gave them a nice view. The afternoon sun was still high enough over the bluffs to make the porch warm and pleasant.

"Annie, I was so sorry to hear about Jack. Rita called me just before she and Thomas drove out to be with you."

"Thank you. It's crazy how life can be going along fine and then, in a heartbeat, it changes forever." Tears welled up; her eyes grew red around the rims.

Betty reached over and rubbed her back in small little circles. "Only time will help. Time and a safe sanctuary like home and Door County."

Finally, Annie turned toward Peter. "I'm sorry, Peter; I didn't mean to act like this. How's Paula?"

Now it was Peter's turn. He turned away. When he turned back, his vision was blurry.

"Right after I talked to Rita about you and Jack, Paula and I had to go to Bimini to bring a sailboat back to Miami. There was some heavy weather developing over the Gulf of Mexico, and we didn't think it would be more than typical stormy weather, but it quickly intensified into a hurricane. We got stuck in it while we were coming back, and Paula was washed off the boat when a large wave crashed on top of us. I was lashing down the main sail and had a safety harness on. She came up to help me but she didn't have her harness on and got swept away with the wave. I lost her." He wiped at the tears rolling down his cheeks with the back of his hand. "I guess we both came back here for similar reasons."

They looked at each other, their emotions raw and exposed. Annie reached over and slid her hand gently over his, squeezing it. "Peter, I am so, so sorry."

Peter looked towards Betty and saw tears on her cheeks, and then felt her hand rest on top of his and Annie's.

"Oh honey," she said, "I'm so sorry for you. It's not fair what's happened to both of you."

Just then, a waitress came up and asked what they'd like. It was a blessing, because it got them back to the present.

Wiping away the tears with his jacket sleeve, he looked up at the honey blond waitress. *She's probably wondering why I'm crying?* Peter smiled. "I'd like one of your world famous root beer malts." Looking at Annie, he said, "If you don't know how to make it, this lady can help you."

The waitress turned and looked at Annie, puzzled.

Annie smiled. "I used to work here. That's how we met. He taught me how to make root beer malts."

"Oh, then you got married and you're back here to celebrate. How romantic."

Their eyes met, but neither Peter nor Annie said anything.

"What would you like?" She asked as she looked at Annie.

"I'll just have some of his malt, and a tuna fish sandwich. Isn't that what we had on our first date?"

Peter laughed. "It was, but if you'll remember, I made them. I'm not sure they could duplicate my secret recipe."

"And you?" The waitress looked at Betty.

"Oh, give me a chocolate ice cream cone."

Annie and Peter looked at each other and smiled.

Over their food, they talked about what was going on locally. Annie brought Peter up to speed on the schooner Garibaldi's progress. She had started working there two days before, she said, and decided she wanted to work on the figurehead. She explained she had done some work with wood figures years ago and was going to try her hand at it again.

Peter said he was going up tomorrow. He needed to rent a car. Then he was going to see Mr. Peterson and Jim Erickson.

The food was just as Peter remembered it. Annie and he split their lunch and Betty had her cone. Then they walked back to Evergreen Beach Hotel. It had been a while since Annie and Betty had been in the Evergreen, so they came in and visited Peter's room.

"Here it is, right around the corner from our house, and I bet I haven't been in here in twenty years," Betty said. "It's got a very nice view of the Bay. I wish we had a view of the water, but the forest is nice in its own way. And in the spring, we have all the water we want to look at when the snow melts and the creek runs high."

Peter decided he'd walk back to their place just to see how things looked. Nothing had changed except they had a newer car. Betty cut Peter a big piece of cherry pie and gave him one of Darrell's beers to take back to the hotel. "He won't miss it, and you'll probably want one later. Remember, Ephraim is dry."

He thanked Betty and gave her a hug. Then he gave Annie a hug. Finally, Annie raised up on her toes and gave Peter a gentle kiss on the cheek.

"It was good to see you again, Peter. It gives me comfort knowing you're around. I'll see you at the boat works tomorrow."

"I'll be there, but I'm not sure exactly when." Waving goodbye, he took his beer and pie and left.

**

Dennis got up early the next morning and drove the 30 minutes north to pick up Peter.

"How you doing, buddy?"

"Fine. Thanks for picking me up. I should have done this yesterday, and it would have saved you making the trip."

"Don't think about it. What did you do after I dropped you off?"

"Went to Wilson's and had a malt. I ran into Annie and her mom. She looks good, considering."

"Hey, she always looked good to me." Dennis said. "But then she was your girl and I had Rita. They were two pretty hot chicks." He broke into a big smile. "I won't see you this weekend. Going to Brew City to see Connie. Man, that woman loves to screw. I'm not sure we'll even get out of her condo. I'm just glad I'm the guy who helps her feel good."

"Well, I can see nothing has changed in your life, Mr. Jamison."

"Na, what can I do? They love me. I don't have to love them. I just have to make them feel good. Do you know George Strait has a song he sings about a guy like that? *The Fireman*. That's me. I just go around helping put out the fire that's burning inside them."

Peter rolled his eyes. Once they reached Sturgeon Bay, he thanked Dennis. "I'll see you Monday. We'll have a beer at The Stein, and I'll buy."

Peter rented a Chevy pickup at the local dealership. He liked driving a truck. With a truck, he could haul stuff. What stuff he'd haul around he didn't know, but he wanted it all the same. The truck was beat up and it was cheap to rent. He drove up on the lakeside of the peninsula along highway 57, just because he usually didn't go that way.

He stopped at the Blue Ox in Baileys Harbor for coffee. He loved the place. It had so much antique stuff on the walls; saws, old rifles, tools. If it was used in Door County, it was on the wall. The Blue Ox was known for good chili, good beer, and good music, but since it was early, all he wanted was strong coffee.

That they had. He laughed at some of the locals who were having a shot of brandy or whiskey and a beer. It was fall, and that meant that the salmon and trout were coming in to spawn and die. He watched the fishermen from the bar, as they jerked their rods, trying to snag big fish with their treble hooks. Fishing was a big part of the economy this time of the year.

Peter listened to the other patrons as they bitched and boasted about the fishing that morning, and the banter helped him forget. He liked their company. Made him think of Mahoney. He smiled. Mahoney would like Door County. He might have to bring him up sometime.

After two cups of coffee, he'd had enough company and fish talk. It was time he was on his way to Sister Bay. It had not changed much since July when he was last there. It felt good as he drove down the hill into the village.

He smiled as he saw the goats at Al Johnson's grazing on the traditional grass roof. The gift shops and cafés were doing a brisk business. Unlike summer, most of the people walking around now were adults. Fall brought an older crowd. Food and shopping were the main agenda items for most.

He soon reached the marina where Garibaldi was being constructed. They had made significant progress since his last visit. They had most of the frames in place and were working on one of the bow sections as he drove up.

Ken Judd stood near the bow, pointing at something he wanted moved. "Jesus Christ, can't you guys read plans? It goes higher." He turned and when he saw Peter, his face lit up. "Well, look who's here. What brings you all the way from Florida?"

Peter smiled as he shook his and then brought his hand up to shade his eyes against the morning sun. "I wanted to see how things were progressing. Actually, I needed to get away from work for a while. Let's go over to Base Camp, and I'll buy you a cup of coffee and fill you in."

Mr. Peterson saw Peter walking with Ken. He walked over and gave him a hearty handshake. Peter asked him to join them. He thought it best to tell his story, as few times as possible, since it ripped him apart each time he had to relive the story. He knew that after telling Ken and Mr. Peterson, he would not have to explain why he was here. The story would get around and he could get some semblance of normalcy.

It seemed to take hours to tell his friends about Paula, but in reality it was only about ten minutes. "I need to be here now because this place is filled with good memories and gives me strength. I also need to be doing something to keep myself busy. Using my hands and energy on Garibaldi is what I need." He could feel his eyes getting misty. Every time I think about her, I tear up like now. I miss her so. "I'm not a carpenter or Boatwright, but I can do anything you guys want me to do."

Mr. Peterson smiled. "Seems to me you were good at cleaning up boats. I know we can always find a broom and paint brushes for you." They laughed. "We'll keep you busy. The rest is up to you."

"Thanks, Mr. Peterson," said Peter.

Ken looked at his watch and then at Peter. "Well, if you're serious about working, I'd say it's time to get at it. If we sit here any longer, people are going to think were just a bunch of gossiping women."

"I'm ready. Let's go," said Peter.

Ken slapped him on the back. "Follow me. I'll introduce you to some of the guys. We'll get you working on that bow section. Lots of work has to be done there. Those guys will help you learn what boat building with wood is all about." He raised a finger and shook it. "Watch out for Gary and Bob. They like their beer when the day's done. They'll bend your ear for as long as you listen on and off the job."

"Thanks, Ken."

Chapter Twenty-Nine

Annie started jogging that fall in Door County after Jack's death. She'd walk down toward the water's edge each day to see the sun's first rays strike the limestone bluffs across the bay. Somehow everything seemed better, clearer, in the morning light. Then she'd jog. Both things got her mind off of what happened. It gave her hope and helped stave off the image of the Towers. They'd creep into her thoughts without warning if she weren't diligent.

While jogging, her thoughts drifted to old times, and to Peter. She knew she shouldn't think of him, but Peter was Peter, and he was hurting like she was. She could see it in his eyes. She could hear it in his voice. Her heart went out to him.

Before Jack, there was Peter and yes, Dennis, she had to admit regretfully. But after a brief fling with Dennis in college, it was really Peter. There was no question of her love for Jack. She deeply loved him and always would, but she missed the touching, and caresses, that said, I care, I love you.

Her mind snapped back to the present as a car buzzed by. *Shit, just what I need, to get hit by a car.* She jogged past Wilson's and thought back to that day when she and Peter first met, the race and their first kiss at Newport Beach. It was so many years ago, a lifetime it seemed. She slowed her pace as she came around the turn towards her parent's road.

I wonder if Peter is around, she thought as she jogged past Evergreen Beach Hotel. She decided it was time to get back to some type of a routine. She decided to take a shower and drive to Sister Bay. Just take one day at a time.

Betty was making coffee and had just put a pie in the oven when Annie came in from her jog. "Did you have a nice run, honey?"

"Yeah, it was good to get out. I'm going up to work on the Garibaldi. I'll see you later for dinner."

"Have fun. Say hi to Peter if you see him."

She went upstairs. After her shower, she slipped into some comfy jeans and a Wisconsin sweatshirt. She opened her jewelry case looking for some earrings. While digging around, she spied the *Falcon* boat charm and chain Peter had given her years ago.

I guess it is too early to wear this, but it makes me feel good just knowing it's here. She knew Jack would not be upset if she wore it. She knew if it were the other way around, she'd want him to get on with his life. This would be one of those steps towards healing. She instinctively started rubbing *Falcon* just like she used to. *Yes, Peter. I'm thinking of you.* I'll know when it's right to wear it again. Then she put it back in the case and smiled.

As she looked into the mirror, she noticed a few gray hairs. "I guess I earned those," she said with a wry smile. "I'm not as young as when he gave me the necklace."

**

Connie sat on the large breakwater limestone stone, touching Dennis's waist where he stood. Wrapping her legs around him, she pulled him closer. "This is the perfect spot. I love sex outside." She said. "I love to feel the wind caress my body along with the excitement of possibly being discovered." She unsnapped his jeans and reached in.

"Let's do it now. No one can see us here," she said with a gleam in her eyes. A warm breeze blew on them. She wrapped her arms around his neck and gave him a deep kiss, their tongues intertwined.

She stripped Dennis's fleece and T-shirt off over his head, and then scraped her nails across his chest.

"Take me. Take me now. I want it now."

Dennis grabbed her thin cotton sweater at her neckline. In one violent movement, he ripped it off. Next he tore her bra off, exposing her breasts. Her nipples stood at attention, excited by his frenzied action as he lowered his head to feast on her.

Her moans cried for more. "Yes. Yes. OH, yes!"

He reached for her jogging pants. Slipping his forefinger and thumb on each side of her pants and thong. He jerked both down in a swift movement.

"Yes, baby! That's it. That's what I want."

He slowly kissed his way down to her waiting love triangle.

"Yes…that feels so good." Connie arched her back and squeezed her legs tight against Dennis's head. "Now I want the rest of you."

Dennis slid his jeans and underwear down around his ankles. He wasted no time. Connie wrapped her legs around him, pulling him in. His hands worked her breasts and nipples as they made love.

Dennis was sure some of the boaters could hear Connie's vocal coaching. Maybe a few could even see what was going on like the guy on the bike overpass. The guy had binoculars and was them watching them the whole time. He didn't care.

After they finished, they got dressed. Connie wore Dennis's fleece home. Climbing back along the sea wall, Dennis looked at the overpass again. He was still there. What's with that guy? He thought. Creepy guy!

"What are you looking at?"

"Some guy with binoculars. I think he enjoyed our show. He's going now."

"Sick. Come on, I'm getting cold." She threw the tattered remains of her ripped sweater and bra in the garbage can as they walked past the fish cleaning station and went home.

**

Monday morning, Annie showed up at the building site and heard Ken Judd explain to Peter how they needed to build the bow section stronger. She heard Ken bellow some instructions to some of the shipwrights standing with Peter. Annie saw a slow smile come to Peter's face when he saw her standing off to the side. After all the years, the look he gave her whenever he saw her was the same. His eyes twinkled and he always smiled. It was the first time she had seen him since their chance meeting at Wilson's. She was glad he was here.

Annie saw Ken notice her. Then she saw him notice everyone's attention had shifted from him and the boat building to Annie. That's when she heard Ken say, "I can see you guys aren't going to get anywhere here for a while since our chief resident artist and figurehead sculptor is here. Let's take a coffee break." She laughed. She watched them all move away towards the back of the building to the coffee pot. That is all except Peter.

"Hi."

"Hi, Sounds like you're going to be doing some heavy work on the bow. That's good, because I need to get an idea on how big I need to make Miss Garibaldi."

Peter took off his cap and ran his hand through his hair. He smiled. "Do you want a guy's opinion on what the figurehead should look like, or is it a sculptor's license?"

"What do you think?" She smiled. "If it was up to you guys, there would be two big boobs and not much more."

"That's not true. Any head would do. You don't even have to sculpt one. No one looks at the head anyway." He was chuckling.

"Well, my sculpture is going to be realistic. Matter of fact, driving over I came up with a brilliant idea to get a little publicity for the boat. We'll have a contest open to any female who would like to be the model for the figurehead. She has to wear the same clothes and hairstyle I'm going to carve. There will be a community vote, with each vote costing a dollar. The contest can be held at one of the sponsoring bars or restaurants this fall. The contestant having the most dollars cast for her wins. They can wear as much or as little as they want, but they need to realize they'll be displayed on the boat for years to come. It should be fun, and we can use the money."

"What a great idea. Let's tell Ken and the guys. We'll have to call the local paper. When are we going to have the contest?"

"How about Halloween?" Annie said with a smile. "Everyone will be in a party mood. I'll get the word out. We've only got three weeks until then, but that should be enough time. This will generate a lot of excitement for the local girls, plus the winner will have a place in history."

**

It was mid-October and unusually warm as the day came to a close. Peter looked out across the bay and thought how wonderful it would be to take Red Baron out for a quick last sail. He turned to Annie and, without thinking, said, "Isn't it beautiful out? I thought I might take a quick sail. I don't know how many more days we're going to get. Would you like to go?"

She smiled and then looked pensive. "I'm not sure I'm dressed for sailing. I mean I just have a sweat shirt and my jeans."

"You think I don't have warm clothes on board? I always have extra jackets. Come on. It will be fun. We haven't done anything like this since that summer sail. We need a break."

She looked up with a smile. "Okay, but not for too long. I'll call Mom, so she doesn't hold dinner. You'd think I was a kid. Since 9/11, she worries about me."

Afterward, she looked at Peter and said, "Mom said it was okay, but have me home before midnight." They both laughed.

"I'll just pick up a few beers at JJ's and we'll head out," said Peter.

He got four beers and a bag of ice, and in five minutes, they motored out of the marina and were sailing. There was a light chop from the southwest, and they made a nice reach out into Green Bay.

Peter tied in the rudder, balancing the head and mainsail so it sailed on a relatively straight course. With the boat slightly heeled, they sat next to each other. Their legs touching, Peter opened a beer for each of them.

"This is really nice," Annie said. "I can feel the tension oozing out. I guess I didn't realize how tense I was. Being here with you, I don't feel like I have to be on my guard."

Peter raised the beer to his mouth. His eyes were locked on the shore as it slowly passed.

Annie watched as he lowered the can. She expected him to answer or agree with her, but he just stared at the shore.

Finally, after what seemed like several minutes, he turned to her. "You know, Annie, when Jack went off to work on September eleventh, no one would have thought that an act of terrorism would take down the Twin Towers and take his life. You had no control over what was going to happen that day, but that's not true for Paula and me. If we had taken proper precautions, she would still be alive. We screwed up, and it cost Paula her life. I can't forgive myself for losing her."

"I understand but I think you are too hard on yourself. It was an accident and if Paula could speak to you now she'd tell you the same thing." He saw her reach for his hand and hold it. After a few minutes, she said, "Peter, you didn't think the risks were deadly. From what you told me, she was trying to help you. She probably knew she should have her harness on, but she just acted. It was an accident, just like Jack's death was an accident. They were in the wrong place at the wrong time. No matter how I turn things over in my mind, it isn't going to bring Jack back. You can't bring Paula back, either. We both need to build our lives from here. We need to stop beating our heads against a wall. We need to live, to enjoy each moment for what it is. The past is history. We can't control the future. We need to enjoy the present because it's all we have." She laughed. "I sound like one of those preachers on TV."

Peter chuckled. He leaned over and kissed her softly on the cheek. "Thank you, Annie. You're right." He reached over and pulled the jib sheet in a bit. Leaning back, he finished his beer.

"Before the accident, one of the big charter companies offered to buy me out. At the time, I had no interest in selling the operation, but now I have no interest in going back. I called yesterday and accepted their offer, with the condition that Mahoney has a job for as long as he wants it. Dennis offered me the national sales manager's job at Deacon's, and I think I'll take him up on it. It allows me to stay in boating, which I love. I can travel around the country and be based in Door County, a place that is near and dear to my heart."

"Oh, Peter, I'm so happy for you. We can keep in touch and see each other more."

"Yes, I know. If I had done that years ago, instead of being so damn stubborn, we probably would have gotten married."

Annie blushed. "You know, Peter, it was just as much my fault as yours. I was stubborn, too."

"Well, we know a lot more than we did back then."

"In a lot of way we do. But now we have different challenges facing us. You. Me. Us. How do we work through all that has happen to us over the last six weeks? I'm afraid. How do we move forward and make it feel right. I just don't know what to do about us. I almost feel like I did after Smithback's summer party when I didn't know what to do."

"You didn't know what to do about what? Me? My parents? Or about Dennis?"

"Oh God. You knew?"

"No. I didn't know about Dennis, and what happen that night but I had my suspicions."

"I'm sorry Peter. I was so confused back then about what I wanted. I'm still not sure about your parents. Are they still difficult?"

"I had no choice in my parents. Mom's never going to change. Dad's mellowed but can still get difficult but not like mom. Let's just try to work on you and me, okay?"

"Okay. I'll try but I afraid it's still too soon."

"Too soon, too confused. It almost sounds like that first summer. I'm just trying to get you to think about the possibility of getting together. You aren't still thinking about Dennis are you? He's in Sturgeon Bay just like old times. Is that what you're telling me?"

She slapped him. "How can you say that?"

"I'm sorry. I guess I'm still bitter."

Looking at his watch, he said, "We better come about. The mood out here just got as chilly as the weather."

**

Halloween was a fun time on the building site. Everyone dressed as pirates or wore traditional sailing costumes from that era. The kids wore eye patches and scarves.

The highlight of the day was the Miss Garibaldi contest. About 20 lasses from the area showed up in full costume. Full costume consisted of revealing peasant blouses that helped expose their beautiful assets. Some of the more modest had a shawl over their shoulders.

Angelina Cabala from Egg Harbor captured the hearts, lust, and dollar votes of the male dominated crowd. It didn't hurt that she was of Irish and Italian decent.

Annie was thrilled because Angelina, the winner of the Miss Garibaldi contest, had great curves and an outgoing personality. She bartended at one of the local bars in Egg Harbor and knew this would be her claim to fame. All told, $758.00 was raised for the boat.

The next day, boat construction continued as usual. Several of the volunteers and workers drifted in later than normal. All seemed to hover around the coffee pot, nursing their headaches or talking about the contest.

"Annie, you should carve a figurehead every year," one of the volunteer shipwrights said. "They could be displayed at one of the local bars, kind of like a figurehead hall of fame, complete with glossy pictures and a bio of the winner. What do you think?"

Annie laughed. "Well, it's a fun idea. If you can get a sponsor, I'll do it."

Now with a subject for the figurehead, Annie was spending more of her time at her studio with Angelina. Time passed in a relaxed, pleasant way for both. Annie could feel the black cloud from Jack's death lifting and her life progressing. She still thought of him every day, but the hurt did not overpower her as it once had.

Still, little things brought back memories of her time with Jack. A song, a phrase, or seeing someone wearing a Mickey Mouse watch, made her think of happy times from the past and she'd cry. Fortunately, Angelina kept her rolling with laughter as she described the guys who were after her.

"I know I want someone who's good, kind, trustworthy, and good-looking, but you know who really gets me hot are the bad boys. I know I'm going to be hurt, but somehow I just gravitate toward them. Isn't it stupid?"

Annie smiled. "Don't be too hard on yourself," she said as she thought of Dennis. "They get the heart fluttering, but you'll find someone who's just right for you. If you're lucky, you might find a couple guys, and then you can have some real fun."

"I guess you're right. You think I have enough of the right equipment?" She pushed her breasts up to show a little more cleavage. "Maybe I should talk more? You know, I'm an accounting major at UW Green Bay."

"You don't say?"

"I haven't found a bad boy that likes to talk about debits and credits." she said sadly and looked at her watch. "Wow, I can't believe what time it is. I've got to get to work. Happy hour is where I make most of my tips. The older guys with the money like to fantasize about me, the others just drink, but they all leave good tips. Got to go. See you later."

"See you next week, Angelina. Have a good night."

Annie worked a little longer on the figurehead before calling it quits. After cleaning up the wood shavings, she sat down in an old stuffed chair. She added a few cubes of ice to a coke she had been drinking. Reflecting on the day, she idly watched the weekend cars stream past. Ok, it was Friday. She wasn't looking forward to spending another evening with Darrell and Betty. They meant well, but she needed a life of her own again.

Fridays were a time to get out and have fun. Maybe she'd call Peter and see what he was doing. *He's been kind of cool towards me since I slapped him. What the hell, I'm an adult. I just want company tonight, at least for dinner.*

She picked up her cell phone and dialed his number. When he answered, "Peter Franklin." She laughed.

"Hey, what are you doing for dinner? Want to keep me company?" There. She said it fast and to the point. There was a pause.

"Annie?"

"Yes, it's me." She felt nervous. Maybe she was too forward. Maybe he wasn't ready yet. After the tiff about Dennis on the boat, things were strained. She hoped dinner might help ease the strain. At least she hoped so. Besides, its time she showed people she was alive and trying to get her life back in order.

"Dinner sounds great. Why don't I pick you up about six-thirty? That will give me a chance to get cleaned up."

"Okay."

"We can go to the Greenwood. How's that?"

"Sounds good to me. I love their fish."

Chapter Thirty

When Peter arrived, Darrell was watching the Packer report on Channel 5. "Dennis tells me you've accepted the national sales manager's job at Deacon's," he said. "That's great."

"Deacon's is a great company, and I'm excited to work for them."

"Well, we're glad to have you. You'll do a great job, I'm sure. Who could have guessed when I first met you guys that someday you'd be my bosses."

Peter smiled. Just then, Annie and her mom came downstairs. "Hi, Betty. Hi, Annie. You look great. Like a model."

"I know. Jeans and a Norwegian ski sweater make me look stunning," she said with a smile. "It seemed cool out driving home, so I thought it would be okay."

"Let's go. I'm really hungry."

"Have a nice evening, you two," Betty said.

As they walked out to Peter's truck, Annie said, "My mom was so excited you'd think I was going to homecoming or something."

"She just wants you to be happy and so do I." Peter squeezed her hand.

The Greenwood was packed, as usual. The locals and tourists knew about the place, so it was always busy. They ran into some of the volunteers and had a pleasant time until their table was ready. Both ordered the area's famous whitefish and had a nice bottle of Riesling. They had a piece of cherry pie with ice cream. It was good, but not as good as Betty's.

Driving back, Annie patted Peter's thigh. "Why don't you park the truck at your place, and walk me home? It's nice out and we could walk along the shore and then cut up through the old Hotel Ephraim property."

"You sure you'll be warm enough?"

"Yes, this sweater is really warm. Besides, you can always put your arm around me like you used to." As soon as she said it, she regretted it. She knew she'd like to feel Peter's arm around her, but she wasn't sure if he was ready. It had been a slow easy time for them. A small step in rebuilding their relationship. She knew he had feelings for her as much as she had feelings for him.

"Okay, that would be nice. I miss the walks along the beach holding a pretty woman." He smiled at Annie. "Besides, I haven't walked that way for quite a while."

They got to The Evergreen Hotel and parked the truck. It seemed colder than they realized. Annie saw an old blanket in the back of the cab.

"Why don't you bring that blanket along and we can drape it over our shoulders if it gets too cold?"

Peter grabbed it and they started walking, their breath creating mist as they talked. The water level was lower, so they were able to walk along the beach instead of the highway. Looking north, the lights of Ephraim illuminated the shoreline and bluff. The Moravian church and Wilson's seemed to stand out from the rest.

"You know, Peter, I never get tired of that view. I like it even better than the Chicago skyline."

"It really is special," he said.

When they finally got to the old stonewall of the Hotel Ephraim property, it was a little warmer. Peter turned to Annie. "Are you cold or do you want to sit here for a short while? It brings back good memories. Remember when we'd sit next to this wall out of sight of the guests and kiss?"

Annie laughed. "Yes I remember." She had been thinking the same thing. "We could sit for a little while."

Peter took the blanket and spread it out on the sand next to the rock wall. As he turned to grab Annie's hand, a car drove by, catching her in its headlights. At that moment, the *Falcon* charm slid out and dangled in the glare. Peter couldn't believe it. *She's wearing it again.... after all these years.* When she sat down, he remained standing.

"What's wrong?"

"Nothing. I just noticed you're wearing the *Falcon* charm."

"Yes, I am. I needed something that brought back good memories." Taking the *Falcon* between her finger and thumb, she rubbed it. "I rubbed it every time I thought of you. If you look, you'll see it's starting to look polished."

Peter slowly reached for the charm. He looked at it and then he looked at Annie. Slowly, ever so slowly, he moved his lips to hers. He trembled as they touched.

She let out a sigh. Her hand slowly slid up his back to his neck and finally into his hair. Their lips lightly touched like a mayfly dancing across the water on a warm summer evening. Peter moved his lips across her cheek, tasting the salty tears as he moved to her warm neck.

"Oh, Annie," he whispered. "I'm sorry. I probably shouldn't have done that."

She laughed softly. "No Peter I wanted to kiss you as much as you did. It's just that I'm conflicted about Jack. I can't let myself go. Maybe it's too soon to be doing this. I miss the feeling of Jack holding me, caring for me, waking up in the morning and seeing him next to me. I'm still in love with someone who is never coming back. I'm sorry if I led you on. Once again, it's not you Peter. I hope you know that. It's me goddamn it."

Peter pulled her close. "I know. It's just when I'm with you, I feel better. My life's not so empty."

She rested her head against his chest and sighed. "Empty. I think you're right."

The sound of a police siren speeding past the beach, and the reality of the cold, broke the spell. They stood, and Peter shook the sand from the blanket and put his arm around Annie. He draped the blanket over their shoulders for the walk to her house. Illuminated by the front porch light, Peter kissed her. Holding her tightly, enveloped in the blanket, he whispered in her ear, "I'm so glad we're back in Door County."

"Me too." Annie turned, still holding his hand as she moved to the door, and then she slowly released her grip. "Tomorrow," was all she said as she gently closed the door.

**

It was almost a week before Christmas, and it was cold even for Door County. The cross-country skiers got what they wanted, a foot of nice dry snow for perfect skiing at Peninsula State Park. Annie called Rita to see if she could come up for a few days.

"That would be wonderful," Rita said. "I need to relax and be with friends. I love my family, but I just want to be someplace like Door County, if you know what I mean."

"I sure do. Come on up. You can stay at our house. Mom would love it, if you don't mind getting the twenty questions routine. Speaking of twenty questions, how's your love life?"

"I knew you'd ask that. It sucks. Oh sure there are some nice guys, lots of doctors who want to get in my pants, but there's no one that I really care about."

"That's too bad, Rita. I was hoping you had some hot hunk."

"Sadly, no. Speaking of hot hunks, how's Dennis? I hear he's seeing some old flame from high school. I thought I saw him a couple of times when I was driving to work at Columbia Hospital. He was with a blond."

"Might be. I don't know, and I don't think Peter knows much either."

"How is Peter?"

"He's okay. He sold his business and bought one of the condos on the old Hotel Ephraim property. He's so happy with the place. He'll be national sales manager of Deacon's when the current guy retires next year. He's going to start in January and work weekends on the project. Right now, we see each other every day, working on Garibaldi. It's really helped both of us."

"Oh, really?" Rita said.

Annie could imagine a huge smile on her friend's face. "I'll fill you in on what's happened along those lines when you get up here. You can keep guessing until then. When are you coming?"

"How about Thursday the twentieth? That gives me a long weekend with you and whoever else is around." She cleared her throat loudly. "Maybe you could tell Peter I'm coming, and he could let asshole know, just in case he'd like to see me for old time's sake."

"I'll do just that, Rita! For old time's sake, as you put it." And they both laughed.

**

Peter was putting things away in his recently purchase condo when the phone rang. Peter recognized the voice. "Hi Annie. What's up?"

"Well, Rita is coming up Thursday for a few days. We were thinking it would be fun for the four of us to go out together?"

"That would be fun," Peter said.

"Do you think you could let Dennis know? Maybe he'd like to spend some time with us instead of going to Milwaukee.... just for old time's sake," Annie continued. "It would be fun for us all to be together over the holidays. It's something we've never done."

"Let me ask him. He happens to be right here visiting."

Dennis looked at Peter with a questioning expression.

"Thanks, Peter. Just so he knows, Rita's coming either way."

"Okay, I'll see what he says."

Dennis looked at Peter as he sipped his beer. "Annie?" he said.

"Guess what? Rita is coming for a visit before Christmas. Annie thought it would be fun if we all got together. Think you can tear yourself away from Connie for few days?"

Dennis smiled at the thought. "You know, I think I might like that. I always liked Rita. Between you and me, buddy, I liked her the most."

"The most? You mean the most of all the women you've been with? Wow!" *More than Annie, even?*

Hunching his shoulders, Dennis looked at Peter. "Right from the first time we started going out. There was something about her. Sort of wild like me, but she's good. Let's do it! Connie can go on the back burner for a while. Besides, she'll have enough to do with the holidays coming up. I'll just tell her I want to stay up here with Mom. That should satisfy her. I'll drive down on Christmas Day and bring her an extra present. How's that?"

Peter shook his head. "Jeez! You really use women for your own gratification. Don't you ever care how they feel?"

"I'm not sure. I probably have, but I can't remember when."

"Just a friendly reminder, in the Christmas spirit, Annie's off limits old buddy."

"I'll remember that, but didn't you say, Rita came on to you once upon a time?" He smiled. "Don't you be going after my date."

**

As the week progressed, Dennis found himself thinking more and more about Rita. He knew she had divorced Zach and split time between Chicago and Milwaukee. God, he had fun with her. She was about the only one who could go toe to toe with him. Vegas might have been only a few hours, but God, it was good.

He could hardly wait to see her. It was fun to be excited, he thought. It's what drove him to be the way he was. He better go to one of the gift shops in town and get her a Christmas present.

Actually, he realized, he really wanted to get her something nice. That was something new for him.

**

Thursday came, and it was almost like Christmas. The anticipation was high.

Rita arrived about three in the afternoon. She and Annie were so happy to see each other. It was a tearful reunion at first but a happy one.

"Come on, you can put your stuff in my room," said Annie. "If things work out right, I hope you'll be spending time with Dennis. Peter tells me he got a room at the Eagle Harbor Inn. Peter offered him an extra bedroom, but he said he didn't want to bother him if he came in late."

Rita laughed. "Well, I hope that means that things are going to get lively."

"Oh, yes. We both know Dennis," Annie said. "So what did you bring to blow his socks off?"

"Just a few necessities I bought at Victoria's Secret. I even brought the outfit I wore in Vegas. Do you think he'll remember?"

"I doubt it. He probably had only one thing on his mind."

"We both felt that way. So, what's on the agenda?"

"Peter is going to pick us up here, and then we're going to meet Dennis at the Northern Grill. It's close to his mom's nursing home. He wanted to see her early in the weekend, so he wouldn't be bummed out the rest of the weekend thinking about her. Seeing her makes him think a little more about his own mortality. At least that's what Peter said."

Chapter Thirty-One

When Peter showed up at the Wilson's house, Darrell had just gotten home.

"Hi, Peter, want a beer?" He reached for two beers. "There's lots of laughing and hollering going on upstairs. Betty and Annie are helping Rita get ready. All I'm hearing is 'try this and oh, that's sexy and he doesn't stand a chance'. It hasn't been this busy around here since Annie's prom days. I think we're really going to have a good seat in just a few minutes. God, I wish I were thirty years younger so Betty and I could go along. You know Betty was a real looker…. And still is!"

Peter smiled.

They didn't have long to wait before the three women descended the steps. First Betty, then Annie. Annie looked great in a tight pair of jeans, red turtleneck and an unbuttoned ski sweater. Her shoes were red and her hair was twisted and tied up revealing her attractive neck. The *Falcon* charm was around her neck. Peter smiled as she turned the corner leading from the kitchen to the living room.

Finally, Rita made her entrance. It was like waiting for the bride to walk down the aisle.

"Ta Da!!!" Peter and Darrell's jaws dropped. You could hear a barely audible "Christ" from Darrell. Peter thought, *Dennis, you don't stand a chance.*

Rita had on red high-heels, skintight soft black leather pants and a leopard thong that just peeped over the back of her leather pants just to let Dennis know what was there. Her white silk blouse had no buttons and was tied in a knot. A sexy leopard cami showed her ample breasts, so they looked like they were going to explode. Her red lips, gold hoop earrings and a gold chain completed the look. Her bright red hair was loosely curled and hung down, giving her a mysterious look, as she held a short red leather jacket in her left hand.

She twirled around. "How do I look?" Rita asked. "Do you think Dennis will think I look okay?"

Peter looked at Rita and then at Annie. "I think Dennis will think you look very, very nice. What do you think, Annie?" he said and smiled.

Darrell jumped in. "If he doesn't, he's blind."

"Dad, I couldn't have said it better. Should we go?"

Rita slipped on her red jacket. "I'm ready."

"Have fun, be careful," Betty said as they were leaving.

**

As they got closer to Sister Bay, Peter suggested they drive around and make sure Dennis was at the Grill before they arrived.

"Great idea," Rita said. "I want to watch his expression as I walk in."

When they pulled in to the Northern Grill parking lot, Peter saw Dennis's Tahoe. "Yep, he's here. Let me go in first and then you two come in. I want to be up close to see his reaction, too. Just give me twenty seconds."

"Hey, Peter," Dennis said. "Where are the girls?"

"Oh, they're coming. Annie couldn't find her purse so they were looking under the seats. Here they come." When Rita made her entrance, it went cold silent in the bar for about three seconds as all heads turned to look at her. Then things went back to normal.

"Jesus Christ," Dennis said, as his eyes opened wide. His hand went to his upper lip.

Rita walked straight up to Dennis, never taking her eyes off him, and gave him a long, lingering kiss. "Hi, Dennis. Long time no see. I thought you were dead. You never called or even wrote me a card. I thought I meant something to you back in Vegas?" She waited, looking him up and down.

Dennis's mouth opened, closed, opened, closed, and finally he stammered out, "No...No I'm alive as you can see. I should have called. It has been a long time. Too long, you look great! Ah here, sit here. What can I get you?"

"How about a Cosmo," Rita said. "You look like you put on a few pounds. Must be middle age creeping up."

"What? No, I don't think I've gained any weight, must be the shirt, European cut or something. You really look great. How do you stay so trim?"

"Oh, that's easy. I work ten to twelve hour shifts five or six days a week in the emergency room. When people get shot, cut up or mangled, I put them back together. When I make a mistake, it usually costs someone his or her life. High stress. The stress keeps the weight off."

"Well, you sure look great."

Dennis kept his eyes on Rita. He hardly ever looked away. After a while his hand moved to the small of Rita's back, and he gently moved his fingers in a small circular motion just above her thong. It felt like old times to him, Rita was enjoying him touching her when all of a sudden she turned to Annie.

"Annie, I have to go to the restroom. Do you have to go, too?"

"Oh, yeah, I do. Be right back boys. Order us another drink, will you?"

"Sure," Dennis mumbled. "Bartender, another round please."

Turning to Peter, "Wow, I can't believe how great she looks. My God, she looked great in Vegas, but... she looks even better now."

"Easy, boy, easy," Peter said, but he was enjoying it as much as Rita and Annie were.

**

Annie and Rita started laughing as soon as they got to the restroom.

"Rita," Annie said, "I know you missed Dennis, but you're like a dog that caught a scent of a fox. Take it easy, will you."

"I thought I was cool considering. I have to calm down. I'm so excited to be with him. It's been such a long time. I just have to remember, this time he's going to pay for his past. I wonder how long we can both hold out?"

They came out of the rest room, laughing. All the guys' heads turned in unison and followed them as the girls walked thru the bar. Rita came up to Dennis and gave him a short peck on the cheek. "Miss me?"

As their eyes connected, he leaned in close. "Rita, I did miss you. I didn't realize how much until I saw you tonight. We've been apart too long."

"Nice line, Dennis, but you forget that I know you. I know how you act."

"No, really. I mean it. I really missed you. When you got married, I was really pissed. I thought, now I've done it. Missed the only woman I really cared about. I went on a three day-drunk."

"Oh, do I look impressed? I'm glad you're happy to see me, but we'll just have to see how things progress from here. I have a social life, too. Just like you do, I'm sure. "

"Time to go to JJ's for a little Mexican. Rita would you like to go to JJ's in my truck or ride with Dennis in his Tahoe?"

"Oh, I think I'd like to ride with you guys. Is it alright if Dennis rode with us?"

"What! Are you kidding me? I thought you'd like to ride with me." Dennis said.

"Not tonight Dennis. I like to spend time with my friends that didn't leave me high and dry several times in the past, so if you want to ride with me, hop in with us!"

Dennis was forced to pile into Peter's truck or ride alone.

The four had a great dinner at JJ's but when it was time to head home Rita surprised everyone but especially Dennis. "I think I'm going to ride back to Annie's with Peter and Annie. I'll see you tomorrow. Have a nice night Dennis." She said.

**

Peter could only guess how horny and frustrated Dennis was. Especially after he had spent all the money for the room at Eagle Harbor Inn. "It even had a whirlpool in the room." He had said. When Rita said she was going home with them, Peter could tell Dennis was pissed by the force of the slammed Tahoe door, but he also told Peter earlier in the night, he didn't want to lose Rita by throwing a fit, so Peter was impress by how he tried to control himself after that.

It had been a fun night for all. He laughed to himself as he watched Dennis drive back to the Eagle Harbor Inn. Alone.

**

The next day started with Dennis picking everyone up, starting with Peter, then Annie and Rita. Everyone wore jeans, heavy boots and warm sweaters. They went to Al Johnson's for breakfast. Next was the snowmobile rental in Fish Creek. It was a bright, sunny day, mid 20's, and not a cloud in the sky. Perfect for just about anything.

They went snowmobiling through Peninsula State Park's trails first and then hit other trails. They made the rounds of the bars that were open for the winter. There were plenty of people up for the holidays. The bars were hopping.

The day went by quickly. They turned the snowmobiles in and headed back to Dennis's hotel and whirlpool. After collecting their suits at Annie's they finally got to the Inn. Annie and Rita moved to the bathroom to put on their bikinis.

Annie said to Rita as they changed in Dennis's bathroom, "Rita, Leopard Bikini? You're really into the animal look this weekend."

"I know. I read where guys love the leopard look. Tomorrow, I have one that's red and the last one is cobalt blue. It's a one piece, but very revealing. This is so much fun. I'm going to hate to see it come to an end."

Annie looked in the mirror at her legs and bottom. "How do I look? I've been jogging since I got up here. Do you think it's helped?"

"Jeez, Annie, you look great. You looked great before, and you look even better now. Peter can't get enough of you. When I see the way he looks at you...you know, he loves you. It's very apparent."

"I know. We both love each other, but it's still too soon. People will talk, don't you think?"

Rita paused before she answered. "How long is long enough. It only matters what you and Peter think. You'll both know when the time is right. If I know Peter, he feels the same as you do. Just enjoy your time together."

"Let's go out and enjoy that whirlpool. Dennis said he had some beer and white wine. I'm ready, if you know what I mean." Rita flung open the door.

Dennis stared hard. "Well, don't you both look fabulous?"

They poured their drinks and slowly slipped into the whirlpool.

"Oh, this feels so good after the cold and the bouncing. I can feel it in my back," said Rita.

Dennis looked at Rita. "I can feel it someplace else, and the warm water feels good there too."

Peter smiled as he watched Rita's hand slid under the bubbling water. Peter knew what was happening. Envy is what he felt. Taking a chance he grabbed Annie's hand and moved it under the water. "Oh, Sorry. I guess you want some attention too." It was ok, but he wanted more. Much more. He was ready to get physical later. It was the holiday. The spirit of sharing was in him and he wanted to take that next step. He hoped Annie was ready?

After water sports, the four had Sammy's pizza delivered to the room. "It's 10:30 P.M.," Peter said, "We decided to called it a night. With a full moon, we'll walk the short distance back to our homes."

"Dennis said he would take me back to your home later," Rita said.

Peter watched Annie smile at Rita, guessing that Rita would never make it back until the next morning.

**

Morning came with 3 inches of fresh powder. "I love Cross-country skiing." Annie said. "Cooking out in the woods, having wine and just enjoying Door County's wonderful winter is what I'm looking forward to today. Everyone got the stuff we'll need in the daypacks?"

She saw them nod yes. The drive over to the park only took about five minutes.

"The Bay's not frozen over. Look how brilliant the sky is. The water looked especially blue here at the observation tower in the park. The snow from last night has covered the branches, causing them to bend." As they skied through the park's inner trails, the four got into an easy rhythm. They saw parts of the park they wouldn't normally see. They enjoyed stopping, seeing the tracks of the many animals. "Look, something happen here. Looks like a rabbit met its untimely end with a hawk or owl. See the red spots and ruffled snow." She said.

"What are you this morning, a park ranger?" Peter asked smiling. "Come here. Let me give you a kiss?"

"Smarty." She moved over. Their lips touched and she got a burst of warmth. "Nice."

They stopped around noon for lunch. The men got dry birch twigs and wood, built a nice fire in one of the campsite stoves. They brought wine and brats that were pre-soaked in beer, so the package claimed. There was a small can of sauerkraut, some ketchup and mustard. It was a simple meal. For dessert, the girls made s'mores.

They spent about an hour and half enjoying the trail before reversing their way back to the truck. By the time they got back, they were warm and decided to use the Eagle Inn's indoor pool.

That night, for dinner, they went to the bowling alley for fish and steak. They even bowled a few games. Peter and Annie beat Dennis and Rita. The difference was the three strikes Peter made in the last frame to edge out Dennis and Rita by seven pins. They had a good time and headed back home. Dennis dropped Annie and Peter at Peter's condo, then Rita and Dennis went right to the Inn.

Peter built a roaring fire in the fieldstone fireplace. He opened some wine. Then they curled up on the Native American blanket Peter had purchased at one of the local gift shops in Ephraim. With their backs against large throw pillows, they watched the flames flicker. Lying on the floor with Peter gave Annie peace like she had with Jack back in her loft in Chicago. *Jack would like this place.* Lowering her head to Peter's chest, she felt finally at ease, something she had not felt for months.

She felt Peter's hand gently caressing her hair. She must have dozed off, waking to his gentle kisses on her forehead.

"Ah, that feels nice. Sorry. I dozed off. I guess I'm really relaxed. It's been a fun time with the four of us."

"I know," Peter said as he stroked her hair and the back of her neck. "I like it. It reminds me of years ago when we were all so young. It's better now because we both now know how good things can be. Annie, this is one of those times I don't want to stop." He leaned in and touched his lips to hers.

At first she was gentle, but as they continued to kiss, Annie became the person she wanted to be with Peter. Her passion simmering just under the surface manifested itself as she gave herself to his kisses, exploring as their tongues danced and their hands caressed. Annie felt herself going toward the edge and then gently pushed herself away.

"Peter, we have to stop." She said it in such a way as not to embarrass him but to get some air and let their emotions calm. "I want to do this as much as you do. Believe me, I do….but not now. I'm not ready yet."

"I know. I guess I'm not ready yet either. It's just…"

"I know you love me." Annie looked at him. She felt the tears welled up in her eyes.

He got up and put more wood on the fire. When he turns back to her, he said, "the reflection of the fire dancing across your face makes you so beautiful."

"We don't have to do anything more, but don't leave right now. Let me hold you. I need to hold you, Annie."

Annie, placed her head on his chest, closed her eyes. She hoped peace would come soon for both of their sakes. After about thirty minutes, she decided she needed to go home. She didn't want to, but she knew at this stage it was the only thing to do. *Pressure. Tell me Jack, is it okay yet?*

Walking home with Annie, Peter made a snowball and threw it at a tree limb.

"That looks like fun." She said, and made one herself, but instead of aiming at a tree limb she aimed at Peter, hitting him in the back of his head. "I couldn't help myself." She giggled.

"Really?" Peter said. "How's this?"

For the next few minutes, they were in a good old snowball fight. The tension of love turned into teenagers having fun. Finally Peter tackled Annie, wrestling her to the ground, threatening to give her a face wash with snow. When she pleaded with him not to, he gave in. He gave her one last long kiss before helping her up. They walked the rest of the way with their arms around each other, heads tilted and touching.

**

That night, Peter sat in front of the fireplace, alone, and thought about the next day. It was Sunday, their last day together before he had to drive to Saint Louis and visit his parents. Tomorrow was shopping day. He knew it would be fun, though he didn't like to shop and wasn't sure he could shop a whole day. After all, it usually took him only a few minutes to find what he needed. He had known women who considered three to four hours a short period of time to shop.

Thank God, all four of them were going. He was sure they could find some stores near a sports bar or something. Rita and Annie wouldn't expect the guys to spend all day shopping, would they? And wasn't it football Sunday? He knew Dennis would be on his side. Surely he wouldn't cave in to shopping all day just for a piece of ass? He laughed to himself. On second thought, Dennis would!

But the Packers were in the hunt for the Super Bowl. That was like a special Christmas present all by itself. Surely they'd at least take some time off to watch the game. He went to the fridge, got a Bud, and sat down on the couch to watch the last few embers burn out.

He thought of the last few days. He was happy. His thoughts drifted to Paula, then he thought about Annie again. He was comfortable with how their relationship was going. Parts of his body would like to see it move faster, but he knew the right time was getting close. He could wait. He waited this long. He could wait as long as he had to. There weren't many second chances in life.

He finished his beer. Pulling an old blanket resting on the back of the couch over him, he closed his eyes. Instead of sugarplums, images of Annie, Rita, and Dennis danced in his head that night, as they cavorted in the snow, laughing and enjoying each other.

Chapter Thirty-Two

P eter woke to pounding on his door. He looked at his watch. Was it really 8:30? He couldn't believe he slept so long. He stumbled to the door and opened it to a smiling Dennis.

"Man, I'm hungry! Did you eat already? Hey, aren't those the same clothes you had on yesterday?"

"Yes, I fell asleep on the couch. You just woke me up."

"Sorry. Someone keep you up to the wee hours?"

"No, I was just tired."

"Too bad. I didn't get much sleep, that's why I'm hungry."

"Well then, you can make breakfast, Mr. Stud. I'm going to take a shower and shave. Food is in the refrigerator. Scrambled eggs and toast are fine with me. Don't forget the coffee."

"Fair enough."

They finished breakfast by 9:30 a.m. Peter was impressed with Dennis's scrambled eggs with Tabasco sauce and cheese. Dennis even did the dishes as Peter finished his second cup of coffee.

"That was great. Guess we all become good cooks when we live alone," Peter said.

The phone rang. Peter answered. "Hi. Yes, we're ready. Okay, we'll be right there." He hung up and said, "Let's go, they're hot to trot. They have a list of places they want to hit before the Packer game. Darrell and Betty are going to make food and stuff for the game, so we have to get going."

Dennis smiled. "I can hardly wait. This ought to be worth something later. What do you think?"

"I think you might be right."

They drove to Egg Harbor to the All I want for Christmas shop, Made in Britain, LTD, Jane's designs. Then it was Fish Creek for On Deck Clothing Company, Fish Creek Basketry, J. Jeffrey Taylor Jewelry & Fine Arts, and Pure Joy at the Hill shops. Next it was to Sister Bay and Ecology Sports, across the street from JJ's. Rita had seen some glass art at Clayton's glass studio, so they stopped in.

Just south of town, they went to the Blue Willow shop. Annie liked the 125-year-old log stable that housed everything. Then it was to the Quilter's Quest and finally to Al Johnson's to look at sweaters and have a snack.

By this time, the guys were climbing the walls, so they stopped at the Bowl, had one quick beer and headed to Darrell and Betty's for food and the game. It was a great game. The Packers beat up on Cleveland 30-7.

Once the game was well in hand, Rita, Annie and Betty moved into the kitchen to discuss the day's shopping. Betty was very interested in the places they went and what they liked. The guys just watched football and talked about the Packers' chances of getting to the Super Bowl. It was a fun day, but the next day, Monday, everyone was going someplace except Annie.

Dennis was going to Milwaukee, Peter to St. Louis, and Rita to Madison and then on to Chicago. Annie wanted to go to Chicago and be at the shops with Thomas, but she decided it was too much travel. Besides, she knew her parents would be disappointed if she was not with them to go to the Moravian Church on Christmas Eve. It was a tradition she always looked forward to. Then it was home to open presents and have boiled shrimp, herring, raw beef and cookies, and watch "It's a Wonderful Life" while drinking eggnog. That was Christmas in Door County and she always loved it. After the game, Annie was going to Peter's condo to say good-bye. He was leaving at dawn to give him time to get a jump on the holiday traffic. Tomorrow was Christmas Eve, and he wanted to get to St. Louis around four in the afternoon.

**

Annie and Peter walked hand in hand to his condo, and then he built a roaring fire. The shadows danced across the ceiling. She leaned her head back against the couch, closed her eyes while she thought about the future. How was everything going to work between her galleries in Chicago, her gallery here, and her personal life? She had to get a handle on what she wanted.

Peter snuggled up next to her on the Indian rug.

She ran her hand across the rug. "Maybe it was made by the Hopei Tribe and would give her hope?" She smiled at her play on words then pressed her head to his shoulder as he pulled her close.

"I wish I could stay up here with you for Christmas," he said, "but duty calls. I hate traveling on the holidays. It seemed like we were always going someplace when I was little, and I hated it. I used to say, "When I get older I'm not going anyplace on the holidays. But here I am, traveling again, away from you and Door County." He gave her a kiss.

They felt the emotions of the holiday. They sank together as one, the fire crackled, and the wind rustled the snow against the windows.

"I love you, Annie."

Looking at the fire reflecting in his eyes, she said, "I love you, Peter." They held each other close, not wanting this moment to end.

**

Dennis was up and moving around by 8 a.m. He was surprised he felt so energetic. He and Rita were up until close to 3 a.m. when he finally took her to Annie's. As he kissed her goodbye, he got a surprise as he held the Tahoe's door open after she got out. "I have something I need to say to you. I really had a good time with you these last few days, Dennis. I don't know if I'll see you much anymore. I guess that depends on you. I know you and your ways. It's up to you, but I will tell you I'm not going to wait forever for you to decide if it's me you want to be with or someone else. If it's me, you have to make a commitment to me, and only me. I know there are others, but not if you want me. I won't stand for it." She leaned against him, kissed him one long lingering kiss, and then she slowly walked to the house, opened the door and stepped in.

He walked around and sat in the Tahoe, looking at the house, before he finally turned the ignition key and drove off. He went back to the Inn for a few hours sleep, but the bed seemed so empty, so unfriendly. He tossed and turned, unsettled by her words. In the morning, he paid his bill at the Inn and then stopped by his house in Sturgeon Bay to get a few things for the next few days. He picked up the presents he had for Connie and took off.

The drive to Milwaukee was uneventful. The only problem was that he kept hearing Rita's words and he wasn't sure what to do. Then his mind shifted to his image of Connie and he smiled. Humming and singing the words to *Here Comes Santa Claus*, he knew he would have a Merry Christmas.

**

Annie was glad to be back in Chicago after the Christmas. She loved her apartment with all of Jack's things. It made her happy seeing his smiling face in the photos of the two of them. She'd curl up on their rug and closed her eyes. She was at peace with herself.

Peter called enough to keep her from being lonesome for Door County and him. They made a date to have dinner in Chicago on Valentines' Day. He was going to be calling on some clients there and decided to stay an extra day to be with her. He said he'd stay at the Sheraton on the river, close enough to walk to her place. She wanted him to stay with her in the loft, but he said he felt uncomfortable doing that at this stage. She didn't push it. It would be nice to have him there. She looked forward to showing him her Chicago.

Rita didn't have much time to relax once she got back to Chicago. Violence never takes a holiday. She scarcely had time to think about Dennis. When she did, it made her sad because as much as she loved her time with him, she thought he would never change his womanizing ways. She remembered his call saying how much he enjoyed being with her. "Enjoyed! Is that what he called it, the asshole?" She simmered down and thought about it. Actually for Dennis, that was a lot. Just calling her was something new for him, she realized.

**

Dennis had made a Valentine's dinner date with Connie back in January, but since Christmas, his thoughts had been more focused on Rita. He still saw Connie, but it wasn't the same. The sex was great, but it wasn't enough for him anymore and he knew why.

He had thought about it long and hard on the drive down to Milwaukee from Sturgeon Bay. He had taken half the day off so he had enough time for dinner and something else that needed to be done. He smiled to himself as he thought about something he had never done before. It was going to be an unusual day for Dennis Jamison, he thought.

**

Annie enjoyed getting dressed for Valentines. She chose a red silk wrap dress with a black lacy chemise that she knew would reveal just enough to keep Peter excited. Next, she wore black thigh-high stockings and garter. Secretly, she liked being naughty. She had on red high heels with a fake diamond decorating the toe. As usual, she wore the *Falcon* necklace Peter had given her so many years ago, and she brushed on some new sparkle powder.

She smiled as she looked in the mirror. The powder made her think of how the water sparkles when they went sailing. Her hair was pulled up in a twist showing off her diamond earrings.

Peter picked Annie up at 7 p.m. in a cab. She looked stunning, he thought, but then she always did to him. Peter made reservations at Gibson's. "After dinner, I thought we could walk on State Street or Rush Street," he said.

He looked at her, smiling up at him, and then heard her say, "I am really looking forward to this, Peter." She gave him a gentle kiss just before entering the cab.

They had a wonderful dinner with champagne, Caesar salad, perfect filets, and finally, cherries jubilee with a nice bottle of Cabernet Sauvignon. For an extra surprise, Peter arranged for a horse-drawn carriage that was waiting for them at the curb after dinner. It was a wonderful night for a carriage ride.

**

Dennis had made reservations for dinner at Moe's steakhouse. He and Connie had a glass of bubbly at Connie's condo before they left. Dennis left his Tahoe with the attendant, giving him ten dollars and telling him he'd be down shortly. After about an hour, they came down feeling very relaxed. They got into the truck for the short drive to Moe's. A black car pulled out immediately behind the Tahoe as the two drove away. The black Lincoln Town Car turned on its bright lights and followed right on Dennis's bumper. "What's with this guy? Asshole!"

Chapter Thirty-Three

A nnie was enjoying the carriage ride. The blankets kept her warm, the white holiday lights flickered, the smell of the working horse all added to the moment. Annie's cell phone rang as Peter paid the driver. Her night changed abruptly as she listened. "Rita, what's wrong?"

"Oh, Annie, it's Dennis. He's been shot. I don't know if he'll make it. Can you come up to Milwaukee? Columbia Hospital's ER."

"Of course we'll come. I'm with Peter."

"I didn't know who else to call. I mean, his mom's in the nursing home. I didn't want to call her until I knew more. You and Peter were the first people I thought of."

"We'll be right up. Will you be okay?"

"I have to be. I'm the main doctor here tonight. Most of the staff begged off for Valentine's Day. I did the surgery on Dennis myself. My combat training paid off. I focused on what I had to do and that's all. I was able to block out who he was until I was done. Then I broke down and cried. My surgical team couldn't figure out what was up. I've done hundreds of procedures and never once cried."

"Oh my god!" *9/11. Now this. I'm not sure I can take any more death.* "Rita, we're on our way. We'll be there in ninety minutes."

**

When Peter and Annie got there, Rita was waiting. Two of her surgical nurses were keeping her company. Seeing Peter and Annie, she turned to them. "Thanks for staying with me. I'll be okay now. These are the friends I was telling you about. Come and get me if any emergency comes up."

"I will, Doctor Gallagher. Try to get some rest." one said. "We'll call some of the other doctors to see if they can come in, though they probably have their pagers off."

Rita smiled. "I would if I was out on Valentine's night"

"What happened?" Annie asked as she gripped Rita's hand.

"Here's what I know: Connie and Dennis were on their way to Moe's restaurant for Valentine's dinner. They had just parked Dennis's truck and were walking to the restaurant when Connie's ex-husband, Jason, blocked their path with his car.

"An off duty detective, Tim O'Malley, was walking right behind them and saw the whole thing unfold. This is what he told me. The ex-husband stepped out of his car. He must have been drinking because Officer O'Malley saw him stagger slightly. Then he heard him swear at Connie saying, 'You bitch! I'm tired of you whoring around. I'm tired of you making a fool of me. If I can't have you, no one's going to have you.' Jason raised his arm, revealing a pistol. That's when O'Malley saw the gun."

"Then what?" Annie asked.

"Connie hid behind Dennis, he said. Dennis lunged to try and grab the pistol, but he was too far away to do anything. Officer O'Malley heard Jason say, 'Sorry fella, nothing personal.' Then he shot Dennis three times, once in the arm, once in the head, and once in the stomach. The shots to the arm and head were superficial, but the shot to the stomach did most of the damage. Luckily, it went right through, missing all the vital organs, but there was a lot of internal bleeding." She caught her breath. "I was able to clean up the wounds to the head and arm and stopped most of the bleeding."

"And Connie?" Peter asked.

Rita shook her head. "Connie wasn't so lucky. Jason emptied three rounds into her, which killed her almost immediately. Officer O'Malley yelled for him to put down his weapon and, when Jason raised the gun again, O'Malley shot him in the heart once and killed him."

"Is Dennis going to be okay?" Peter asked.

"I don't know. I stitched him up as best as I could. We'll just have to wait and see."

Annie looked at Rita. "How long until we know?" *I feel like the grim reaper is following me around, and just when I was feeling better about life.*

"It's one o'clock now. Hopefully, we'll know by morning. That's not all. When I came to work for my shift tonight, look what I found waiting for me." She pointed to a dozen red roses and a letter.

"Who's it from?" Annie asked.

"They're from Dennis. Can you believe it? Read the letter." Her hand shook as she handed it to Annie. "Go ahead, read it out loud, so Peter can hear it." Her eyes misted over as she sat with her hands folded in her lap.

Annie slid the letter out of the soft pink envelope. Written on fine stationary, Annie was startled at the neat, carefully written words.

Dear Rita,

I hope you like the flowers. I'm sorry I can't be there personally to deliver them to you, but I have a dinner date with Connie tonight. Before you go and get your Irish temper riled up, I just want you to know that I made this date weeks ago and it will be the last date I have with Connie for the rest of my life.

I gave a lot of thought to what you said to me at Christmas that Monday morning. You've always been unequaled, Rita. When we were together in Door County those first few years, you made me feel special and you were simply unbelievable. I know I haven't been faithful to anyone but myself. It's not something I'm really proud of, but maybe we can talk about it.

You see, Rita, I want to be with you from now on. You are the one I've been looking for. I knew that when we were together in Las Vegas, but never really got a chance to tell you. Then when you married Zach, I thought I lost my chance.

This Christmas, I realized how much I really missed you. How good we are together. I don't mean just sex. I just feel so much better with you than anyone else I have ever been with. I love you, Rita. I've never said those words to anyone. Even in the heat of passion, I've never said them. I'm writing them now to you, and I'll say them to you when I see you tomorrow.

I love you, Rita Gallagher. I am looking forward to seeing you tomorrow, so we can talk about where we go from here. I'm willing to make the commitment you want if you can wait one more day. We'll talk and see if we can make this work for both of us. I love you, Rita.

Dennis

"Wow," Peter and Annie said almost as one.

"I didn't think I'd ever live to hear Dennis say those words," Peter said.

"He's got to live," Rita said. "I've waited my whole life for him, it seems." She lifted her gaze to the ceiling. "Please, God, let him live." She leaned her head on Annie's shoulder and cried.

**

Peter and Annie stayed with Rita through the night. Near morning, Rita reached for Dennis's hand, then leaned forward and tenderly kissed his forehead and his lips. "I love you, Dennis. I've waited my whole life for you, and now you go and get yourself shot. You better not go and die on me."

Dennis's eyes moved and his lids fluttered open. They all watched as he tried to focus. When one of Rita's tears landed on his lips, he moved his lips together to capture her worry.

The early morning sun streamed in through the window behind Rita and surrounded her with glowing light.

"Where am I? I hope its Heaven?"

Rita gave him another loving kiss. "Oh, Dennis, I was so worried about you. I thought, I'm sorry, we thought we were going to lose you."

"We?"

Yes, We. Annie and Peter are here too." She stepped aside so he could see.

"I'm sorry. I guess my timing was bad with all this. How is Connie?"

"I'm sorry, Dennis. She didn't make it."

"I kind of guessed that. All I remember is this guy yelling at us, pointing a gun. I know she got behind me. He must have shot me. I don't remember much except her screaming, and I remember hearing more shots before I passed out. The next thing...here you are."

"I've been here the whole time, Dennis."

He smiled. "Did you get my flowers and the letter?"

"Yes I did. They were beautiful, especially the letter."

"I know this might not be the right time and place, but...Rita, I love you. I want to spend the rest of my life with you. Will you marry me?"

Her eyes lit up. She blinked twice and slowly leaned down to give him a long kiss before she pulled back. "Yes, Dennis, I'll marry you."

Driving back to Chicago with Peter, Annie felt exhausted and drained after the evening events. "Thank God it turned out the way it did." She said, "Dennis gets shot, Rita saves him and then he proposes and someday he and Rita will marry." She smiled as she thought about them marrying after all these years. Why couldn't it be that simple for her?

Forty-five minutes later, Peter pulled up in front of her loft. "Here you go. Home sweet home. Do you want me to come up?" Peter asked.

"No." She said softly. "I'm sorry the night didn't turn out the way you planned. It was wonderful until we got that call. I'm exhausted. I just want to take a shower and lay down. I'm sorry Peter. I'll be up in Door County soon, and then we'll get together. I promise."

"I understand. I was hoping we could make love but it always seems like Dennis or something is getting in the way. I'll be waiting."

She kissed him, "I'm sorry Peter, but I'm just not ready yet!" She caressed his face and then turned and went in. Annie did not realize how tired she was until she got out of the shower. Putting on her favorite robe, she got two sheets, a pillow, and a down comforter. She laid down on the bearskin rug and was sound asleep in a few minutes.

That night, she dreamed she and Jack were walking, shopping, eating, and doing all the things couples do. It was a beautiful day in her dream, as they walked hand in hand, to Grant Park, and the Lakefront. Then she looked ahead and saw Peter walking toward her. What is he doing here? She thought. As he came closer, Jack turned to her and said, "Annie, it's time for me to go. Peter is a good man; he'll take care of you and make you happy. I think you should spend the rest of your life with him. I love you Annie." He kissed her, turned, and walked away just as Peter arrived to take her hand.

**

That weekend, Annie drove to Door County with a purpose. She called Peter as she drove. "Peter, it's me. I'm coming up to see you. I had a wonderful dream last night.

It's Friday. Let's go to The Inn at Kristofer's and have dinner. I can tell you all about it."

She picked him up and went to the restaurant. She wanted to have a table near the window, overlooking the bay. They each ordered the cashew whitefish and a bottle of Riesling.

After dinner, Peter asked about the dream. Annie told him. He sat very still as she recounted everything. When she was done, he simply took both her hands in his and kissed them tenderly.

"Jack was a wonderful man. You were very lucky to have him. I am honored that he came back to tell you it's okay for us to be together. I'm sure Paula would feel the same way."

They sat holding hands and looking into each other's eyes. Not saying anything. They didn't have to. It was in both of their hearts.

They went to his condo, built a fire, and Annie made some hot chocolate. They snuggled on the couch, wrapped in a blanket and looked into the fire. Finally, Peter turned to her. "You know I love you as much as any man can. I know you love me the same way."

Annie nodded. She nervously reached for the sailboat around her neck and rubbed the charm.

"I don't want to miss you a second time." He said. "Annie, will you marry me?"

Dropping her hands to her lap, she looked deep into his eyes. "Peter, it is time for us. Yes, I'll marry you."

**

On June 21, Peter and Annie were married at the Moravian Church overlooking Ephraim Harbor. Throughout the short service, an eagle perched on the steeple of the church. As the bride and groom left the church, the eagle took off, climbing high into the clear blue sky. It banked hard to the right before swooping low over the couple's heads, making slow graceful circles as it gained altitude and flew across the bay to the bluffs.

The locals could not remember seeing an eagle perched on that church steeple in Ephraim before, but Peter knew and he smiled. "Thank you, Paula."

Wilson's catered the small reception. Following tradition, the bride and groom feasted on tuna sandwiches and root beer malts.

Afterward, Peter led Annie by the hand the short distance to the municipal dock. Looking out on the water with its many boats, he turned to her. "See anything you recognize?"

Annie raised her hand, shielding her eyes against the sun. "Hey," she said. "Isn't that *Falcon* out there on its old mooring? It hasn't been here for years."

Peter smiled. "Yes, it is *Falcon*."

"Really? It's nice to see it again. It brings back good memories. It's on its old mooring, too."

"It does. Do you remember the promise I made to you years ago about that boat?"

Annie looked at him, confused.

"I said, someday I'd buy you that boat if I could. Well, today's that day. I hope you like your wedding present." He smiled as he handed her the boat keys.

"Oh, Peter," she said, wrapping her arms around him, she kissed him. "I love you."

The End

Made in the USA
Monee, IL
18 November 2021